BELIEVE

Jill
Thanks for your
support. I hope
you enjoy the
book. Jon
Walters

Believe

Jan Walters

iUniverse LLC
Bloomington

BELIEVE

iUniverse books may be ordered through booksellers or by contacting:

iUniverse
1663 Liberty Drive
Bloomington, IN 47403
www.iuniverse.com
1-800-Authors (1-800-288-4677)

ISBN: 978-1-4759-9777-4 (sc)
ISBN: 978-1-4759-9776-7 (hc)
ISBN: 978-1-4759-9775-0 (e)

Library of Congress Control Number: 2013912038

Printed in the United States of America.

iUniverse rev. date: 7/30/2013

Chapter 1

THE MOMENT ANN SPOTTED the decrepit-looking bookstore, her life turned upside down. Ann normally avoided this area of town because of the high crime rate and the number of strange-looking characters lingering about the streets after dark. But after a late night out with Stacy, a coworker and her best friend, Ann had missed her turnoff. In a hurry to get home, she drove through the warehouse district. Suddenly, she hit the brakes. To her right, nestled in between towering buildings, sat a bookstore. The bookstore stood out from amongst the surrounding buildings. Most buildings in the area appeared to be undergoing major renovations—probably more downtown condos or strip malls.

Ann couldn't help but notice the odd bookstore. It had a steep tile roof. Missing tiles revealed portions of the roof with an unnatural curve. "Water damage. What a shame," she muttered aloud. Patches of dirt glazed over the store's windows, giving it a dreary appearance. Even the painted sign outside had faded away, leaving only the word "Bookstore" in view. The metal sign inside the door, showing the hours of operation, was just as battered as the outside of the building. The store would be open tomorrow. Maybe she'd stop by. In daylight, she was sure the store wouldn't look quite so dilapidated. She couldn't help but wonder what the inside looked like. Was it as neglected inside as out? What kind of books were inside? She loved antique books. Ann had always felt a kinship with the past. Maybe that was why she enjoyed researching genealogy.

Unable to resist a quick look inside, she parked the car in front of the bookstore. As it was after midnight, the store was dark. Ann glanced around the area before getting out of the car. Mark, her son, would throw a fit if he knew his mom was traipsing around darkened streets in the middle of the night. Ann had divorced her husband when the kids, Mark and Jessica, were very young. She had caught him cheating with a neighbor woman. Now that the kids were out of college and on their own, Mark seemed to think he was responsible for his mother. At times, she was lonely—a third wheel. She didn't date much, and the kids had their own lives to live. However, she was determined to move on.

Not seeing anyone loitering nearby, Ann deemed it safe enough to quickly check out the store. She wiped the window with her hand. Dark smudges stained her fingertips. Pressing her nose against the cold pane, she saw rows of tables. Each table was stacked high with books. It was hard to tell whether they were old or not. She wished she had a flashlight.

A sudden breeze blew the pile of dead leaves at her feet into the air. They whirled around her. Around and around they flew. It was as if she stood in the middle of a whirlwind. Ann hit the leaves with her hands, trying to bat them away, but they continued the circular motion. A loud noise from the nearby alley caused Ann to jump. The leaves collapsed in a pile at her feet again. "Who's there?" Hearing nothing, she clutched her car keys and ran to the car. Once inside, she locked all the doors. Her harsh breathing filled the car. She was safe, she kept telling herself. Her pounding heart finally began to slow. A cat had probably knocked over a garbage can. She looked at the clock in the car. It was two in the morning, too late for moms in their forties to be out alone. Turning the ignition, she drove away, resisting the urge to turn and look at the bookstore one more time.

∞

The next morning, Ann stumbled to the kitchen. It wasn't even eight o'clock, yet the sound of the neighbor's lawn mower filled the air. Grabbing her favorite mug, Ann poured the coffee. Thank God for automatic timers! She opened the front door and picked up the paper on the stoop, waving to the guy mowing the yard. Didn't he realize that some people liked to sleep in on Saturdays? Ann tossed the paper on the kitchen table before getting a banana to eat. What she really wanted to eat was a big warm chocolate croissant. Maybe two of them. But no, she had to try to lose some weight. Her doctor said she was premenopausal, which was causing her to put on weight around her waist. Since she wanted to start dating again, the extra weight had to go. She had even started jogging again.

Gazing out the window, Ann caught a glimpse of herself in the reflection and saw that her green eyes were framed with dark shadows. Her thick red hair fell to her shoulders, the curly locks outlining her heart-shaped face. Her head pounded from lack of sleep. Hopefully, the caffeine would kick in soon.

Ann's thoughts returned to last night. A chill ran down her arms. She should just forget about going back to the bookstore. Based on the appearance of the outside of the store, they most likely would have only junk, nothing of any interest. Ann put her empty cup in the sink before climbing the stairs to the bedroom. By lunchtime, Ann had changed the bedding, dusted, and vacuumed all the rooms. Restless, she went outside to see if the mail had come yet. By this time of day, most of the neighbors were outside. Many were raking up the piles of leaves that littered the yards every autumn. Ann wrinkled her nose at the layers of leaves covering her grass. Just looking at the leaves caused her to think about the bookstore. Darn it! She couldn't quit thinking about it. She decided that since she had nothing else to do, she might as well go there and get it over with.

Ann found herself poised in the bookstore doorway later that afternoon. With her hand on the doorknob, she hesitated. A slight tremor shook her body as she thought about the events of last night. Above, dark clouds blotted out the sun. There had been a rash of severe thunderstorms in the area, but today's forecast indicated only rain showers. A sharp wind blew her long tendrils across her face.

With a deep sigh, she entered the store. There was little light inside the store. Dust motes floated through the air, almost like fairy dust. Large white globe lights were suspended from the ceiling by dust-covered chains. Long, narrow planks of scuffed wood covered the floor. They were so old that the floor stain was obliterated. A long cluttered counter was nestled in the far back corner. Ann walked toward the ancient-looking cash register perched on the counter.

"Hello. Is anyone here?" Biting her lower lip, she couldn't help but wonder what she was doing here. The store was outdated and obviously empty. Ann questioned whether it had been a good choice coming here to look for books. She didn't even see a phone. Feeling a tingling sensation roll down her spine, she whipped her head around, trying to find the source of her unease. As she turned to leave, a large album peeking out of a stack of old books caught her attention. The weathered red leather cover glittered like a diamond in a pile of coal. It looked familiar, but how could it? Butterflies fluttered in her stomach. Her hand shook as she drew it toward her. She slowly opened the album's cover.

By the style of clothes and hairstyles of the people in the pictures, it appeared they were taken at a formal English society event. She wondered about the age of the pictures. Turning the pages, she stared at one amazing picture after another. The dresses the women wore were beautiful. This had to be some sort of family album. How sad it was to think that there were no family members alive today to cherish these photographs. How did the album end up in Iowa? Feeling like an interloper, Ann started to close the album, and that's when a large picture caught her attention.

She was staring at a picture of the most gorgeous man she had ever seen. A soft sigh escaped her lips. *Oh, baby!* Dressed in black formal wear, the man presented a formidable presence. Masculinity radiated from his athletic frame. His dark hair glistened from the light above. A chiseled jawline showed that he was a determined man. He almost had a stern, unrelenting look—if it hadn't been for his captivating eyes. Something in his gaze tugged at her heartstrings. His eyes glittered with laughter or perhaps a titillating secret. Was he looking at someone over the shoulder of the photographer? Whoever he was, Ann couldn't quit staring at his picture.

A nearby noise caused her to jump. Holding a hand to her throat, Ann sighed with relief as an elderly woman shuffled from behind the counter. Her cane tapped on the worn wooden floor as she came toward her. Her floral dress fell below her knees, and she wore a pair of black leather boots. Coarse gray hair haphazardly stuck out from a bun pulled on top of her head. "Hi. I hope it was okay to come in and look around. You are open, aren't you?"

The woman hobbled closer to Ann, her bent frame obviously the result of osteoporosis. Tilting her head, the woman smiled, showing gaps between yellowed teeth. "Oh, yes, dearie! I was expecting you."

"You were?" Ann shuddered. Thrusting the album forward, Ann rushed on. "Er … I found this. I was wondering if you knew anything about the family or the history of the album."

The woman's grin grew larger. The wrinkled face grew more pronounced. She pulled a wadded floral handkerchief from a pocket and dusted off the red cover. Faded gold script was revealed. Ann could see "Lady O'Neil's Memoirs" on the cover.

"The O'Neils were a prominent English family in the late nineteenth century. The lord and his lady were a lovely couple. I think they had several children."

"Wow! My great-grandmother was an O'Neil, but I'm sure it's not the same family. I wonder how the album ended up here in Iowa."

The woman shrugged her bony shoulders. "Fate has a way of finding those destined to be together. Don't you think so?" The old woman's cloudy eyes focused unblinkingly on Ann.

The hair on the back of Ann's neck rose. She had a sudden urge to leave. "I guess so."

Not wanting to spend another minute in the store, Ann yanked out her billfold. "The price tag shows twenty dollars. Here you go."

The bill fluttered to the counter as if a supernatural breeze flowed through the dark recesses of the store. An eerie whisper sounded in her ear: "Believe." Turning her head, Ann saw no one else in the store.

The woman reached for a sack. "Don't be late."

Ann froze. Did she dare ask what that cryptic comment meant? No! She wanted out of here.

"Never mind the sack; I can carry it. Thanks again." Ann forced herself to walk to the doorway. No running! She was so proud for not glancing back.

If she had, she would have seen the old woman straighten and lay the cane aside. A large gray cat jumped up on the counter, purring as a withered hand rubbed between its ears. "Well, Moonbeam, it's time for us to go to work. We've been called to help."

The cat purred in response as the two of them retreated to the back of the store.

Chapter 2

EACH NIGHT THE DREAMS were the same.

"Damn you, damn you," the man in the picture raged. "Stay—I can protect you!" His clenched fists rose to the heavens. A roar wrenched from his throat as his broad shoulders shook with pain. Thick ebony hair curled about the back of his neck and fell to his brow. Startling green eyes reflected his frustration.

Murmuring in her sleep, Ann thrashed about the bed, causing the covers to wrap around her legs.

The man's fury was tangible. She could see the taut muscles in his neck and how his jaw was tightly clenched. He called, "Come back to me!"

His white shirt gaped open, revealing a bronzed chest that tapered to a lean waist. Black pants hugged narrow hips and powerful thighs. He looked like a man used to being in control.

"I'm here. I'm here," Ann mumbled sleepily.

With a start, Ann sat up in the bed, pushing back the tendrils tumbling across her face. Intense pain and longing ripped through her. The depth of his despair was so real that tears dampened her cheeks. Her heart felt as if it were breaking.

Wiping an errant teardrop, Ann warily stared at the album on her nightstand. She had been able to do some research on the Internet and had learned that the album was Lady O'Neil's chronicle of nineteenth-century life in London. The photos in the album had become a source of foreboding. She half expected the album to levitate across the room. Shaken from the dream, she thrust the album in a drawer. The sooner it was out of her house, the sooner her life would return to normal.

Ann kicked off the covers and hurried to the bathroom. Green eyes stared back in the mirror. She ran a hand through her auburn hair, which was sticking out at odd angles. The dreams worried her. Her mind was made up. On Monday, the book was going back to the eccentric old woman who had sold it to her. Ann had to get the book out of her house or lose her sanity. The obsession with the dark stranger in her dreams was eerie. Since her divorce twenty years ago, Ann hadn't obsessed over any guy. Her ex-husband had successfully turned off any romantic emotions. At least he had left the state; she had never heard from the womanizer again.

At the office the next day, Ann's thoughts constantly drifted to the closed desk drawer where the album was stored. Her job as an accountant was great. Her boss was easy-going and gave her lots of flexibility in her work hours, so she could leave early or come in late. There could be no more procrastinating. She would return the album before the bookstore closed tonight. Starting tonight, she would be dream-free.

Ann left the office to have lunch with Stacy. Also divorced, Stacy frequently expressed her views on men, sex, and life without inhibition. Watching her approach the table, Ann smiled, noting Stacy's new hair extensions and color. Stacy was so vivacious. At times, Ann was envious.

"Hi there. How's it going?" Stacy sat down next to Ann and adjusted her short skirt, showing her legs at their best advantage.

Ann had to smile in amusement. "Your hair looks great. I love that skirt. I wish I could wear something like that."

Stacy raised her hands and fluffed her hair. "Oh, Ann. You could. Let me take you shopping."

"You would have me dressed in something that's crazy. What looks good on you doesn't quite work for me, you know."

Their laughter drew the looks of several businessmen seated nearby. Stacy seemed to bask in the attention. Ann shook her head. Even though she was in her midforties, she considered herself somewhat in shape and attractive. Maybe not as much as Stacy, but her friend was truly unique.

The downtown restaurant with its fifties' motif was their favorite meeting place. The female servers blew huge bubbles with their gum as they walked by, their wide poodle skirts swishing back and forth as they hurried to keep up with the bustling lunch crowd.

"I just love my hair color. I've always wanted to be a blonde."

"It looks great on you." Ann's smile faded, and she nervously twisted her napkin. "Can I talk to you about something? Something weird is going on."

Stacy's hands fell to her lap as she leaned forward. "Sure, what's wrong?"

"I found an album last week called *Lady O'Neil's Memoirs*."

"OMG! Don't you have some relatives named O'Neil?"

"I do. Because of that, I thought I'd do some digging and maybe discover new information about my family. I know this is going to sound crazy, but it's as if the album called to me. To top it off, there was a little old woman at the store who warned me not to be late. And then—"

"You're upset about a woman at the bookstore who told you not to be late?"

Ann fought back the tears of helplessness. "Oh, Stacy! You wouldn't believe what's happening. I'm having really strange dreams about the guy pictured in the album. It is as if he's calling to me."

"Whoa, sweetie! You're getting upset about a dream?"

Ann shook her head. "No, there's more. You remember the IT guy I dated for a while?" Seeing Stacy nod, she continued. "David is calling at all hours of the night to harass me."

Stacy gripped Ann's hands. "First, they're just dreams. You probably saw a movie or met someone who looks like the guy in the album. You need a vacation. I warned you that you were working too hard. Even your boss told you to take some time off. For God's sake, you're losing your vacation time. Second, if David is giving you problems, go talk to human resources. You don't have to take his crap!"

Exasperated, Ann leaned back. "That's a good idea. I will do that today. But the album ... I'm really worried about it! I swear it's possessed or something."

Stacy laughed aloud. "Possessed? Like in *The Exorcist*? Ooooohhhh!"

Ann tossed her napkin across the table. "Great. My best friend thinks I'm a raving lunatic. By the way, your ghost sound sucks!"

"Okay. Now I feel guilty. How can I help?"

Ann gave her a tentative smile. "Come with me tonight to return the album."

"I can't. I have a date, a very special date. How about doing it during lunch tomorrow?"

Insistent, Ann shook her head. "No. I'm getting rid of it today. I'm afraid to even open it again."

Stacy frowned. "Hey, just wait until tomorrow and I'll go with you. You're all pale and look kind of shaky. I'm worried about you." Stacy reached across the table and patted Ann's clasped hands. "It's a dream, Ann."

"I know," Ann whispered.

The women quietly finished their lunch. After a quick hug for Stacy, Ann returned to work. During her afternoon break, she stopped by human resources, but the person she needed to speak to was on vacation. Sighing, she returned to her desk. This is the way her life went.

Later that day, Ann pulled in front of the secluded bookstore. The store didn't look like it was open. Hesitantly, she pushed open the door. Looking around the dimly lit store, it appeared empty.

"I'm not scared, I'm not scared," she chanted softly.

The odor of incense permeated the air. "Oh, hell, here we go again." She let out a squeak when the black curtain behind the counter suddenly parted. A young man with thick glasses walked toward her. "Can I help you?"

Funny, she hadn't noticed the curtain last week. Ann nervously cleared her throat as she slid the album toward the clerk. "I want to return this."

He studied the cover, slowly flipping through yellowed pictures. "This isn't our album. You must have bought it somewhere else." He pushed it back to her.

Ann paused. Was this some kind of joke? "I bought it here last week. A gray-haired woman waited on me."

His quizzical look increased her nervousness. With a half smile, he said, "I'm the owner of this store, and I'm telling you that we didn't sell you the album. No old women work here either."

Her stomach twisted into knots. Ann wiped her damp palms against her skirt. Her lips stretched into a taut line. "I'm telling you the truth. If you won't give me a refund, then you can keep the damn album and sell it to someone else."

The owner's smile faded. A hint of red tinted his pale cheeks. "Maybe you should take the album and leave, miss. You really should keep the album."

Something brushed against Ann's legs. Startled, she glanced down. A large gray cat wove between her feet, purring loudly. When Ann looked up, the man had disappeared.

Frustrated, Ann called out, "Hey! Sir, you need to come back. I want to return this book." An uncomfortable silence filled the store. Even the cat quit purring, only to sit at her feet and peer up at her.

Minutes later, she grabbed the album in frustration, muttering under her breath as she marched out of the store. Tossing the album in the back seat, she slid behind the wheel. She'd come back later.

As Ann sped away, a withered hand lowered the blinds in the front window of the bookstore. A closed sign now faced the street. The watery eyes watched Ann's car turn the corner. "Come on, Moonbeam. It's almost time."

Living in a small town only twenty minutes from work, Ann found the drive home to be her favorite time of day. She switched to a local classic rock station and tried to enjoy the soothing beauty of the rolling green hills and country fields. She refused to dwell on the album and the weird bookstore. Instead, a mental image of the man from the album abruptly appeared. Ann's body tingled just thinking about his piercing eyes and towering frame. What would it be like to have a man like that run his hands down her body? To kiss her as if he had to have her right then or die? To press into her with a deep, hungering thrust? Nothing like that would ever happen to her. She was just an average middle-aged woman.

With a quick glance in the rearview mirror, her eyes narrowed. The dark shadows around her eyes were prominent. She had to get some sleep tonight. She was not a femme fatale like Stacy, but she was more than passably attractive. Several guys in accounting had asked her out, but she'd turned them down. One smoked. Another sniffled all the time. She could have a date every weekend if she wished to date an accountant, which she didn't. But she did enjoy her time alone. It gave her an opportunity to relax and read books, even though the last purchase at a bookstore hadn't gone so well. Pushing away the negative thoughts, she sighed. Almost home.

Pulling into the driveway, she saw a white Mustang sitting in front of her house. "Just what I need."

As she got out of the car, David waved. Pasting on a smile, Ann walked toward her unwelcome visitor. "David. What a surprise."

"I thought I'd just stop by and see if you wanted to go out for pizza or something."

"I thought I mentioned that I'm pretty busy this week."

With a classic model's face and an athlete's build, David exuded confidence. His golden tan accented his lean facial features and blue eyes. He wore his blond hair clipped short on the sides, leaving the crown longer to settle on his brow. Fastidious about his looks, he smoothed back his hair, which had become slightly windblown during the drive.

"Hey, you still have to eat, and I did drive all the way here to see you. C'mon, Ann. What do you say?"

He flashed a smile. Ann knew that he watched her at work. She made a point of avoiding David's office. If she did happen to meet him in a hallway or the break room, he would be overtly friendly, often invading her personal space. Everyone at work thought he was wonderful. She knew differently. She had seen a violent side of his personality while on a date. Another driver had cut in front of them while driving. David had raged and ended up cutting off the other driver. Both men got out of their cars and were ready to exchange blows by the time a police car pulled up beside them. It had scared Ann. She didn't need that kind of drama.

Her elderly neighbor sat on her front porch, staring at the two of them. Mrs. Whitson was a busybody. By tonight, everyone would know that she had a man in her house—that is, if she asked him to come in. Her hands tightened around her purse strap when she noticed that David had moved closer. Since he seemed to be congenial, Ann decided to invite him in.

"Let's go inside for a second. How about a Coke or iced tea?" Goose bumps crawled up her arms as David followed her inside. He was too close. She already regretted her decision to invite him in the house.

She returned from the kitchen with the drinks and saw David leaning back comfortably on the sofa. He patted the cushion next to him, making it clear that he expected her to sit next to him. "Hon, sit over here."

With a weak smile, she sat in a nearby chair. "Thanks, but this is good. Listen, David. We had a few dates and some good talks, but I told you several times that I don't want to be involved with you or anyone else right now."

David set his glass on the end table with a loud thud. He stood, advancing toward her. "Ann, Ann," David cajoled in a silky voice. "You're just like the others. I try to be nice, but suddenly you don't want to see me anymore." He shook his head.

Ann leaned back in the chair, forcing herself to remain calm.

"David, I made it clear that I only wanted to be a friend. I thought you understood."

David came closer, now towering above her. He pressed his muscular legs against her knees, pinning her to the chair. His eyes blazed with suppressed fury. With his face inches from hers, he ground out, "What about the way I feel? Since I did not agree to terminate this relationship, it isn't over. Not until I get what I want." He sneered contemptuously. "You do know what I want, don't you? Or are you stupid besides being a tease?"

Ann was paralyzed with fear. She couldn't move, let alone think. She heard a car door slam outside. Peering out the window, she saw her son, Mark, walking up the sidewalk. Alert to the new arrival, David quickly backed away from the chair.

Mark rang the doorbell several times and bolted through the doorway. "Mom, where are you?"

Ann sprang out of the chair and walked over to give Mark a hug.

"I wanted to see if you wanted to get dinner tonight, but I see that you have company." He started to turn toward the door. "We can do it another night."

The tension in the room vibrated off the walls.

"Stay!" Ann blurted. "David just stopped by for a minute and was leaving."

David glared at Mark before turning to meet Ann's gaze. "I'm leaving, but this isn't over." The door slammed behind him.

Ann fell back into the chair with relief.

"What was going on just now?"

"Nothing. David stopped by and asked me to dinner."

Mark grunted. "He's that guy from work, isn't he? He looked really pissed off. Are you sure he didn't hurt you?"

"No, he didn't hurt me. He gets upset when things don't go his way. He's such a control freak. If a pencil is out of place on his desk, it upsets him. I can't believe I ever went out with him in the first place."

"Then why did you let him in the house?" Mark chided.

Ann got up and wrapped her arms about his broad shoulders,

hoping to erase the worried look on his face. Mark had grown into a wonderful young man. Slightly over six feet, he towered above her. He inherited his slender build from his father's genes. No one in Ann's family was tall or thin. Even though he was built like her ex, Mark had her coloring, reddish hair and all. "You know me. I thought if I was nice, he'd get the picture and leave."

"Maybe I should spend the night? If he shows up here again, he'll meet Mr. Right and Mr. Left." Mark held up his two large fists.

Ann groaned. "Oh, great! That's just what I need, for you to be arrested. Let's forget David and go get something to eat."

Mentally exhausted from her encounters at the bookstore and with David, Ann suggested they eat at a nearby café on the square, a favorite hangout of the local farmers. Its informal style and relaxed atmosphere would soothe her disquieted nerves.

Despite her reassurances to Mark, Ann's thoughts kept returning to the unpleasant scene with David. His flattery and attention to detail had originally impressed her, but it hadn't taken her long to figure out that he was obsessive and controlling. He had recently started harassing her with late-night phone calls and lots of deep breathing. How juvenile!

As if reading her thoughts, Mark touched her hand. "Mom, are you sure everything is okay? You've hardly touched your food."

"I'm fine. Just a little tired. I've been staying up too late working on the family history again."

"It's kind of neat that you can document that our ancestors came to America in the 1840s. I'd hate to be alive in Ireland during the potato famine."

Ann sipped her Diet Coke. "Me too. I know you and Jessica think I'm crazy spending all my spare time on this project, but it's addictive. Enough about me. Any special girl in your life now that you've reached the ripe old age of twenty-six?"

Mark's eyes twinkled at her. "Yep."

Ann chuckled as she playfully punched Mark's arm. "Is that all I get? When I was your age, I had two kids. You were six, and Jess was five. C'mon, give me the details."

Mark rubbed his bicep, pretending to be in pain. "I'm not jinxing things. Her name is Deb. She works in the financial industry. She's smart and gorgeous. Don't worry—you'll meet her soon."

"Geez. It's like pulling teeth to get you kids to tell me anything."

After they finished their dinner, Mark picked up the bill and drove her home, chattering about his job and the chances for promotion.

As they pulled in her driveway, Ann pressed a kiss on his cheek. "Hey, if you don't mind, let's call it a night. I'll give you a call soon."

He sat in the car until she was in the house. She waved at him as he pulled away.

Renewed by a long, hot shower, she turned on the computer and reviewed the latest information. She had recently discovered that Michael and Alice O'Neil, a distant branch of the family, had a son. Her thoughts returned to the album hidden in her room. She remembered the exhilaration in finding the album about the O'Neil family. But was it really a coincidence?

Being a history fanatic, she wanted to learn everything about life in the nineteenth century and the O'Neil family. Ann stared at the family tree on the computer screen and frowned at a blank space. Why was the son's name so elusive?

A cool breeze rustled the curtains. Shivering, Ann went to close the windows. As she neared the window, a moaning sound drifted in. Startled, she looked about the darkened yard. She'd probably imagined the sound. Then she heard it again. "Ann, Ann," the wind whispered. Was that David's voice? Ann cranked the window shut and closed the blinds. Was he trying to scare her? Tomorrow she would contact the police and secure a restraining order.

Turning off the computer, Ann jumped into bed with the covers pulled up around her neck. She lay still, listening to the sounds of the night. For once, she wasn't dreading a reoccurrence of "the dream." It would be a welcome relief compared to a dream about David. Ann punched the pillow in frustration as she tried to get comfortable. A few weeks ago, her life had been completely normal, dull in fact.

"Why me?" she wailed softly. "I just want an ordinary life."

For one night, the dream was absent.

Chapter 3

ENGLAND
1870

"EGADS," PATRICK MUMBLED AS he rose from the large poster bed. His head throbbed from lack of sleep. Once again, he had dreamed that Lady Victoria Montgomery was in danger. There was nothing in real life to substantiate his dreams, and he was puzzled as to why he was continually plagued with the same nightmare.

Patrick hoped to see Victoria at the upcoming costume ball. Her father, Baron William Montgomery, owned the adjoining estate. Patrick's home, Epsom Hall, was the largest estate in the county.

Mary, his aunt, breezed into his darkened room, her cheery voice a soothing tonic for his frayed temper. "Oh dear! You are looking quite dreadful. Did you have another one of those dreams where Victoria is in trouble?"

Patrick attempted a smile. "Please, Auntie, you must let me dress before barging into my rooms. I'm a grown man. And the answer to your question is yes."

The gray curls bobbed as she drew back the heavy drapes. "I should remind you that I changed your nappies, but I won't. Now quit fretting. I am sure she is safe, for her father never lets her out of his sight."

Patrick rang for his valet, Carrick. His grin grew as Mary continued to grumble about the baron. "Stop!" he finally said. "Now you must take yourself off. We have servants to take care of my needs. You do not need to draw the drapes for me."

His aunt pinched his cheek. "Let me spoil you. You are my only remaining relative. Humor an old lady." Before he could respond, she resumed her rant about their neighbors. "Besides, it's not proper the way that man treats his daughter. Sometimes I think she is unable to make a decision on her own. Poor dove. I daresay she is probably forbidden to venture outdoors. The entire family is strange, if you ask me."

Patrick's head pounded with a vengeance. He sighed wearily. "Aunt Mary, you know that I care for Victoria. If her brother and I had remained friends, perhaps the family would not be in such dire straits today. I should have been a better friend and helped Malcolm avoid his gambling cronies. He appears to take after his father. Poor Victoria has been forced to bear the brunt of her family's poor financial decisions."

A servant brought in a tray and set it on a nearby table. Mary handed him a steaming cup of black coffee. In a motherly tone, she offered, "Here you go. Why not sponsor the girl by sending her to her cousins in Cornwall? I hear they are nice people. I'm sure they would care for her."

His back rippled as tension set in. He knew that his aunt only wanted what was best for him. Patrick stared lovingly at the robust woman, his father's older sister. Never married, she and Patrick had enjoyed many escapades when he was young. Sometimes her opinionated views were trying. He had to remember that she was used to looking after him.

"Perhaps I could marry her myself. I don't fancy anyone else, and I am of age to get an heir. Who knows, I may even come to love her, and I could be a dutiful husband."

Mary's hands clasped her large bosom. Her thick gray curls bobbed, as her displeasure at his suggestion was evident. "No, no, my dear boy. Do not entertain such a thought. In time, you will meet your true love." Collapsing in a wing-back leather chair,

Mary massaged her temple. "I cannot countenance having the baron as a relative."

Patrick walked over and planted a kiss on Mary's cheek. "Dear girl, you must calm yourself. 'Twas just a thought."

At twenty-eight years, Patrick had enjoyed many different women, yet he had never felt an overwhelming desire to spend his life with anyone. While he had concentrated on diversifying the family's financial interests and increasing his fortune, Victoria had matured into a young woman poised on the brink of womanhood.

Mary sighed and left the room, wise enough to leave Patrick to his musings.

Patrick finished dressing and dismissed his valet with a nod. As he entered the sitting room, he stared up at his parents' portrait above the fireplace. Every time he looked at the picture, his chest hurt with grief. Their sudden death a year ago had been a shock. Prior to their death, he'd lived in the family townhome in London. It was hard living in the family home knowing that his parents would never return. If and when he married, he longed for a close relationship like his parents had enjoyed. His parents had truly loved one another, even though they had come from entirely different backgrounds. His mother had been the coveted daughter of a wealthy English shipbuilder. His father, a member of the Irish aristocracy, had been forced off his family land in Ireland, but he became very successful when he joined his father-in-law's business. Now Patrick headed up the family shipping business and had expanded into railroads as well.

His father had been determined that Patrick would fit into English society. He made sure that Patrick attended the best schools that England had to offer. With his Irish heritage, Patrick frequently endured the brutality and taunts of schoolmates, and in the end, he was stronger for it.

Over the years, Patrick had become fiercely independent. His cynical mind knew that whatever the *ton* thought of him and his Irish background, they would never dare speak it aloud. The women appreciated his wealth and handsome looks, which opened many boudoirs doors that would normally be closed.

Hungry, he hurried into the dining room, where his aunt was sorting invitations that had arrived earlier in the morning.

"Mr. McAlfry would like to meet and discuss a business matter with you."

Dabbing jam on his toast, Patrick nodded. "Hmm. Probably wants more money for his railroad. Give that one to my secretary to handle. Anything else of importance?"

Mary's brow arched as she waved a note under his nose. "It seems that Lady Paxton requests your presence as soon as possible."

Patrick leaned back in his chair, silently counting to ten. "Auntie, we've had this conversation previously. Please let me open the invitations addressed to me. As you've noted on numerous occasions, it normally makes little difference. I do appreciate your help managing the household, but my personal business is of no concern to you. You may continue to open business documents only."

"Well!" Mary slapped her napkin on the table. "I was trying to be helpful. Lucky for you that I did not toss that woman's note into the fireplace. No good will come from a relationship with her. Mark my words!" With that, Mary pushed back her chair and marched from the room.

The doorman slipped a note to Patrick. Montgomery had accepted his invitation for dinner. He remained at the table, deep in thought. He recalled his return a year ago, when he had chanced upon Victoria, the baron's daughter.

As children, he had frequently played with Victoria's brother, Malcolm. Victoria always seemed to tag along, following the boys.

One day he had seen her in the forest where they used to play. "Wait! Please stay," he requested as she started to rise from the fallen log.

She continued to stare at the moss-covered ground. "I must return home."

Patrick tugged at the sleeves of his gray morning coat. He studied the elegantly dressed woman with the reddish curls.

Blushing, Victoria smiled. "Lord O'Neil. Papa said you had returned. Please accept my condolences regarding your parents. I will miss them."

"Thank you. It was quite a shock to me. They were so young. Mother always spoke highly of you. If you don't mind, I'll join you on your chair. Remember how you, Malcolm, and I used to ride our horses through the forest?"

Patrick studied the loose tendrils framing her oval face as they blew gently in the morning breeze.

"I do. We had a grand time. You always let me win the races."

Patrick's laughter rang out. "I wondered if you would figure that out."

This unplanned meeting had laid the foundation for renewing their friendship. They continued to meet once a week in the forest. They discussed everything from the latest fashions from Paris to the education of children.

Every time he broached the subject of her family, she would become evasive. Why would she not talk about her father or brother? What had happened to the Montgomery household while he had spent the past ten years in school and living in London?

A couple of weeks ago, the rendezvous abruptly ceased. There had been no note or explanation. Patrick was worried about her. Dinner tonight would give him an opportunity to see the baron and judge for himself if the man had changed. Plus, he could see Victoria again and reassure himself that she was fine. But what if she wasn't fine? What was he prepared to do about it?

Chapter 4

VICTORIA AND HER FATHER arrived early. Directed to the parlor, she patiently waited for Patrick to join them. Her stomach churned as she watched her father.

Victoria looked around the room. No wonder her father's eyes had lit up like a candelabra. The Italian marble fireplace glowed with dying embers, casting an amber hue over the room. A red Oriental rug covered most of the floor. The white brocade-covered chairs had silver strands woven into the fabric. Priceless paintings covered the walls. This was a stylish room.

Hearing footsteps, Victoria turned and saw her father stride toward Patrick with his hand outstretched. "Good evening, O'Neil. It's a pleasure to see you again."

"I'm pleased that you came," Patrick replied. Victoria stood quietly at her father's side. Patrick's observation caught her attention, and she truly smiled for the first time in days.

With a bow to her, he remarked, "Lady Montgomery. It is a pleasure to see you again."

Victoria glanced at her father to gauge his reaction. She never knew how he would react. She returned his smile. "Thank you. Will your aunt be joining us tonight?"

"No, I'm afraid not. She had a previous engagement."

Patrick took her arm and led the way to the dining room. Hearing the front door open, they all turned to see her brother,

Malcolm, standing in the hallway, preening and plucking at his clothing like a peacock. Patrick's smiled faded.

Malcolm tossed his head, allowing his fashionably long hair to fall over his brow. Victoria was embarrassed. She couldn't say anything; to do so would bring her father's wrath down on her head.

"Patrick, ol' boy, you look like an old man frowning like that. One might get the impression that you are not pleased to see me."

Patrick's eyes narrowed. "I'm surprised that you left London and your usual pursuits."

Malcolm put his arm about Victoria's shoulder and gave her a light kiss on the cheek. "I truly missed the clean air and the joys of country life." He clutched Victoria's hand, adding, "After sampling London's most beautiful women, I find that none of them can surpass my darling sister."

"Yes, yes," interrupted William, "we can continue this discussion later. Dinner is waiting."

Victoria shook off Malcolm's arm so that Patrick could escort her to the table. After a shaky beginning, dinner was served. Several varieties of wine were offered during dinner. Victoria pressed her lips into a tight line when her father emptied his fourth glass and requested more. Patrick's sympathetic eyes met hers. She smiled back. Rather than retreating to the library for brandy, the men joined Victoria in the music room after dinner. Malcolm went to the piano and toyed with the keys. He appeared bored with the conversation and was content to indulge himself with the bottle of port.

It wasn't long before William drifted off in a drunken stupor near the fireplace. She and Patrick sat on the settee, quietly conversing. Suddenly, Patrick stood and offered her his arm. "Come, let me show you the garden."

She hesitated for a second. "That would be lovely."

Malcolm glared after them.

The night air was heavy with the aroma of hundreds of roses. But Victoria was distracted, making it difficult to enjoy the beauty of the garden. Malcolm's behavior was becoming more alarming. He took every opportunity to brush against her hand or sit near her. His bold stares were unnerving. Her brother's angelic golden looks hid the dark side of his personality from society, but she knew what he was capable of.

She turned to study the towering man next to her. He was kind and represented safety, something sadly lacking in the Montgomery household. Patrick stopped next to a white wrought-iron bench. Dusting off the seat with his handkerchief, he offered her a seat.

She was not fooled by Patrick's recent attentions. There was no love between them, only friendship. She was intimidated by his dark looks and physical size. He was too powerful. Too intense.

Sitting beneath the trellis, covered with golden roses, Victoria felt shielded from her family.

"You look like you are a thousand miles away."

"Excuse me. What were you saying?"

Smiling down at her, Patrick inched closer. "I was remarking that your thoughts seemed far away."

"I'm sorry. I did not mean to be rude."

"Your behavior is perfect. I was just teasing you." He gently squeezed her hand.

"Father never teases," she whispered, nervous that such a handsome man was flirting with her.

"Well, a little humor often makes a tense situation more tolerable." Patrick rushed on. "Victoria, I have known your family for many years. I'm sure by now you realize that I care about you. I consider it the highest honor to offer you the protection of my name."

Her response was barely audible. "I would be greatly honored, Patrick."

Her mind swirled with many unanswered questions. Satisfaction coursed through her. He had offered for her! Yet fear and assorted questions crept in. What would be her father's reaction? Would she ever come to love Patrick or know the physical pleasures that others whispered about? Did she want to?

Gingerly lifting her hand, he caressed her skin with his warm lips. She had the sudden urge to pull away. Patrick gently placed his hand on her neck. His fingers grazed her skin. Afraid that she would do something wrong, she stared into his eyes, noting that they altered between green and gold.

"Your eyes are the oddest color. They remind me of a tiger."

He pulled her closer, murmuring in her ear, "And when was the last time you saw a tiger this close, Victoria?"

Giggling, she broke from his embrace. "It tickles when you talk in my ear."

"Let it never be said that I failed to amuse a lady." He stood and offered her his arm, leading her back to the house. He gave her an odd look. Did he know that she didn't love him? She couldn't let him kiss her. Could not!

"I'm not sure whether Father will give his blessing."

He patted her hand reassuringly. "I'm never deterred once I make a decision. Your father will see things my way."

Upon entering the house, Victoria drew back from Patrick. William looked angry as he paced about the room.

Spotting her, William charged forward. "Victoria! You forgot to ask my permission to stroll in the garden."

The censure in her father's voice dashed her good mood.

Patrick interrupted, "Sir, if I could have a few minutes of your time, I would like to discuss something of importance to both of us."

Victoria watched as William followed Patrick to the study. A calculating smile spread across her father's face. Victoria knew that her father's gambling debts had dramatically reduced the family income. She wasn't blind. One by one, the horses, artwork, and jewelry had disappeared from the estate. Her father constantly ranted about Malcolm's gambling beyond his means and throwing money away on mistresses.

Malcolm scowled at her before walking out of the room. Alone, Victoria's hands twisted together. What if her father refused Patrick's offer? She wanted to escape his unstable moods and the impending poverty. She had to know what was being discussed. But how? Tapping her foot impatiently, she had an idea. Secretively gliding along the walls of the hallway, Victoria saw the study doors cracked open. Standing to the side, she could see Patrick sitting at his desk and her father sitting across from him. William helped himself to a brandy and a cigar.

Patrick's dark eyes hid his emotions. "I assume that you know why I wished to speak to you?"

William blew a ring of smoke in the air. "We're here so you can state your intentions toward my dear lovely daughter. Am I correct?"

Patrick growled, "I will say this just once, so let me make myself perfectly clear. I intend to marry Victoria, and I do not expect nor desire any dowry. I will assist your family by covering all outstanding debts because I do not want her embarrassed or feeling guilty about leaving. I have decided that we will be married as soon as possible. After that, any contact with one another will be limited. Are my terms clear?"

Victoria gasped, swiftly covering her mouth. Her father had to be furious. He would surely refuse Patrick's offer now.

William stood and ground the cigar in an ashtray. "Do you think that I care so little for my only daughter that I will agree to your terms?"

Patrick sneered at his future father-in-law. "You care for your pocketbook, not her feelings. Name your price."

Victoria could see her father's rage. His face was vivid red. Her heart was pounding with anxiety. After a minute or two of hesitation, William muttered, "I accept, but I will require a suitable living allowance. I must keep up appearances until I remarry or Malcolm marries."

"Thank God," Victoria whispered. This time his greed would result in a favorable outcome, something that actually benefited her.

A look of satisfaction shone in Patrick's eyes. "Done. I will have the necessary papers drawn up. They will be delivered to you within the week."

As Patrick rose from his chair, Victoria scurried back to the music room.

Victoria rose as Patrick strode toward her with outstretched arms. Enveloped by his strength, she leaned her head against his broad chest. She felt so safe and secure in his arms. If only life could stop at this moment, she would surely be content forever.

"I have good news, my dear. Your father has consented to our marriage. If you agree, I'd like to be married within the month."

"A month? I need more time … to prepare. Several fittings will be needed for the dress, and there are so many details to attend to."

"Sweeting, I will ask my aunt to help you with the planning. She will follow your every wish. We will have the perfect wedding. I believe I heard your father order the carriage. I wish we had more time to visit tonight, but we will talk soon. I promise."

Numb, she nodded in agreement. Her heart pounded with fear. She was terrified at the thought of intimacy. If her father and brother were any indication of how men and women interacted, then she would soon come to hate Patrick. How could she tell Patrick that what she most wanted was someone to protect and comfort her? The thought of unbridled passion frightened her.

Her father and Malcolm waited near the door. The sounds of a jiggling harness and the clumping of hooves indicated that the carriage was ready. Patrick helped her with her cloak. He took her hand in his and pressed a warm kiss on her pulse. His eyes glittered with an unnamed emotion. "Good-bye. I will see you soon."

Surrounded by darkness, Victoria leaned back on the carriage seat as they drove home. Her evolving relationship with Patrick and the feelings toward marriage added to her confusion.

Malcolm's sarcastic voice broke the silence. "So congratulations are in order, *Lady O'Neil.* I suppose you think that you're too good for us now?"

Victoria looked at her father for assistance. His steady snores rumbled off the sides of the carriage, a result of the overindulgence in brandy.

Malcolm inched nearer. The smell of alcohol washed over her. "I've seen you watching O'Neil. Do you imagine him touching you?"

Disgusted by his insinuations, she snapped, "Why are you tormenting me? I'm your sister, your own flesh and blood. If you don't cease, I will tell father."

Laughing harshly, Malcolm grabbed her hand, capturing it in his. "You stupid chit. Haven't you ever wondered why father has always treated you different from me? He is your stepfather. There is no blood between us!"

Tears welled up in her eyes. "Stepfather? No! Mama would have told me. You're a liar!"

"She was waiting until you were old enough to understand."

She lunged forward and swung her arms as hard as she could, wanting to silence his hateful words.

Startled by the noise, her father woke to see her flinging her fists at Malcolm. His booming voice startled her. "Stop it! What is all this fuss about?"

Lights from the manor house loomed ahead as the carriage rolled up the long tree-lined drive. William shook his hands at both of them, silencing further discussion. They climbed the steps to the entryway and walked past the servants, who faded into the darkened hallways, not wanting to be a target of their employer's wrath. William marched them straight to the study. Sitting behind a massive desk, he glared at the two of them. "Do you want to create a scandal? Victoria, a young woman in your position must be careful. We do not want O'Neil to reconsider his offer."

Angry, Victoria's voice rose. "Malcolm said you're not my real father."

"Young lady, I suggest you curb your rebellious tongue. It is unfortunate that you discovered the truth, but it changes nothing. Go to your room. I will deal with Malcolm."

Blinded by tears, she ran to her room. She couldn't stay here. Malcolm's behavior scared her.

Dismissing the maid, she curled up into a ball in the center of the canopied bed and rocked back and forth. She was trapped. A marriage to Patrick provided a means of escape. She had no choice but to go forth with the wedding plans and hope that there would be a better life waiting for her.

Chapter 5

THE WEEKEND ARRIVED AT last. As Ann cleaned house, she couldn't shake the feeling that she had met the man of her dreams before viewing the album. But where? When? Anyone pictured in that old album had been dead for years.

After constant urging, Ann finally agreed to meet Stacy for dinner. Maybe this was just what she needed, something to keep her mind off her dreams.

Glancing at the clock, she muttered. "Crap, late again." After getting a jacket, she rushed out the door.

Ann walked into the Italian restaurant and saw Stacy with a man she hadn't seen before. From the cut of his suit, she knew it was expensive. He was immaculately groomed. His sable hair gleamed in the dimmed lights. His hazel eyes consumed her friend.

"Ann, over here." Stacy stood and waved.

Half of the men at the bar turned to stare at Stacy, who looked striking in a black knit dress that hugged her thin but well-defined body. Ann wished she had worn something dressier. Her tan slacks and tweed blazer felt dowdy.

"Sorry I'm late."

Stacy held the man's hand as she introduced him. "Ann, I would like to introduce you to Kevin Fazio. He and his brother own the restaurant."

"Kevin, it's nice to meet you. Will you be joining us for dinner?"

Her eyebrows quirked upward as his hand slid down Stacy's back and rested on her slender hip.

"No, thank you. I was keeping Stacy company until you arrived. I can't have a beautiful woman sitting alone in my restaurant. It might ruin my reputation." He gave Stacy a friendly kiss on the cheek and excused himself.

Amused, Ann watched Stacy's eyes follow Kevin as he walked away. Stacy sighed in mock surrender. "Have you ever seen a better-looking butt?"

Ann leaned back and folded her arms across her chest. "Okay, give me the details."

"I was sitting by myself—waiting for you again, I might add. Kevin just walked up and introduced himself. You wouldn't believe the things we have in common."

Laughing, Ann replied, "Let me guess. He probably has a sports car and a healthy bank account?"

Stacy tilted her head to cast another glance at Kevin. "Well, he does have a black Mercedes." Turning back to Ann, Stacy remarked, "You still have the dark circles. Girl, you need a good night's rest. Please tell me that you took that album back to the store."

Ann shrugged. "No. Something always comes up. With David calling all the time, I haven't had a decent night's sleep in weeks. Did I tell you that I got a restraining order?"

"About time. That should keep David in line. He'll get bored and move on to some other unsuspecting woman. By the way, are you still working on your genealogy?"

"Yeah. It seems that most of the O'Neils came to America, but Michael O'Neil moved to England with his wife, Alice. They died in some type of accident."

"That's too bad." Stacy flashed Ann a puzzled look. "I don't understand why ..."

"Michael?" Ann supplied.

"Yeah, Michael. Why would he leave Ireland and move to England?"

Ann leaned forward, brushing her hair behind her ear. "I'm

far from an expert, but from what I've gathered on the Internet and from family journals, Michael O'Neil owned a large estate in Ireland. Due to high taxes, they leased out their land. The O'Neils were trying to help those who had no land and no way to support their families. When the potato crop failed several years in a row, the tenants had no way of paying the rent, and O'Neil had no way to pay his taxes. Rather than let some stranger take his house and belongings, he sold everything he could and gave the money to his brothers, who were leaving the country. Then he went to England to help Alice's father run the family business. She was an only child, so her parents' estate fell to her. They had a huge interest in the shipping industry."

Ann paused as the impatient server took their pizza order. A large group celebrating a birthday was seated nearby. The server was obviously interested in a bigger tip from the other table.

Ann resumed her story after the server hurried off. "The last thing O'Neil did was burn the house and all the outbuildings in Ireland to the ground. Apparently, the new English owners were really ticked off."

"My God, that sounds like a script from some movie."

"Can you imagine never knowing if you would see your family again? From what I've read, anywhere from one and a half to two million people died from hunger or disease during that period in Ireland."

"At least now I know why you've been so busy lately."

Ann tightly clasped Stacy's hand. "I don't know what I would do if you weren't here for me. I love you."

Wiping her eyes, Stacy retorted, "Honey, I'm your best friend. Numero uno! Okay, enough of this mushy stuff. Let's eat and get to the movie on time for a change."

Several hours later, they emerged from the theater. As they lingered on the sidewalk comparing their reactions, Ann stopped in midsentence. "Look! There's David's car." She latched on to Stacy's arm to keep from running away.

Stacy quickly looked around the half-empty lot. "Are you sure it's David's?"

Ann gaped at the quickly emptying lot. "I saw a white Mustang!"

Stacy looked around the dimly lit area, where there wasn't even one white car. "Uh, I hate to tell you, but I don't see anything."

Ann's eyes swept the area. Sure enough, the car was gone.

"Are you getting paranoid on me?"

Taking a deep breath, Ann placed her hand over her racing heart. "Maybe I overreacted, but I'm sure that when we came outside, there was a white Mustang."

In an effort to reassure her friend, Stacy rationalized, "Did David know where we were going tonight? No! Is there more than one white Mustang in town? Yes! There is no way that he would know you were here."

"I know, I know. You're right. Let's just go."

After separating, Ann couldn't shake the feeling of being watched. She checked her rearview mirror constantly to make sure no one followed. After opening the garage door once she reached her home, Ann pulled inside and hurried into the house, immediately bolting the door behind her. She moved through the house, checking the window locks in each room.

Confident of her safety, she decided to take a shower. Ann went upstairs to her bedroom to get a nightgown. Noticing the open blinds, she quickly closed them.

From outside, hidden in the bushes across the street, observant eyes waited and watched. Once she entered the bedroom, he approached the house, creeping along the side to avoid being seen. When he reached the back door, he slowly grasped the handle in his thick palm and turned it. Damn! It was locked. Glancing up, he saw that the bathroom light was still on. Slipping a pick into the lock, it opened easily. No alarms sounded. There was nothing but silence. Pleased at how his plan was coming together, he stepped inside the kitchen.

Suddenly, the neighbor's backyard light flooded the blackness. Dogs started barking, and the sound of voices grew louder. He cursed and quickly slithered into the night shadows. Another time.

Flushed from the hot shower, Ann went downstairs and switched on the kitchen light. She saw the open door and froze. Her heart thundered in her chest. She had checked the door earlier. Someone had broken in! Was someone still in the house? She grabbed the phone and dialed 911. Within minutes, flashing red lights lit up the neighborhood. A thorough search of her house confirmed that no intruders were present. From the muddy footprints outside on the patio, the police were sure that someone had gained entry but had left for unknown reasons.

Huddled in a chair with a blanket draped about her shoulders, she somehow managed to complete the necessary paperwork. The police thought that the most likely motive was burglary. They asked whether she had any ideas about who would break into her house. David's name immediately flashed through her mind. Could he be this unstable?

Ann described David's recent behavior, and the officers took his name and address.

"Ms. Roberts, I would suggest that you spend the night with a friend or have someone stay here," the senior officer politely advised.

Her voice shaking, Ann asked, "C-could you stay until my family arrives? I need to call them."

"No problem. We'll just complete our paperwork out in the car while we wait."

Ann picked up the phone and dialed Jess first. "Hi, Jess. It's Mom," she whispered.

"Mom, what's going on? You sound funny."

Ann started crying. "Someone broke into my house tonight. I—"

Jessica interrupted. "Are the police there?"

"Yes."

"Good. I'll be there in about an hour. I'm packing an overnight bag. Scott won't mind. He won't have to share the remote."

"Scott's a good husband." Ann attempted a laugh but broke into another sob.

"Mom, Mom, I'll call Mark. Don't worry. Everything will be okay." Ann sat on the sofa so she could see the police car. She wrapped her arms across her stomach, letting the tears course down her cheeks. What if David had come upstairs while she was showering? She wasn't even safe in her own home. Filled with the urge to lash out, she punched the sofa.

In less than an hour, footsteps echoed outside. She looked out and saw Mark and Jessica running up the sidewalk. Throwing open the door, they rushed to her side.

"Are you okay? What the hell happened? Was it David?" Mark demanded angrily.

"Calm down. You're upsetting Mom," Jessica reprimanded.

"Please, kids, not now. I gave the police David's name and address. They checked for fingerprints. I guess we wait and see what they come up with."

"Well, if he's involved, I hope you plan on pressing charges." Mark paced about the kitchen.

Jessica, always the nurturer, started heating water for tea. When the tea was ready, Jess pulled up a chair next to her and began rubbing her tense shoulders. Ann felt guilty for disrupting the kids' evening.

"Hey, listen, guys. I'm feeling much better now. The shock has worn off a bit. I want you both to go home since you have to work tomorrow." Jessica was an administrator at a local community college, and Mark was in the insurance industry. "I'll call Stacy to come stay with me."

Jessica shook her head. "We're not leaving, are we, Mark?"

Mark resolutely stated, "Hell, no, we're not leaving. Mom's upset."

Jessica filled a mug and set in front of Ann. "Mark and I have talked about David. We're glad you got the restraining order. If he's the one who broke in tonight, you're coming to live with Scott and me for a while."

Ann kissed Jess's cheek. Her daughter was just like her. She had a take-charge manner. A younger version of herself, with the exception of hair color, Jess was a powerhouse. She didn't back down from anything.

"We'll talk about things in the morning. Let's turn out the lights and go to bed. I'm exhausted."

She fell asleep before her head hit the pillow, comforted by the presence of her children. Minutes later, the phone rang, jolting the entire household.

Jumping out of bed, Ann bumped her foot on the dresser. "Ouch!" She hobbled to the phone and mumbled a hello. She waited for a reply, unsure if the caller had already hung up. "Hello. Is anyone there?"

The only response was the eerie sound of someone breathing heavily. By this time, her children had joined her.

"Who's on the phone?" Jessica whispered.

Once again, Ann demanded to know who was calling.

Mark moved closer to stand by his mother. "Mom, hang up! Don't talk to him."

Ann knew better than to indulge a prank caller, but she thought that if she could hear just a sound, she would know whether it was David. After a few seconds of silence, she slowly lowered the receiver.

"Damn you! Don't you hang up on me," she heard David roar. She reluctantly put the receiver back to her ear. "You're not getting away with what you've done. I'm going to make you pay and enjoy doing it!"

Ann's anger boiled to the surface. "What I did to you? I've done nothing to you. We hardly know each other and you want to control my life. I've had enough. If you show your face anywhere near me again, I'll have you thrown in jail so quickly that you won't know which way is up. Understand?"

Hysterical laughter was his response. "Oh, Ann, do you think your threats frighten me? This isn't over." The phone went silent.

Chapter 6

ANN LET THE PHONE drop on the table and retreated downstairs as if in a trance. Both kids fell in close behind her.

"I need another cup of tea," announced Ann.

"It was David, wasn't it? Did he threaten you?" Jessica asked, her voice trembling.

Ann nodded.

Mark stormed around the kitchen. "Damn it, we need to let the police know that he called. I'll go call them." He took his cell phone into the front room.

Jessica got a Kleenex and wiped away her tears. "Mom, you're not safe here. Please pack your stuff and move in with me for a month or so. After that, we can reevaluate the situation."

Ann's hands began to tremble. She tried not to panic. Jess's idea made sense. Her impulse was to start packing, quit her job, and leave the state—go somewhere where he couldn't find her. Then her anger resurfaced. She loved this house. This was where she had raised her children. Why should she leave?

"Sorry, Jess. I'm going to stay here. This is my home."

Seeing her daughter's tears, Ann hugged her tightly. "Sweetie, don't cry. I'm fine. Really!"

Jess's sobs turned to laughter. "I'm supposed to make you feel better, not the other way around."

Determined to put David behind bars, she and Jessica joined her son as he talked to the police.

During the next week, repair people came and went. The doors and locks were all upgraded, and a security system was installed. The police reported that they had searched David's house and office. He had vanished. Even his bank account had been closed. The police assured her that it was only a matter of time before they had him in custody. Mark and Jessica took turns spending the night. The kids had encouraged her to purchase a gun, but Ann was adamant that guns provided more danger than protection. She did, however, purchase several canisters of pepper spray and a stun gun.

Weeks drifted by, and Ann began to feel comfortable and safe again in her daily routine. David had probably realized that he'd crossed the line and left the state.

Stacy's involvement with Kevin drastically cut the time the two women spent together, so Ann devoted her time to delving into her family history. Summer dissolved inevitably into fall. The mighty maple and oak trees that lined Ann's street showered their multitude of crimson and golden leaves on the frosty ground. In this season of transition, Ann found herself more absorbed than ever in the nineteenth century.

There were so many places on the Internet to look for genealogy information that it was overwhelming. She checked out a couple of well-known sites like Ancestory.com and several others with archival records from England. Ann just didn't have time to do the research herself, so she hired a genealogist to do the work for her. Ann was lucky to find a woman in England to help her locate information that could identify O'Neil's son. Ms. Marshfield specialized in British genealogy. After several weeks, Ann received documents from Ms. Marshfield in an e-mail, including a report on the O'Neil family.

Several of the pages appeared to be from a diary. Excitement filling her, Ann eagerly printed the documents. After reading them, she learned that the pages were out of a diary belonging to Alice O'Neil and were dated 1842. Awestruck, she tried to read the faint handwriting. It appeared to be written shortly after the birth of Alice's son, and it described a difficult birth.

The name of the child was Patrick O'Neil. Suddenly, the missing piece of the puzzle jumped off the paper. After twirling around the room with joy, she hurried to the computer, eager to enter the information.

Without warning, lightning flashed outside and booming thunder shook the house. The lights flickered. Ann tried to stand, but dizziness overwhelmed her. Her vision wavered as she fought to remain conscious. A damp gray mist shrouded the room. As her sight cleared, she found herself in a strange room. Light was diminished, as heavy velvet drapes covered the tall windows. The smell of lemons filled the room. It reminded Ann of her grandmother's house. The wood-paneled room was furnished with Victorian antiques. The Tiffany lamp on the end table looked very expensive.

Ann squeezed her eyes shut. "This can't be real. I'm dreaming. It's a delayed reaction to all the stress." She pinched her arm. "Okay, that hurts."

She slowly opened her eyes and saw that she was still in the same odd room. Where was she? When she tried to move, she found that her feet had become lead weights that wouldn't budge. What was happening? Even her body felt different.

Heavy footsteps echoed in the hallway. Ann felt a level of fear never before experienced. Her anxiety increased as the sound drew nearer. She pushed her tousled curls out of her face, bracing herself to meet who or what lurked on the other side of the door.

The footsteps paused near the door. Seconds later, the door burst open, allowing a gust of wind to rush into the room. Ann jerked with fear, muffling a scream with her hands. A man filled the doorway. A heavy black coat billowed about his formidable frame. He whipped off his outer garment and threw it on a chair, creating a whiff of intoxicating musk that caressed her senses. His emerald eyes locked with hers. His dark evening clothes were austere. His chiseled facial features held a strained, intense expression.

Was she confronting a phantom or a real man? Terrified, she covered her face with her hands. Thunder continued to echo throughout the house. Would this nightmare ever end?

The man studied her, fixating on her hair. Slowly he moved over to her and ran his fingers through her curls. She jerked away. With ragged breathing, she met his stare. When his regard traveled down her body, he paused, staring at her chest. Surprisingly, he began choking. She was freezing, which caused her nipples to harden into little nubs. Embarrassed, she folded her arms across her chest. His lips curved into a half smile.

Why was he smiling at her? His heated gaze made her even more nervous. Now she knew how Little Red Riding Hood felt when she came face-to-face with the big bad wolf. His hand shook as he reached out to touch her cheek. What was his game—to seduce her? If that was his intent, it was working.

As they stared at one another, she was afraid to break the magical spell that surrounded them. The need to run into his arms was overpowering. Her legs grew weak. Was it from fear or desire? His smoldering scrutiny was overwhelming. Breaking through the haze of passion, her brain finally began functioning. He looked familiar. But how? Somehow, somewhere, she had seen him before.

Immobilized by the intensity in his eyes, she huskily whispered, "Will you tell me your name?"

Chapter 7

THINKING SHE WAS PLAYING a strange charade, he winked at her. "I am whoever you want me to be, darling."

Patrick had arrived home after just missing the storm that swirled outside, and he had started for the stairs. That's when he heard a strange sound coming from the sitting room. It had been his mother's favorite place in the house. After her death, he had ordered staff to close off the room. When he threw open the door, nothing could have prepared him for what he saw. Victoria! At least, he thought it was Victoria. He saw no carriage at the front drive, and none of the staff had alerted him of her presence. She was trembling. Was she afraid of him?

He reached out and touched a curl covering her breast. His hand slowly squeezed. Her swollen nipples drew his undivided attention. Unable to stop himself, he weighed her breasts in his palms. Her quick intake of breath was the only sign that she was aroused. She leaned into him, pressing into his warmth and his arousal. His lips met hers, slowly tasting and savoring the scent that was hers. He reached one arm around her bottom and tugged her toward him. He wanted to sink deep inside her. His hips began a slow back-and-forth cadence. A moan broke the silence. Was that his voice or hers? He felt like a schoolboy, unable to control his arousal and passion. He realized that he could not take her on the floor. He broke the kiss and took her hand. His empty bed was mere steps away.

Ann backed away from him. She folded her arms across her chest in a defensive move. "What do you think you're doing? Just answer my question and tell me your name."

Was she trying to confuse him? Then it dawned on him. She was playacting! That had to be it. His deep husky laugh filled the room. "If you are trying to excite me, you have succeeded. Come here and let me give you a kiss."

"Ooooh! Are you always such an ass? Just because you're good-looking and obviously rich doesn't mean you need to be crude."

Her language was appalling. His smile faded, but he was secretly pleased that she thought him attractive. "Let's not get too carried away with your little game."

"Game? You're totally losing me."

Patrick slowly assessed her every curve. "Enough! My patience with this game has ended. You have a choice, Lady Montgomery. Shall we finish what we started upstairs in my bed or do you prefer to wait until the wedding?"

"Wedding? What are you talking about?"

Patrick carefully studied Ann. Her flushed cheeks suited her coloring. He had never noticed her full breasts before. She seemed so different tonight. She even lacked the appropriate undergarments. She wasn't herself at all. Her manly costume and huskier voice puzzled him. But he had to admit that he was intrigued.

The storm outside gained momentum, and thunder rattled the windows. Without warning, her figure grew hazy. Uncomprehending, he gasped as she became transparent. He frantically tried to grab her hand. His eyes widened with terror as his hand passed through hers. A gray mist consumed her body, making her disappear.

From a distance her voice pleaded, "Will you tell me who you are?"

"Where are you?" he called frantically.

Flashes of lightning were blindingly close. Her voice drifted out of the mist. "Are you Patrick O'Neil?"

"Yes, you know I am," he cried impatiently. "Why is this happening? Victoria! Victoria! Come back."

Patrick winced as thunder reverberated, rattling the windows. He glanced around the room. It was empty. Was he losing his mind? His hands tore through his hair. Victoria hadn't been here after all. She wouldn't have dressed like a boy. Maybe the wine he had consumed earlier in the evening had dulled his senses. With his head pounding and manhood throbbing, Patrick sighed in frustration. He gripped the door handle and peered around the door once more, hoping to see her again, but there was only darkness and the whisper of her alluring scent.

The dizziness lifted, and the sound of thunder faded in the distance. Ann's vision cleared. She was home. She felt relief and a sense of loss. Her throat tightened as tears threatened. She stumbled to the bathroom and splashed cold water on her face. Had she really traveled back in time and met Patrick or was it another dream? If it was a dream, it was the most vivid one yet.

The vision was like a scene from a sci-fi movie. Ann had felt betrayed by her body. She wanted him to carry her to his bed, tear off her clothes, and make wild, passionate love until they could not do it anymore. Her womb pulsed as she pressed her legs together. "Stop it," she chided herself. "You're not sixteen anymore, so act your age."

Things like this didn't happen. She was just an average woman, nothing special. Perhaps the entire episode was a figment of her overly active imagination, yet it had seemed so real. He had seemed so real—the raindrops on his clothes, the coal-black hair, the fire in his eyes, and the heat of his body pressed against hers.

Ann gulped. He had mentioned a wedding to her! That could be a dream come true. She sighed, fantasizing about Patrick. Hmm. Hot sex with a hot guy for the rest of her life. Wait! What about love? What about the fact that this was all a dream? After all, her common sense argued, Patrick was not even alive. She choked back the urge to laugh hysterically.

As she pulled the T-shirt over her head, Ann took a deep breath. A hauntingly familiar musk scent assailed her. If it had been a dream, then why was everything so vivid? Ann's fear returned. What if she dreamed of Patrick again and woke up in that other house? Exhausted, she finally succumbed to weariness and restless dreams.

Chapter 8

RAYS OF SUNSHINE WARMED his face. He ignored Carrick as the valet let in more of the blinding light.

"Breakfast is ready. You asked me to remind you that Lord Aylesbury is expected to arrive this morning."

He rolled to the edge of the bed, barely able to open his eyes. His head pounded from the large amount of port consumed last night after seeing Victoria. A certain part of his body remembered Victoria's lithe body in the tight shirt and trousers, and it now stood at attention. He could have sworn that it was Victoria who had spoken to him, but the woman who had stood before him had more spirit than the Victoria he knew. Her words and behavior intrigued him. His loins tightened as he remembered how she had looked in those strange clothes. His arms ached with desire to hold her. Victoria was usually so reserved and timid that he would have never supposed her ready to venture into the realm of lovemaking. After last night, his opinion had changed. But how did he feel? True, he didn't love her. His proposal had been impulsive, not like him at all. But he did feel the urge to protect her.

Yet the woman standing before him last night did not need saving. She needed a man to show her how to unlock the passion that simmered just below the surface. The Victoria he saw last night had a fire within. He could grow to love a woman who filled him with such desire.

He finished dressing as his best friend, Anthony Collier, Lord Aylesbury, was announced. Patrick entered the dining room to find Anthony helping himself to a large plate of sliced ham and biscuits.

Patrick's sarcastic tone welcomed his friend. "Thanks for waiting. If I had been any later, I doubt you would have left me any breakfast."

"Hmmm," Anthony murmured as he bit into the flaky biscuit dripping with jam. "I believe I will steal your staff so I can enjoy all this delightful food at my table. Mother constantly complains, so our staff finds it a challenge to see how many ways they can destroy a meal."

"So Lady Aylesbury hasn't changed. You're always welcome here, even if you do eat enough for ten men."

After breakfast, they rode out to check the property and exercise the horses. Anthony's lighthearted conversation entertained Patrick. As they rode side by side, the dirt lane provided stark contrast to the lush pastures on either side. Sheep and horses dotted the landscape as they grazed.

"Are you still fencing daily?" Patrick asked.

Anthony grinned. "The major insists upon it. He's a stickler for routine. Besides, it keeps me fit."

Patrick snorted, taking note of his friend's new sideburns and cut of his hair. Fastidious about his looks, Anthony always had a mistress at his side in public. "Yes. Fit so you can escape irate fathers and brothers when you toss their sweet daughters or sisters aside. What is your aversion to marriage? At thirty, you should be thinking of starting a family."

Anthony pretended to have a wounded heart. "My God! My best friend, my old chum from Oxford, whom I looked after, might I add, is lecturing me like my mother."

Patrick grinned as he increased the pace, leaving Anthony to catch up. He lapsed into silence as his thoughts returned to Victoria.

After several miles, Anthony broke into his thoughts. "What the devil is wrong with you today? You haven't heard a word I've said in the last half hour. You look like hell. What happened after you left the ball last night?"

Debating how much to reveal, Patrick reined in his horse and dismounted. Dark green hills surrounded a nearby pond. A flock of geese took flight as their voices broke the peaceful silence of the morning. Patrick stared toward the neighboring Montgomery estate. "As you know, I proposed to Victoria last weekend." After Anthony's nod, he continued. "Victoria's actions have led me to believe that she is not completely committed about our marriage. She will not confide in me. One minute she is a desirable woman, and the next she becomes a timid girl again."

Dragging his fingers through his hair, Patrick groaned. "I'm at a complete loss on how to handle this situation. Then there's her family. I'm not sure if I'm doing the right thing."

"Well, we know that Malcolm isn't to be trusted," Anthony stated. "He is a miscreant by all standards. He is hardly welcome at any social event in London. The rumors of his debts and other excesses have circulated widely."

"Most of the rumors are true. Her father is just as bad. He spends most of his time gambling. Perhaps it would be better for Victoria to move in with me until the wedding."

"Has your brain turned to mush? Your reputation as a rake would be carved in stone."

"Devil take them all! People may think what they want."

"Is there something you aren't telling me? I haven't seen you this edgy since we took our finals at Oxford."

Patrick's eyes remained riveted on the shaded path that led to the Montgomery estate. "I've got a lot on my mind. Between the engagement and the odd dreams, something isn't right. I want to visit Victoria. Let's go."

Each intent on his own thoughts, the riders paid little attention to the wildflowers growing along the edge of the trail or to the beauty of the ancient limbs draping themselves over the path to create an arch. A short ride brought them to the Montgomery manor house. Patrick frowned at the extent of disrepair that had fallen on the once-stately manor. It had been almost ten years since he had visited the Montgomery family.

After several knocks on the weathered door, the butler finally opened the door, disapproval evident upon his stern face, for it was too early in the day for visitors.

"Please inform Lady Montgomery that Lord O'Neil and Lord Aylesbury are here," Patrick tersely demanded.

The butler reluctantly opened the door and led them to the drawing room. "Wait here. Lady Montgomery shall be with you shortly." Like the house, the butler's clothes were faded and worn. A faded rectangle on the wall revealed where a painting had been taken down and most likely sold to pay off gambling debts.

Patrick turned as Victoria entered the room. She glided across the marble tiles. Her yellow gown brought out the reddish glints of her riotous curls as they swayed back and forth. Her mannerisms were not that of the woman who'd infatuated him last night. Feeling off kilter, he forced a smile.

Patrick kissed her hand, trying to discern whether she would behave similar to how she'd been last night. He didn't know if he was relieved or disappointed that she didn't greet them in the costume she had worn last night.

"My father and brother are out. Shall I send someone to fetch them?"

Frowning, Patrick had to lean forward to hear her subdued voice. "No. I wanted to visit with you, not them."

While the maid poured the tea, Patrick saw Victoria sneaking glances at him. He was glad he had decided to call on her. He also watched her when he thought she was unaware. There was something different about her. She was nothing like last night.

Anthony entertained them with stories from London until all three of them dissolved in laughter.

Patrick rose, reluctant to leave, but the length of their visit had already extended the bounds of propriety. Anthony excused himself in order to allow the two of them a few moments together.

"I hope we have not imposed too long. I was worried about you after last night."

Victoria met his gaze. "Last night?"

"I was surprised and delighted to see you last night. If I had known that you wanted to be with me, I would have made it a point to arrive home much earlier. I'm curious how you made your way home."

She stared at him with a blank look. He felt uneasy. Why was she pretending that she hadn't visited him?

"Please do not make fun of me." She spun away, hiding her tears of disappointment.

He gently turned her toward him. With a touch of his finger, he raised her chin. "Forgive me. Those clothes you wore last night were wonderfully provocative. You created havoc in my dreams last night."

"You keep insisting that I visited you last night, but you are mistaken."

The confusion in her eyes gave Patrick pause. He impulsively swept her into his arms. He had to know whether the feelings he'd experienced last night were real. She gasped as his lips met hers. He pressed her against him hungrily, ensuring that she felt the outline of his arousal.

She pushed him away, tearing her lips from his. She visibly trembled. "Lord O'Neil, that was ill-advised. What if we had been discovered?"

He silently assessed her. Something was very wrong. Where was the woman he'd held in his arms just hours ago? Or was he mistaken? Had he experienced a vision last night?

"Believe me, I would never hurt you. I will honor your request. I will never force you to do anything you do not want to do."

Tears welled up in her eyes. Filled with regret, he quickly took his leave. His self-control was stretched beyond recognition. Her unresponsive body weighed heavily on his mind. Did she truly desire marriage? More importantly, was he doing the right thing for both of them?

Chapter 9

VICTORIA HURRIED TO HER bedroom window, humiliated by Patrick's actions. She watched the men riding down the lane. Patrick's accusation puzzled her. Why did he keep insisting that she was at his house? Was her future husband unbalanced? She was so scared.

The rest of the day, Victoria flitted aimlessly about the house. She was grateful for Malcolm's absence. Now that she knew the truth about her parentage, many past mysteries were resolved. She had never understood William's rejection until now. She remembered her mother as a sad figure, often crying alone in her room. Losing her mother at ten years old had altered her life. Any opportunity for joy or happiness had disappeared. Victoria was told that her mother had lost control of her mare and fallen, even though she had been an expert rider. Out of fear, Victoria never learned to ride.

Victoria rang the bell to clear away the serving tray. She felt like a ship without an anchor. She wanted to scream from frustration, but she would not. She was a lady at all times. Her stepfather had drilled that in her mind. She began to think that she had made a mistake accepting Patrick's offer. Though what choice did she really have? Victoria knew that her dowry was gone. William had spent the funds to pay his debts. Once she was married, there would no longer be a need to worry about money. She never knew from week to week whether there would be funds to pay the grocer. Patrick was wealthier than she had ever imagined. Life would be so much easier.

A wispy smile graced Victoria's features as she walked outside, hoping a breath of fresh air would shake away the melancholy. When she reached the orchard, she gently pulled a large yellow apple from an overloaded branch. Wiping the dust off on her skirt, she took a bite out of the sweet apple. A trickle of juice ran down her chin. Laughing, she wiped it off with the back of her hand. She spread out her skirts as she sat down. Leaning back, she watched the clouds skip by. Her eyes grew heavy in the warmth of the afternoon sun.

Victoria's eyes flew open as warm breath hit her face. Malcolm was crouched next to her. His cobalt eyes twinkled at her. When she struggled to rise, he pushed her down in the tall grass.

"Relax, I won't hurt you. We need to talk. You have misunderstood my intentions."

Her fear increased as he pressed closer.

Slowly he straightened, putting a few inches between them. "Now that's better. I know I haven't shown it recently, but I want to make amends." His voice cracked. Surprisingly, he looked contrite. "I have protected you for years. I was the one who made sure that you didn't do without. I should be your husband, not that Irishman. I love you more than he ever will."

She shook her head in disbelief. "How can you even think of becoming my husband? You're my brother."

His coarse laughter rang out. "You are naive if you think Patrick loves you. Oh, he may be infatuated, but that, my dear, is far from love. I should know, for I have loved you for years." He pressed his cheek against hers, urgently whispering, "Leave with me today. We will go somewhere and start a new life together. I can make you happy."

Why was he trying to destroy her chance for happiness? Victoria jumped to her feet and backed away from Malcolm. Couldn't he just love her as a sister?

"Malcolm, please. You know that the family is in danger of

losing everything. You and your father have spent every dollar, including my dowry. I could never be with you as you want."

Shaking his head, Malcolm grabbed her hand, wrapping her in an embrace. His lips pressed against hers. With all her strength, she shoved at his chest, breaking away. The sound of her slapping him was the only sound heard.

Malcolm stared at her. His shoulders drooped. "Your wish is my command, Lady Montgomery." Without a backward glance, he mounted his horse and rode toward the house.

A male voice caused her to jump with fright.

"Sorry, m'lady. Me and my son heard loud voices. We didn't know if there was trouble or not. Can we help?"

She wanted to sink into the ground and disappear. "No, thank you. I appreciate your offer of assistance, but I can manage well enough now."

Tipping his cap, the farmer turned and walked away. A sigh of relief escaped her. Once she was married, Malcolm would treat her like a sister again. He had to! Why would he even think that she loved him and wanted to marry him? She couldn't tell her father or Patrick what Malcolm had proposed. It would just create more turmoil.

As she returned to the house, she thought about her appearance. Her mouth felt bruised. She decided to enter through the servants' entrance to avoid discovery by her stepfather.

Blanche's voice startled her. "Dear child! Whatever happened to you? You look a fright."

Unable to control the tears any longer, she buried her face in one of Blanche's familiar plump shoulders.

"There, there, don't cry. Nothing can hurt you now."

Blanche hustled her up the stairs and into the bedroom, chattering incessantly. Blanche laid a cool rag on her face, gently wiping away dried tears. Feeling more composed, Victoria sat on the edge of the bed.

"I think I'll rest for a while, but thank you for your help and support." Blanche gave her another hug and left the room.

After Victoria woke several hours later, Blanche knocked on

her door and slowly entered. "Oh, you look much better. The nap must have agreed with you. This may not be a good time, but have you forgotten that the O'Neils' costume ball is only days away? We still must find you a costume to wear."

Victoria sighed as she brushed back the curls framing her face. She dreaded the thought of the ball, for it meant that her wedding night was that much closer. "I did forget all about the ball with the plans for the wedding and all. We must find something special to please Patrick."

"I have an idea. I'll send word to the seamstress."

"Whatever you think best. I trust you, Blanche. Please tell my stepfather that I am unable to come down for dinner." Victoria locked the door after her maid left. She wanted to ensure that there would be no surprise visits from Malcolm. In a way, it was a relief to know that William was her stepfather. Victoria had always been bothered by his lack of affection. Now she no longer cared, for in less than a month, she would no longer be a Montgomery.

Chapter 10

THE MORNING OF THE ball arrived, the clouds dissipating as the autumn sun reigned in its glory. Patrick's servants busied themselves preparing for the biggest party of the year. Guests would begin arriving by early evening.

Hearing voices in the foyer, Patrick opened the library door to see Anthony.

Patrick warmly greeted his friend. "Aylesbury, it's good to see you. Have you come to help with the floral arrangements?"

"Ha-ha. I'm here to lend you moral support. Besides, my mother was lecturing me again about the benefits of matrimony."

"Even though it's still morning, come and have a drink with me. I've been working on correspondence from the bookkeeper. I swear, sometimes it becomes quite tedious."

Anthony followed Patrick to the library. After discussing generalities, Anthony set his glass aside. "I need to tell you the latest rumor at the club. Your dear friend Lady Paxton is planning to attend tonight."

"Damn her! I informed Katherine weeks ago that our relationship was over. I thought that once she saw the engagement announcement in the papers, she would become enthralled with someone else who had deep pockets." His fist tightened dangerously about the glass.

"I'm thankful that my former paramours are not as persistent as yours. Perhaps it is your winsome charm that they cannot bear to part with ... or maybe it's your talent between the sheets."

"Careful, Anthony. I can still beat you in the ring."

Anthony smothered a chuckle. "How do you propose to keep her from Victoria? If Katherine catches Victoria alone, she'll make mincemeat of your fiancée."

Patrick paced angrily about the room as Anthony sipped his drink quietly.

Patrick turned to his friend. "Do whatever it takes. I'm counting on you to make sure Katherine and Victoria do not come face-to-face, even if you have to dance with Katherine yourself."

Anthony flinched. "Hell, you do realize that Katherine will have her claws in me when she realizes that you are avoiding her. People will still talk. Victoria may overhear some careless remark. Perhaps you should warn her."

Patrick shook his head, ruffling his hair. "No, it would be too upsetting for her. This night is for the two of us. I do not want it marred in any fashion."

Anthony nodded. "You know that there is bound to be a scene."

Patrick shrugged. The events of the evening would most likely cause a sensation that London society would talk about for years.

"I need to check to see how the arrangements are progressing. Come with me."

As the men walked to the ballroom, Patrick had to smile at his aunt busily ordering around the horde of servants. Maids carried large bunches of fresh flowers in painted French vases, placing them throughout the house. Pausing in the doorway, Patrick could see that the floor gleamed from a recent waxing.

Mary looked up and saw them, waving them to her side. "Patrick, there you are. Anthony, it's nice to see you again. What do you think of the room so far?"

The smell of sweet roses and lilacs filled the room. A banquet of food and wine was being arranged on tables covered with pastel linen cloths. The musicians were busy tuning their instruments; the sounds of various instruments echoed about the room.

Patrick kissed his aunt's rosy cheek. "You have created a masterpiece. Thank you for your help with everything. Victoria will love you for it."

Without responding, Mary bustled off to see that the servants were being attentive to the details that she had planned.

After luncheon, Patrick excused himself, as Anthony had decided a nap was in order. Patrick had to finish a few letters before the guests began arriving. As dusk settled, Patrick stood and stretched after being hunched over his desk for the past few hours. He headed up the stairs to his room to dress for the evening.

Apprehensive about how the evening would unfold, Patrick was fidgety. His valet, Carrick, threw up his hands.

"My lord, if you don't stand still, you will go downstairs looking like an escapee from Bedlam. I refuse to accept the blame."

Patrick winked at the old man. Carrick had been his father's valet and had worked for his family for the past thirty years. "I would look like a bedlamite if I wore that damn pirate costume that my aunt picked out for me. I refuse to look so shabby. So I advise you to hurry before she comes up here and makes me wear the thing."

Minutes later, Patrick descended the stairs wearing traditional black evening clothes and a crisp white shirt. He wore an emerald paisley waistcoat. His aunt raved about paisley. He couldn't wait to see her reaction to the waistcoat. Besides, it would serve as a peace offering for not wearing that horrid costume. As he walked past several women who had arrived early, he heard a sigh or two. He fought back a smile. He was not ignorant of the speculation as to why he was attracted to the Montgomery girl. Her looks were not that of a typical London beauty. Her family's reputation was tarnished to the point that many men would have found her unacceptable. Men had placed bets at the club that he would have a new mistress within a year and would keep Victoria isolated in the country to raise the children. He would prove them wrong.

He joined his Aunt Mary near the entryway to greet the arriving guests. She glanced at his waistcoat and winked. "How apropos, O'Neil."

Victoria frantically called for Blanche. She still had to dress, and they were scheduled to leave within the hour. Her costume was far more revealing than she desired. It was a harem costume. A golden silk veil covered her face and hair. Blanche had convinced her that there would be so many layers of silk that it would be quite acceptable. Besides, the golden shade of the material highlighted her coloring.

Almost giddy with excitement, Victoria finished dressing. She stared into the mirror and was amazed at the transformation. She felt like a different woman. Still, a feeling of dread nagged her. She hadn't seen Malcolm all week. The servants reported that he had left for London several days ago. Though he was invited to the ball, she prayed that he would not attend.

William bellowed from below. "Victoria, you must not keep Lord O'Neil waiting! For the last time, hurry up."

Victoria rushed downstairs. For the past week, she had remained in her room in order to avoid her stepfather and Malcolm. She had read in the newspaper that her upcoming wedding was the talk of London.

William had ordered a new carriage to be delivered the next week, in time for the wedding. He was already spending money that Patrick had given him for the marriage settlement.

Overcome with nervousness, Victoria twisted her handkerchief as they approached Patrick's home, Epsom Hall. It was intimidating. The prestige and influence of the O'Neil family was evident by the appearance of the estate.

William glanced at Victoria. "Quit fidgeting. Now remember, you are a Montgomery. You are honoring them by attending. Stay close to me; I want to ensure no blunders occur."

Victoria stared down at the carriage floor. Why did he always ruin any opportunity for her happiness?

William assisted her out of the carriage. Victoria stood and gazed at the towering limestone walls. Epsom Hall was where she would soon live and be safe. No longer would she have to fear Malcolm. Why couldn't he be the loving brother from her childhood?

∞

Patrick stood in the doorway waiting for her. The light shining behind him poured out into the night. He felt like her prince, and she looked like a princess.

Patrick wouldn't have recognized her if William hadn't been at her side. She was beautiful yet appeared to be distressed. Taking her hand, he brought it to his mouth for a gentle caress.

"You have arrived at last." Patrick wrapped her arm in his. He glanced at William and nodded. "Welcome. Please come in and join the festivities. I want to take Lady Montgomery inside where it's warmer. Excuse us."

Patrick and Victoria wove their way through the crowd, reaching a secluded corner of the ballroom. Patrick's admiration was mirrored in his actions. "You look beautiful." Pressing her hand over his heart, he whispered, "Just a few more days and we'll be joined in marriage. Are you sure this is what you want?"

She squeezed his hand. "I assume you want a traditional marriage. Once we have a child, I plan to live here. I realize that you may wish to live in London."

Warning signals went off in his brain. His lips pressed together. "Traditional marriage? What are you suggesting?"

She nervously twisted her veil. "Surely you comprehend my meaning. I dislike mentioning such a personal subject." She leaned closer and whispered, "I know that you need an heir. I'm willing to perform my duty. Once that duty is fulfilled, we can live apart."

Patrick bristled with rejection. No woman had ever dreaded coming to his bed. He had hoped that with tender nurturing, her desire would match his own. Patrick straightened, trying not to frighten her. "I will not rush you, Victoria, but we will share a room and have relations more than once a year. I cannot accept otherwise."

He could not live in that manner.

Chapter 11

LADY KATHERINE PAXTON WATCHED Patrick's and Victoria's every movement. Her eyes narrowed in contemplation. "I couldn't have planned this any better myself," she crowed as Victoria ran out of the ballroom.

Katherine made her way to Patrick's side, letting her fingers brush against his as she offered him a glass of champagne. She'd dressed to impress Patrick. Her long white Grecian gown laced with a silver ribbon beneath her breasts pushed the ivory mounds nearly out of the dress, as was her intent. She wore a matching ribbon weaved through her upswept golden curls. Several guests remarked on what a striking pair they made—he in black and she in white. Society ignored her promiscuous behavior. As a widow and heiress to a large old estate, her influence was formidable. A year ago, everyone had assumed that she and Patrick would marry. Without warning, he had broken off the relationship. Katherine missed his demanding touch and fiery lovemaking.

She let her gaze dip below his waist to the slight bulge in his trousers. "Your body remembers me. Why not admit it? Victoria is not the woman for you. If she saw what was between your legs, the poor thing would faint with fright."

Ignoring the warning glare from his eyes, Katherine leaned closer, giving Patrick full view of her breasts. Confidence growing, she brazenly caressed the length of his thigh. Her tongue darted eagerly over her lips.

He calmly grabbed her hand and drained his glass. After handing the glass back to a passing servant, he said angrily, "Remember, you are a guest in this house. Our relationship is over and has been for several months. If you do not want to be thrown out, I suggest you locate your escort and leave."

Glaring at his retreating figure, Katherine tapped a finger against her pouting mouth. There was more than one way to skin a cat. If she couldn't have him, she would make sure that he couldn't have Victoria.

She searched the room for her escort, Edward Marshall. She had known him for years. He was always there for her after she broke off relationships. He'd been her constant companion after Patrick terminated their relationship.

"Edward, don't you disappear on me now!" she whispered. Just then, she spotted him. At slightly less than six feet tall, his solid frame stood above his companions. Edward's tough exterior didn't fool his friends. Though he was a boxing enthusiast, he was a devoted supporter of many social causes.

Minutes later, she saw Victoria sitting alone near an open window.

"Excuse me, gentlemen. I have need of Edward." Katherine wrapped her arm about Edward's. Without giving him an opportunity to speak, Katherine pulled him outside, near the window where Victoria was sitting.

"What are you up to, Katherine? Why are we lurking about?" His brow rose as he assessed her face.

Theatrical as ever, Katherine placed a hand to her forehead and spoke loudly. "I have a dilemma which requires your advice, Edward. I need a man's perspective."

"What can I do?" His eyes narrowed.

"It's Patrick. You know he is to be married soon." Ignoring Edward's sudden glare, she rushed on. "I once loved him. He hinted at marriage, but I enjoyed being his mistress. Such a considerate lover! Imagine my surprise when he approached me tonight and asked to resume our relationship. Naturally, I was surprised and taken aback by the proposal. I pity the Montgomery girl. They're not even married and he's looking for a mistress."

Edward turned away from her. Katherine felt a twinge of regret. She didn't like using Edward like this, but this was her opportunity to win Patrick back. As he turned to face her, she paused, noticing his sudden pallor.

"That seems unlike Patrick. I thought him a man ready to settle down. Are you sure you understood his intent?" Edward ground out.

"I know what Patrick proposed. Are you insinuating that I'm fabricating his proposal?" Worried that he would see through her tale, Katherine turned to leave.

Edward grabbed her arm. "I trust you to make the right decision. If Lady Montgomery knew that Patrick did not love her, it could destroy her."

Katherine snapped, "Why do you care about her? Shouldn't you care more how I feel?"

Removing his hand, she whipped around to return inside. She was determined to see how her scheme played out.

Chapter 12

VICTORIA SAT PERFECTLY STILL. Unfortunately, she had heard every word of Lady Paxton's conversation. She rose, pulling the veil over her face. She had to find her stepfather before the tears became unstoppable. Patrick was no better than Malcolm was. How dare he ask that horrid woman to be his mistress! She was a fool to even think their marriage could work. She would break the engagement with Patrick as soon as possible. Thinking of her stepfather's reaction brought trepidation. Hopefully, he would support her decision until another match could be made.

Victoria scanned the ballroom one last time. Her stepfather was nowhere to be found. She had seen him hours ago, arguing with Malcolm, who had decided to attend the ball after all. Malcolm had been loud and unsteady on his feet, thus attracting unwanted attention. Her stepfather had probably sent him home. She could wait no longer. She couldn't face Patrick now that she knew what kind of man he really was.

Glancing at the elegant house one last time, she sent for their carriage and quietly slipped away. As the carriage pulled away, Victoria spotted Katherine standing on the terrace, watching her leave. The woman had the audacity to raise a glass in her direction. That was the final straw! She broke down in tears.

∞

The sound of ragged sobbing woke Malcolm. Holding his throbbing head, he bellowed, "For God's sake, stop that wailing. And stop the coach immediately!"

When the carriage lurched to a stop, he opened the door and leaned out. The sounds of his retching echoed through the carriage. After a few minutes, Malcolm wiped his mouth with the back of his hand. Gingerly, he leaned back on the seat. The carriage continued at a more sedate pace.

"Well, well, what a surprise. It's Victoria."

"H-how did you get in here?" she stuttered.

"It *is* the family carriage. Father thought perhaps I should wait here until the two of you were ready to leave."

"But you were in London. Why did you come back?" she hiccupped, dabbing her tears.

"And miss the biggest social event of the year? Besides, O'Neil always serves the finest drink and has the richest guests." Sensing her dismay, he continued to chisel away at the thin veneer protecting her emotions. "May I ask why you left so early?"

He flinched as a tear trickled down her cheek. "Patrick isn't aware that you left, is he? Oh my, trouble with the two lovebirds."

"Be quiet. I shan't discuss it with you."

Victoria's chin trembled before she turned away. Malcolm was mesmerized by Victoria and her golden costume that clung to every curve. He knew the silky material would be as soft as her skin. He didn't want to hurt her, but he had to convince her that he loved her more than Patrick did.

When the carriage stopped at the front entrance, Malcolm quietly assisted Victoria into the house. Malcolm convinced her that hot tea would perk up her spirits. Sitting on the settee next to Victoria, Malcolm held her hand, trying to calm her.

"I don't mean to pry, but what happened tonight?"

Her eyes filled with tears again. "I overheard Lady Paxton talking to someone."

Malcolm nodded and encouraged her to continue. His vision

was blurry. Damn it! He wished he hadn't had so much to drink tonight.

"Patrick has asked her to be his mistress. I am so humiliated. I shall be the laughingstock of the season. I cannot bear it! I cannot."

She took Malcolm's hand, gripping it tightly. "Perhaps you or Father could marry and help our family recover."

He shook his head. "I know that Patrick and I have had our differences, but I can't imagine that he would say that. Katherine has always been a troublemaker."

Surprisingly, Victoria rose and poured herself a brandy. Rebelliously, she threw back her drink. Her eyes widened as a fit of coughing overtook her.

"So you don't believe me?"

Malcolm wished he could think straight. "No, I didn't say that. I've told you my feelings, Victoria. Maybe this is fate's way of helping us be together."

He wrapped an arm around her waist, drawing her nearer. His lips lowered ever so slowly toward her mouth. He pressed into her, the pressure increasing as his passion grew. Her body was still. She wasn't rejecting his advances. Encouraged, he held her tighter. This seemed right. They were meant to be together.

Malcolm's head flew back as Victoria hit him with her fist. Her wild eyes stared back at him.

"How dare you betray my trust!"

Taking his thumb, he wiped a trickle of blood from his split lip. He snapped, "You were willing a minute ago! For God's sake, Victoria. What do you want from me?"

Her body crumpled. "I want to feel safe in my own home. I want you to be the brother I loved all these years. I see now that my wishes and my dreams will never be a reality."

Malcolm tenderly patted her shoulder. "Don't cry. I am sorry. Let's have another brandy. It will help calm you."

A shadow of a smile brightened her pale complexion. "You are right, of course. You and Father are always right."

Her tears and sobs resumed. She was becoming hysterical. He pleaded, "Victoria, calm yourself."

She picked up the empty glass and flung it at his head. In evading the flying object, he fell and hit the floor with a thud. "Crap! What are you doing?" Malcolm yelled. By the time he struggled to his feet, cursing every second, the room was empty. Racing to the foyer, he saw the front door standing open. He gripped the doorframe, turning his fingers white. "Victoria, come back!"

He had to find her. All his good intentions had failed. He wanted to show her that he did love her. He could never hurt her. He just needed time to demonstrate that he could fulfill her dreams.

Filled with fear, she ran toward the woods. Distorted images flew by. Her chest burned as she tried to breath. The sound of ripping fabric did not slow her down. Escape was her only thought. Escape from the unbearable tension of living in the Montgomery household. Escape from the humiliation of being put aside for a mistress before she was even married. Escape from a man she loved as a brother but who wanted more from her. It was too much to bear.

Low supple limbs struck his cheek, stinging his skin. A light drizzle in the air mixed with the dead leaves and bare ground, creating a dangerously slick surface. Running down a steep slope, his feet slid out from underneath him. He fell hard on his back, and a large gush of air rushed from his throat. He lay immobile for several minutes, his chest heaving in and out as he tried to breathe. Mud soaked the back of his clothes.

An unearthly silence greeted Malcolm as he struggled to his feet. He was torn between returning to the house to get help and continuing his search. He cautiously made his way through the dark. He called out her name every few seconds but heard nothing in response. His heart pounded erratically. He felt light-headed. He staggered on, barely able to see more than a few feet in front of him. Damn it all! What had he done?

Minutes later, his foot caught on something, throwing him off balance. Pitched forward, he touched a piece of material and gasped in alarm when he saw that it was a piece of Victoria's costume. Dropping to his knees, he crawled along the damp moss-covered ground, valiantly searching.

"Victoria, it's Malcolm. I'm here to help you." Hysteria mounting, he continued to call her name.

Sliding down an incline, he found her body twisted unnaturally. He gently lifted her head to his lap. His hand trembled as he stroked the muddy tendrils away from her face.

"Oh, God, don't let her die, please! Give me another chance to do things right." Tears coursed down his cheeks. Victoria moaned and tried to turn her head. "Don't move, my love. You'll hurt yourself."

Malcolm met her gaze. He could feel his tears tracing down his face. She gasped and then gripped her chest.

"Malcolm," she murmured, "don't cry. It's not your fault. I've been foolish in so many ways. I'm sorry. You must forgive me." A trickle of blood flowed from the corner of her mouth as coughs racked her battered body. He wiped the blood from her pale face.

"Don't speak. I'll go get help. You must try to stay awake until I return. Victoria, do you hear me? Victoria!"

He knew the bleeding was not a good sign. The way her body had been positioned when he'd found her, he had suspected internal bleeding. Now he knew.

Her eyes fluttered. She was murmuring. He bent lower, trying to hear her words. He couldn't understand what she was saying. Frozen with despair, he watched helplessly as her spirit drifted away from this world.

Malcolm leaned down and reverently kissed her cold lips. Her chest rose one last time, and a small sigh escaped her lifeless body. He threw his head back, screaming to the heavens for the injustice of her death. He raged until he could utter no further sounds.

Malcolm held her body throughout the night. The sun was

peeking through the horizon when he finally rose, clutching her still body. No one would believe that Victoria's death was a terrible accident. How had things gotten so out of control? He had only wanted to make her realize that he truly cared for her. Now the only person who had ever cared for him was gone. He was alone, truly alone. His life was over, but he was too much of a coward to kill himself. Not knowing what else to do, he decided to hide her body deep in the forest. He would get a shovel and bury her. No one would notice a fresh mound of dirt here amongst the trees. He could come here and mourn alone.

The blackness of this night must remain his secret … but never be forgotten. His heart turned to stone. How could he explain Victoria's disappearance? He had to leave, get away from his father's influence. No one would notice his absence. He was the most horrible creature that had ever walked the earth. Surely he was condemned to hell.

Chapter 13

ANN ROLLED OUT OF bed, staring at her haunted reflection in the mirror. The dark circles under her eyes were more pronounced. The dreams were becoming too real. Her meeting with Patrick had been a dream, hadn't it? Yet Patrick had stood in front of her, talked to her, and touched her. He was flesh and blood. But how could he be? Pouring her morning cup of coffee, she plopped at the kitchen table, too exhausted to think any more. She needed help.

She phoned Stacy a few hours later. "Hi there. Are you doing anything this afternoon?"

"I have a date with Kevin at six."

"Kevin? It's starting to sound serious between the two of you."

"He's really special. You wouldn't believe how kind and thoughtful he is. I don't want to jinx this relationship, but I think I'm starting to fall in love."

Surprised, Ann asked, "Are you sure?"

"Oh, Ann, how does anyone know if she's sure? All I know is that he's the best thing to happen to me in years."

Ann was happy for Stacy, yet she was also envious. It seemed that everyone else was moving on with their lives—except for her. Sighing, she wished that there were a man like Patrick in the real world.

Stacy rushed on. "I do need to run by the mall. Let's meet at two?"

"Great! I'll see you then."

Ann moaned after hanging up, for a glance at the clock confirmed that it was already half past one. She'd thought it was closer to one. Throwing open the closet doors, Ann grabbed a pair of jeans and a mauve knit shirt. Five minutes later, she was out the door and in her car.

On the way to the mall, Ann noticed the forbidding black clouds that rolled across the sky. She changed the radio over to a news station so she could listen to the weather report. A storm watch for their area was announced.

In record time, Ann parked the car and hurried toward the mall entrance. Just as she reached the door, Stacy ran in after her. "Talk about timing. I can't believe you're not late," teased Stacy.

"I only have two speeding tickets to show for my punctuality," Ann joked. "Let's go get a Coke and something chocolate."

They waded through the throng of people, managing to find a table where they could sit and visit. Stacy glanced outside. "I hope it doesn't rain tonight. I want to dazzle Kevin. I found a sexy teal dress. It's very fitted and strapless." Pausing, she asked, "You seem a little down. Tell me what's been going on. It seems like weeks since we've talked."

Ann flipped her curls back over her shoulder, pondering her words. "Stacy, I have something serious that I need to discuss with you. I trust you to keep this confidential."

"What's wrong? You're not sick, are you?"

"No, it's nothing like that. Remember that terrible storm last night?" Ann paused as Stacy nodded. "During the storm, my lights went out. At first, I thought it might be David trying to break in. One minute I'm sitting at the computer, and the next minute I'm in this strange house. I couldn't move. It was as if I were paralyzed. I heard footsteps coming closer, and the door to the room swung open. You'll never guess who entered the room."

"Wait a minute. You make it sound as if it really happened."

Ann shook her head with frustration. "I don't know what to

believe anymore. Let me finish and then tell me what you think. This man walked into the room. I don't mean *walked*—I mean, he *really* walked, like in the movies. It was a can't-take-your-eyes-off-him walk. It was the guy pictured in the album. He was so real that I could see the raindrops on his black hair, see his piercing green eyes, and even see the frown on his face. When I asked him his name, he thought it was some game. The weirdest part was that he called me Victoria."

Stacy stared at Ann. "You're not serious, are you? It was just a dream."

"I thought it was a dream at first, but he was too real. His touch was very real."

Stacy's eyes widened. "Like hubba-hubba real?" Stacy chortled. "C'mon, Ann. Don't pull my leg."

Ann rolled her eyes at Stacy. "It was real. When the thunderstorm outside grew more intense, my vision started to blur. As I started to disappear, he asked me to stay. Here's the best part: he said he was Patrick O'Neil."

"No way! Not *the* Patrick O'Neil from your research. Let's be rational about this. Who knows about your research? If someone found out, this could be a hoax. You could've been tricked into believing this whole dream thing."

"I wondered the same thing, but this is way too complicated for someone else to imagine. I doubt I was hypnotized into believing that I met Patrick. No one but you knows that he is pictured in the book and appears in my dreams. The more I think about this, the more I believe it really happened."

"Whoa, girlfriend! Do you realize what you're saying? I'm really trying to understand, but how could you meet Patrick O'Neil? He was born ages ago."

Ann shivered. "There's only one explanation. I traveled back in time."

The last statement hung in the air, and both women were silent as if afraid to say a word. Minutes stretched out like hours as they ignored the mass of people shuffling past them.

Stacy took a deep breath. "That's crazy! Besides, why you?

If time travel is really possible, how did it happen? Time travel is something you see in movies or cartoons."

"I've asked the same questions. It all boils down to that damn album. Ever since I learned Patrick's name, the dreams have become weirder." Hands shaking, Ann managed to take a sip of her soda without spilling.

Stacy slapped her hands on the table. "I don't believe it. I just can't accept the fact that time travel is possible."

"What else can explain this mess? I've tried to think of every angle, but I keep coming back to the same thought. The man I saw was as real as you are," Ann argued.

"Maybe you should contact someone from the university, like the science department. They could tell you if time travel is even possible."

Ann rolled her eyes, pretending to hold a phone to her ear. "Hello, can you help me? I think I traveled back in time, but it might have been a dream. How can I verify what I think is real?"

Stacy laughed. "Okay, I get the picture. They'll think you're a nutcase."

Leaves whipped against the glass surrounding the food court of the mall, breaking up their discussion. The threatening skies looked as if buckets of rain could fall at any minute.

Quickly glancing at her watch, Stacy frowned. "I hate to leave. Why don't I call Kevin and tell him I can't make it tonight?"

Stacy started to call Kevin, but Ann took her hand. "No, you go ahead and have fun. I'll be fine. We'd better run to our cars before the rain starts. I'll call you tomorrow."

Giving her friend a quick hug, Ann reassured Stacy that everything would be fine. Not ready to go home, Ann got in her car and drove. As hard as she tried, she couldn't ignore the album in the backseat. She was going to return the album today, right now. Minutes later, she pulled up in front of the bookstore. Greenish-black clouds rushed by as if on fast-forward. Ann felt the hairs on the back of her neck rising. She wanted to hurry and get home so she could call and check on the kids.

The gray-haired woman stood behind the register, smiling at Ann. The woman's piercing gaze gave Ann goose bumps.

"Did you find what you were seeking?" quizzed the woman.

Ann dropped the book on the counter. "I wasn't looking for anything. You can cut the riddles; I'm returning this. The album has given me lots of nightmares. By the way, the young man you have working here told me that no older women work here."

The woman's cackling laugh startled Ann. "The album is yours," she said. "Remember this always." Her smile fading, the woman fondly patted Ann's hand. "We will not see each other again in this lifetime. Believe that anything is possible."

Ann backed away from the counter, freeing her hand. The woman gave her the creeps. Ann practically ran to the doorway. At the last minute, she stopped to glance back at the counter. The woman was gone! Ann looked about the store. It was empty. The album remained on the counter. Shit! She couldn't leave it there. After all, the pictures were her distant ancestors. Maybe she could pull out a few pictures and burn the rest. There was no way she was ever coming back here again! With her luck, next time a mummy would probably shuffle out of the back room.

Letting the door slam behind her, Ann hurried to the car and sped home.

Night was fast approaching. The rumble of thunder drew closer. She pulled into the garage and retrieved the album. Once inside, she locked the door behind her. Even though there had been no word from David lately, she wasn't taking any chances. It was as if he had disappeared from the face of this earth.

For some reason, she couldn't leave the album alone. Stretched out on the sofa, she reverently turned the pages. Women wore beautiful gowns and elaborate hairstyles that were foreign to today's style. It wasn't long before Ann was drawn into another world. She no longer believed that a coincidence had caused her to discover the album and the pictures of Patrick. Was there such a thing as fate? The more she thought about the possibilities, the more questions she had.

The radio, playing songs from the sixties, was barely audible from across the room. She reluctantly set the pictures aside and picked up the packet sent by Ms. Marshfield. The woman's research surpassed what she could have done. The materials included diary pages and additional pictures. It was amazing.

Hours later, the telephone rang. Rubbing her tired eyes, she lifted the receiver.

"Mom, are you okay?" Jessica breathlessly asked. "A tornado moved through here a while ago. The neighbors lost their roof."

"Storm?" Ann was shocked when she lifted the curtain. She had been so absorbed in her work that she hadn't realized the weather conditions had worsened. The wind howled, and lightning lit up the sky. The trees swayed back and forth as if they were twigs. The electricity in the air created a crackling sound on the telephone line. Feeling nervous, Ann pulled the desk drawer open and found a flashlight and some candles.

"I think we'd better get off the phone. The storm seems to be headed this way. Jess, I'm glad you called. I have something I would like to talk to you about. Let's try to get together for lunch this week?"

"Great idea, Mom. I love you. You'd better head for the basement before the storm gets there. Call me if you need anything. Bye."

No sooner had Ann set the receiver in place than the phone rang again. This must be check-on-Mom night. Sure enough, Mark's voice came across the line. After she reassured him that everything was fine, he clearly relaxed.

"Mom, I have great news. You're the first one we've called."

"We? Deb must be with you. How is she doing? Did she get that job offer in Kansas City?" Bracing herself, she said, "Tell me—I'm dying to hear the good news."

"Deb and I are going to get married, probably next spring. Are you up for a wedding?"

Ann shrieked, "That's wonderful! I love you both. I was beginning to think you would never settle down. Where will the wedding and reception be held?"

Mark chuckled. "I told Deb that you'd be excited. We're not

sure where we'll hold the wedding. Deb wants to visit a few places first."

Mark paused, which gave Ann concern. "You got quiet all of a sudden. What is it?"

"Deb got that job offer in Kansas City. It's a great opportunity for her. For us! I've talked to a few people in my company, and I can transfer with no problem. We hate to move away from you and Jess, but an opportunity like this doesn't come along very often."

"Kansas City?"

In a low voice, he murmured, "Mom, you can visit any time you want, and we'll come up to see you at least once a month."

She knew that Mark and Deb would be happy. Not wanting to dampen their high spirits, she said, "I'm glad your company will let you transfer. I'll come and visit you two whenever you want me."

Mark cleared his throat, his voice sounding husky. "I'll always want you, Mom. You're not upset, are you?"

"Heavens, no. I think it's great. With both of my kids so successful, one in insurance and the other one working at a college, I will expect a cruise once a year."

The tempo of the storm outside gained momentum.

"Listen, sweetheart," she said, "this terrible weather is making the line crackle, and I can't hear you very well. Let me call you back tomorrow. Tell Deb that I love her. I love you too."

Afterward, Ann felt strangely disquieted. She hurried downstairs to gather up the usual storm provisions. With an armload of candles, matches, and flashlights, she marched back upstairs to work on the computer. The warning sirens were silent, so she felt safe enough upstairs. Besides, her basement was wet, damp, and creepy. She could always run down there if there was an actual tornado.

Sitting at the computer screen, she continued to work. A short while later, she paused to take a stretch break and rub her eyes. She traced Patrick's name with her finger. She wondered what his life was like. Did he ever marry? Have children? She had so many questions.

The windows rattled from the force of the wind. Ann jumped when small branches raked against the glass. The lights flickered on and off, as if a warning. A moment later, the lights went out. Ann waited to see if they would come back on, but minutes later, there was still only the dim light from the computer screen. Not wanting to drain the battery, she saved her work and shut down the laptop. Darkness now surrounded her.

From downstairs came a sound that resembled breaking glass, making Ann jump. "It's just a tree limb hitting the window," she rationalized aloud. "Where are those darn candles?"

Using the wall as a guide, she reached the other side of the room and the candles. Barely able to control her tremors, she finally managed to light a candle and set it on the table. She shoved the laptop in her gym bag with her Nikes and jogging clothes.

A thumping noise from the foot of the stairway penetrated the sound of the storm. She stood in the doorway, trying to decipher the noise. The harsh sound of someone breathing drifted up the stairs. Galvanized into action, she slammed the bedroom door and turned the lock. Ann scrambled for the phone. She couldn't believe this was happening. The floorboard creaked from the other side of the doorway. The only time it made a sound was when someone was standing on it.

Ann took several deep breaths, trying not to hyperventilate. Her sweaty palms covered her mouth, blocking cries of terror. Maybe it was one of the neighbors coming to see if she needed help. A booming crash of thunder shook the house. She dug though her bag and snatched a key ring with a can of pepper spray attached.

Tension rippled through her. She leaned against the door, listening for sounds. Holding the spray in her hand, she gripped the knob. Before she could open the door, the knob started to turn from the other side.

"Who's there?" she challenged. No one answered. "I've called the police, so you'd better leave!"

The rasping sound of laughter came from the other side. David! She'd recognize that voice anywhere. As quickly as the laughter stopped, the pounding of fists on the door began. Ann retreated to the farthest corner, away from danger. She lifted the phone one more time. Maybe, just maybe, it would work. Dead silence.

David pounded furiously on the door. "Open up," he raged. "If you don't, it will be worse for you."

She clamped her hands over her ears, blocking the sound of his voice and the nearby tornado sirens blaring out a warning. Refusing to be intimidated any longer, Ann approached the door, armed with her pepper spray.

With a loud splintering sound, the doorframe gave way. The door flew open. Ann stared at David. As his arm lifted toward her, she instinctively lunged for his face, aiming the nozzle toward his mouth and eyes.

Screaming in pain, he covered his eyes, trying to wipe away the spray. He fell to his knees, reaching out blindly for Ann.

Backing away, she realized that there was no way to reach the door without stepping over David. Determined to incapacitate him as much as possible, she plugged her nose and squeezed her eyes shut as she sprayed again.

"Take that, you creep!" Ann screamed, full of bravado.

Without warning, his hand shot out and pulled her down on the floor. With one eye partially open, he wrapped an arm around her neck. His grip tightened, blocking her airway. The pepper spray fell and rolled across the floor during the struggle. He pulled her closer, gaining leverage over her body.

David stared down at her. His eyes were red and swollen. What was he waiting for?

"Now I have you where you belong—under my feet. You're just like all the other women."

Hoping to stall for time, Ann pleaded, "No, David. I'm not like the others."

"Yes, you are! You left me, just like my mother and my other girlfriends did."

Spittle flew from his mouth as he talked. Without warning, he reached down and began choking her. Ann tried to scream, but the pain in her throat was too severe. Coughing, she tried to pull his hand away.

He continued with his rant while shaking her. "You ruined my life! I've lost my job, my house, everything. All because of you! Damn you!"

Unable to breathe, blackness threatened. Suddenly, she felt his hand loosen from her neck.

"Don't die yet. We have unfinished business," he hissed. "I'm going to take what I want. I'm going to be the last thing you see before you die."

He looked out the window as the storm tempo increased. Ann frantically looked for something to use as a weapon. Her foot brushed against the key ring. She inched the ring closer, so intent on moving the object that she failed to see the fist aimed at her face.

"Lie still," he threatened, "unless you're anxious to die."

A desire to live overrode caution. "You're sick! Everyone will know you did it. Why don't you let me go? If you go away and never come back, I promise not to tell anyone."

"Yeah, you won't tell anyone," he snarled. "What do you think I am, an idiot? There is only one ending for tonight, Ann, and you know it."

Despair filled her. If only she could reach the spray. It was her only chance. She said a silent prayer and concentrated on getting free. Ann began to sob hysterically, hoping to distract him.

"Stop that crying! No one will hear you. If you think tears are going to make me change my mind, think again."

David leaned over and reached for the telephone cord in order to tie her hands.

While he concentrated on getting the cord, Ann grabbed the pepper spray. The second he turned his face, she saturated him with a steady stream of disabling spray. He rolled off her, clawing at his fiery red face. She coughed as the spray filled her airway. She managed to stagger to her feet before she was assailed by dizziness. Why couldn't she see? What was happening?

The storm seemed poised directly above the house. The entire foundation rumbled, and the thunder made it nearly impossible to hear anything else. The windows shattered, scattering shards of glass across the hardwood floors. It appeared as if crystals of ice lay strewn about. The rain-soaked curtains whipped about wildly. A cold mist seeped through the broken windows. Soon a grayish shadow filtered throughout the room. Ann remembered seeing the mist before—the first time she saw Patrick face-to-face. She inched toward the doorway. David rose to his feet and pulled a hunting knife from a slit in his boots. Ann silently screamed. Her heart pounded so fast that it made her feel light-headed. She would not collapse. Somehow she remained upright.

Blinded, he wildly jabbed the deadly blade inches from her body. He bumped into an overturned chair and stumbled to his knees.

This was her opportunity to escape. Ann grabbed her bag with the computer and ran for the door. Tornado or not, she was getting the hell out of here. With luck, she could make it to the police station. Even though ajar and the lock broken, the door wouldn't open more than a couple of inches. The hinges were frozen into place. A shiver of fear consumed her. She clutched the knob and pulled. It wouldn't open! Using both hands, she tried until red welts were imprinted in her palms. Slowly turning, she saw that the mist had encircled David. He stood angrily waving the knife, screaming threats. He seemed unaware of the mist and the electrical charge in the air.

Frantic, she tried the door once more. This was unbelievable! Pounding on the wooden barrier, she screamed, "Let me out of here. Someone help me! God, please help me."

She stilled as warm air blew across the back of her neck. David's body pressed her against the door. This time she knew there would be no escape.

"It's over, Ann. It could have ended differently between us. If only you had trusted me. If only you had listened. Now it is time for you to die."

Exploding backward, she shoved against him. As he struggled to retain his balance, she raked her fingernails down his cheeks. Rivulets of blood formed, splattering red drops amongst the slivers of glass scattered about the floor.

"You bitch! I'll make you pay for that." He tightly gripped a handful of her hair, exposing her neck. She saw him bring the blade closer. Flashes of lightning lit up the room, allowing Ann to see the blade glimmering dangerously close to her body. The plunging blade signaled the end of her life. She stared in disbelief as it drew closer to her chest.

When the blade was within a fraction of a second from entering her body, she screamed her last conscious thought: "Patrick!"

Time stopped. She stared at David, his motionless arm poised near her chest. He stared blankly at her. His breathing was shallow and irregular. She tried to slip away, but his hand still clasped her hair. The tip of the blade was so precariously close that she was afraid to make any sudden moves.

"Someone please help me." Her voice fell away as the enormity of her precarious situation hit her.

A cold draft chilled her body. Ann shivered as the now-familiar mist wrapped about the two of them. The objects in the room began to waver. Moisture coated her skin. Her eyes closed. She was tired, so tired. It was as if she floated adrift somewhere in time. She couldn't open her eyes. Yet she somehow knew that David was no longer a threat. Surprisingly, she wasn't afraid. How long she remained in this state of nonexistence, she couldn't guess.

What seemed hours later, she was finally able to open her eyes. Pain throbbed across her brow. Staring at her body, she saw that she lay crosswise on a large overstuffed damask-covered chair. She gaped in total amazement. "Oh my God, I don't believe it!"

She was back in the same strange room. Sounds of music and laughter drifted in from the other side of the door. Terrified at being discovered, especially in her current state, Ann looked for a means of escape.

If her hunch was right, then this was the nineteenth century and there was no logical way to explain her presence or the way she dressed. Spotting long green velvet drapes, she quickly hid the laptop bag behind the curtains. Ann checked the windows to see if they would open. After a few moments of straining the muscles in her arms, she knew it was futile. The latches were stuck.

Ann collapsed on the sofa and stretched out. She needed to

regroup, to think. She had to come up with a plan. Physically drained, Ann drifted off to sleep.

The noise from the party abruptly grew louder. She jolted awake and peeked over the arm of the sofa. Crap! Patrick stood in the doorway, his hawkish looks dark and intent. Afraid to breathe, she pressed her face down in the cushions. The door clicked shut, and she sighed with relief.

"Good, he's gone." She couldn't handle any more stress tonight. She flipped over on her back and stared up at the crystal chandelier. In the next instant, Patrick's stormy face loomed into view. Ann screamed and rolled onto the floor with a resounding thud.

"Victoria! Where have you been? Everyone has been looking for you. My God, what happened to you?"

Numb with shock, Ann stared into the most captivating green eyes she had ever seen. How could she rationally explain her presence? And who in the heck was Victoria?

Chapter 14

PATRICK HAD SEARCHED FOR Victoria for the past hour but had no luck. Her absence was creating significant speculation about their engagement. Sympathetic glances and whispered comments cast in his direction were quickly becoming a source of irritation.

Anthony came up beside him, offering a drink. "I hate to be the bearer of bad tidings, but I just overheard our dear friend Katherine telling others that your wedding will be postponed."

Patrick felt his jaw tighten. "Where is that witch?"

He scanned the crowd until he spotted his former mistress in the middle of a swarm of young admirers. She had tried to make him jealous on numerous occasions, with no success. By the time he had terminated their relationship, he no longer cared what she did or with whom.

The conversation ceased as he approached the group. Instinctively, those closest to Katherine stepped away. He made little effort at hiding his anger. Without a word of acknowledgment to the men, he gripped Katherine's elbow. "Madam, may I have a moment of your time?"

Without waiting for her response, he led her away from the crowd. Their departure set off a flurry of speculation. Firmly shutting the door to the library, he motioned for her to have a seat.

Katherine rubbed her arm, visibly seething with resentment at his treatment. "Suppose you tell me what is the meaning of your bullish behavior. You were never like this before, except in bed." Her tongue traced her lower lip.

With his legs braced apart, arms folded across his chest, Patrick glared at her. "What have you done?" His body threatened to explode at any moment, yet she had the gall to sit there batting her eyes at him.

"Whatever are you referring to? I have been with Edward all evening. Is there some juicy gossip? I would love to hear it."

Unleashing his anger, he seized her by the arm. He simmered with controlled rage. "Do not take me for a fool, Katherine. I know how malicious you can be. If you've hurt Victoria in any manner, I will see that you are ruined, financially and socially."

Her eyes narrowed. "You wouldn't dare. Is it my fault that the simpering miss has run off?" she hissed.

Sickened by her disregard for others, he flung his arm away from her. "If she has run off, as you've said, I swear that I will learn the reason why. If you had anything to do with her leaving, you will rue the day we ever met."

He stormed from the library via the balcony doors. He didn't want to face his guests in this state of mind. The stricken look on Katherine's face when he threatened to destroy her social life provided little satisfaction.

As he gripped the railing around the balcony, the sound of thunder rumbled in the distance. Rejoining the assembly, he tried to remember to smile as he walked through the crowd. As etiquette dictated, he stopped and smiled. Another brief glance out the windows revealed that the storm would soon be upon them. Hopefully, it would not detain any guests for the night. At this point, he wished they would all leave.

William rushed to Patrick's side, his bulging stomach heaving in and out. He paused to wipe his brow. "I cannot find Victoria. There's no sign of her. My carriage is gone, but none of the servants recall seeing her." William wrung his hands together. "What do you suggest we do?"

"Find her!" Patrick lashed out. Lowering his voice, he said, "Don't worry, I will still marry her."

Although he heard William speaking, the sound seemed muted and distant. Patrick turned to stare at the sitting room door. The memory of the recent storm and finding Victoria in his mother's former sitting room came to him. Brushing off Williams's hand, he strode toward the locked room.

Patrick paused outside the doorway, his hand inches from the handle. He always carried the key to this room. He could escape here with complete solitude and recall memories from his youth. Why did he have this urgency to enter the room? He pulled the key from his pocket and unlocked the door. Upon opening it, he stood in the doorway and studied the room. Nothing appeared out of the ordinary. As he was about to shut the door, a pair of eyes peered at him over the arm of the settee. They quickly disappeared. Relief flooded him. But it was quickly replaced with anger. Where had the bruises on her arm and face come from?

What was the little minx up to? She needed a good scare. He pretended to leave the room. Waiting quietly in the shadows, he crept behind the settee. He couldn't believe it. She had changed into those outlandish clothes again. Her pert rump was prettily encased in trousers. Hmm. Maybe the trousers were acceptable.

Ann stared up at Patrick. "Well, say something. You wouldn't believe what just happened to me."

He knelt down beside her, laying a hand on her forehead. "No fever, but where did you get those bruises?"

"As I said, you wouldn't believe me," she muttered. "Do I sound different?"

Worry lined his furrowed brow as he studied her strange garments and disheveled appearance. She had an odd look about her. "No, you don't sound different. Why would you ask? I will call for a physician."

Ann sat up. "No, I'm okay." She wiggled her legs and arms to illustrate the fact.

Patrick snapped at her. "All that movement is quite unnecessary.

Be still before you hurt yourself. Now, where are the clothes you wore earlier? If we hurry, we can still join our guests."

Ann cocked her head to the side. "What clothes?"

He smoothed her ponytail, frowning as if it were a dirty rag. "We will get someone to do something with your hair."

"Hello! I just asked you a question. Leave my hair alone." She yanked her hair out of his hand. She proceeded to fold her arms across her chest and glare at him.

What had he done wrong? He was trying to salvage the evening. There was no reason to point out the torn clothing and blood on her shirt. He needed to remain calm and learn the reason for this escapade. After ringing for Maggie, the housekeeper, he sat down and studied his potential bride. He wanted to kiss away the frown that marred her brow. Yet he also wanted to turn her over his knee for a good spanking.

Moments later, Maggie bustled into the room. She saw Victoria and drew a deep breath of relief. "Sir, we were so worried. When you rang the bell from this room, we were all hoping that Lady Victoria had been found."

"Yes, yes. As you can see, we need a few things to make her presentable." Patrick quickly clipped off a list of requests. With a brief nod, Maggie scurried off to order the servants to gather the needed items. Minutes later, another servant knocked and entered, carrying a tray with tea. Pouring a cup of the hot liquid, Patrick handed the cup to Ann.

Slowly sipping the tea, Ann watched him over the rim of the cup. A pleasant-looking young woman brought in a gown and personal articles of clothing. Bobbing before her, the young maid asked, "Is that blood, my lady?"

"Let's not dwell on that now," interrupted Patrick. He calmly stroked Ann's hand. "You look exhausted, Victoria, but if you could dress, we can put in a brief appearance together and then you can retire for the evening. I've sent a note to your father, indicating that the two of you will be spending the night here. You clearly have suffered some sort of shock and need to rest."

"Victoria?" Ann asked. "Who's Victoria?"

Patrick glanced at the maid and shook his head. "You, dearest."

As Ann drank her tea, she didn't notice the odd looks between him and the maid. Until this spell passed, he would watch over her. He knew that his servants wouldn't repeat anything said this night.

Speaking in a low, calm voice, Patrick patted Ann's hand. "Your maid will assist you with the dress and do your hair. Stay here until I return for you."

"Got it. I'd probably get lost if you weren't with me."

She lifted the gown and rubbed the luxurious fabric against her cheek. "This has to be a dream. I can't wait to see what the dress looks like on me."

Lightly kissing her pale cheek, Patrick reluctantly left the room. What could have happened to cause this memory loss? What if she never recovered from his episode? What kind of future would they have?

Chapter 15

ANOTHER SERVANT ARRIVED AND locked the door. "Oh my!" the elder servant said, mouth open. The woman stared at her jeans.

"Hi. Who are you?"

The servant paused. "Quit teasing, m'lady. We must get you dressed."

"Seriously, I must have hit my head tonight. I don't remember you."

"You poor lamb. I am Blanche. I've been your maid for years. Now, we have to get you dressed."

Ann spotted a screen in the corner. Behind it was a basin of warm water and towels. Still shaky from David's attack, she took the dress and disappeared behind the screen. This was only a dream. Time travel was impossible. No matter how many times she repeated these words, she still didn't believe them. She just needed to relax and go with the flow. What choice did she have? After washing, she quickly tossed her jeans and T-shirt to the floor. She couldn't wait to try on the expensive gown.

Blanche gasped as Ann came out from behind the screen in her underwear. Blanche stared as if she had never seen an underwire bra and bikini pants. This red pair was her favorite. Oops! She forgot where she was. What underwear did women wear in this century?

Ann squeezed her eyes shut, willing away her headache. When

she reopened them, she remained in the beautiful room with Blanche and a maid staring at her as if she had grown another head.

She didn't know when she would return to her own time, but she couldn't ignore her attraction to Patrick. Her last foray to the past only lasted a few minutes. She could disappear at any time. She planned to make the most of this adventure. Pondering whether she could take Patrick back with her, she quickly dismissed that thought. He wouldn't have a social security number, much less a driver's license. What kind of work could he do besides modeling? Ann cringed thinking about hordes of sex-starved women ogling pictures of Patrick. No, that wouldn't do. She wanted to keep him for herself.

Her mouth quirked upward as she imagined all the explaining it would take to tell Stacy about this little adventure. She was torn from her reverie by a sudden jerk on the back of her head.

Blanche brushed, pulled, and twisted the long reddish locks into an elegant French twist. Small tendrils framed Ann's oval face. Blanche motioned for the removal of her sassy red undergarments. The maid then tugged her into layers of undergarments. Holding up what appeared to be a bodice, Ann was instructed to hold it as Blanche laced from behind.

Unable to catch her breath, Ann pulled away. "Stop. Are you trying to kill me? I feel like a sardine."

With a deep sigh, Blanche undid the laces. Ann snatched the offensive garment to get a better look. "This is a corset! I can't believe you were trying to get a corset on me. This is too bizarre. Stacy will never believe this."

"But, my lady, every woman wears a corset," Blanche pleaded. "You must have a waistline of eighteen inches. I wouldn't being doing my duty if I did not dress you properly."

"Right," she muttered sarcastically. "I can imagine how many women are envious of my figure. I haven't had an eighteen-inch waist since I was fourteen years old. I know it was before I had any children."

Blanche held the corset up. "My lady, please. We must hurry."

Ann folded her arms across her chest, defiantly shaking her head. Blanche surrendered and tossed the offending corset on the chair.

The dark blue silk gown was the most gorgeous gown Ann had ever seen. It was very modest in front and dipped slightly in back. The waist was gathered and had velvet trim with a bow in back.

Unable to hold back a squeak of fright, Ann faced the mirror. Nothing could have prepared her for what she saw in that floor-length mirror. She sensed that she had stood in front of this mirror before. It was such an odd feeling. Her smile faded as she gazed into the reflecting glass. She saw herself ... but didn't. A younger and much more voluptuous Ann stared back. The fine lines around the eyes were gone. The thickening about the waist had also disappeared. It looked as if she did have an eighteen-inch waist. She ran her hands across her flat abdomen. It was amazing. She looked and felt twenty years younger. She turned to view herself from every angle. Perhaps this was the reason people addressed her as Victoria. How had this transformation taken place? Victoria must have taken her place in the future. She could pretend to be Victoria. No, that was dishonest. Yet why did it feel so right? She felt as if she belonged here. She could be flashed back to the future at any minute. Damn it all! She would be an imposter for now. At least she would have the memories of Patrick and this lifestyle.

She noticed Blanche's reflection in the mirror. The maid gave her a big smile.

Ann clapped her hands together and laughed aloud. "I can't believe this! Look, I'm young again." She whirled about the room, careful to hold the edge of the skirts up to prevent herself from tripping

Noticing the silent figure standing in the doorway, Ann came to an abrupt stop. Flushed from the excitement, she met his penetrating eyes. They gazed at one another for several minutes. A shiver of excitement coursed through her.

She watched as he opened the black case in his hands. A luxurious ruby necklace lay in a nest of velvet. He carefully placed it about her neck, kissing her bare shoulder as he fastened the necklace. The pear-shaped jewel nestled between creamy mounds.

Rattled by his scrutiny, she stepped toward the mirror. His assessment unnerved her. "It's beautiful. Do you want me to wear it?"

"It's a wedding present. I want you to know how much you mean to me. Besides, I want every man out there to know that you belong to me."

Oh no! Victoria was supposed to marry Patrick. Ann couldn't marry him and then disappear. Besides, Victoria probably loved him. Ann was not going to be the other woman. She pulled away, biting her lower lip. "I think I should stay here. I'm not feeling very well."

"Come now. You were dancing around the room a moment ago. I'll be right next to you."

And that was what Ann feared the most. Being close to him made her hormones go into overdrive. It was much safer to admire him from a distance or in her dreams.

Patrick's stern gaze made her feel like an errant schoolgirl. "We need to make an appearance together." His look did not invite argument. As they were about to join the guests, Blanche hurried forward, carrying long white gloves. "You mustn't forget these, my lady."

Without thinking, Ann asked, "Are they really necessary?"

Patrick flashed a surprised look. With a sigh, she pulled them on. She felt like Napoleon being led to her Waterloo.

Patrick looked perplexed. What did she do wrong now? He grumbled, "Could you please smile? You look as if you're being led to the guillotine."

If he only knew the torture he was inflicting on her. Her body tingled with every brush of his hand, every look, and even the husky tone of his voice.

A man watched them approach. His silky laughter greeted her. "Is your betrothed being a bore, Lady Montgomery? If so, may I offer you a dance?"

Ann stared back at the attractive man who'd addressed her.

His devilish good looks and sense of humor calmed her. She didn't realize that she was staring until she felt Patrick's eyes upon her. She felt like a child caught with her hand in the cookie jar.

Massaging her temples, she whispered, "No, I have a slight headache. I'll just stand here and watch." Now that she wanted to be alone, she had two amazingly handsome men who refused to leave her side.

Ann was transfixed by her surroundings. Numerous tapered candles cast a golden hue over the room. Elaborate jewels graced every neck and wrist. She would bet that those weren't the costume diamonds and rubies that were so common in her day. The music was surprisingly soothing, not the usual rock 'n' roll that she normally listened to but the slow hypnotizing rhythm that brought two lovers together. The kind of music her grandmother used to listen to.

Patrick's breath fanned her neck. "I believe this is our dance, my dear."

Ann's knees locked together. She couldn't dance, let alone perform a waltz. Years ago, her grandmother had tried to teach her how to dance for a school party. Ann couldn't convince her that teenagers no longer danced the waltz. If the band played a two-step, she might be able to manage. She had to get out of here before they discovered that she was an imposter.

"I don't think I can. I can't dan ..."

Patrick drew her to the dance floor, refusing to release her arm. His grip was unyielding. The warmth of his hand about her waist sent tremors through her body. When the music began, she panicked and tried to pull away. "I told you I can't dance," she snapped.

He looked down in disbelief. "Of course you can dance. Just relax and breathe. Follow my lead and you will do fine."

Seconds later, her foot trampled his toes. He grimaced and glanced down at her.

Oblivious to Patrick's discomfort, Ann tried concentrating on the beat of the music, only to step on the same toes again.

"Sorry, I'm really trying. I told you I can't dance." Ann ducked her head, hiding a grin.

His gruff voice sounded suspiciously strained. "Apology accepted. Try shutting your eyes and letting your body relax. I'll lead, and you follow."

"You Tarzan … me Jane," she muttered, rolling her eyes.

"Excuse me?"

"Nothing. I was talking to myself."

Deciding it wouldn't hurt to try his suggestion, she let the tension flow from her body. Within minutes, she realized that she was actually dancing. His touch guided her without further mishap. She leaned her head on his shoulder, letting out a little sigh.

Patrick's muffled laughter caught her attention, and his low voice rumbled through her body. "We are creating quite a scandal dancing so close to one another."

Ann raised her head and glanced around the room. "Hmm. This is wonderful."

All too soon, the dance ended. Breathless, her eyes sparkled with delight. "Oh, we have to do that again. It was wonderful. My grandmother would have loved this."

Ann saw that Patrick had that puzzled look on his face again. Another faux pas on her part.

Several elderly matriarchs stared, watching them intently as they drew nearer. Ann didn't have a clue if she should curtsey or nod. It didn't seem appropriate to walk up and shake their hands. Ann smiled at the women. Nodding their heads in her direction, they offered her a chair. She stared at Patrick's retreating figure as he was pulled aside by a guest. His wide shoulders set off a lean tapered waist. His black hair brushed against the collar of his jacket. If Stacy were here, she would most certainly voice her opinion about his butt. Barely stifling a giggle, Ann drew the attention of the regal-looking woman sitting next to her.

"Tell me, young lady, how are the wedding plans progressing?"

Unsure of what to say, she strived for words that wouldn't raise any suspicion. "Uh, fine. Patrick is handling everything. He is so good about these things."

The older woman gaped at Ann. "Surely you do not mean that Lord O'Neil is handling the arrangements."

Red flags instantly waved in front of Ann's face. She had goofed. "Oh, no. That's not what I meant at all. It's just that he is so efficient about everything. I rely on his judgment in these matters. A woman must put her faith and trust in her husband."

Where had that bunch of drivel come from? After the experience with David, she didn't know if she could ever trust any man again. Only time would reveal Patrick's true nature, and Ann didn't plan to be here long enough to find out.

Hands folded in her lap, Ann waited for Patrick. An attractive woman gazed at her from across the room. At first, Ann thought the woman was staring at someone else. When she realized that she was the focus of the woman's attention, Ann straightened her shoulders and stared back at the stunning blonde. Ann attempted a smile, but the woman quickly turned away, ignoring her effort at a greeting.

The older woman next to Ann renewed their conversation. "I understand that you are without female relatives. If there is anything that I can do, please call on me. I would be glad to provide you with advice."

Ann stared back at the grandmotherly woman. If the woman only knew that she already had two children and knew all about the birds and the bees. Appreciative of the offer, Ann graciously replied, "Thank you."

Patting the younger woman on the hand, the older woman smiled and turned to join her friends. Ann glanced anxiously about. Where was Patrick? She felt like a wallflower. Heedless of the speculative glances of several young men, Ann slowly made her way across the crowded room. The long skirt hampered her efforts to walk gracefully across the dance floor. It kept tangling about her legs, forcing her to alter her long strides.

Caught up in her surroundings, she had to veer quickly to avoid a servant, only to bump into a man carrying two glasses of wine. The deep red liquid created a puddle on the waxed wooden floor.

Her hands fluttered to her throat. "Oh, I'm so sorry. I didn't see you. Did any of the wine spill on you?" Horrified, she saw a trail of liquid running down his leg.

Laughing, the man set the half-empty glasses aside. "Don't worry. I clean up quite nicely."

As she bent down to wipe up the mess, the man grasped her arm. In a jovial tone, he said, "Heavens! There are servants to clean up the mess. It isn't your concern, Lady Montgomery."

Her ears perked up. Montgomery! So that was Victoria's last name. She felt like a detective, trying to find out all she could before she was returned to the twenty-first century. Straightening, she started to offer an apology again, and that's when she saw the unpleasant woman from earlier in the evening slithering toward them.

"Edward, what is taking so long? I've been waiting for my drink. Have you forgotten?"

Clearly chagrined, he kissed the woman lightly on the cheek. "How could I forget? We've had a slight mishap here, and I was reassuring Lady Montgomery that there was no harm done."

Katherine stared down at the red stain on his pants. Her nose wrinkled in frustration. "Fine. Please make yourself presentable. It is time to leave." With a swish of her skirts, she left the two of them staring after her.

"I must apologize. Katherine is usually quite gracious. I don't know what came over her. Thank you for the wonderful evening. We wish you congratulations on the upcoming nuptials."

Ann attempted to put him at ease. "Thanks for coming. It was nice to meet you."

Edward politely smiled back at her. Ann's smile faded, noticing that he was giving her an odd look. She really had to be more careful.

Later that evening, after the guests had departed, Patrick returned to her side with a ruddy-skinned man accompanying him. The older man greeted her with a hug and kiss. Someone else she was supposed to know. How long before someone realized that she was a fraud?

"Victoria, we were all so worried about you. You should be ashamed of scaring your father like that."

"It was just a misunderstanding," Patrick said.

Patrick whispered in her ear, "Come, I will show you to your room. It's late, and I'm sure you wish to retire. My aunt Mary would like to meet with you tomorrow to review the arrangements for the wedding."

"So soon? Can we wait a couple of days? I'm really exhausted." Instinct told her to run to the nearest door. It was only a matter of time before Patrick discovered that she was pretending to be Victoria.

"The next week will seem like an eternity. I think it's wise to finalize the preparations."

When they reached the doorway of her room, Patrick opened his mouth as if to say something and then appeared to change his mind.

Her hands reached up to unclasp the necklace. Patrick leaned closer. She felt his warm breath on her ear. She unconsciously moved closer to him.

"Keep the necklace. It will be yours soon enough. I can't imagine how I will get through the next few days."

Surprised at her own daring, she reached up and let her fingers drift down his cheek. Rising up on her toes, she gently kissed him on the lips. "Good night. I'll see you tomorrow."

Ann turned and retreated inside her room. Dormant sensations came roaring back to life. That man was dangerous! His potent masculinity jumbled every coherent thought in her brain. Her legs felt like Jell-O.

Focusing on her surroundings, Ann looked about the room. It reminded her of something out of *Better Homes and Gardens*. A stately four-poster bed occupied the center of the room. The yellow spread and bed ruffle matched the curtains. Brightly colored pillows were artfully arranged on the bed. She immediately felt at home. A knock at the door startled her. Ann peered around the door.

"Blanche, it's you. What do you need?"

"I'm here to help you undress. Turn around and let's get you out of this dress."

Ann never had anyone help her dress and undress before. It was embarrassing. "There's no need for that. If you undo the top buttons, I can finish the rest myself."

"Hush now. I know you are tired." Minutes later, Blanche had the gown off and a nightgown pulled over her head.

That night, Ann lay in bed reliving every second with Patrick. She wanted to memorize everything about this evening. The waltz with Patrick would always be a special memory. She wouldn't marry him, so why was she making herself a nervous wreck?

Ann hoped that the element of time was different in this century. If time was passing at the same rate in the twenty-first century, her family would be frantic at her disappearance. She wished there was a way to communicate with them. When she returned, the first thing she would do is contact the police about David. He needed to be locked up in a psychiatric facility.

Her thoughts kept returning to Patrick. He was overpowering. The dreams didn't do him justice. She was not put off by his dark, moody looks. She had felt the tightly leashed emotions trembling through his body—the slight quivering of his arm about her waist and his firm lips when she kissed him. To her, he was like a volcano, his body coursing with molten passion. But was she the right woman to release that fire and energy? Or was it Victoria?

Chapter 16

ANN DREW THE COVERS from her face as Blanche opened the curtains, allowing the morning sun to fill the room. Why did the servants come in and wake her? She hoped this wasn't customary. She was not a morning person.

"Ugh, what time is it?" She opened one eye and looked about the room. So yesterday hadn't been a dream …

"Miss, the day is half gone. Your father wants you to join him for breakfast."

Perhaps she should take advantage of the time with William. She wanted to learn more about Victoria. Ann tossed off the covers and stretched, causing the back of her legs to cramp. The pale, slender calves reminded her that this wasn't her body. This body wasn't used to physical exercise.

Blanche helped her choose a demure violet dress to wear. Ann was amazed at the layers of clothing that were required—camisole, petticoat, corset … The latter she still refused to wear. It still baffled her how she could fit into Victoria's clothes. Blanche insisted on pulling her hair up, and she used a matching ribbon to keep the unruly curls in place. Ann was amazed at the transformation.

When she entered the dining room, William and Patrick rose to their feet. Blushing, she met Patrick's warm gaze. Patrick held the chair for her as she was seated. The adventure in the nineteenth century was awesome so far.

Patrick stared at Ann's face. She wanted to avoid his attention as much as possible. She didn't need any unnecessary scrutiny.

Sitting next to her, he asked, "Would you care for anything special to eat?"

Since soy milk and blueberries weren't an option, she hesitantly replied, "Tea and fresh fruit would be nice." William sat back down and resumed wolfing down a plate full of ham, eggs, and several huge flaky biscuits coated with real butter. She wondered if this was the reason that the expected life span was so low for this century.

Startling her from further speculation, Patrick cleared his throat. "You look rested. If you feel up to it, my aunt would like to talk with you. I assume the invitations met with your satisfaction."

Damn, the wedding again. "Yes. Everything looked great." Abruptly, she turned her attention to the sliced peach on her plate. She didn't want to think about his marrying Victoria.

This charade may prove harder than Ann had originally imagined. Apparently, Victoria allowed everyone to make decisions for her. Good grief! Didn't the woman have a mind of her own? The least that Ann could do was to establish some independence for her so that when Victoria returned, she would be pleasantly surprised at the changes that Ann initiated.

Patrick watched Ann as she picked at the fruit on the plate. "Are you sure you wouldn't care for something else?"

Ann choked down her fruit and shook her head. Her throat tightened as guilty feelings consumed her. She forced a brilliant smile when the men rose and left the dining room.

Tossing down her napkin, Ann reluctantly went in search of Mary O'Neil. She didn't want to be making wedding plans for Victoria; it made her very uncomfortable. Yet she couldn't resist adding several healthy entrees to the menu. Ann was able to get Mary to change some recipes, leaving the sauce off the meat.

Once they finished, Ann entered the main hall and saw Patrick and William talking.

William approached her with his hat and gloves. "Are you ready to leave?"

"Where are we going?" She nervously glanced at Patrick. She didn't want to leave.

"Nothing like sleeping in your own bed, I say. We'll be home within the hour and you can rest up."

Rest up? Is that all the poor girl did? All this inactivity was getting on her nerves. Taking a step backward, she stated, "If it's okay with everyone, I'll stay here." William made her nervous. In addition, by staying, she could learn more about the O'Neil family.

Patrick's mouth fell open. He quickly stepped forward, grasping Victoria's elbow. "There would no inconvenience if she were to stay. I'm sure that any rumors could be quietly quashed."

Ann's interest was piqued. "Rumors? What kinds of rumors?"

"That is none of your concern, young lady," William gruffly remarked.

Ann's chin jutted upward. "Well, excuse me. I have a right to know what would be said if I stayed here."

Patrick shrugged. "People would question our relationship if you stayed here before we were married. Even with a proper chaperone, gossip will reach the ears in London."

"Some things never change. Well, I suppose I should go home." Her foot tapped with annoyance. Ann caught an amused glimmer in Patrick's eyes. "What's so funny, Lord O'Neil?"

Gallantly, he lifted her hand to his lips. "I never realized what fire was contained in that small frame. Yet we must be practical." In a lower voice, for her alone, he teased, "I am very pleased that you want to stay here with me. I'm looking forward to seeing this same spirit on our wedding night."

Oh, baby! A wedding night with him would be full of hot, steamy sex. Her knees almost buckled imagining what his lips could do to her body.

She pulled her hand from his and followed her father to the carriage. As she attempted to step up into the carriage by herself, the overabundance of material in her skirts wrapped around her ankle, throwing her backward.

Effortlessly Patrick caught her and lifted her into the carriage. "Allow me to assist you." His hand slid up the back of her skirt and gave her bottom a little squeeze.

"Oooh!" She flashed him a look, daring him to do it again.

With a sly wink, he added, "We don't want any nasty bumps or bruises before the wedding."

Before she could fire back a retort, he shut the carriage door, urging the driver on. She literally tumbled onto the seat. His rumbling laughter echoed behind them. Arrogant man! He was too handsome for his own good. Unable to resist, she leaned her head out the window, yelling back at him, "Hey, O'Neil, I owe you one! Just wait until next time!"

Chapter 17

ANN THOUGHT WILLIAM WAS going to have a heart attack after she yelled back at Patrick. Her "father" gave her quite a lecture as they rode toward home. Finally, they drew up to the Montgomery estate, and Ann peered at the house. It definitely needed a face-lift. William hurried from the carriage, leaving Ann on her own. With yards and yards of skirts to worry about, exiting the carriage was a trial. She felt lucky not to be lying on the ground right now. Inside the house, Blanche hurried to Ann's side and removed her wrap.

"I can't believe this is where Vic … where I grew up."

Blanche gave Ann an odd look. "My lady, are you well?"

Ann hadn't felt this young and carefree in years. "Heavens, yes."

Ann hurried up the stairs, anxious to explore the place where Victoria grew up. This would allow her to learn about the Montgomery family and figure out where Victoria had disappeared to.

Blanche followed. Completely out of breath by the time she reached the top of the stairs, Ann lapsed into giggles.

"Miss, you must restrain yourself. Your father will have apoplexy if he hears you."

Ann laughed even harder. Really, these people were uptight.

Ann's room was smaller than the one she had occupied at Patrick's, but it was just as cozy. Ann ordered a tray for lunch, as she wanted to check out every room in the house. A row of portraits of long-deceased ancestors graced a secluded hallway. Although the bones of the house were good, many areas showed neglect.

The clock chimed five o'clock as she hurried to the main hallway. Blanche took one look at Ann's rumpled dress and moaned. "My lady, you must change."

"Don't tell me that I am expected to change my dress just to have tea?"

"Of course you are. You seem surprised."

With all this changing of clothes, no wonder women needed domestic help to do the laundry. It was crazy. It was so much simpler to wear a T-shirt and jeans.

Thirty minutes later, she joined William in the drawing room. Glaring at her, he growled, "You're late, young lady. This type of behavior won't do at all when you are Lady O'Neil. You have been brought up better, and I expect better. Do I make myself clear?"

Ann frowned. This father thing wasn't quite as she remembered. She hadn't been lectured by anyone for twenty years. Even her real father hadn't been this dictatorial.

"I do not appreciate that face of yours, miss. I strongly suggest you alter it quickly or return to your room."

Acting the part of a dutiful daughter was going to be tough. She demurely folded her hands in her lap. "Yes, Father."

"Much better. Now I want to enjoy my tea." William peered at Victoria. "Are you ill? Your voice seems hoarse."

Ann shook her head, biting into a bland cookie of some sort.

"Hmm. Well, take care of yourself. I don't want the wedding delayed. We need the money that O'Neil is offering."

Ann bit back a retort. Greedy man!

After enduring tea with William, Ann excused herself and went outside. The gardens had fallen into decay, like many other things in the house. For some reason, it saddened her.

The stables were a different story. Compared to the house, she was amazed at the superior quality of the facility and the horses. As a child, she had always wanted a horse. With several stables in the area, she had been able to ride frequently. Eyeing the sidesaddles, Ann laughed. No way would she attempt to use those.

Ann returned to the house. Inescapably, her thoughts returned to Patrick. She knew she should tell him the truth, but fear won out. Visions of being homeless and penniless in 1870 England were enough to make her hide the truth.

Ann quickly dressed for dinner. She didn't need another lecture about punctuality. At dinner, Ann absently mentioned the lack of fresh vegetables.

William shook his head, his jowls quivering. "I don't want my digestion ruined. We will not change the menu or the way food is prepared. That's the trouble with young folks today, always wanting to change things. I want things kept the way they are."

He continued eating, ignoring her presence. Exasperated, she asked to be excused. "What a nasty person," she mumbled softly.

As she left the room, she began counting to ten. She was ready to explode.

His faint voice sounded from the dining room. "What's that? Are you sassing me, Victoria?"

Ann smiled as she walked up the stairs. Having William as a father was going to be challenging.

The next morning, Ann hurried to the stables, hoping to avoid another encounter with William. The groom brought out a sidesaddle. After convincing him that a standard saddle would be much safer, she hoisted herself up, smiling at the worried groom. The feisty mare pranced sideways, anxious to be turned loose.

Taking the reins, Ann nudged the animal forward at a sedate pace. Once they were out of sight, she gave the horse its head. Within seconds, they were flying across the meadow. The wind tore through her hair. Her laughter filled the air. She leaned forward, urging the horse to go faster yet. Minutes later, Ann pulled up on the reins, slowing the winded mare.

A grove of trees lay ahead. Beads of sweat dotted her brow. Brushing her dampened curls from her face, Ann was drawn toward the cool shade ahead. She jumped down and loosely tied the reins to a bush. Ann breathed deeply, relishing the peace and solitude of the moment.

Patrick's anger finally cooled to a low boil. He had stopped by the Montgomery residence a short while ago, in hopes of taking a pleasant ride with his future bride. Instead, he was informed that Victoria rode out earlier, by herself! His concern for her overrode the dressing-down the guilty groom deserved. Patrick mistakenly assumed he could catch up with her. At the top of a hill, he stopped, trying to catch sight of his fiancée. He had been about to turn back to the house when he saw her. If it hadn't been for her vivid hair color, he would have never believed that it was Victoria riding in such a dangerous fashion.

Numb with fear, he watched her horse gallop at breakneck speed. Afraid that she no longer had the horse under control, he rushed to rescue her before she broke her neck. Sweat beaded on his forehead. His heart pounded in his chest. Never had he been this afraid for anyone in his entire life.

Suddenly, her laughter rang out across the meadow. In disbelief, he watched as she pulled the remaining pins out of her hair, allowing her curls to blow wildly in the wind. All resemblance of a fashionable lady had disappeared. He then realized that she had never been in danger. She was actually enjoying it! He dismounted, trying to contain his anger. Little hoyden. Didn't she know the horse could have stumbled? Or she could have fallen and lain injured on the ground, where no one could find her.

He fumed with fury and something else he hadn't felt before. He stalked toward her purposefully, having only one intent. Ignoring her gasp, he yanked her off the horse and pulled her against him. Running his hand through her tousled hair, Patrick pulled her head back until her wide eyes met his. Without uttering a word, he ground his lips to hers. His anger melted as his senses focused on the woman held tightly in his embrace.

After several minutes, the intensity of the kiss dimmed.

Trembling, she laid her head on his chest. His pounding heart matched hers.

Eyes closed, her head tilted back, she whispered, "Patrick."

Lifting her in his arms, he reverently laid her beneath a towering oak. He jerked off his jacket and threw it to the ground. Her passion-filled eyes and lush lips fueled his fire.

His eyes never left hers as he tore at the front of his shirt. Buttons flew to the ground in his haste to join with her. He dropped to the bed of meadow grass, where his body instinctively pressed against her lush curves. His lips worshipped her mouth, and his hands worshipped her heavy breasts.

A soft moan escaped her when she ran her hand across his bare chest. His muscles twitched with the touch of her fingers. His hand crept up her thigh and palmed the heat between her legs. Her hips pressed upward, seeking what he offered. Her swollen nipples tightened through her dress as his hot breath brushed across the tips. He swore he stopped breathing when she brazenly reached down and unfastened his trousers. His cock was rock hard. She slowly massaged the length of his member. He moaned his pleasure, pressing into her hand.

His hips pumped into her hand, sliding up and down in her hot grip. He drew back and stared down at Victoria. Who was this woman? Her head tossed from side to side, uneven breaths escaping her parted lips. This was no timid virgin who thrashed in the throes of passion. Heat clouded his brain, making it difficult to think anymore. He urged her hand to pump harder … faster. He was so close to a climax. Just a few more seconds.

Realizing the path they were on, he tore his lips from hers. The way that Ann stared at his parted mouth stoked the fire in his lower body. The feel of her rosy lips was enough to melt any man's resistance.

Ann shoved at him and struggled to her feet. She wouldn't meet his gaze. He watched as she picked the twigs and leaves out of hair. Patrick stood to fasten his pants and tuck in his shirt. His ragged breathing echoed in the air. He reached up, smoothing the hair off her neck.

Batting away his hand, she demanded, "What was that all about?"

He watched the sunlight play upon her riotous curls. He gently raised her chin so she would be forced to look at him. "Your reckless behavior is unacceptable. I think the image of you racing like a wild woman will haunt me until the day I die. However, your reckless behavior between the two of us is perfectly acceptable. I must ask you a question. You indicated that you wanted a marriage of convenience. It appears that you have changed your mind. Why?"

She jerked away from his touch. "A marriage of convenience? Whatever gave you that idea? Besides, I am an accomplished rider. Everything was under control. I suppose you thought I would fall off the horse?"

He folded his arms across his chest. "Now that you mention it, the thought did cross my mind."

Turning on her heels, Ann marched to where the horses waited. Patrick grabbed her hand when she reached for the reins.

"I don't see why you're upset. I'm the one who should be angry. You could have been killed. I forbid you to ride in that manner ever again."

Tears welled up in her eyes. "You want a wife who sits in the house knitting or doing whatever women do these days. I'm different. I can't be the wife you want."

His brows drew together. Tears made him feel helpless. "You will not be a prisoner. I want you to be happy, but I want to protect you. Surely that is nothing to cause you grief."

"This is so hard to explain. I know that you're trying to understand." Gripping both of his hands, she said, "I've changed. I'm not some fragile porcelain figurine that will break at the slightest touch. You must have faith in my abilities and judgment. Would I have jeopardized my own life when our wedding is only a few days away?"

Patrick raised her hands to his lips. "Very well. I will try to withhold comments in the future. However, society is not as tolerant."

As they rode back to the house, neither spoke about what happened under the oak tree. Upon reaching the Montgomery stables, Patrick turned toward home, deciding it was too risky to be near her in his current condition. He wanted nothing more than to carry her to his bed and finish what they'd started in the meadow. He turned to take one more look at his fiancée, more confused than ever.

Chapter 18

THE GROOM TOOK HER reins. "Miss, we was real worried about you. Thank God Lord O'Neil found you. He was mighty upset when I told him you were riding alone."

Ann patted his arm. "Next time you'll have to keep my secret, so I won't get in trouble." Ann chuckled at the perplexed look on the groom's face.

As she walked toward the house, myriad thoughts coursed through her mind. Victoria was going to marry Patrick, not her. What was she thinking—or not thinking, as the case may be? Things were moving too quickly. Their mutual attraction was blotting out all reasonable thoughts. She couldn't have sex with him and then go back to the twenty-first century. That would not be fair to him or Victoria.

Later that afternoon, the smell of apple dumplings greeted her as she left her room. She followed the wonderful smell and ended up in the kitchen. She'd always found a kitchen to be the warmest and coziest room in the entire house. The warm sun filtered through the windows, and the servants teased one another as they finished their duties. Several of them stole glances at her while they worked. Ann selected an apple from the bowl on the table and sat in an empty chair. One of the servants opened her mouth to say something, but the cook raised her brow and shook her head. It wasn't their place to comment.

Ann smiled at the cook. "The dumplings smell delicious. When will they be ready?"

"Soon. If you would like, I could have a maid bring one to your room."

"That's too much trouble. I'll just wait here until they're done."

"Lady Montgomery, you mustn't stay here. It's not proper. Your father will have my head if he discovers you here."

"Never mind him. He won't find out."

Pointing to the bowl of apples, Ann asked, "Do these need to be peeled?" Without waiting for the answer, Ann started peeling the sweet-smelling fruit.

The cook frantically wiped her hands in her apron, twisting the material over and over. "My lady, you really mustn't do this. It isn't right."

Ann observed the stricken looks on the faces of the servants and decided that maybe it would be better if she left. "Well, if you need anything, please let me know."

As she left the room, she saw the servants staring at each other in complete bewilderment. She knew that within an hour, every servant in the house would know about her visit to the kitchen.

It hadn't taken Ann long to figure out that she should stay away from Peter, William's valet. He had been with the household for years, and he lorded his power over the other servants. According to Blanche, he took personal pleasure in reporting the misfortunes of others to Baron Montgomery.

As Ann undressed for bed, her mind raced. She felt like a character in a soap opera. She tossed the covers aside, trying to sleep. She needed to keep her wits sharp to survive this adventure.

Ann was famished the next morning. Dressed for her morning ride, she breezed into the dining room. Without waiting for assistance, she helped herself to tea and reached for the newspaper. Although it was over a week old, it was still news to her.

William snatched the paper from her reach. Surprised, she stared at him. *How rude,* she thought.

His pudgy fingers tapped on the table until the servants left the room. "I have been informed about the incident with the servants. The servants have been gossiping about your behavior. This kind of behavior will not be tolerated, Victoria. I have threatened to dismiss anyone who allows it to happen. There will be no association with those people. If this unladylike behavior of yours reaches O'Neil, the wedding could be canceled."

Ann pushed back the chair and tossed the napkin on the table. "I was just getting to know them. They're really nice, and you should appreciate all they do for you."

Without warning, William closed the distance between them and brought his palm to her cheek. "Your insolence will not be tolerated."

Ann's eyes watered from the stinging sensation. She wanted to jump to her feet and poke her nails into his face. He was a horrible brute. Little wonder that Victoria was such a timid woman.

"I forbid you to leave this house until the wedding. Your maid will deliver all meals to your room."

Great! Now she was in time-out. Having a parent again was a real downer.

"Let me remind you that you are a Montgomery and I expect you to comport yourself in the appropriate manner. Now leave my sight."

Heat burned her cheeks. "Touch me again and I'll make you regret your actions." Stomping past him before he could react, Ann retreated to her room, slamming the door loud enough to be heard throughout the house.

William secluded himself in the library and quickly reached for a brandy. He ran his fingers through his thinning hair. His face was beaded with sweat. Mopping his brow, he absently stared at a pile of statements from Malcolm's creditors. He shoved Malcolm's bills into a desk drawer. Moneylenders had called yesterday wanting money. The last of his funds had been used to purchase a suitable wardrobe for Victoria. William expected to recover those funds soon enough, and he didn't want Malcolm drawing attention to their dire circumstances. Ungrateful whelp! Both children were such disappointments.

Victoria's rebellious behavior was becoming bothersome. Perhaps a little opium in her tea would calm her down and allow him to retain control.

Her mother had also ignored his requests. After her constant threats to leave him, he had purchased opium in the East End of London. In a constant drugged state, Victoria's mother stayed in her room, leaving the estate in his hands. Without her interference, he was able to spend the money as he wished.

There was much more at stake this time. The entire O'Neil fortune could be his. Victoria would cooperate one way or another.

Chapter 19

WITH HER CURRENT CONFINEMENT, the days dragged by for Ann. Blanche smuggled in books to help her pass the time. The wedding was fast approaching, and she was still in the wrong century. She had to get back to Patrick's house to get her computer and bag. She didn't want people asking questions that she wasn't prepared to answer. Thank goodness they didn't burn people at the stake anymore.

Although she tried not to think about it, she started to imagine what life would be like if she stayed and married Patrick. Would she ever see her two children again? With Mark and Deb marrying and Jessica already married, what about grandkids? Would she and Patrick have any children? In her brief stay, she'd found him courteous and caring. The longer she stayed, the more she felt that she belonged in this century. She had to remind herself constantly to ignore any feelings she had for Patrick. When Victoria returned, she would be the one to marry Patrick, not her.

Thinking of all the possible complications was driving her crazy. She needed to get outside and get some exercise. William had left the house earlier in the morning. Ann estimated that she had at least two hours of freedom and rang for Blanche.

"Bring my riding clothes, please." Not waiting for an answer, Ann started undressing. She turned around and saw Blanche standing there with empty hands. "Is there a problem?"

"Miss, your father left strict orders that you are to stay in your room. I don't feel right disobeying him."

Ann threw open the doors of the armoire. "I feel great disobeying his orders!" Slipping on the riding skirt, she watched as the maid nervously paced about the room. "You need to have faith. Just because my father says something doesn't mean he's right. Men do make mistakes. You probably won't believe it, but someday women will have the same rights as men."

Blanche warily glanced toward the door. "If your father heard you, he'd be furious. You'd best be careful."

"Wouldn't you like to vote for the best person to represent you in Parliament? Can you imagine a woman representing you in Parliament?"

A ghost of a smile spread across Blanche's face. "Now that would be worth seeing." Without further argument, Blanche hurried to find Ann's boots.

With the exception of Peter, all the servants were willing to help her circumvent William's orders. The groom cheerfully saddled her mare. Enjoying her freedom, she automatically headed for the O'Neil estate. Galloping down the path that connected the two estates, Ann saw a man riding toward her. He was slumped forward in the saddle as if injured. His clothes were tattered and dusty, as if they had been worn for several days. Ann hesitated and considered turning around. Chiding herself for being silly, she decided that it was probably someone down on his luck. Even though she continued forward, she wished she had her pepper spray.

The man slowly raised his head. The sun prevented her from seeing clearly. Ann's eyes widened. The sight of his blond hair sent fear coursing through her. Was it David? She drew up on the reins, staring ahead. A second look confirmed that it wasn't David. The man was smaller, not as muscular.

The horses drew next to one another. Both riders stared silently at each other. His haunted gaze convinced Ann that this was a troubled man. Suddenly, the man slid out of the saddle and stumbled to a nearby tree. The man slipped to his knees, his head bent and deep sobs shaking his body. The heartbreaking sound touched Ann's heart. Poor man! What could have happened?

Walking over to him, she gently laid her hand on his shoulder. He turned and gazed up at her. Tears glistened in his eyes. Clasping her hand, he held it tightly, seeming unable to speak.

She softly asked, "Is there anything I can do to help you?"

He just sat and stared at her. Trying again, she probed, "Are you okay? Do you need a doctor? Please say something."

Tears streamed down his cheeks. "God, forgive me. I've changed. I'm truly sorry. I'll do whatever it takes to prove that I've changed. Take the ghost away."

Ann stared at the distraught man. What terrible thing had happened to make him beg for forgiveness? Did he really think that she was a ghost?

"Don't be frightened. I assure you that I'm as real as you are."

He seemed lost in a fog of despair, staring blankly into her eyes. Ann took a step backward, but he gripped her hand as if she was an anchor to sanity. His eyes never wavered from her face. His face remained unreadable.

Anxiety mounted when he refused to let go of her hand. "I suggest you let go of my hand this instant."

After a moment of surprise, he began to laugh hysterically. He fell back on the ground, holding his sides as fresh tears ran down his face. Holding up his hand, he tried to speak. Deciding the man was emotionally unbalanced, she hurriedly moved toward the horses.

"Wait, please. I must talk to you."

"Fine. I'll stand here and you talk. Be quick about it. People will be out looking for me soon."

He mopped his face with a yellowish handkerchief from his pocket and rose to his feet. "Forgive me for the outburst of emotions. I wasn't trying to alarm you. I've had a terrible shock recently and fear my mind was playing tricks on me."

"Great. If you don't mind, I'll be leaving." As he walked toward her, she quickly mounted the waiting horse.

He came closer, standing next to her horse. His hand rubbed the horse's neck as Ann watched, ready to bolt if necessary. He started to hand her the reins. "Let me introduce myself. Sir Malcolm Montgomery at your service. I would like to know the name of the kind Samaritan who helped me today."

Surprised at the mention of the Montgomery name, she asked, "Are you related to William Montgomery?"

"He's my father."

"Father!" Without thinking, she blurted, "Then you're my brother!"

Before she could utter another word, he yanked her off the horse. His blue eyes reflected the turbulence growing within. His red face pressed nearer.

He growled, "You are not my stepsister. What game are you playing?"

"My name is Victoria Montgomery. You can ask anyone at the house if you don't believe me."

His hands gripped her shoulders. "If you're her, then explain why you didn't know me."

What a blunder! How could she explain why she'd failed to recognize him? Unable to think of an answer quick enough, Malcolm interrupted her thoughts.

"Aha! You look enough like Victoria to fool most people, but I know you are an imposter. You must have heard about Victoria's engagement to O'Neil and decided to impersonate her. Luckily, I came back to prevent this injustice from taking place."

She was torn with indecision. Should she try to explain what really happened? Could he even understand the possibility of what happened?

"How did you know that I wasn't Victoria?"

Clearly surprised at her admission, he hesitated for a moment. "Several things. Your eyes are greener than hers. Your voice is deeper, huskier. And you are also rather outspoken."

"You love her, don't you?"

"Yes," he moaned. "It isn't what you think. She's my stepsister.

She is an angel. Never would she consider any improper behavior. I was such a fool not to realize it sooner. Now I have lost her."

"You speak as if she's dead."

Malcolm abruptly turned away. "She is not dead. She and I will be together soon."

Ann struggled to find the right words. "My name is Ann Roberts. I'm from America. There was a terrible thunderstorm with lots of lightning, and—"

Blatantly skeptical of her explanation, he interrupted. "Let me guess. Some mystical force transported you here to England."

She raised her chin defiantly. "If you let me finish, I'll explain, though you probably won't believe me."

"Pray continue. This fairytale has me spellbound."

"There was a man, David, whom I used to date. I told him I didn't want to see him anymore. He became angry when I told him that I didn't care for him. On the night of the storm, he broke into my house and tried to kill me."

She braved a glance at Malcolm. He was staring at her, appearing to be seeking the truth in her words. "He tried to kill me with a knife. During that time, a huge storm was shaking the house. Just when I was about to give up, I screamed. When I woke up, I was in Patrick's house. Everyone assumed I was Victoria."

He snorted in disbelief. "Where were your parents and servants while all this was taking place? Your scheme will not work. Are you some poor man's daughter trying to catch a rich husband?"

"I live alone. Where I live, only the very rich have servants. My children ..." Stopping, she clasped her hand over her mouth. Her desire to convince him had just taken a detour. Maybe he hadn't heard her last statement.

A sly smile graced his face. "Children? Just how many do you have, madam? How were you going to convince Patrick that you are a virgin on your wedding night?"

The half-truths were creating havoc with her brain. She had to tell him everything. Ignoring the risks, she continued. "I have two children, a boy and girl. My son is close to your age."

He snorted. "If you have a son my age, then I am the king of England."

"I'm going to tell you the whole truth. I am from America, and I've told you my real name. There was a man trying to kill me. What I haven't told you is that I traveled back in time to be here. The whole thing started when I bought an album to help me investigate my family history. Patrick was pictured in the album. I'm in my forties, so it is reasonable to have children the same age as you."

She paused and took a deep breath. Malcolm was still scowling at her. "Does this mean you don't believe me?"

"I quit believing in fairy tales before I was out of the nursery. You expect me to believe this preposterous tale of flying through time and somehow taking over the body of a woman less than half your age?"

She stomped her foot on the ground. "Well, you can go to hell. I don't care if you believe me. It's the truth. If I had my choice, I would be back in the twenty-first century, where we have all kinds of conveniences and women have the right to be heard. England won't even allow women to vote until 1928."

Clearly fed up with her lies, he grabbed her shoulder. "Women are not interested in politics. You're trying to confuse me with these wild tales."

"I suggest you check in London. Women are already working for the government. This is only the first step. Once we start working and earning money for ourselves, you men don't stand a chance."

Rubbing his forehead, he muttered, "Now that you bring it up, I have heard that Parliament hired women clerks to work in government offices. So it's true? Women do get the right to vote?"

Nodding, she sat down beside him. "It's not really the end of the world. We take our rights quite seriously."

"I don't suppose you Yanks have elected a woman for president?"

Surprised at his congeniality, she found herself rethinking her opinion. He was much better company than his father. "No, not yet."

"Good. It shows you Americans still have some sense."

They both burst into laughter, and she felt that their distrust of each other was gradually fading. They rode home side by side.

As the house came into sight, Ann muttered aloud.

Malcolm eyed her curiously. "Is anything wrong?"

"Your father ordered me to stay in my room. I see he has returned. I think you should know that I dislike your father."

Surprisingly, he winked at her. "I don't care for him much either. He can be a little overbearing. Don't worry—I'll protect you. Slip in the servant's entrance while I cause a distraction at the front."

She felt better than she had in days. She hoped she could spend time with Malcolm, but there was so little time until the wedding. Maybe the reason she had traveled back in time was to help Malcolm. At least she now had a confidant.

Chapter 20

RECENT RAINS DAMPENED THE grassy slope. David slowly regained consciousness, moaning in pain. The blinding sunlight compounded his headache. Mud coated his cheek, along with most of his clothes.

The hum of flies hovering nearby buzzed in his ears. He tried to turn over, but every muscle in his body rebelled at the effort. He groaned, rubbing his temples. "Damn, what happened?" It felt as if someone had beaten the crap out of him and left him for dead.

Once on his feet, he hobbled to a nearby tree. Nothing looked familiar. Not a house in sight. He tried to remember what had happened. Desperate for a drink of water, he stumbled down the dirt road. The warm sun caused sweat to trickle down the back of his neck and between his shoulder blades. Frustrated, he kicked at the ground. Dust swirled up around his face. He choked as the cloud of dirt surrounded him. For a city boy, this was like being on another planet.

He blinked as an old-fashioned carriage with four bay horses came barreling down the road. Maybe it was used for some country fair or historical reenactment event. But at least it was a ride. He stood in the middle of the road, waving his arms. One way or another, he was getting on that thing. It was too damn hot to walk.

∞

The startled coachman pulled up, and seeing a man blocking the road waving like a madman, he reached down to make sure a pistol was close at hand.

Lord Edward Marshall peered out the carriage window. "Why are we slowing down, Jenkins?"

Leaning down, Jenkins answered, "Sir, there's a man in the middle of the road. Do you want to stop?"

Edward leaned farther out the window. The stranger stumbled as if he were on the verge of collapsing. "See if he needs assistance but be careful."

Jenkins left the carriage and cautiously approached the semiconscious man. Besides being filthy, the man had bruises on his face. The poor bloke had been beaten to a pulp.

"Can you help me? I need a ride to town. I'm not sure I can ma ..." Before he could finish, he slumped forward.

Edward opened the door and stepped out to help Jenkins lift the stranger into the carriage. Opening a bottle of wine from the luncheon basket, Edward held the glass to the man's lips. Greedily, David drank the entire contents.

As he refilled the glass, Edward wondered about the quality of this man. Who was he? With all the dirt and blood, it was difficult to determine the quality of his clothing.

"I'm Edward Marshall. It seems you were in an accident. I will be glad to drop you off somewhere. Do you live nearby?"

David leaned back on the black leather cushion. "Sure, I've got an apartment in Des Moines. Just drop me off at the nearest phone and I'll get a ride the rest of the way. How about another drink?"

Edward's mind tried to filter the stranger's accent and words. Des Moines? If he was correct in his geography, that was a city somewhere in the States. He had no idea what a phone could be. "Des Moines, you say?"

"Yeah, you know ... in Iowa." David joked, "You do know that you're in Iowa—the Tall Corn State and all that stuff. Personally,

I prefer Chicago or New York. The farmers can keep the pigs and corn to themselves."

Perplexed, Edward succinctly asked, "Do you think that you are in Iowa now?"

"Of course, unless I've been abducted by aliens." Sounding unnerved by Edward's piercing gaze, he quizzed, "Where do you think we are?"

Edward couldn't tell if the man was deranged or injured from a blow to the head. He tensed, watching for any sudden movement. "Right now, we're outside London, England."

David smirked. "Right. Next you'll tell me that it's not the year 2013."

Edward decided that the man was in need of medical attention. "I do not know if you jest or not, but the year is 1870. Perhaps we should have that cut on your head looked at. I'll take you to Lady Paxton's. I heard tell that she was inquiring about needing a stableman."

David arched off the seat, slamming his head into the roof of the carriage. "You're crazy. Yesterday was 2013. Today is 2013. Look around! This is Iowa. Just stop and let me out before I really get pissed off."

Edward remained calm, not wanting to alarm the man seated before him any further. Still, his astute gaze took in every movement and nuance of the stranger. "I assure you that this is reality. You have suffered a head injury. Do you know who you are?"

"Damn it," David muttered as he sat back. Flakes of dried mud flew from his clothes onto the leather seats. "Of course I know my name. I'm David Stewart. I remember everything, so I know I'm not the one confused."

Wisely, Edward kept silent. It was no use arguing with Mr. Stewart. The man would soon remember the correct year.

David stared out the window, his fists clenched together. Could it be possible that he really was in England? What happened last night? When he tried to remember, the pounding headache returned. All he could remember was a woman with reddish hair.

He was an avid fan of science fiction. He knew that some physicists thought that it was possible for time to travel backward, but no studies were documented. There was always the possibility of another dimension. Whatever had happened to him, it appeared that he needed Edward for the time being.

The carriage pulled up a circular drive. Towering sandstone walls stood before David as he stepped down. An elderly gentleman dressed in black-and-white livery quickly met Edward on the steps. "Good to see you, my lord. Lady Paxton was worried that you would miss this evening's engagement."

"Thank you, Albert. As you can see, we had a diversion on the way." Turning slightly, he ordered Jenkins to take David around to the servant's entrance.

David felt embarrassed. He had been prepared to walk in with Edward. Instead, they treated him like some kind of bum. There was no choice but to follow the coachman.

David soon found himself in the kitchen. He saw several women preparing food. They wore long black skirts with starched white blouses. Open windows did nothing to cool the overheated room. There were no fans or electric lights anywhere.

Jenkins turned to one of the cooks. "Martha, bring us two bowls of stew and some bread." Nodding at David, he gruffly added, "If you want to wash up, there's a pump and towel outside."

"I don't suppose you happen to have some soap and bandages?"

"Water will be enough. I'll lend you one of my old shirts in the meantime. You best be moving before the food gets cold. They'll not be warming it."

Heading outside, David let the door slam behind him. Damn, who did Jenkins think he was? Scrubbing the dried blood from his face, he grimaced. What he wouldn't give for a nice hot shower.

All conversation ceased when he returned to the kitchen. What was wrong with these people? He ate the congealed mixture, ignoring the curious glances cast his way. He had to get out of here, but he had no clue where he was. If only the horrible headaches would go away, he was sure he could remember what happened.

Chapter 21

KATHERINE'S EYES NARROWED AS Edward approached. His boyish smile enhanced his youthful appearance. His jaunty steps gave credence to his amiable nature. A boxing enthusiast, his whipcord frame was proof of his time spent in the ring.

Until Patrick was safely snared, she would have to be careful to avoid Edward's scrutiny. Edward represented respectability. If she hadn't met Patrick, she would have married Edward, for they dealt quite well together—better than most married couples. Except she couldn't forget the way Patrick made her scream with pleasure.

Edward's lips grazed her hand. "I'm sorry to be late. There was an unexpected delay. We found an injured man on the road." Shaking his head, Edward went on. "I've sent Jenkins after the physician. The man has a head injury and believes the strangest things."

Katherine set her wineglass aside. "Pray tell, what does he believe?"

"He says he's from the States. His accent may support his claim."

Ringing for the maid to remove the tray, Katherine had already lost interest in the tale. "If he needs employment, put him in the stables. I am sure that the help would be welcome." She rose, gliding toward Edward. Her fingers ran down his roughened cheeks, and then her lips tugged playfully on his.

Edward smiled knowingly. "What are you up to Katherine? When you're like this, I know that you want something."

Donning her most innocent look, her lashes fluttered. "How can you say that? I'm just looking forward to our night together without any interruptions. I've dismissed the servants."

With a low growl, he pulled her closer. "Be warned, my dear. If it is mischief brewing under those golden curls, I might not be around to put the pieces back together for you."

Peeved that he could so easily discern how her mind worked, she walked to the window and peered out. She liked when he took control. His calm mannerisms misled many of his boxing opponents. They mistook his quiet demeanor as meekness. Katherine knew that he could be as hard as the situation warranted.

And she loved it when he was hard.

David followed Jenkins to the stables. They entered a room that had a blanket for a door.

"Here's your room. You can help me with the horses. Just do what you're told and stay out of trouble."

After Jenkins left, David kicked a pile of straw. "Damn." He didn't know anything about animals. He wasn't a farmer. He knew technology. And from what he'd seen so far, there was no such thing as technology here. Nada!

From a dust-covered window, he watched Edward and an attractive woman embracing in the window on the second story. David's calculating eyes followed her movements. She seemed like an appropriate adventure for a man stuck in the wrong century.

A strange dream interrupted his sleep that night. He was chasing a woman with auburn hair. The blanket twisted about David as he thrashed on the bed. He woke up clutching his chest. He remembered nothing but a sense of uncontrollable rage. Who was this mystery woman?

The next couple of weeks were agony for David. His hands were covered with blisters from working twelve hours a day. He was pitching hay, rubbing down the horses, hauling feed and water, and the list of chores went on and on. He learned how to handle the reins of a carriage like an experienced driver. Each night, he threw himself on the cot, asleep before his head hit the pillow.

David frequently saw the woman that he now knew was Katherine. She and Edward seemed to be a couple. They spent time doing such things as walking in the garden or taking tea on the terrace. They acted as if he didn't exist. His bitterness festered each time he spotted them.

Katherine watched David when Edward's attention was engaged elsewhere. She was very much aware of his existence and let her fantasies grow. David's taut muscles strained the back of his shirt to reveal a masculine physique. His blond hair appeared almost white in the late day sun. His attitude was anything but menial.

Edward planned to return to London tomorrow. A wicked thought took hold. Mr. Stewart would be a pleasant diversion until she was back in Patrick's arms.

Edward left early the next day and planned to return in time for Patrick's wedding.

She put her scheme into motion before Edward's carriage was out of sight. Katherine called for her maid.

"I wish to go out. Have the new man prepare the carriage."

"Are you sure, my lady? Jenkins could take you. Mr. Stewart is an odd sort of man."

"Odd. What do you mean?"

"Most of the female servants are afraid of him. Nothing has happened, but several of us feel that he is off his cork, if you get my meaning." Her maid paled as if regretting her statement.

"I want the carriage brought around front. I do not want to hear any more stories." If the servants were afraid of him, then it became essential that she meet and judge him for herself.

David readied the carriage as instructed and drove to the front of the house.

Katherine knew she was a beautiful woman. She was tall and slender yet voluptuous. Her hourglass figure accentuated her full breasts. She made sure all her clothing showed her figure to her advantage. She relished the look in men's eyes when they watched her.

David held out his hand to assist Katherine into the carriage. When their fingers touched, her pulse quickened. Her lips parted. Katherine met his gaze and trembled. He looked as if he wanted to rip off her skirts and plunge deep inside her. How intriguing.

Arranging her skirts, Katherine took a good look at him. His clothes were sadly lacking, but there was potential underneath. What was a little dalliance? She had to be discreet, however. She couldn't afford to lose both Patrick and Edward.

After they'd been driving a sufficient amount of time, Katherine tapped on the roof. "Driver, pull over. I wish to stretch my legs."

David opened the carriage door. Katherine held out her hand so he could assist her.

Katherine strolled over to a large tree, toying with the ribbons on her hat. She glanced over her shoulder and smiled. David stood by the carriage, looking unsure of whether he should follow. Couldn't he see that she wanted him to follow?

The brim of the hat hid her eyes. If she tilted her head just right, she could watch him. Standing in the sunlight, she wished she had her fan. The midday sun was warm. Likely drawn by the scent of her cologne, a pair of bees buzzed near her face. Afraid of being stung and ruining her appearance, she lifted her skirts and ran.

"Don't just stand there—help me! A swarm of bees is attacking me."

David ran to her side and grabbed her arm to stop her flight. There was one lone bee perched on top of a silk flower that adorned her hat. Katherine continued to hop about and wave her hands. David broke out laughing.

Humiliated, she drew back her hand and slapped his face, wanting to erase the smug smile spread across his face.

Seizing her wrist, he twisted her skin. Furious, she raised her other hand. Anticipating her intent, David intercepted her arm. He tightened his grip, even when she gasped from the pain.

Attempting to pull free, Katherine snapped, "Let me go this instant, you fool."

"Fool? I'm not the fool; you are. No woman hits me and gets away with it."

One glance at his hardened eyes and she knew that she had made a mistake. Her impulses always got her in trouble. There was no recourse except to pacify him. "Forgive me. I was upset. Bees terrify me. Besides, I hate being laughed at."

Wordlessly, he dragged her toward the grove of trees.

Katherine's heels dug into the grass. "I wish to return to the carriage immediately!"

They moved farther away from the road and from any help that would happen by. In all of her past escapades, she had always been the one in control. His bizarre behavior frightened her. He was like no other man she knew. The specter of death flashed through her mind. No man in his right mind would harm her, but what if David was insane? Then her life was truly in jeopardy!

He shoved her to the ground. She lay still, paralyzed with terror. He drew off his shirt. His golden skin glistened in the afternoon sun, rippling over an abundance of well-defined muscles, yet his piercing blue eyes were like daggers of ice.

He smirked. "You women are all alike. You pant after any man, regardless of how he uses you."

Incensed, she attempted to rise. As if she were an animal, he pushed her back onto the punishing ground with his foot. She writhed with pain as a rock poked through her dress, breaking the skin on her back. He pulled out a rope and bound her hands. Before she could protest, he stuffed a dirty rag in her mouth. Shaking her head wildly, she tried to kick him.

He jerked her upright, tying her to a nearby tree. Removing a large knife hidden inside his boot, he proceeded to slit the bodice of her dress, letting it gape open. He toyed with the knife, running the deadly point down her cheek.

Tears of pain and fear dampened her face. She was ruined. Patrick was marrying someone else. Edward would leave her.

Society would reject her. Why did she allow her impulses to govern her decisions? Now even Edward would despise her!

She shut her eyes, not wanting to see the carnal gleam in his eyes. Minutes later, feeling no insidious hands pawing her skin, she slowly opened her eyes and stared down at her slit-open dress. His back faced her. What was he doing?

He whipped around and stalked toward her. He pressed his body against her, his hot breath warming her ear. His fingers twisted her nipples until she shuddered with pain.

"I have a proposition for you, Katherine. Seeing that you can't speak, I'll continue. I detest being poor and treated as if I'm nothing, so I'll make you a deal. I'll become your long-lost cousin. I will live with you and have all the benefits of your money. You can introduce me to a rich heiress."

Violently shaking her head in disagreement, she vowed not to do anything to help him.

He ran the tip of the blade down her arm. "Option two is that I'll continue to remove your clothing, rape you, and leave you tied to this tree. It may be days before anyone finds you. With no water, you may not survive. If you do survive, I'll explain that I was attacked and couldn't help you. You will be dirty goods. No one will want you." Eyes gleaming from madness, he awaited her response.

She nodded her head, dropping her chin to her chest in shame. Katherine had no choice but to agree to his demands. No one must learn of her humiliation. At some point, he would make a mistake. Then she would get her revenge. After agreeing to his demands, David untied her. She hastily covered her exposed body, sickened by what she had become.

As they arrived home, Katherine quickly wrapped a cloak about her torn dress. Albert assisted Katherine from the carriage to the house. David jumped down from the carriage. His gaze darted nervously between Katherine and the servants.

Jenkins came around the corner of the house. He yelled, "Stewart, get those animals to the stables right now. Can't you see they're thirsty?"

David walked to Katherine and took her arm in his. When his fingers tightened about her arm, she shrilly announced, "I have the most unexpected news. I have learned that Mr. Stewart is none other than my cousin. Our grandfathers were brothers. I'm so happy."

Shocked expressions were evident on those who stood about. Clearly disbelieving the tale, Jenkins spit near David's feet. David glared at the groomsman. "I'll let that go for now. Next time, be sure that you demonstrate proper respect."

Katherine's legs shook as they walked into the house. Would the servants believe her? More importantly, would Edward? Albert followed them into the house. Bowing slightly, he asked, "Shall I show Mr. Stewart to a room?"

"Yes. Put him in the west wing, Albert." She wanted him as far as possible from her room.

David smoothed back his hair, looking like the cat that ate the canary. "I will need a hot bath and a good tailor. Please see to it, Albert."

His requests made her bristle in anger, but she would play the game to keep her reputation intact.

In the following days, Katherine refused to leave her room. Her maid informed her that David had turned the household upside down. He had tormented one poor maid until she quit. He had ordered a year's worth of clothes from the most expensive tailors in London. Of course, he had to have a suitable riding mount, which led to a new carriage with matching black horses. Katherine was at her wit's end trying to find a way to expose him.

She had written several letters to Edward, urging him to come as soon as he could. Edward finally arrived the day before Patrick's wedding. She rang for her maid, quickly changing into a violet muslin dress and matching ribbon for her hair. Her waist-length hair was braided and wrapped into a sleek coil. Anxious to speak to Edward, she flew down the stairs.

"They're in the library, my lady." Albert nodded toward the closed door.

"They?"

"Lord Marshall and Mr. Stewart."

Afraid for Edward's safety, she burst into the room. Startled, the two men drew their attention to the doorway. Edward came forward and pressed her hand to his lips. "I missed you. I just heard the most surprising news from Mr. Stewart—or should I say David? Let's be seated. He was just explaining how his good fortune came about."

Katherine saw the silent warning in David's eyes before he turned toward Edward. "As I was saying, Katherine and I were talking, and one thing lead to another. Our grandfathers were brothers. My parents didn't marry, so I took my mother's name. She died when I was very young, but I remember her telling me that I came from a wealthy family. Before I ramble on, I must apologize. I can't believe how confused I was the day we met. All that nonsense about coming from the future ... I even had myself worried."

Edward's gaze assessed David. Would Edward be fooled by David's speech?

"What about the rest of your family, brothers or sisters, perhaps?" Edward's brow quirked upward.

David set down his drink. He softly murmured, "All dead. Smallpox outbreak. No survivors." David expelled a choking sound and covered his face.

Edward cleared his throat. "Well, that's all in the past now. With Katherine and me backing you, you will have no problem gaining the proper introductions. In fact, we are attending the O'Neil wedding tomorrow. It will be the event of season. You must accompany us."

Katherine's chin trembled as she fought back the hysteria. "No, David will feel out of place."

Edward kissed her forehead. "With us making the necessary introductions, David will do very well. I doubt he will lack for dancing partners."

David snickered. "I can always dance with you. I'm sure Edward wouldn't mind."

She shuddered and excused herself, unable to bear David's effrontery any longer. Later in the evening, she sat at her desk, staring at a piece of blank paper. Maybe she should send a letter to Patrick, stating they wouldn't be attending the wedding. She tried several times to pen a letter, only to become frustrated and throw wads of paper to the floor.

She had to attend the wedding, just to see Patrick one more time. She had to know that there was no chance of renewing their relationship. She had tried to be faithful to Patrick and failed. Now he was marrying that mousy Montgomery girl.

A large hand reached out and snatched the half-written letter in front of her. Katherine's scream died as she turned to see David standing behind her.

Scanning the paper, David shook his head. "I can't have you upsetting my plans. How will I meet a nice rich girl? Look on the bright side: you'll get rid of me if I marry." He viscously twisted her wrist until it reddened.

Katherine whimpered with pain. "Let go of me! Get out of my room before I call Edward."

In one swift movement, he jerked her from the chair and pinned her to the bed. He ran his finger across her taut lips. "If you do that, my dear cousin, I will kill him. That would be a shame, for I'm beginning to like ol' Eddy."

"Please don't kill him," she pleaded. "I'll do whatever you want."

"Just follow my instructions and no one will get hurt. We'll go to the wedding like one big happy family. If you do anything to mess this up, you'll regret it. Do I make myself clear?"

In a trembling voice, she whispered, "Yes. Now get out."

Straightening, he smoothed back his hair. Glancing into the mirror, he glared back at her, a silent threat to cooperate or else.

Who could she tell? There was no doubt that he would kill anyone attempting to thwart him. She must stay calm and gain David's trust. She would pretend to cooperate ... for now.

Chapter 22

Malcolm grinned as the butler opened the door. His mouth opened and closed like a fish gasping for air. Patting the man on the shoulder, Malcolm breezed past. "Send Peter to my room to prepare a bath and lay out fresh clothes. Where's my father?"

Malcolm saw the butler wrinkling up his nose as he went by. Maybe he should take a bath first. Instead, he followed the butler toward the library.

William glanced up at the interruption. His father frowned at Malcolm's disheveled appearance.

"Well," he growled, "how much do you need this time? Damn, look at you. Disgraceful! Did the neighbors see you?"

Malcolm smiled and dropped in the chair across from the desk. "It's nice to see you too. You're looking at a new man." Reaching into his pocket, Malcolm pulled out a large handful of twenty- and fifty-pound notes.

William pawed through the pile of money. "It looks real. Did you steal it?"

Malcolm's smile faded as he jammed the money back in his pocket. "Must you always think the worst? I won it. I've repaid most of our debts. I need a fresh start, so I've come home to manage our affairs."

William's bushy brows drew together. "We have a steward to handle things. If you want to do something, control your sister.

She wants to delay the wedding. With us working together, we will soon have everything we need."

Anger seared Malcolm's cheeks. "Forget about O'Neil's money. I can produce a tidy profit from the estate."

William slammed his fist on the desk. "No! I won't discuss this. Just talk to your sister. If you cannot drum some sense into her, then I will," he threatened.

With the door slamming behind him, Malcolm took the stairs two at a time. Why had he returned? His father was a tyrant. His own mother had died when he was born. Victoria's mother had tried to bring joy into their lives but had died when Victoria was eight years old and Malcolm was a young man of sixteen. Malcolm often wondered how she had died. An excellent rider, it seemed odd that she had fallen.

As a child, Malcolm had had few friends other than Patrick. Only two years younger than Patrick, he and Patrick had enjoyed many youthful pastimes together, from fishing to riding. Now his one-time friend Patrick had rejected him. After years of dissolute behavior, it was little wonder that society excluded him from most functions. Victoria had been the only person who ever cared for him. In the end, he'd destroyed her. It had only been a few weeks since her death. He had to prove to himself that he could be respectable. It was ironic that he found himself with a sister again. Maybe God was giving him another chance to prove that he had changed.

Quietly knocking on Ann's door, he heard her call out. He was pleased that she had kept Victoria's room the same. "I see that you managed not to get caught."

"Yes, thanks to you. I'm so glad you're here. I could really use a friend."

Unaccustomed to praise, Malcolm shifted uneasily. "I've spoken to my father. He insists that you are an impertinent chit and says that I must control your impulsive behavior."

Ann chuckled. "Now you see why I dislike him so. I hope all men in this century aren't so horrible …"

"Don't worry. Patrick is quite pleasant, for a nineteenth-century man," Malcolm unabashedly grinned. "Does he know who you are?"

"No, I thought about telling him, but since I won't be marrying him, why bother?"

"What do you mean? Are you leaving?"

Ann sighed. "Yes. Victoria will surely return in time for the wedding. She must love him very much. If Patrick suspects that I'm not Victoria, he'll probably have me locked up."

Malcolm turned away, hiding his emotions. He knew he had to convince Ann to marry Patrick. Victoria would never return.

The next morning, Malcolm left the house early and rode to the village. People greeted him with stony glares. He politely tipped his hat and nodded to those watching him. Expecting the worst, he was pleasantly surprised when one or two returned a smile. Malcolm entered the general merchandise store, determined to turn over a new leaf. He was going to start by repairing tenants' homes.

The store owner greeted him with a noticeable lack of enthusiasm. "Good day, sir. Can I help you?"

Malcolm flashed the stern-looking owner a smile. "Yes, I would like a load of shingles delivered."

"How much would you like?"

"I don't have any idea. The material is for the tenants. Several of the roofs are in need of immediate repair."

The storekeeper rubbed his chin. "The materials aren't cheap. I need to have payment up front."

Malcolm slapped the notes on the counter. "This should more than adequately cover the expense. The rest can be credited to my account."

Mr. Smith beamed. "The goods will be delivered by the end of the week, if that's fine with you?"

"Perfect. If there are any delays, notify me immediately." He turned and headed outside. He hadn't felt this good in years. His only regret was that Victoria wasn't here to witness the change in him. He now had a purpose in life. He wanted to erase the memory of the past several years. He had to redeem himself. He simply had to.

Malcolm hurried to his room to change for afternoon tea. Since Ann's door was open, he stepped in and surprised her with a brotherly peck on the cheek.

Ann smiled back. "You look pleased with yourself. What happened today?"

"There is so much work to be done. The estate is practically in shambles, but repairs are under way."

She grasped his hand. "That's great. Your father will be surprised."

He flashed a grin. "I can't begin to express how good it feels to do something positive."

Malcolm continued to regale her with his plans over tea. The two of them bantered back and forth, chuckling aloud at each other's jokes.

Malcolm's smile faded when he spotted William standing in the doorway.

"What's so amusing? All the noise is distracting."

Ann held out a cup of tea and offered it to William.

"Tea? A man needs more sustenance than that! Pour me a glass of port."

With a sigh, Malcolm finally rose to get the liquor.

"Son, sit down and have a drink with me."

"No, thank you. I prefer tea at this time of day."

Raising his brows, William glared at Malcolm. "Since when do you prefer tea? What has gotten into you?" he grumbled. "You are as soft as your sister."

Ignoring his father's insults, Malcolm turned and stared out the window. He peered through the glass to see a familiar figure riding up the lane. Smiling, Malcolm walked over to Ann's side. After a gentle nudge, she took the hint and followed him to the window.

Malcolm saw Ann's face light up as she watched Patrick. Obviously, his fitted black riding coat and gray waistcoat that emphasized his broad shoulders impressed her. He could tell that she had feelings for him. He was reminded of his feelings for

Victoria. If only he hadn't ruined it. He wanted to ensure that Ann and Patrick had a chance for love.

They saw Patrick toss the reins to a waiting servant. Patrick glanced up and waved to Ann in the window.

As Malcolm watched Ann trying to contain her excitement, he could barely choke back his laughter. She appeared to hop from foot to foot. He winced as a linen napkin hit him in the face as Ann hurried to return to her seat.

Minutes later, Patrick strolled through the doorway. Ann blushed as Patrick turned to stare at her.

William stood to greet his future son-in-law. "Well, well, what a surprise. Nothing is wrong, I hope?"

"No. I had a sudden desire to see my bride-to-be."

William guffawed and winked. "Come, Malcolm, let's leave the two of them alone for a few minutes."

Malcolm flashed a sly smile at Ann as he drew the sliding doors closed.

Chapter 23

ANN WAS UNSURE OF what to say or do. She nervously asked, "Would you care for some tea?"

Each time he saw her, she was afraid that he would figure out she was an imposter.

"Not really." Patrick came toward her, his eyes never wavering from hers.

His warm gaze glided over her body. Unable to bear the scrutiny of his heated look, she walked to the window to try to steady her erratic breathing.

Suddenly, his hands gripped her tense shoulders. He gently turned her to face him. "You're shaking," he whispered seductively in her ear. His hot breath caused a sensation of shivers to course through her body. Her hands clenched his jacket as a pool of heat between her legs threatened to unnerve her.

"You make me nervous."

"Really? No other woman makes me tremble with desire as you do." His hands continued their exploration at her hip, pressing her forward to feel the outline of his penis. He was very well endowed. Ann hid a soft smile. It was so easy to imagine his hands lingering over her breasts while his hips thrust in rhythm with hers. Stop it! She couldn't climax standing here. He'd think she was a slut with a crazy libido.

Ann buried her face against his chest, trying to slow her

breathing. Why couldn't she have met him in the right century? Life was so unfair. She was falling in love with Patrick and couldn't marry him.

Patrick tenderly tipped her chin so he could see her face. "What's wrong? Have I upset you?" He led her to the sofa, pulling her into his embrace.

"I ... I need to tell you ... something." She focused on his firm mouth inches away. What she wouldn't give to indulge her need. The pressure between her thighs was increasing.

His kissable lips broke into a grin. "Shhh. Don't speak." He leaned closer, inhaling her scent.

Helplessly, Ann pressed into him. "You're too damn hot for your own good."

As he tenderly nipped her earlobes, he huskily whispered, "You have a rather odd manner of expressing yourself. I am assuming that hot is a compliment."

She wanted to marry him. Her spirit felt that he was her other half. Could she take a chance? Love didn't come along every day, and in her experience, not even every decade. She couldn't lie to him. He would hate her duplicity. What if they got married and then she was sent back to the future?

"What if we could only be together for a few months ...? Would you still want to marry me?"

He pressed his lips to her forehead. "Of course. If I had only one hour with you, I would take it. You consume my every thought. With every breath, I dream of you and our future together."

Ann's guilt surfaced under his words of devotion. "But sometimes things aren't as they appear. We're not always in control of our own fate. I would give anything to spend the rest of eternity with you."

He held her tightly against him. His mouth trailed down her cheek to her lips. The glimmer of passion she felt earlier burst into an inferno. She threw her arms about his broad shoulders, melting as the flames of desire were stoked by his touch.

"My preference is that we continue this upstairs, but there is something to be said for anticipation," he murmured.

She drew back before her resolve crumbled under his smoldering look. She smoothed his ebony hair back into place. The glossy strands wrapped around her fingers.

"Will we go to London?"

"Would you like to?"

"Yes, I've never seen ... I mean, I cannot wait to see your house. Can we attend a ball?"

His eyes twinkled back at her. "You sound like a child at Christmas. There will be so many balls that you'll beg me to decline the invitations."

A knock on the door drew their attention. Malcolm jauntily entered, a satisfied look emblazoned on his face. Patrick glared at Malcolm, nodding toward the door.

"Malcolm, come join us. Patrick is making fun of me. Tell me, do you think I will tire of attending balls?" Ann scooted away from Patrick. The heat was radiating off his body. All she could think of was how his lips could work their magic on her naked body.

Lounging against the mantel, Malcolm unbuttoned his jacket. "I don't think you will tire of anything. You are too full of life."

Ann was puzzled as to why Patrick frowned at Malcolm. What had brought about this mood change?

"Patrick, what's wrong? Are you upset?"

"I'm fine. Malcolm, I heard that you were in London recently. Did you put in your usual appearance in at the gaming halls?"

Malcolm stared at Patrick, visibly struggling to maintain his composure. "Yes, I did. Luck was with me. If I must say so, I did quite well."

Patrick smirked, "I'm sure you did."

Ann was taken off guard at the coldness in Patrick's tone. "Aren't you being a little hard on Malcolm? You don't have a clue what he's done and ..."

Malcolm straightened, seeming to bristle with outrage. "Enough! I'm sure Lord O'Neil is not interested in my actions. It appears I am intruding. Please excuse me." Without another word, he strode out the door.

Ann was bewildered. What brought about this standoff between the two men?

"I can't believe you were so rude. For your information, Malcolm purchased roofing materials for the tenants and has paid off many of the family's debts."

Patrick massaged his temples, allowing his hair to fall across his brow. "Forgive me. I know the real Malcolm. Have you forgotten what he's really like?"

"I don't know what you're talking about. I would appreciate it if you would try to get along with him."

His deep voice purred, "It seems I need to reacquaint myself with your brother."

"It would seem so."

Feeling like a shrew, Ann turned the conversation to less volatile subjects for the remainder of their visit. After Patrick left, a feeling of uncertainty came upon her. What was she doing here? Why couldn't God send a clue? Could life be any more frustrating?

Hours later, Malcolm found Ann near the pond, throwing rocks across the water. She had taken the pins from her hair, letting it fall down her back. Her shoes and stockings were tossed in a pile.

"Whatever are you doing? I must say, you are the most unconventional woman I know. Do you ever sit still?"

Without smiling, she growled, "Watch out—I'm feeling crabby. This wedding has me on pins and needles."

After several minutes of silence, she did grin. "I can skip a rock across this pond of yours. Are you up to a challenge?"

At Ann's insistence, Malcolm took off his boots and socks and waded near the water to choose a rock. Mud oozed between his toes. Ann's laughter rang out. He didn't see what was so amusing. It was a damn mess, but if it cheered Ann, it was worth it.

That evening, as Malcolm joined the family for dinner, he found the usual commotion. Inebriated, William sloshed wine all over the table and himself.

Malcolm could barely keep his emotions under control. All

the talk of the wedding reminded him of Victoria. Although Ann was not his stepsister, he had grown very protective. For Patrick's sake, he hoped that Katherine was no longer his mistress. Victoria wouldn't fight for her husband. Ann was another story. He would not put it past her to challenge Katherine to a duel. What a stir that would cause!

Wiping the hair out of his eye, William attempted to stand. "Why are you two so gloomy? It's a great occasion. No more worries for us." He doubled over with laughter, losing his balance in the process.

Malcolm slid the brandy bottle under the table. "Father, perhaps you should prepare for bed. You want to look your best tomorrow, don't you?"

William leaned on the chair for support. "Quite right. Off to bed."

Peter appeared out of nowhere to guide his employer up the stairs. Sighing simultaneously, Ann and Malcolm looked at each other and rolled their eyes.

"Thank goodness he's gone. How can you stand that man? If you were like him, I would have run away the day we met."

A shadow crossed Malcolm's face. "If you had known me a few weeks ago, you would hate me." Moving to the fireplace, he poked at the dying embers.

"You seem somewhat melancholy tonight. Is there anything I can do to help?"

"No one can help me."

"Not even God?" Ann moved to Malcolm's side. "Don't say that. Nothing is so bad that God cannot forgive. Perhaps you should talk to a minister or priest. That may help you feel better about yourself."

"Maybe. It seems odd that after tomorrow, you'll be gone. I've just become used to having you around." Attempting a smile, Malcolm teased, "See, I just feel sorry for myself."

Linking her arm with his, Ann walked to the stairs. "Tomorrow is a big day. I need you there for moral support." She lightly kissed his cheek before retiring.

His hand touched his skin where she had pressed her lips. Malcolm stood gazing at the empty stairway. His vision blurred. Wiping an errant tear, he choked back a sob. There were so many regrets. He wished he could turn back the hands of time. His only chance at redemption was to be a brother to Ann and bring dignity back to the Montgomery name.

Chapter 24

ANN TOSSED AND TURNED all night. Flashbacks from her first marriage haunted her dreams. Waking with a start, she rose and looked out at the morning sun slowly rising. She'd survived his betrayal. As kids, Mark and Jessica were lucky to even get a card at Christmas. Patrick seemed the exact opposite—possibly the man of her dreams. But could she trust him? How much time did she have to find out?

Out of breath, Blanche hurried in the room. "We need to get you ready, m' lady."

"Do you think it's too late to cancel? Tell Patrick that I've changed my mind." Ann flopped back on the bed, clamping the pillow over her head.

Blanche tugged her hand and pulled her off the bed. "Hush. You must hurry. Your father is pacing about the dining room snipping at everyone. You need to eat something before we dress you."

"Fine." Grabbing a dressing gown, Ann trudged downstairs. The nightmare about her ex unsettled her. Doubts assailed her. Her stomach rumbled as she sat down to breakfast.

Hours later, she and Malcolm took a walk outside. Ann gripped Malcolm's hand. "I can't do this! I'm lying to Patrick. What will Victoria do when she learns that I've married her fiancé?"

"I know that you and Patrick have deep feelings for each other.

You're doing the right thing. Do not worry about Victoria. This is what she would want. Trust me. I will always be here for you. If you ever need anything, just send word and I will be there."

Ann squeezed his hand. "That means so much to me. My only regret is that you and I won't see each other as much as I'd like. I've never had a brother. I don't think I could have found a better one than you."

Malcolm leaned down and pressed a kiss on her cheek. "Thank you."

When they returned to the house, the carriage was loaded and ready to go. Ann quickly freshened up and hurried down the stairs. William was yelling again. At least he planned to ride separately, as he had to address a business matter.

The ride to the O'Neil estate was over in a heartbeat. Patrick's aunt met her at the doorway. "Come, come, we have much to do. I hope everything meets with your approval. It was so kind of you to allow me this boon. After all, Patrick is my only nephew."

Ann hugged the beaming woman. "I'm sure it will, Mary. I really appreciate all your efforts."

They walked toward the stairway. The musicians were setting up in the ballroom, the sounds of their instruments echoing throughout the house. Servants scurried about polishing and cleaning every inch of the house. The glass doors to the gardens opened, and several men entered carrying armfuls of white and dusty-pink roses. Mary excused herself, scolding a servant who dropped several of the flowers. Ann made her way upstairs, where she found Blanche unpacking her clothes.

When Ann offered to help, Blanche waved her away. "You need to rest for tonight."

Mischievously, Ann asked, "Rest for what? I plan on sleeping like a log tonight. You wouldn't believe what I've been through."

"Shame on you. Think of Lord O'Neil's disappointment. After waiting all this time, then to have you fall asleep, all limp-like."

At the word "limp," Ann began to laugh uncontrollably. A loud thumping noise at the door finally drew their attention. Ann dabbed her tears and saw Patrick lounging in the doorway, as gorgeous as ever. Without his waistcoat, Patrick's powerful frame was even more overwhelming.

The way he stared at her left little to her imagination. She could tell exactly what he was thinking—if the bulge in his trousers was any indication.

He dryly remarked, "I thought brides were supposed to be nervous. Though I'm glad you are enjoying yourself. Out of curiosity, did I hear you say something being limp?"

Ann dissolved with merriment and fell back on the bed. Blanche busied herself, attempting to cover her smile.

Arms folded across his chest, Patrick leaned against the doorframe watching her. His smile grew. He walked to the bed and took her hand, pulling her off the bed. "Let's take a walk."

Ann wiped the tears of amusement from her face. "I think Blanche could get more work done without us around."

Ann's stomach felt as if a hundred butterflies were fluttering inside. She cast a curious glance at Patrick as they strolled through the garden. It was hard to imagine that he would be her husband in a matter of hours. A wavy lock of ebony hair fell over one brow. She reached up to brush it off his face. As her hand touched his face, she paused. A muscle in his jaw flexed. Lifting her other hand, she lightly caressed the dark stubble near the corner of his mouth and chin. His chiseled lips parted slightly. Heat from his gaze made her tremble.

"I love the feel of your whiskers. They're so sexy," she whispered.

"I'll have to remember that and never shave." Patrick crushed her to his chest. "I love the feel of your hand on me. If I don't take you back to your room this minute, both of us may miss the wedding."

Hand in hand, they walked back to the house. Mary was coming down the stairs as they entered, still holding hands. "We don't have time for this mischief making. You'll have plenty of time for that later."

Ann was whisked upstairs. She hadn't had this many jitters at her first wedding. She tried not thinking of all the reasons that she shouldn't marry Patrick. In her heart, the marriage felt like the right thing.

For the next two hours, Ann endured the attentions of several giggling maids, letting them arrange her hair and dress her. With the last of the pearl buttons fastened, Ann stared at the mirror in amazement. Who was this woman? The vision before her was the epitome of Victorian fashion. Glossy auburn curls artfully cascaded down to her shoulders. French lace exposed just enough neckline to tantalize the groom. The heavy train, made from numerous yards of delicate lace, had to be carried by two maids. The dress was the height of fashion for the nineteenth century, and it was more elegant than any dress Ann had ever seen.

Ann chewed her bottom lip. She had to find a way to tell Patrick who she really was. Patrick would hate her for hiding the truth, as much as she believed the wedding should take place. She was still an imposter, taking over a stranger's life. How could this be happening? In each one of her dreams, Patrick was the one person who stood out from everything else. The love she felt for him was etched deep into her soul. She knew that if she were to die today, fate would bring her and Patrick together again. A sound at the doorway drew her attention.

Malcolm's eyes widened in amazement as he greeted Ann. She was radiant.

Ann gave him a feeble smile, "Well, how do I look?"

Malcolm's hands shook as he placed them on her shoulders. He kissed Ann lightly on the cheek. "You're beautiful. I don't remember ever seeing a more beautiful bride."

"Don't you think you're overdoing it? Besides, how many brides have you actually seen? I see by your smile, not many. Is your father here yet?"

Malcolm glanced at his watch. "It isn't like him to be late. Especially when he's been scheming for the past several years to have this wedding take place. I should send someone to look for him. My fear is that he drank himself into a stupor."

"If he doesn't show, then you can escort me down the aisle. He's so obnoxious. I'd much rather you walk with me."

After discussing William's absence with Patrick, Patrick sent a rider in search of Malcolm's father. Malcolm watched Patrick pace back and forth while his best friend, Anthony, lounged in a chair.

Anthony quipped, "If your former paramours could see you now. Lord O'Neil, the most evasive bachelor in all of London, pacing like a schoolboy. It does my heart good to see that you are indeed human. What do you think, Malcolm?"

Patrick ceased his pacing and cast a curious glance at the two of them. "I wouldn't have believed it myself. Who could have guessed a few months ago that I would be in this predicament? For a time, I thought that Victoria was not in favor of our betrothal."

"I think you two will get along quite well."

Patrick grinned back at him. "Thank you. Now, I must admit that I'm weary of this excessive waiting."

Anthony rose and patted the nervous groom on the back, motioning toward the door. "I believe it's time to put in our appearance." The men entered the foyer.

Malcolm anxiously looked out the window. "Patrick, any word from the rider yet?"

"I'm afraid not."

Muttering, Malcolm glanced toward the men. "Something must have delayed him. Do you want to wait until he arrives?"

Patrick shook his head. "I don't believe that would be wise. I don't want Victoria to change her mind. I'm sure your father will agree with me on this. Are you prepared to assist your sister?"

Feeling somewhat defensive at Patrick's last comment, Malcolm scowled. "Of course I will walk down the aisle with my sister. I will go tell her the change in plans."

Malcolm walked in to see Blanche adjusting the veil. Tears trickled down the maid's face. "Oh, my lady, you are so beautiful. No one will be able to take their eyes off of you."

Blushing, Ann embraced the woman. "Thank you. Without you, I would have fallen apart."

"Enough of this gushy female gibberish. Are you ladies ready? The groom is impatient."

Taking Ann's arm, he escorted her to the carriage. The ride to the chapel was a short one. He stoically stared out the window. From the corner of his eyes, he saw Ann fidgeting with the veil. He had hoped to be married one day, but that dream was gone. Taking a deep breath, he let out the tension he felt. He needed to focus on Ann to ensure that her dream wedding took place.

Once inside the church, Ann came to an abrupt halt. "I thought we were having a small wedding. This place is packed. I can't do this," she said.

Pulling her off to the side, Malcolm chuckled. "I keep forgetting that you're not familiar with this lifestyle. O'Neil is one of the wealthiest men in England. His friends and associates could have filled a church ten times this size. As a man of wealth, an appropriate ceremony was called for."

Flinging her hand toward the front of the church, Ann moaned. "But there are so many people! How did I ever think that I could marry Patrick? I don't have the foggiest idea what's expected of me."

"Calm down. You're doing just fine. Patrick believes you are Victoria or he wouldn't be marrying you."

Ann flung her arms in the air. "Gee, thanks. That doesn't help. What will Patrick do when I tell him who I am? Let's delay the wedding. I need to tell him before we get married."

Malcolm wrapped his arm about her shoulders. "Oh, no, you don't. We will continue with the wedding."

Breathless, Blanche rushed up to them. "The ceremony is about to begin. Lord O'Neil sent me to tell you that your father still hasn't arrived."

Arms shaking, Ann took Malcolm's arm. "It's now or never. Lead on."

"My dear, you must learn to curb your speech if you want to fit in."

Walking slowly down the aisle with Ann at his side, he stared at Patrick. With his black formal attire accentuating his striking looks, he definitely looked like a groom. Patrick's possessive gaze fixated on Ann. Malcolm was so proud of her. She looked like a princess.

Ann trembled as they approached the altar. She gave him a beseeching look. She may not know it right now, but he was helping her in the best way possible.

Chapter 25

His heart practically ceased beating. She was a vision in white. The silk skirts swirled about her as if she walked on a cloud. Her silky curls peeked from beneath the veil. He wanted to pull the pins from her hair, letting his hands slide through the auburn curls.

Noticing her pallor, he whispered in her ear, "Are you able to stand?"

Unable to speak, she nodded.

Patrick only half listened as the minister droned on. Worried about Ann, he studied her pale face. He was so concerned that he failed to hear the minister ask him to repeat his vows. A jab in his ribs brought a quick smile. So she was as anxious as he was to have their vows sealed in front of God and man. At last, they were pronounced man and wife.

Lifting the veil, he lowered his face until their lips met. Patrick savored the kiss, reluctant to release his wife from his embrace. The minister had to clear his throat numerous times before the noise registered in his brain. The guests laughed heartily. Flushed, Patrick turned and bowed to the guests. His action brought more robust cheers and laughter.

Several of Patrick's closest friends surged forward to congratulate the new couple. Anthony kissed Victoria lightly on the cheek. "I want to be the first to congratulate you. May the two of you have many happy years together."

"Thank you. Come and visit us whenever you like. Our home is your home."

"That's very gracious, but I'd better wait a few weeks or Patrick will toss me out on my ear."

Patrick walked over and draped his arm over Ann's shoulder. "Did I hear my name mentioned?"

Anthony smiled. "I was trying to convince your bride to leave you, but she won't hear of it. You must have impressed her somehow."

Ann playfully slapped Anthony's arm.

Patrick flashed a quizzical look. "I believe our presence is required at the house." He was surprised at how relaxed his wife was around his friends.

After an hour of standing in line, Patrick tried to see if he could see the end of the receiving line. It was still quite long. Ann shifted her weight. His bride graciously welcomed every guest. He was proud how she had taken to her role so quickly.

A short while later, Patrick whispered in her ear. "Would you care to sit down? I think we've stood long enough."

"You must be a mind reader."

As they walked through the crowd, well-wishers continued to congratulate them. They managed to escape to the sitting room. He was tempted to lock the door and not join their guests. But after all the work his aunt had done, he did not want to disappoint her.

The door had barely shut when Patrick pressed Ann against the door, forging his lips to hers. Passion racing, he thickly muttered, "I think I'll get us something to drink before I overheat. Would you care for anything?" Shaking her head, Ann reached for the nearest chair. Patrick soon returned with a drink in hand.

The time away from his new wife had not cooled his ardor, not that he expected it would. He was unable to take his eyes from her. Draining the glass, he set it aside and sat down beside her. He reverently took her wrist and ran his tongue along the inside. "You're blushing again. Are you nervous?"

Ann stared at Patrick's mouth. "A little. I never realized that you were so important. You have so many friends."

Ann babbled as if she couldn't help herself. In fact, she looked quite flustered. There was a becoming flush to her cheeks.

"Half of those people came to ask favors. I only claim a small group as friends, and you'll have opportunities to meet them in the coming weeks."

He stood and pulled her to him. His mouth brushed against her ear. "We need to rejoin our guests. One second longer and I'll consummate our marriage right here. Though I can be convinced to stay if that's your desire."

Her lips tingled from his kiss, while her mind whirled away with thoughts of all that had happened. Married! She was married to the most wonderful man imaginable. But she knew that she had to tell him the truth about who she was and how she came to England. Once they were alone, she would explain everything. She would to do it before they retired for the night, for once they were alone, all logical thoughts would vanish.

Ann's eyes widened as he pressed against her. "I heard there is something to be said for anticipation." Smiling, she took his hand and led him from the room.

The party continued throughout the evening. Patrick and several gentlemen retreated to the balcony for a round of drinks and cigars. Ann noticed a few late arrivals and went to the door to welcome them. She paused to stare at a familiar couple that entered.

Edward took Ann's hand. "I apologize for arriving so late. Business kept me longer than I had anticipated. Katherine has been berating me for the last two hours."

Ann frowned, trying to remember how she knew them. Then it came to her. Katherine was the rude woman from the ball.

"Come, Edward. Let's join our friends," Katherine pleaded.

Katherine acted as if she hated her. But why?

Ann turned toward the door as another guest entered. His head was turned so she couldn't see his face, but his profile looked alarmingly familiar. He slowly turned toward her. Recognition struck her like a bullet. It was David! Had he traveled back in time with her? If so, where had he been the past couple of months?

He slowly approached her. "I hope Edward explained why we're late. Let me introduce myself. I'm David Stewart. Katherine and I are cousins."

Ann tried to speak. Her voice cracked with anxiety. "Arrr ... are you staying with Katherine very long?" Her heart pounded. He didn't appear to recognize her. How did he get here? Could he truly have traveled through time with her? Surely he wasn't related to Katherine.

Rubbing his chin, he smiled. "I haven't decided. It depends on my opportunities."

"Don't let me detain you further. I'm sure you wish to join your family."

Without another word, she turned and fled the room. Flying up the stairs, she slammed her bedroom door. She had recognized him immediately, even with the longer hair and sideburns. A choked sound escaped her throat. Was he only pretending not to know her? How could she tell Patrick that she was afraid of David when he didn't even know the events leading up to her being in England? The pot of lies was quickly spilling over. The question was, who was going to get burned?

Chapter 26

DAVID MASSAGED HIS POUNDING head as Lady O'Neil hurried away. She had a strange look on her face when he'd approached her. She looked as if she had seen a ghost. Why?

The blinding headache had returned. He downed a glass of champagne. What had triggered it this time? The headaches normally occurred after he woke from the enigmatic dreams. Something wasn't right. Lady O'Neil's reaction to his presence was too pronounced. He would snoop around and try to quell the uneasiness that enveloped him.

Patrick waved to get Anthony's attention. His friend excused himself from a bevy of mothers and young women, and they didn't look happy about it.

"You are looking much too serious for a man just married."

"I've misplaced my wife. I haven't seen her for the past half hour."

Anthony glanced at the crowd. "She is probably exhausted and sought a reprieve somewhere. Did you ask her maid?"

"You're right. The strain of the wedding is a bit much." Spotting Blanche near the servants' passageway, Patrick walked over to her.

"My lord, may I help you?"

"I haven't seen Lady O'Neil for a while and hoped you would know where she is."

Blanche tittered. "Oh, sir. She probably wanted to freshen up a bit. Shall I go upstairs and check her room?"

"No, you're busy here. I'll go check. If you see her, please mention that I was asking."

This habit of disappearing was worrisome. Taking the stairs two at a time, Patrick threw open their bedroom door. Standing frozen in the middle of the room was his missing bride.

Patrick sauntered forward, perplexed by her odd behavior. "I turned my back and you disappeared again. Is this becoming a habit?"

Ann retorted, "No! Can't a person have any time alone?" She marched to the window, turning her back to him.

Patrick was unsure of what to do. Couldn't she see that he was concerned for her welfare? Before he could apologize, she turned and ran into his waiting arms.

"I'm sorry. I know I sound like a crazy woman. There's so much I need to tell you, but I'm afraid."

He guided her to the bed and gently wiped her tears. "There is nothing to be afraid of. If I'm overbearing at times, forgive me. This husband business will take some getting used to."

"No, it's me. You've been wonderful. I couldn't have wished for anyone other than you. It's just so hard to adjust to everything here in ... in ..." She hesitated, wanting to tell him the truth. "Here in England."

Unable to contain his mirth, Patrick snickered. "England? I didn't know that you had such a strange sense of humor."

Flushed, she stared at him. "I'm serious. I need to tell you something that is very important to our future."

Patrick's smile faded. Something was seriously amiss.

She swallowed hard. "I haven't always lived here."

"Victoria, I know all about it." Seeing her astonishment, he continued. "I know all about your family. If it weren't for your mother's ability to manage things as well as she did, your family would have been destitute years ago."

Frustrated, she shook her head wildly. "No, that's not it. I'm from America."

A knock on the door sounded. Blanche entered the room. "Excuse me, my lord. Lady O'Neil's father has arrived and is asking to see his daughter."

"Tell him we'll be there shortly." Waiting until the door closed, Patrick quietly asked, "Do you really believe that you lived in America? Ah, I see that you do. If that is true, how do you explain your British accent? We were childhood playmates. Remember how you followed me all the time? You were like a shadow."

"That wasn't me. I'm trying to explain, but it's so incredible that I don't know where to begin."

"Dearest, I assure you that I want to understand, but we need to return to our guests. We'll talk later this evening, I promise."

He helped her to her feet. What had triggered her fears? He was damn well going to find out.

For the next couple of hours, Patrick hovered at her side. Everywhere Ann turned, he was there. Feeling smothered, she eventually convinced him that she was fine and that he needed to visit with the guests.

Malcolm rescued Ann from an elderly widow's discourse on proper behavior for the wedding night and led her outside to the balcony.

"Thanks. It's so hot and stuffy. I was about to wilt. You're not lacking dance partners. Is there anyone you're particularly interested in?"

Malcolm groaned. "Now that the most beautiful woman I know is married, I'm desolate. Most women are like leeches, wanting to attach themselves to any man who has a title or wealth."

Ann slapped him playfully on the shoulder. "They know a catch when they see one. If I weren't married, I'd go after you myself."

Clicking his heels together, he raised her hand to his lips. "Thank you. You know how to raise the spirits of any man."

Glancing over his shoulder, he muttered, "How long do you think we can hide out here?"

The two of them joined in laughter. Sudden movement in the nearby bushes gave them pause. A man's shadow drifted along the edge of the garden. Ann's heart pounded. A stream of light revealed a man with blond hair. A web of evil hung over the gardens.

Ann shivered. "It's getting chilly out here. Let's go inside before Patrick thinks I've disappeared again."

Arm in arm, Ann and Malcolm walked toward the house. Patrick stepped from the door, grinding his cigar on the walkway with his heel. His glance darted from Ann to Malcolm and back again.

"Where have you been? I thought something had happened to you."

Worried about his terse tone, Ann joked, "Malcolm and I have been hiding from all the single women who are searching for husbands."

"After our earlier talk, I hoped you would be more considerate. Come, I believe this is our waltz." He led Ann to the dance floor.

Before Patrick could take his wife in his arms on the dance floor, Katherine stepped between them.

"I want to offer my congratulations. I'm sure your wife won't mind if we dance. Will you, my dear?"

Katherine stepped into Patrick's arms, nudging Ann aside. Ann clenched her fists and took a step forward. She had never backed down from a challenge and wasn't going to start now.

Patrick neatly positioned himself between the two women. He reached out and squeezed Ann's hand reassuringly. "Let's not make a scene. Katherine needs to understand that I am no longer interested." With a wink, he whispered, "Don't disappear."

Katherine rolled her eyes as she followed him. She blatantly adjusted the neckline of her gown, showing more of her breasts.

Silently, Ann mouthed, "Bitch!" toward Katherine. Seeing her shocked look gave Ann a moment of satisfaction.

Ann was startled from her reverie by a familiar voice. "You must excuse Katherine's boldness, Lady O'Neil. She's used to having her own way and finds it difficult to accept the truth sometimes."

Ann glanced up to see Edward standing beside her. "Believe me, I'm not worried. She's the one who should be worried."

Edward stared moodily after Katherine. "I hope to make her my wife someday. Now that O'Neil is married, I hope she will discover what I can offer. Don't misunderstand me—I love her greatly, but she is like a butterfly that flits from flower to flower, trying to find the sweetest nectar."

Edward's crooked smile melted Ann's anger. She rested her hand on his. "If I can help, let me know."

"I believe that half of the women here would assist me in my quest so they wouldn't have to worry about their husbands. Ah, here they come now. Please excuse me. I think Katherine needs to dance."

Watching Edward and Katherine, Ann sighed. Life was so confusing. Edward was loving, caring, and could provide for Katherine. Yet she sought someone who was already taken. The truth could not be denied. She was jealous and in love with a man from a different century. And then there was his temper ...

Warm lips caressed her neck before she was trapped in her husband's arms. Giggling, she whispered, "Behave yourself."

"When you're near, all thoughts of proper behavior are remarkably absent. You and Edward were enjoying an intimate conversation."

"Jealous? Since you were so taken with Katherine's breasts, I decided to look for a replacement."

His laughter faded. Sudden pain flared in his eyes. "Katherine means nothing to me. Never question my devotion to you or the sincerity of my feelings."

Unable to calm her racing pulse, Ann touched his cheek. "I was just joking. I'm not interested in Edward."

The guests were beginning to leave. His thumb skimmed her bare arm. "I'll be right back. I have to bid good night to our guests."

Ann watched Patrick cross the room as the guests gathered

their wraps. Ann felt a tap on her shoulder and was handed a piece of paper. Who could be writing her a note? *Must see you at once in the stables.* The note was unsigned. Looking around the room, she saw William totter over to a chair. Malcolm, who had been watching William all evening, was noticeably absent. Malcolm probably wanted to say good-bye privately. She glanced around the room once again. Patrick had disappeared from view. She should let him know where she was going. She nervously tapped her foot. She hated to keep Malcolm waiting. Damn it! Ann quietly slipped from the house, avoiding discovery. She would be back before Patrick even noticed.

Chapter 27

THE HINGE ON THE heavy wooden door creaked as Ann pushed it open. "Malcolm, it's me, Ann." A single lantern hung on a nearby hook, casting shadows against the stark walls. She called out again.

David reached out of the darkness and gripped Ann's wrist. His hand muffled any sounds she would have made. His harsh breathing echoed in her ear. She jerked her head back and forth, trying to loosen his hand. She bit his hand. Swearing, he drew back and swung his fist, knocking Ann onto a pile of hay. She squeezed her eyes shut, moaning aloud. David jumped on top of her, pressing his hips against hers.

He growled, "Any further noise and you won't see that new husband of yours again. I actually did forget who you were. The fear on your face helped loosen my memory. You've undergone quite a makeover." He held a loosened curl and rubbed it against his face.

Ann jerked her hair out of his hand. "If you leave now, no one will know what you've done. Leave before Patrick finds us."

In a calm voice, he continued as if he hadn't heard her. "I can't believe we both traveled back in time. These rich society people are just as bad as the corporate jerks at work. Some things never change. But I've found the golden cow. You remember Katherine, don't you? She's going to make me rich."

Ann quickly rolled over, trying to escape his grasp. The bodice of her gown tore while they thrashed on the ground. He jerked her back so they lay side by side, their faces only inches apart.

David relished the look of fear in her eyes. "I warned you. You led me on for months. I saw you watching me at work. Now that you've somehow turned back the clock, you're even better looking."

Her nails raked his cheek when his hand skimmed up her thigh, leaving him filled with the need to punish her.

"I know you want me. I bet you're wet." He pressed his lips against her neck.

"Unhand my wife this instant!" Running toward them, Patrick blocked any possible escape. "Stand up or I swear I'll kill you where you are."

After sparing a quick glance at Ann, Patrick faced him again. "Victoria, what happened? Do you know this man?"

Ann struggled to stand, grasping pieces of the bodice together. Tears welled up in her eyes as she nodded.

David laughed as he jumped to his feet, brushing the hay from his clothes. "Victoria? Is that the name she's using this time?" David watched Patrick's face turn a bright shade of red. "Ann, tell Patrick how we came to England. She always swore that she would marry someone with money. I would say she has done quite well for herself, wouldn't you?"

David swelled with satisfaction as Patrick flashed an odd look at Ann. He loved causing Ann trouble. After what she put him through, he owed her big time.

Before he could blink, Patrick grabbed his shirt. A fist shot forward, smashing David's nose.

"You have said more than enough. Consider yourself lucky that duels are illegal, though you'll wish yourself dead by the time I'm through. I'll ruin you."

Releasing his hold, Patrick shoved David against the wooden railing. "Get off of my property before I change my mind and shoot you."

David covered his throbbing nose and left the stables. Pausing at the cracked doorway, he overheard Patrick speaking to Ann. "I'll send your brother to you. I want to be alone tonight."

David chuckled. He hadn't accomplished his goal, but his actions definitely hurt Ann and the rich bastard who was her husband.

He'd love to see Ann poor and homeless in this century. Then how would she survive?

Chapter 28

THE NIGHT AIR SEEPED through the torn wedding gown, causing chills to rack her body.

Malcolm ran to Ann's side. "What happened? Patrick stormed into the house and locked himself in the library. Father and I have tried to talk to him, but he refuses to see us."

The pain was too intense. Sobbing, Ann clung to Malcolm. It was several minutes later before she could speak. "I'm so afraid. Patrick hates me. If I tell the truth, he'll know that I've lied and that he's married to an imposter."

Malcolm held her tightly, patting her back as if she were a young child. "I'm not sure I understand what happened."

Ann wiped her tears with the back of her hand. "The night that I traveled back in time, a man named David tried to kill me. He showed up tonight with Katherine. He's trying to kill me. He'll never give up."

Malcolm's jaw dropped. "This whole story would be preposterous if I didn't know that you had in fact traveled here from a different century. David must be locked up. We will contact the authorities at once. The Montgomery and O'Neil families are not without influence."

"No. He'll tell the authorities who I am. Patrick despises me. He'll probably file for divorce. I don't even know if a divorce is an option in this century," she wailed.

"You need sleep and so do I. Because of what's happened tonight, Patrick has offered father and me a room here tonight. I'm so sorry. I should have urged you to tell Patrick the truth sooner. More than your marriage is at stake here."

Arms entwined, Ann leaned her head on Malcolm's shoulder as they walked to the house.

After kissing Malcolm good night, Ann retired to the room adjoining Patrick's. Blanche prepared the bed, pulling back the covers and plumping the pillows. "Anything else, Lady O'Neil?"

Ann started. Lady O'Neil? The question was whether she would remain Lady O'Neil. She was disappointed in Patrick. He'd closed down emotionally and never even given her a chance to explain. Punching the pillow a few moments later, Ann blew out the lamp.

She heard muffled sounds of male voices drifting from Patrick's room. Malcolm? What was he doing in Patrick's room? The voices grew louder. Were they arguing about her? Someone slammed a door. She held her breath. She couldn't bear to talk to him tonight. Hours later, the tension and stress of the day took their toll, allowing Ann to drift off to sleep.

Just before dawn, Ann stirred at the sound of the door to the adjoining room being edged open. Ann barely opened her eyes and saw Patrick slipping into her darkened room. Standing at the side of the bed, he stared down at her. Clenching his hands, he drew back before he touched her tousled hair fanned out on the pillow. He turned to leave. He looked so confused that Ann felt bad for him. Why didn't he touch her? Was he still thinking about the scene that transpired in the stables?

As he turned to leave, his knee slammed into the trunk. A groan escaped his tightly closed lips. Patrick limped back to his room. Ann bit back a giggle. Hope blossomed as Ann rolled over. Perhaps there was a chance for their marriage after all.

Patrick was the prominent focus of her dreams when she fell back asleep. Did the album bring them together? How did the old woman fit in? It was as if fate was telling her that she and Patrick belonged together.

Hours later, the bright morning sun filtered through the windows, spurring her to decide to go out for a jog. Ann jumped out of bed, determined that this life was her new beginning. Exercise cleared her mind better than anything else did.

She crept downstairs to get the bag she had hidden when she'd arrived in this century. Luckily, it was still there. She needed to move the bag to a new hiding place. Opening the parlor door, she quietly locked the door behind her. Tiptoeing across the room, she anxiously opened the computer case. Everything was as she had left it. The sound of voices nearby almost caused Ann to drop the computer. She clutched the case to her chest. Peering out of a crack in the doorway, she saw that the coast was clear. She ran up the stairs, praying that no one would stop her.

Her heart pounded with excitement. She had hidden the clean clothes in the bag. Tossing the nightgown on the bed, she slipped on jeans and jogging shoes. Anxious to get going before the entire household was up and about, she put on a long robe to cover her clothes. She slipped out of the house and ran to the stable. Once the groom was out of sight, she stuffed the robe underneath a saddle. Ann stretched and started slowly toward the woods. It didn't take long to discover that this new body of hers wasn't up to rigorous exercise. Stomach cramps assailed her. She slowed the pace but kept running until every muscle ached. Wiping the beads of sweat from her brow, she eventually turned back toward the house. She ducked into an open stall and snatched her robe, quickly covering her clothes. Jubilant at her successful adventure, Ann entered unnoticed through the servants' entrance.

Muffling a cry, she darted into a nearby closet when she spotted Patrick at the end of the hallway. His footsteps paused in front of her hiding place. Patrick was already angry at her. If he found her now, her marriage could be over. What was she thinking? Her impulsiveness would bite her one day.

A feather duster hung from a hook inside the door. Every breath brought the feathers closer to her nose. Her cheeks puffed outward as she held her breath. She could see his shadow from the crack under the door. *Go away. Please go away,* she silently prayed. Finally, his footsteps moved down the hall. Grateful for the reprieve, she ran upstairs to the safety of her room and sneezed.

Her leg muscles throbbed. Dismissing the maid, she eased into the waiting bath water. Submerged in lilac scented bubbles, Ann closed her eyes and relaxed.

Patrick's groin tightened as curvaceous flesh dipped beneath the mounds of bubbles. He hadn't seen her at the breakfast table and thought she had taken ill or, even worse, had returned home during the night. Torn between leaving or watching her bathe, his desire eventually won over his pride.

Rubbing soap in her hair, Ann lustily sang a refrain from some song that he was unfamiliar with. After rinsing, she stood and wrung out her hair. While reaching for her robe, her hand came into contact with his chest. Her screams immediately filled the air.

Patrick covered her mouth with his hand. "Stop shrieking. It's me."

She backed away, clutching the robe to her throat. "How long have you been spying on me?" She stared at the damp fabric clinging to his broad chest.

"Long enough to know that I have married a beautiful woman. I won't detain you now. Get dressed. I would like you to join me in the library this afternoon. We need to talk about our future."

"I can explain."

He nodded and then left without saying another word. He'd seen the frustration on her face and heard the thump of something hitting the floor. He wondered what she had tossed to the floor. A shoe, perhaps?

Twice in twenty-four hours, he'd walked away without giving her an opportunity to defend herself. Did their marriage have a chance? He hoped so, but he needed to hear the truth. Only then would he know whether they stood a chance.

Chapter 29

WILLIAM AND MALCOLM WERE finishing breakfast as Ann joined them. Malcolm rose and pulled out her chair. "Tea?" he offered.

"Sure. Please pass the sugar."

William quit chewing long enough to say, "Sugar? When did you start using sugar?"

Before she could respond, Malcolm interceded. "Patrick has encouraged her to try it. It's how he prefers his tea."

William grunted and returned to his food. Between mouthfuls of food, he watched his children whispering, and confusion clouded his face. He wasn't one who liked being ignored. Malcolm said something to Ann, who shook her head.

From the far end of the table, William eyed them suspiciously. "Why are you whispering? If you have something to say, say it aloud."

"Calm yourself, Father. We're just reminiscing."

"Just remember your obligation to the family." Jabbing a greasy finger in his daughter's direction, William railed, "Now that you have the means, I expect you to help out the family should circumstances arise."

Ann laid her napkin on the table. "I understood that Patrick already provided you with sufficient funds. Why not let Malcolm invest those funds? He is very talented."

William banged his fist on the table. The chair hit the floor as he stood. "Who are you to give me advice regarding financial matters? I will handle the funds in our family, as always. Without me, you wouldn't be married to O'Neil. You fail to remember that there was a time when he wasn't overly excited about marrying you. If I hadn't spent the money on your wardrobe and training, he would have never looked twice at you." His face grew hot with anger. "You have an obligation, and I expect some compensation."

Ann stormed past William, mumbling something about jumping in a lake. Damn uppity girl.

Malcolm broke the quietness of the room. "You were rather hard on her. It's obvious that O'Neil worships her. We're fortunate that he agreed to settle our debts."

William swept his beefy hand across the table, sending his plate shattering to the floor. "You ungrateful whelp! How many times have I paid your debts and gotten rid of unwelcome women who claimed you fathered their children?" Suddenly remembering where they were, William lowered his voice. "A man of my status must keep up appearances. O'Neil has an entire fortune. I'm sure he will want to keep gossip about his in-laws at bay. I need you to talk some sense into your sister. She will have a generous allowance that she can share with us."

Malcolm gripped the edge of the table. "I'm the first to admit my mistakes, and those days are over and won't be repeated. I have learned some hard lessons. I choose to think that I have restored a shred of honor back to the Montgomery name."

"Then I cannot count on you to help me restore the family fortune?"

"Only if it's done honestly. Perhaps you should consider marriage to a wealthy widow." William rushed toward Malcolm.

Malcolm hissed, "Do not do something you will regret. Leave Victoria and Patrick alone. I will not tolerate your inappropriate behavior any longer. You are becoming a pariah."

Stunned by his son's outburst, William's mouth gaped open. He stepped back shrewdly. "Let's calm down. You may have a point. I suppose I could let you try your hand at managing the estate. Perhaps luck will be with us."

The tension between them eased slightly as they shook hands. William hid his rage. Betrayed by his son! He would play out the game. Society would think he had reformed. If an accident befell O'Neil, no one would blame him. He was already beginning to plot his strategy for wealth and success as he followed his son upstairs to get his belongings.

Chapter 30

LAST NIGHT PATRICK HAD watched Ann and Malcolm from an upstairs window as they walked arm in arm from the stables. A pang of regret tore through him. He should have been comforting Ann, not Malcolm. Yet David called his wife Ann. Why? Who was he married to?

The remainder of the morning passed slowly. Patrick met with his secretary to review his accounts. As the man droned on about each minute detail, Patrick gazed through the glass doorway to the gardens. He relived the encounter with Ann in her bath. She was more beautiful than he had imagined. He still could see the bubbles gliding down those long legs. Her fear of David seemed genuine.

Torn with doubt, he anxiously awaited their meeting. Unable to concentrate, he absently dismissed his secretary.

Ann's footsteps echoed down the hall. Patrick knew that his outward appearance was devoid of emotion. He was used to making decisions. He would listen and be objective. Today would set the tone of their marriage.

He rubbed his chin as Ann entered the library. He realized that he'd forgotten to shave this morning. That didn't bode well. He tried to relax his businesslike manner so she would feel comfortable enough to tell him the truth.

She'd chosen a modest sage-colored gown with long sleeves and a high neckline. Sitting directly in front of him, Ann calmly folded her hands in her lap and waited for him to speak.

"Well," he muttered impatiently. "I assume you can explain yourself?" Her pale complexion and dark circles underneath her eyes gave him pause.

"Yes, I can, but I'm afraid you won't believe me."

"If what you say is the truth and logical, I will make every effort to believe you."

Ann leaned forward. "I feel as if I'm on trial. I swear to tell you the truth, but you must look inside your heart. I'm disappointed that you refused to hear my explanation last night. I hope I haven't misjudged you."

Skeptical of any explanation she could offer, he haughtily studied his wife. She'd actually dared to chasten him. "I may have been a little hasty. Now, tell me how well you know Mr. Stewart."

Ann took a deep breath. "First I must ask you something. Have you noticed anything different about me lately? Do you think my looks have changed at all? Do I act any differently?"

"One or two things come to mind, but what does that have to do with last night?"

"Hear me out. You're an educated man and are aware of the scientific advances that are being made. There are things that exist today that didn't exist twenty or thirty years ago, right?"

He shrugged and rolled his eyes. "Of course. In the late fifties, England was linked by the telegraph. We have gas lighting along city routes and new metal pipes for water."

"You see, things are changing so fast that we cannot possibly imagine them all. Anything is possible because new theories are being proven every day."

Amazed at her logic, Patrick fought back a smile. "I'll keep my mind open. Now, where are you headed with this discussion?"

Ann jumped to her feet, pacing in front of him. "My name is Ann Roberts, not Victoria Montgomery, and I grew up in America." She rushed on before he could interrupt. "I'm divorced, have two beautiful children, and have no idea how I ended up here in 1870 England."

Patrick jerked to his feet. The woman was deranged! Why was she trying to convince him that she was someone else? He glanced at her hair, trying to remember if it had been a lighter shade of red. The Victoria he knew was shy and reserved. The woman before him was not. He rubbed his pounding head, studying his wife.

He walked around the desk to stand before her. "If this is a joke, I'm not amused. I understand that you are upset about yesterday. So am I. Perhaps I didn't handle things as well as I should have. I just need to hear the truth about Stewart. Who is he to you?"

Ann hung her head. "This isn't a joke," she whispered. "It may be a nightmare, but it's the truth."

"Then tell me your damned nightmare before I lose my sanity."

She raised her eyes to his. Reaching out, she took his hand. "I used to date David. When I told him I wasn't interested, he went crazy. Then came the phone calls and the harassment. When none of those tactics worked, he became more violent and broke into my house to try to kill me. I th ..."

Patrick's laughter verged on hysterical. On the surface, her story was preposterous. It was as if she talked another language. However, a sliver of doubt was planted in his mind. "Let me see if I comprehend this story. You used to date this man. I assume that means the same as courtship. He called on you, and you didn't wish to see him. Your decision was unacceptable to him, so he physically threatened you. Am I interpreting this correctly so far?"

Ann stomped her foot. Raising her voice, she rushed on. "Yes, he physically threatened me by sticking a large knife under my throat."

He didn't know what to believe at this point. He just knew that he wanted to tear David apart. In one giant step, he crossed the distance that separated them, taking her in his arms. In that moment, all his doubts regarding her fidelity dissolved. She needed his love and protection. Maybe the strain of the wedding caused her to imagine things. Against reason, he still cared for her, and that was all that mattered.

"Where is he staying?"

"I'm not sure. He came with Katherine Paxton, but don't go after him. He's dangerous."

"He needs to understand that you are my wife, and by threatening you, he also threatens me. I should have never let him go."

Ann buried her face in his chest. "Does this mean you believe me?"

His finger trailed down her cheek as he bent to taste her lips. "I believe David is trying to harm you. You have more spirit than the woman I was betrothed to a year ago. Don't ask me to explain any of it. I just want us to go on from here. Let's forget about the past. Today is important, not yesterday."

He swept her up in his arms, carrying her upstairs. Moments later, they were in the middle of his room. He locked the door behind him.

She stared as Patrick's shirt slid to the floor. He was glad that he had a body hardened from years of exercise and physical labor. Her eyes appeared to bore into his body, consuming every inch. Good grief! He could feel himself flushing.

She seemed to cease breathing when his fingers grazed her shoulder. Anticipation gripped him. He loosened several of the tiny buttons cascading down her back. He fumbled for several minutes before ripping the material in a fit of impatience.

"You've ruined the dress. Let me finish."

The sight of her undressing inflamed his senses. Unable to tear his eyes from her voluptuous body, he yanked off his remaining clothes, throwing them haphazardly across the room. Ann slid underneath the covers as he finished undressing.

He had little experience with virgins, but she seemed as eager as he was for their joining. He rained kisses upon her lips, moving to her creamy shoulders, covering every inch of exposed skin in between. Ann trembled beneath him.

"Don't be afraid," he whispered.

She shook her head, not speaking.

He breathed deeply, inhaling her unique scent. Her pulse raced madly under his lips. He ensured that each intimate caress was strategically placed to inflict a desired response. His kisses were tentative at first. Soon they became torrents of fire and passion. She ran her hand down his side. Her touches were enough to make him roar. His mouth devoured hers, encouraging her to continue to explore his body.

Her hand dipped lower. He willed her to touch him. He thrust his hips forward, imagining her fingers tightening around him. His thumb sensuously rubbed her lower lip. "Have I ever told you how beautiful you are?"

Eyes wide, Ann nodded. With restraint crumbling, he molded his mouth to hers. He slowly moved lower, pressing his mouth against her thighs and then into her heat. As he was teasing, in and out, nipping her clit, she thrashed her head from side to side.

Her movements frenzied, Ann wrapped her legs about his waist and pressed upward, taking him deep. When her fingers raked down the middle of his back, a deep growl of satisfaction rose from his chest.

She threw back her head and arched her body, shattering the last vestige of his control. Gripping her hips, he plunged again and again. Her soft moans were fuel to the inferno raging within him. His unstoppable release brought her surrender. Clinging to one another, they drifted back to earth.

Through the sexual haze, he realized that there had been no barrier to their joining. Still, Patrick was reluctant to do anything that might shatter their tenuous relationship. A fierce feeling of possessiveness gripped him. After all, he was the one who'd said to forget the past—that only today was important. Her secrets would be unlocked over time. He could afford to be patient and judge her faithfulness. Until then he would withhold judgment.

Ann woke during the night, seemingly surprised to meet his gaze. He was sprawled out next to her, watching her sleep. He smiled, amazed that they had spent most of the day in bed. She reached up and brushed his hair off his neck. His heavy eyes drifted shut as he flung an arm over her tiny waist.

She snuggled closer, resting on his shoulder. Patrick knew the moment she fell back to sleep. They would face the rest of their ghosts tomorrow.

Chapter 31

ANN HEARD THE DOOR creak open ... then the muffled laughter. She rolled over, reaching for Patrick.

A maid announced, "Lord O'Neil requested that you join him for breakfast."

Ann pulled up the blanket to cover her nakedness. At the sight of Patrick's sock hanging off the bedpost, the two women started laughing.

In the dining hall, Patrick looked up from his paper when he heard Ann's footsteps.

Ann felt herself blushing as Patrick's gaze gravitated to her. Every inch of her body craved his touch. If she were made of chocolate, his gaze would have caused a meltdown.

A servant held out a chair at the far end of the table. "No, thanks. I'll sit here next to my husband."

Patrick raised his brows questioningly. With a smug look, he continued reading the paper. Disappointed at his sudden lack of interest, she rose to fill a plate at the sideboard.

As she passed his chair, he pulled her into his lap and drew her closer. "I haven't had a morning kiss yet, wife. You apparently don't realize that you have certain obligations. The most important is to be by my side and fulfill all my needs. Do you think you can meet my demands?"

Ann tried to look subservient but started giggling. "I'll try, my lord. If I fail, will I be sent to the Tower of London?"

"Nothing as severe as that. I personally prefer dungeon and chains."

"Ooooh! How exciting."

"You're a shameful wife. All this talk of chains has aroused a friend of mine. Perhaps we should venture back upstairs?"

She climbed off his lap, swatting away his hands. "There's time later to fulfill your fantasies. Right now I'm famished."

Muttering under his breath, he strode toward the door, where the butler was holding his coat and hat. "I'll see you at dinner. Unfortunately, I have some business that requires attention. Mary is waiting to show you the household accounts and anything else you're interested in."

Ann walked him outside, where Anthony waited on horseback. "I got your message," he told Patrick.

Patrick nodded. Turning toward Ann, he scooped her up by the waist, swinging her in a circle. After planting a kiss on her lips, he quickly mounted his horse, giving her a jaunty wave. Dazed, she watch the men ride away. Since Patrick didn't seem inclined to tell her where he was going, she didn't ask. Now she wished she had. Was he going to confront David? She would worry until he safely returned to her.

Katherine enjoyed her morning tea in the garden. She relished the time alone, without David. Albert approached her to announce that visitors had arrived. Katherine strolled into the house.

"Patrick! It's so good to see you." Katherine added, "Lord Aylesbury, so good to see you too."

Ignoring any formalities, Patrick bluntly asked, "Where's your cousin, Mr. Stewart?"

Her hand rose to her throat in trepidation. "My, my. Has married life caused you to resort to rude behavior? Do sit down and have some tea." She tried to hide her increasing nervousness. "I take it that you and your new bride are adjusting to married life."

Anthony interjected. "Katherine, we have come to see your

cousin. He presented me with a business offer at the wedding. We want to know if the offer still stands."

Skeptical, she looked from one man to the other. What crazy plan had David concocted? "Fine. I believe he is training the new stallion."

As the men took their leave, Katherine called out, "I would investigate any idea he suggests." Her hands clenched together. She felt sick as she watched the two walk outside. She didn't trust David. She hurried out the door, wanting to ensure that Patrick was safe. Ducking behind a large oak tree near the house, Katherine watched the men approach David.

David held a bloodied whip, lashing out at a towering bay. The cries of the animal filled the air. Katherine grimaced at the man's cruelty, knowing in that instant that David enjoyed threatening those weaker than him. But Patrick was not weak.

The sound of crunching gravel behind David drew his attention. He lowered the whip, wiping off flecks of blood from his cheek. David's lip curved upward.

Patrick grabbed the front of David's shirt.

David jerked in surprise. "Here now. Is that any way to greet someone? Get your hands off of me!"

Katherine couldn't hear every word being said. She moved a little closer.

Anthony tugged on Patrick's arms. "Mr. Stewart, I'm Lord Aylesbury. We were introduced at the wedding. Lord O'Neil and I wish to discuss a private matter with you. Is there somewhere we could go?"

David's face turned bright red. He was probably furious that he couldn't manipulate the men. Straightening his clothing, David puffed out his chest. "I have nothing to say to either one of you. Now get the hell out of here."

Patrick lunged forward. His fist solidly connected with the David's jaw. Patrick growled, "Stay away from my wife. I know everything. I know that you tried to kill her. If you don't disappear, I will contact the authorities. I have no wish to drag the Paxton name or my wife's name through any scandal, but I will do so if you fail to heed my advice."

David rubbed his jaw, smirking at Patrick. What had David done to Victoria? Why would he try to kill her? Fear gripped Katherine.

"So she told you everything, did she? Let me tell you something. She's a damned liar."

Patrick erupted, grabbing David's shirt again and knocking him to the ground. "When a lady tells you she isn't interested, a man of quality never forces his attentions. Now that she is my wife, I'm telling you to leave her alone or I'll kill you."

David lay on the ground, massaging his bruised jaw. "I would love to see her adjust to this lifestyle. Men have all the power here. Too bad it doesn't stay that way. But hey, whatever you say. She wasn't really my type anyway. Perhaps I'll return to America."

Katherine gasped. America? He had changed his story again. Where did he come from?

Patrick stepped back, wiping the blood and dirt from his hands. "Heed my warning. Leave! The sooner the better."

Katherine held back a cheer. Maybe David would take Patrick's warning to heart. Patrick and Anthony quickly left. She scurried back to the house, not wanting to be near David in his current mood.

Katherine sought refuge in the parlor. She jumped as David suddenly appeared in the doorway.

"Did you see Patrick?" Katherine casually asked, noticing the cuts on his face.

His steely gaze pinned her to the chair. "Send up one of the maids and hot water for a bath. I'll need assistance with my bath … or would you like to help me, *cousin?*"

Katherine retorted, "If you need help, Albert can assist you." She rose and drew the parlor door shut, hoping to block the sound of his bitter laughter echoing through the house. He was evil! How could she ever be rid of him? She had been giddy when Patrick had punched David. Now she was afraid of his reactions. Would he lash out and hurt her? Kill her? Patrick was married, so she couldn't ask him for help. Perhaps Edward would help her. She had to ask.

Chapter 32

ANN TOURED THE HOUSE with Mary. Mary would soon be off to tour Europe with friends. Ann wanted to make sure that she could manage the estate like a proper woman in this century. It did amaze her at the number of servants it took to run the household. It was like running a small corporation.

By late afternoon, she found herself with nothing to do. Deciding to take advantage of Patrick's absence, she quickly changed into her jogging clothes—a tank top and shorts. Familiar with the work routine of the staff, Ann knew how to escape unnoticed. She hurried to reach the wooded area beyond the house. Jogging along the worn path that wound through the trees, Ann reveled at the changes in her life. Who could have guessed that only months ago, she was caught up in the everyday rat race of the twenty-first century?

Her thoughts turned to Mark and Jess. Tears blurred her vision. If only she could find a way to let them know she was alive and safe. The battery charge on the laptop may still work. Could she send them an e-mail? She would try; at least it would make her feel closer to them. Too bad Skype wouldn't work from this century.

She turned and retraced her steps, breaking into a run across the open area surrounding the house. As she rounded the corner, thundering hooves ran past her. Patrick and Anthony were racing toward the stables. To her horror, Patrick caught sight of her and her brightly colored attire. His smile slowly faded. In contrast, Anthony hooted with laughter.

Her feet felt like lead. Beads of moisture dotted her face. Instinctively she raced to her room, ripping off the jogging clothes. Frantic, she struggled into a dress. One look in the mirror confirmed her fears. She was a mess. Dampened curls stuck to her neck. Beads of sweat rolled down her neck. A refined English lady she wasn't. Ann ran a brush through her tangled hair. With help from her maid, she was quickly made presentable. She selected a book and waited. There was no doubt that Patrick would come to find her.

Patrick marched into her dressing room and found her sitting on a chaise, properly dressed, pretending to read a book of poetry. He ran a hand through his windblown hair.

"Is Anthony staying for dinner?" Ann innocently asked.

"No. I've sent him home. Don't try to change the subject."

Ann bit back a smile, peering up at Patrick.

"Please correct me if I'm wrong, but it appeared that you were wearing clothes not appropriate for public display. I will not allow my wife to make a spectacle of herself. I didn't say anything the night of the ball when you took it into your head to wear those ghastly clothes. But now you have left me with no choice. Where are the clothes?" With his arms folded across his chest, he tapped his foot on the Oriental rug, waiting for her to give him the offensive garments.

Ann couldn't believe her ears. How could such a loving, wonderful man become so tyrannical? Tossing the book aside, Ann rose to her feet. Her index finger jabbed his chest as she advanced. Patrick backed against the bedpost. "You are not taking my clothes! I have tried to explain everything so you would understand the situation."

Pulling the bag out from underneath the bed, Ann dumped out the contents. The denim jeans, the colorful Bon Jovi T-shirt, and the Nike running shoes lay in a pile. He moved to get a closer look at the strange items strewn about the bed.

He held up the shirt. "Good God!" he roared. "Who would

ever make such a piece of clothing? Of all things." His piercing stare lanced Ann.

Grabbing the shirt from him, she redirected his anger. "Here! Look at these shoes. Do you notice anything strange about these?"

"They are very lightweight. Not at all like the rubber-soled shoes that people wear for outdoor activities." He continued to pull, tug, and turn the shoes every which way to examine them.

"Why would the shoes be made in such bright colors? I cannot fathom purple and gold shoes."

"People like to coordinate the shoes with clothing or show their support of a sports team. I tried to tell you several times that I'm from the future, but I knew you wouldn't believe me. Now I don't have a choice."

Patrick tossed the shoes aside and ventured to the window. Pulling back the curtain, he looked outside. His stiff posture told Ann that he was apprehensive.

Without turning around, he snapped, "Just say the words! End the suspense and tell me."

Ann drew a deep breath. "I've already told you about David and that I lived in America. That's all true. What I didn't explain is that I was born in 1967. I'm from the twenty-first century, not the nineteenth." She paused, ready to gauge his reaction. It was as if time stood still. "Did you hear me? I won't be born until ninety-seven years from now."

Patrick's shoulders began to shake. He sat down on the bed and covered his face with his hands. Ann tentatively touched his shoulder. He peered through his fingers, his eyes crinkling with amusement. She flopped down next to him, scowling as he hooted with laughter.

"Really, my dear. You're very good at inventing these stories. For a second, I almost believed you." Pulling out a handkerchief, he wiped his eyes. "If this is your explanation for wearing those horrid clothes, then you must know that I still forbid you to do so again."

"*Ohhhh!* You bullheaded old-fashioned jerk. You couldn't see the truth if it hit you on the side of the head." Stomping her foot, Ann demanded, "Look again. There is nothing like this anywhere in England or America in the nineteenth century. The first patent for rubber was initiated less than a century ago. There is no way a shoe like this even exists today. As for the T-shirt, it is a common garment for people to wear in my time. This one happens to be my son's shirt. Just look at the labels inside the shirt and jeans. Do you recognize them at all?"

No longer laughing, Patrick's head pounded. If she *was* born in 1967, then he would be dead and buried by that time. If she really was from the future, then that meant that she was Ann, not Victoria. If that was the case, where was Victoria? The questions were endless.

He wrapped an arm about the bedpost, holding on for dear life. "If I believe what you are saying, then how did you get here?"

"I've tried and tried to find the answer to that question. At first, I thought this was all a dream. I was afraid I would wake up one day and find that you had just been a figment of my imagination. Before I knew you really existed, I saw a picture of you in an album called *Lady O'Neil's Memoirs*. Every night, you came to me in my dreams."

The tightness in his chest threatened to strangle him. Patrick stared at her. He also had experienced strange dreams. He'd originally thought that the dreams were of Victoria. Maybe they were about Ann.

Ann jerked open the wardrobe and pulled out the leather case from its new hiding place. He watched closely as she unzipped the case. He eased closer. Flipping up the lid, she pressed the on switch. Within a couple of seconds, a flat object lit up. The whirring sound piqued his interest. Then the words Windows 2008 were flashing in front of him.

Ann talked as she moved a thing that she called a mouse. Like magic, the names of parents, grandparents, and cousins appeared. He stared questioningly into her eyes. "What is that thing?"

"It's called a computer. People use computers to communicate with others around the world by using wireless networks. There are airplanes to fly us anywhere in the world we want to go. Men landed on the moon in 1969. Then ..."

Holding up his hand, he pleaded with her to stop. "All these tales are giving me a hell of a headache. I suppose you have a magic pill to fix that?"

"Now that you mention it ..." Ann dug in her bag and pulled out a bottle of Tylenol. Handing him the bottle, she giggled as he struggled to open it. "Let me help you."

Examining the oblong white tablet in the palm of his hand, he took a glass of water and swallowed it. Patrick lay back on the bed, squeezing his eyes shut. "Even I have read *Celestial Mechanics* by Pierre-Simon Laplace. Did you know he was one of the first scientists to postulate the existence of black holes and the idea of gravitational collapse? Do you believe in time travel?"

"Not until I showed up here, I didn't."

"What about David? How did he get here?"

"I told you that David and I dated. When I tried to break off the relationship, he went crazy. But throughout the whole ordeal, I was drawn to the album with your picture. How I wished that you were real!"

Ann wiped a tear from her cheek. "When I opened my eyes, I was here at your house. You assumed I was Victoria. I was so confused yet ecstatic to see you in person that I pretended to be Victoria. Forgive me?"

Was there an ulterior motive or did she really love him? Her story was impossible. Yet how could he ignore the evidence? Lured by the fullness of her lips, his mouth forged a seal.

The warmth of her arms about his neck silenced further doubts. His arms snaked about her waist. He pressed her deep into the comforter while lavishing kisses down her arched neck. There was urgency in his need for her. Desire raged as he rent the front of her dress in half. Blushing, she tried to cover herself.

"Don't. I want to see all of you, to hold you and know that you are mine."

He moved her hands, touching the swells of her breasts. Lazily his finger brushed across her nipples. As they hardened, his lips lowered, drawing them into the heat of his mouth. Her tremors sent a jolt throughout his body. Her hips thrust upward against him. In his haste to disrobe, the buttons on the front of his trousers flew to the floor. Ann stared at his throbbing member.

"C'mon, baby. Show me what you got."

His laughter filled the room. Flashing a crooked grin, he proudly stood before her, letting her look her fill, silently wishing that her lips would encompass him. When she took too long, he bent over her, pressing his lips to her ankle and making his way up to her thigh. His tongue lavished desire across her stomach. "I plan to show you what I got, my lady. I daresay you will be unable to utter a coherent word. I intend to make you beg for completion again and again, until your moans and screams of pleasure echo about the room."

All thoughts of the past and future were forgotten as the lovers melded with desire, surging to reach the pinnacle of ecstasy together. Words of love were unspoken yet evident in every touch and every breath.

Chapter 33

A KNOCK INTERRUPTED ANN as she pored over household accounts. Malcolm strode toward her. Squealing with delight, she jumped up, hugging him until he groaned.

"Here now. What's all this fuss about? It's only been a few days since I saw you. By the looks of you, married life is agreeable."

Ann kissed his pinkish cheek. He looked so handsome in the hunter-green jacket and maize waistcoat. Working outdoors had improved his complexion to a healthy bronze color. Ann resisted the urge to ruffle his neatly combed hair.

"I heard that you're making progress with the changes to the estate. The servants keep me updated on the local gossip. You're becoming quite respectable. I'm so proud of you."

Malcolm shrugged. "If you compare what I have done to that of your husband, you will find me sorely lacking. Yet things are improving. I started experimenting with new farming methods to increase crop yields. Enough about me. What about you?"

"It's all out in the open now. I've told Patrick everything, though I'm not sure he believes every word."

Malcolm's smile fell away. "You mean he knows that you're not Victoria?"

"Yes, I've convinced him that the differences between the two of us were too great for me to actually be Victoria."

"I just remembered an appointment. Please excuse me; I must leave."

Ann frowned. He looked as white as a ghost. "Do you really have to leave? You seem upset about something. Can I help?"

"No, no." He paused, looking anxious. "Do me a favor. Could you and Patrick keep Victoria's absence a secret for a while longer? People always talk. They will delve into your background, and then you will have to come up with a story explaining your background. Father will blame me for the entire situation."

Puzzled by his logic, Ann attempted to reason with him. "If you explain why Victoria left, I'm sure your father will understand."

Malcolm paced the room. "You don't know him as I do. He's been spending your marriage settlement. I've warned him about throwing away our security, but he laughs about how there will be plenty of money later on."

"What does he mean by that?"

"I'm not sure. You and I both know that he has no concern for anyone but himself. You must be careful. I don't know what he'll do once the money is gone."

She brushed off the shadow of doubt. "Don't worry. I won't give him any money. If he visits, I'll make sure Patrick is here."

After Malcolm left, Ann grew worried. Why did Malcolm refuse to talk about Victoria? Where was Victoria? She sensed he was in trouble. How could she learn the truth?

That evening at dinner, Ann mentioned Malcolm's visit. "He's developing methods to improve the yields on the crops."

Grudgingly, Patrick nodded. "So it seems. I have heard similar reports from our neighbors. They seem to be impressed with the reformation of Malcolm."

"You could be a little more excited. You have to admit that you were wrong about him."

"If you don't mind, I will withhold judgment until a later time. I do miss Malcolm's friendship, but you do not know what he's done. I do. Speaking of your *family*, William has assumed a large gambling debt again. If he keeps throwing money away at the current rate, the annual amount we've agreed upon won't be sufficient."

"Malcolm alluded to the same problem. It seems William believes he'll be coming into a large amount money in the future. By the way, Malcolm asked if we would continue pretending that I am Victoria for now and—"

"I knew it. He is trying to hide something."

Ann threw her shoulders back. "Oh, how could you say that? He was being considerate of me, as there would be all kinds of questions of who I am and where I came from. You and I have never talked about how we're going to answer those questions. Don't you think we should get our story straight before announcing to the world who I am?"

Patrick tapped his fingers on the table. "Right. I will give him that point, but we're not pretending forever. I will also hire an investigator to check into William and see what plans that man is making."

After dinner, Ann joined Patrick in the study. She sat down as he meticulously scanned an annual report from one of the railroad businesses he owned. Would fate allow them to stay together? He had everything she had ever looked for in a husband; he was tender, considerate, protective, and handsome. Although there seemed to be some arrogant qualities, he was hers.

Patrick smiled. "Before you fall asleep in that chair, perhaps you should start packing."

A tremor of doubt coursed through her. "Packing?"

"We," he stressed, "are going to London. You have never experienced a season in London. So as the dutiful husband, I will endure the crowds and parties just for you."

Shrieking with joy, she bounded off the chair and threw her arms around his neck. Bouncing up and down, Ann bubbled with excitement. "I can't believe it! I'm going to a ball! Can I buy a new dress? I want something drop-dead gorgeous."

Patrick gruffly muttered, "Not too gorgeous. I don't want every man gazing upon what is mine. Maybe I should reconsider this idea?"

Punching him lightly on the shoulder, Ann teased, "Oh, no. I've already accepted your offer. Besides, you wouldn't want to live with me if you changed your mind."

"Is that a threat?"

"You can consider it whatever you want, Lord O'Neil."

His movements caught her unprepared. A second later, she found herself tossed over his shoulder. With her head upside down, she saw several servants staring at them in shock. Her head bounced up and down as they made their way upstairs. Giggles echoed throughout the house.

Dumped onto the bed, Ann rolled over to escape her husband's roving hands. "Stop! I'm ticklish. Oh, please stop. I can't stand it."

Before she could utter another word, his warm lips melded with hers. Within minutes, tears of laughter turned to tears of joy.

Malcolm's head throbbed as he rode home. His father's spending habits would force them to the poorhouse if something wasn't done. William's periods of sobriety were becoming less frequent. Malcolm would try one last time to reason with his father. If necessary, he would appeal to the courts and have his father declared mentally incompetent.

Malcolm walked in unannounced to his father's study. Damn, where was the man? Seeing papers strewn about the desk, Malcolm picked up a handful of letters. They were all overdue bills.

From the corner of his eye, a shadow lurked near the doorway. "Father, is that you?"

Peter hobbled forward, bowing slightly. "No, sir, it's me."

Distrustful of the servant, Malcolm demanded, "Why are you sneaking about? Where's my father?"

"I believe he is in his room, sir."

"Good, I need to talk to him." Without a backward glance, Malcolm stormed past the servant. Knocking loudly on the door, he didn't wait for a response. Odors of unwashed flesh and stale bourbon assailed him. Covering his nose with his hand, Malcolm opened the nearest window. After several deep breaths of fresh air, he turned and gazed at his father, who slept unaware of his son's presence. The linens were stained with food and drink, as was his father's nightshirt. He jerked back the covers and watched William struggle to draw them back over himself.

William rolled over. "Peter, shut those damn windows."

Minutes ticked by, and still the cool air streamed through the window. Malcolm watched his father slowly open his eyes. William belched and rubbed his exposed stomach. "Do not try to intimidate me with that haughty look. Get out of here and leave me alone."

"It's afternoon. The day is only half over and you're intoxicated."

"Oh, rubbish. How many times has it happened to you? I'm enjoying life so save the melodrama."

"Father, I've seen the demand letters from the creditors. You have to control your spending. As quickly as I earn a profit, I have to pay off another creditor. You were always so damn worried about the family name. Now you're dragging our name into the gutter."

"Curb your insolent tongue! I'm your father and need no lectures. Look at you! You're working like a common laborer, earning a few pounds here and there. You've lost the desire to go after your dreams. Well, I haven't. O'Neil looks at us as if we're nothing. With all his money and position, he could impart more of his wealth to his relations."

William rose to his feet. His reddened face stood out in sharp contrast with the grimy white nightshirt. Malcolm watched him splash his face and use a dirty sleeve to dry off.

Malcolm wanted to shake his father. No longer able to keep the disdain from his voice, Malcolm bellowed, "O'Neil owes us nothing. He isn't the one who frittered away a fortune. He has been more than generous with us. Patrick genuinely cares for Victoria, and I'll not see you ruin their marriage. I've contacted our solicitor and drawn up papers granting me authority over the estate, due to your unstable condition."

Sweat broke out across William's brow. "I have no condition!

Do this and I'll disinherit you." Quickly pouring a glass of port, he downed it in a gulp and then resumed his barrage. "If you think my actions are reflecting on this family, then I suggest you reconsider your actions before making any further decisions. I warn you—this is my property, not yours."

Malcolm clenched his fists. "Are you threatening me, your own son?"

"Call it what you want. I'm informing you of my position. Get out of here. You sicken me."

Malcolm glared at his father and stormed from the room, slamming the door behind him. At that moment, Malcolm hated his father. He'd never been so angry. He refused to let William destroy him or Ann and Patrick's marriage. If William thought he was an easy target, he should think again. After all, William had raised him.

Chapter 34

AT PATRICK'S INSISTENCE, THE dressmaker had arrived. Ann gazed at the swatches of material, dismayed at the pale blues and lavenders.

She sighed wistfully. "Do you have anything brighter? What about a deep purple ... or gold?"

The dressmaker quickly pulled out samples of dark, bold colors. The two women quickly decided upon the styles and material for five new gowns.

Patrick found Ann in the garden after the midday meal. She carefully laid the fresh flowers in her basket. "Darn it!" she yelped as a thorn pierced her skin.

"Is that any way for a lady to talk?" he teased. He bent down and pulled her injured hand to his lips. "I'm surprised you finished with the dressmaker so quickly."

"I found what I was looking for, but I'm afraid I didn't ask how much it would cost."

"I can bear the cost of a few gowns."

She picked up the basket and flashed him a coy smile. "I can't believe you suggested that I purchase new clothes. In my time, it isn't that often that a man encourages a woman to go shopping."

"I aim to please." Patrick smiled in return, appearing to bask in the knowledge that he had pleased her. He followed her to the kitchen and pulled out a chair to watch Ann arrange the flowers into artful bouquets.

"I had no idea you were so talented. Is there anything you can't do?"

Before Ann could answer, Maggie, the housekeeper joined them. "Sir, a message was delivered while you were out."

"Now what?" Tearing open the envelope, Patrick's frown increased as he read the missive.

"It's from William. He and Malcolm would like to visit later today. They'll probably stay for dinner." Reluctantly, he handed the note to his wife. "Maybe we can decline and say we will not be at home."

She shook her head. "I don't think we have much of a choice. Malcolm is so upset with William. Maybe you can talk some sense into him."

Patrick swore aloud. "William is beyond help. The rumors surrounding him are increasing." He came closer, wrapping her in an embrace. "I'm thankful that you aren't really related to the Montgomerys. Tonight will be a test of my endurance, but for you I'll tolerate anything."

As Ann dressed for dinner, she thought about Patrick. She knew he harbored less than affectionate thoughts for her new family. The tension between Patrick and William was palpable. Perhaps he would see what she saw in Malcolm tonight. She desperately wanted the two men to be friends again, as she viewed Malcolm as a brother she never had in her previous life. From the moment she met him, he was like family.

The announcement of their guests' arrival compounded her worry.

"O'Neil." Malcolm nodded his head. "It's kind of you to have us over tonight. Father was rather insistent that we get together."

Patrick smiled. "Dinner will be ready soon. Could I pour you a drink while we're waiting?"

William stood quietly in the doorway. He was watching the three of them with an odd look on his face. What was he thinking?

William eased next to Patrick. "Good to see you again, O'Neil.

You look well satisfied for a newly married man." Patrick grimaced as William laughed.

Malcolm cleared his throat. "Say, Patrick, I would like to know what investments interest you lately. The recent profits from the estate need to be invested prudently. You always have the Midas touch when it comes to finances. I'd welcome any advice you care to offer."

Ann grinned as Patrick's face lit up. He loved talking about investments for railways and mining in South Africa.

William helped himself to a drink and sat in a leather chair near the wall, observing his son. Scowling, William muttered to Ann, "I don't know what you did to Malcolm, but he is a changed man ... and not for the better."

Rather than getting into an argument, Ann kept her composure and walked over to where Patrick and Malcolm were talking.

Standing on tiptoes, Ann kissed Patrick on the cheek. Malcolm said to Ann, "That peach silk dress is perfect for your coloring. You look radiant tonight, m'dear. If you look like this every night, I see why your husband's friends complain that they no longer see him."

"Don't you know I keep him locked up?"

Patrick bantered back, "If that neckline were any lower, I would definitely keep you locked up! I hope your new gowns are less revealing."

Ann's eyes met William's intent stare, and she couldn't help but notice the heavy bags underneath his eyes and the ruddy color of his skin. "Are you ill? You don't look good."

He grunted before replying, "No, just a touch of dyspepsia. The old stomach tends to act up on occasion. Here now, never mind about me. Let's look at you. You're blooming with good health. I see that marriage agrees with you. I told you it would be fine."

Suspicious of his compliment, she led them into the dining room. Throughout the meal, William's glass was frequently refilled. Malcolm glared at his father at each refill. When Patrick and Malcolm tried to converse about the upcoming season in London,

William interrupted them to discuss his next trip to Brighton for the races.

As her husband's eyes rolled with exasperation, Ann covered her mouth with the napkin to smother her laughter. Malcolm and Patrick seemed to be getting along. She was pleased with the efforts of both men to become reacquainted. After dinner, Patrick suggested they retire to the sitting room for brandy.

William slowly stood and braced his arms against the table. "You two go ahead. I wish to speak with Victoria."

Ann nodded to Patrick, indicating that she would be fine. She trailed after William into the gardens.

"Your husband has been quite generous with you. I don't recognize that dress as one that I purchased."

"Yes, he's very generous. I couldn't ask for a more perfect husband. I hear that Malcolm is doing very well. You should be proud."

"Humph. He is worse than a wife. All the money he makes goes back into the land. He doesn't enjoy life at all anymore, not like you."

Puzzled, she asked, "Pardon?"

"You know what I mean." He waved his hand toward the towering house and lush gardens surrounding them. "The lavish clothes, parties, jewels … You have access to it all. I wager that if you insisted upon a new diamond necklace, O'Neil would send for one immediately."

Ann didn't like where this was headed. "All of this was earned by years of hard work and effort. I wouldn't ask him for something I didn't need."

A strange gleam filled his eyes. "I could always make use of any gifts you felt uncomfortable with. After all, you wouldn't want to hurt his feelings, with you two just married and such."

What an overbearing autocrat! As if she would hand over her jewelry so he could squander the money. If she gave anything away, it would be to Malcolm. At least he would make good use of the funds.

Ann compressed her lips, ready to do battle. "What happened to the settlement that Patrick gave you?"

He quickly closed the distance between them, causing Ann to take a step backward. "Since you have never managed money, I will overlook your remarks. Must I remind you that I spent years raising you as my own child? I put food on your plate and fancy clothes on your back so you could go about in society. Now that you are married, you can repay me."

His look frightened her. "If I thought you would put any money I gave you to good use, I might consider it. Since I know your true colors, I won't even consider it."

William grabbed Ann's upper arm and twisted. Pulling her back into the shadows, he shook her slender frame. "I'm not asking; I am demanding. You will follow my instructions to the letter."

Ann's breathing was labored with fear and anger. "I won't. I'm going to find Patrick and tell him about your threats. I think you had better leave now."

William's mottled face loomed in front of her. "I should have gotten rid of you after your mother died. I have connections with men who have no scruples. A little money given here or there, anyone can be murdered."

"You wouldn't dare!" Chilled to the bone, her body shook.

"Try me! I heard that Viscount Hardin was recently set upon outside London. They took his money and slit his throat when he tried to stop them. I wonder if Patrick would try to stop someone from robbing him? You never know when a second man could appear with a gun and kill an unsuspecting man. If O'Neil died, I would manage the estate until you could be married off again. If you fail to cooperate, you may find yourself married to Lord Warden next time."

"You're delusional."

Lord Warden! Even she was familiar with the gossip surrounding his name. He was at least seventy years old. He had been married three times. One wife died in childbirth. One fell out of an upper window by accident, so it was rumored. The last one vanished and was presumed dead. Although the man had a fortune, no responsible parents would allow their young daughter near the old pervert.

Patrick was in danger. Fear crept into the deepest recesses of her heart. Would William really presume that he could commit murder and not suffer any repercussions? She had to speak to Malcolm. He would know what to do. She was afraid that Patrick would jump to conclusions and think that Malcolm was part of his father's scheme. Since things were going so well between him and Malcolm, she didn't want to jeopardize their friendship.

"Well, what do you say? Do you have a small trinket that you can bear to part with or should I contact my friends?"

Masking her overwhelming terror, Ann hissed, "There are only a couple of small pieces that will not be missed."

He smiled, patting Ann's shoulder. "That's a good girl. I knew you would help your father. Just remember, this is our little secret. As long as you keep your mouth shut, everyone will be happy."

Unable to bear his presence any longer, she turned away. "I will have my maid deliver the package before you leave. Do not speak to me again. You disgust me."

Patrick and Malcolm returned to the drawing room, laughing as if they were old friends once again. As Ann entered the room, Patrick noted her flushed face. "Is anything wrong?"

"No, just a chill in the air. I'll ask the maid to fetch my shawl." Ann sat near the fireplace, rubbing her ice-cold hands together.

The glass doors to the garden opened, and William joined the group. "Son, are you about ready to leave? We don't want to wear out our welcome with the newlyweds."

Patrick was surprised that William hadn't asked for money tonight. The financial situation with the Montgomerys was tenuous at best. Surprisingly, he and Malcolm got along quite well tonight. It reminded him of happier times with his childhood friend. Still, he had some unresolved questions that had to be answered, tonight if possible.

"Malcolm, could you join me in the library before you leave?"

When William started to rise, Patrick shook his head. "I wish to speak to Malcolm privately."

Malcolm shrugged and followed Patrick. What was so important that they had to speak in private?

Patrick quietly shut the library door. "As you know, Ann informed me of the true circumstances of her arrival here in England. I'm sure that you agree with me that her likeness to Victoria is more than remarkable. I must have been blind. Don't misunderstand me—I'm glad that Ann is my wife. I know now that it would have been a mistake for Victoria and me to marry. I cannot believe your father hasn't noticed the difference between the two women."

The tension threatened to choke Malcolm. "Well, as you witnessed tonight, he isn't always clearheaded. The liquor clouds his mind and judgment. I believe only a few people can be trusted with the information regarding Ann. Do you agree?"

With his legs stretched out before him, Patrick studied Malcolm. "Yes. I don't want Ann's role in society questioned. There is one thing I must ask you. Do you know where Victoria is? I'm worried."

Malcolm forced himself to focus on Patrick's face. "I have promised not to reveal her whereabouts. If you remember, Victoria's attitude toward marriage was reluctant. Damn, how was I to know that Father would push her into the engagement? She was helpless against my father. I was little help to her at that time."

"You're judging yourself too harshly. We all make mistakes. God knows I've made my share. I wish her the best. If she needs anything at all, please let me know. If word of this fiasco leaks out, there will be enough gossip to destroy both of our families."

Malcolm rose to his feet, trying desperately to control the tremors raging through him. He should have been man enough to kill himself when Victoria died, but it was too late now.

"Be assured that I will relay your concerns to Victoria. She's in a safe place, and that's all that matters."

After bidding their hosts farewell, Malcolm couldn't escape the house quickly enough. He prayed that Patrick hadn't noticed his shaking hands when he pressed for an answer. Malcolm knew Patrick would hire someone to search for Victoria.

Malcolm sat in the shadows of the carriage, ignoring his father. Mulling over the conversation with Patrick, he feared the consequences if Victoria's death was discovered. All sorts of questions would be raised. How could he ever prove it had all been a horrible accident? No one would believe him! He had to redeem himself for Victoria. He alone would make up for all those long years that he and his father had brought ruination to the family name.

Stuffing a bag into his pocket, William pulled out a silver flask. As the coach hit a rough bump in the road, magenta liquid dribbled down his white shirt. Wiping his mouth with the back of his hand, he leaned out the window and bellowed at the coachman for his clumsiness.

Drawn out of his reflection, Malcolm sighed wearily. "Father, please. It's not the driver's fault for the bumps in the road. Perhaps if you refrained from imbibing until we reached home, you wouldn't slop the liquor."

William poked a finger at Malcolm's chest. "You forget your place. You'll notice that you are riding in my coach and traveling to my home. I have been more than tolerant of your behavior lately. If you wish to play the role of benefactor, so be it. But I will continue to live my life as I want."

Impulsively, Malcolm tore the flask from his father's hands and tossed it out the window. "Damn you. What do I have to do or say to make you understand? Your behavior is shameless. You've become a laughingstock."

Maniacal laughter echoed about the enclosed coach. William leaned forward, spittle spewing from his mouth. "People can talk as much as they want. Once my plans come to fruition, society will regret their actions. Money is power ... and make no mistake—I will have power."

Malcolm threw his hands up in the air. "I wash my hands

of you and your actions. Mark my words: I won't support you if you're brought in front of the magistrate." Williams simply glared in reply.

Malcolm sighed. How could he ever expect to control William's actions when his own life was a mess?

Chapter 35

WOULD THINGS EVER BE normal again? Since Patrick and Anthony had threatened David last month, David had been a terror. Every day another merchant delivered some expensive new item. She would be ruined financially if he wasn't stopped.

Nothing had gone right since that damn Montgomery girl became engaged to Patrick. Katherine had been sure that Patrick would have contacted her by now. It had been weeks since the wedding and still no word from her former lover.

Even Edward had left her. Shortly after arriving home from Patrick's wedding, she and Edward had sat down to relax. An innocent conversation quickly became a major row. As usual, she said things she regretted. Edward stood and rang for the butler. The twitching muscle near his eye was the only sign of his frustration.

Waspishly, she whined, "Why are you leaving? I thought we were going to—"

"Not anymore." Edward yanked on his leather gloves. Although he looked composed, Katherine knew he was livid.

"Your sullen attitude has become quite tiresome. I like Lady O'Neil. It's quite obvious to everyone but you that they are taken with each other. I have offered you my name and heart repeatedly."

Katherine twisted her fingers together, her anxiety building. "But, Edward, I ..."

He held up his hand and shook his head. "No buts, Katherine. Obviously, I'm not the man for you. It's foolish for me to stay and continue to hope that your feelings for me will change. I shall be in London should you ever need assistance."

At the doorway, he turned to look at her. Her tear-filled eyes did not have the impact they had had in the past. She fought for control of her tears.

"I wish you the best, my dear. I hope you find someone who makes you happy."

Just thinking of his leaving tore her apart. He had never treated her this way before. She had too much pride to call him back. All men came back eventually.

Weeks dragged by with not one word or one letter from Edward. She sat down several times to start a letter. Each time, she became frustrated and tore it up. Surprisingly, she missed Edward. He was so much more than a friend. She was beginning to realize how much she really cared for him.

David's actions grew too much too bear. David never let her forget that he would hurt Edward if she failed to give him what he wanted. With no choice, she tossed away any remnant of her pride and wrote to Edward.

Days after she sent her note, Edward finally arrived. Katherine ran down the stairs, almost colliding with the butler. Rushing past the bewildered servant, she hurled herself into Edward's arms.

"You're here! I was so afraid you wouldn't come."

Stunned, Edward held Katherine in his arms. He pressed his lips to her pale cheek. He could only speculate why she had requested his presence. He did not consider himself handsome, but he had many other qualities that were appreciated by the fairer sex. It was about time that Katherine began to appreciate him. He had a family name to carry on and wanted to settle down.

Katherine wrapped her arm about his as they walked to the parlor. "If I didn't know better, I would think that you are not that excited to be here."

With a sarcastic lift of a brow, Edward smiled. "You never change. Tell me why you sent the note."

She nervously glanced toward the closed door. "It's David. He is threatening me. He does as he pleases. I've asked him to leave, but he won't go. I don't know what to do."

He should have known that she was in trouble and wanted him to handle it. Edward rested his hand on her shoulder. "Perhaps you have misjudged the situation. If you like, I will speak to him."

She stomped her foot in rage before grabbing the lapels of his jacket. "No, you don't understand. I'm afraid that he will hurt you. He is devious and underhanded. You cannot trust anything he says."

Edward frowned, gently removing her hands. "How long have these threats been occurring?"

"Since you left."

"Bullocks! You accepted him and made introductions on his behalf. He then repays you in this manner. The man is no gentleman."

Throwing open the door, he called for the butler, barking instructions for staff to be ready to assist him if needed. Returning to Katherine's side, he led her to the stairs. "Go to your room and lock the door. I will handle Mr. Stewart."

While Edward waited in the library, he checked for the knife hidden in his boot. He had learned a long time ago that a man must be prepared to defend himself.

David entered the library wearing an elegantly tailored waistcoat. From the polished boots to his gleaming golden hair, he looked like a gentleman.

Eyeing him speculatively, Edward inquired, "An engagement?"

"Yes. I'm joining friends later for dinner and cards. But, Edward, you surprise me. I thought you had given up your involvement with Katherine. Yet you have returned."

"I'm not here to discuss my personal life. I understand that you've been threatening Katherine. It is time for you to secure your own lodgings. Your welcome here has expired."

David shrugged. "Katherine exaggerates. Like you, I've found that a certain amount of money is needed to see to my comforts."

Edward's determination did not waver. "I have no wish to embarrass you, but you will have to leave. There is a limit to what is acceptable. Due to your lack of family connections, Katherine was kind enough let you stay and you repay her by issuing threats. As a close personal friend of Katherine's, I feel it's necessary to remind you of your station."

David said, "I'm well aware of my station in life. Katherine misconstrues what I said. Why would I threaten her or anyone?"

Edward tensed. David's body movements and stance told him that he wanted to lash out. "Things have changed. I've made my decision. Katherine believes you are a threat, and that is more than enough for me. I will provide you a small quarterly allowance so you can set up lodgings elsewhere. If you're prudent, it should last until you find employment."

"Allowance!" David roared. "I suggest you talk to your whore before you change anything around here. Apparently, she didn't tell you that she came on to me while you were gone. She's one hot number, if you get my meaning."

Edward's breathing sharpened. Based on her previous behavior, he didn't know what to think. "You ungrateful bastard! I won't tolerate your degrading insinuations."

Edward walked toward the door. The next second, his body slammed against the heavy oak door. Unable to catch his breath, he felt a fist pummel his face. Edward writhed on the floor in pain. Through narrowed eyes, Edward studied his attacker.

David's ragged breath echoed about the room. He brushed back his curls, which now lay flat on his sweat-laden brow. His wild eyes darted from Edward to the door.

"Stupid bitch," he raged. "She should have kept her mouth shut."

David looked frantic. Rising from the floor, Edward wiped the blood from the corner of his mouth. He growled, "Pack your bags and be gone within the hour. If you don't, I will personally see that you are escorted off the property. I don't know what your game is, but you've played the wrong card this time."

"I don't think so. You forget that I still hold the upper hand. I have knowledge that will destroy your precious Katherine. One slip of the tongue and all of London will know that she's nothing but a whore."

Although David's words meant nothing to those in society, it still would create an unpleasant situation. He didn't want Katherine's reputation tarnished any worse than it was now.

"You would destroy the only person who cared enough to take you in? My God, man! She's your cousin. Doesn't family matter?"

Strutting over to him, David jabbed his finger at Edward's chest. "Money is all that matters. I see that you still don't get the big picture. Katherine has neglected to tell you one minor thing. I'm not her cousin. We're not even related. So here we have a single man and woman living together in the same household for weeks, all alone, with no chaperone. Can you imagine what people will say?"

Edward gritted his teeth together. He longed to wipe the smile off the bastard's face. Why had Katherine deceived him? He cursed himself for being so gullible. For Katherine's sake, he had to eliminate any association with David. Their names mustn't be connected in any manner.

"What is your price?"

"Ten thousand dollars a month. Plus, I take everything I have purchased in the last few weeks."

"Be reasonable! I don't have that kind of money lying around. Everything is invested. I will give you one thousand of your American dollars. You can also take what you want, as long as Katherine and I never hear from you again."

David chuckled. "There are no options. Play it my way or I'll ruin Katherine."

In the window behind David, Edward saw Jenkins and other servants motioning toward the doorway. Obviously, everyone wanted David gone. Striding toward the door, Edward jerked it open to reveal several burly men ready to fight. Edward instructed Jenkins to fetch Mr. Stewart's belongings and deliver them to a waiting carriage. Edward gestured toward the door. "After you. Everything is being packed as we speak."

David's face became red, his manners stiff. "By all means. I've had enough of this place. I'll check to make sure they load all my things."

Fifteen minutes later, the carriage was loaded. Smoothing the cuffs of his fashionable jacket, David stood and surveyed the house one last time.

"If you're waiting for a fond farewell, you will be disappointed. Don't ever return Mr. Stewart."

"Chill out," he quipped sarcastically. "Have you forgotten something? You still have to pay the piper." With a hand outstretched, David waited.

Edward smiled knowingly. "I think not. Katherine has paid enough. If you need money, you can sell a few items."

To emphasize his intentions, Edward stepped within inches of David. In a lightning-quick movement, Edward whipped the knife from the top of his boot and pressed the lethal blade against David's cheek. "If I hear one slanderous word against Katherine, I shall find you and end your miserable life. If you think that anyone in London will believe your word over mine, think again. Now get the hell out of here before I change my mind."

David backed toward the carriage. "If you think this is over, you're mistaken. I won't forget this, Marshall. You will regret this day." Slamming the carriage door, David shouted at the driver.

Watching until the trail of dust disappeared, Edward sighed. Sheathing the knife, he already regretted not using it. Katherine stood in the doorway. As usual, she had ignored his orders to stay in her room. Her eyes seemed to be lit with admiration. He walked past her, heading to the library. Edward poured himself a brandy, downing it quickly. He then poured another.

"For heaven's sake, Edward. Tell me what happened. You nearly killed the man."

In a hoarse voice, he muttered, "He's gone, but for how long, I can't say. Why didn't you come to me earlier? None of this would have occurred if you had confided in me."

She lowered her head as if embarrassed. "Oh, Edward, please don't lecture me. I'm sorry, but he threatened to kill you … I did what I thought best." She wrapped her arms about his waist. "You were so commanding and took control of the situation with David."

Edward tipped up her chin, meeting her languid gaze. "Katherine, you must be on your guard. I shall post several guards about the property. You must avoid any association with David to discourage any gossip." His thumb trailed down her cheek to her rose-colored lips. "Clarify one thing for me. Did you and he have intimate relations?"

She pulled away, a look of horror on her face. "No! He tried to force his attentions on me, but he was more interested in terrifying me and spending my money. You must believe me."

Raking his hands through his hair, Edward paced before Katherine. "This incident has prompted me to reevaluate our relationship. When David made those terrible allegations, I never felt such intense anger. All these years, I've stood by quietly, waiting for you to come to your senses. I have seen you chase more men than I care to remember."

"I'm sorry, Edward. I never meant to hurt you."

"I realize now that I should have spoken up years ago. I no longer want to be a shadow on the fringe of your life. I want more, Katherine."

Katherine's hand trembled as she touched his face. "You have always been there for me. I'm a horrible, horrible person. Why do you care for me?"

He flung her hand away. In a ragged breath, he uttered, "Katherine, I want more than your friendship. Yes, you have behaved in a horrible manner. Still, I know that deep down inside, you are kind and loving. It is that person inside that I love. I'm asking you, one final time, to be my wife."

Katherine stood silently before him. "I didn't expect you to propose today. You have been by my side since the death of my husband. You've always treated me better than I deserve."

"Katherine, before you respond, I implore you to look to your heart. I desire you, but make no mistake, I won't share you with anyone once we are married. It's your choice." He calmly waited, forcing himself not to sweep her into his arms.

Clasping her hands together, she smiled. "I have wasted years of our lives chasing after something I didn't really want. I will be faithful to you, Edward. Though I do hope you're not going to become a husband who harps about what his wife spends on gowns and jewelry, for I don't plan on changing my spending habits."

Wrapping her in his arms, his lips claimed hers. His hand gripped her hip and pressed forward. Continuing to nuzzle her neck, he muttered, "I want my wife to have whatever she wants. According to my banker, I could afford to keep two wives."

Her lips pursed together. "Two wives? I doubt you can keep up with me, Edward."

Arrangements were made for a quiet country wedding. Without any fanfare, Edward and Katherine were married several weeks later.

Chapter 36

SITTING IN A SMOKE-FILLED tavern, David scouted out the patrons, hoping to find a fool who could be relieved of his wallet. He edged toward two farmers who, according to the bartender, had sold some cows. From the looks of it, they would be easy to rob. One way or another, he needed extra money.

The older farmer nodded vigorously. "Yeah, I heard he got married. I got a cousin working for Lord Marshall, and he gets a bonus each year. People line up to work for Marshall."

The younger man laughed. "I heard that his wife has money of her own. Ain't that the way it always happens? The rich get richer, and we get poorer."

David joined the men. "Excuse me. Did I hear you mention Lord Marshall's name?"

Eyeing him speculatively, the older man straightened. "What business is it of yours?"

"I'm an old acquaintance and would like to wish him well, if what I heard is correct."

The man took a gulp of the ale and wiped his mouth with the back of his hand. "It's true all right. If you're such a good friend, then you know Lady Katherine. They're off to London. He paid all his staff in advance while they're gone. Don't find too many men like Marshall, thinking about their help and all that. How do you ...? Hey, you in a hurry or something?"

Without responding, David rushed out the door, heading to the boardinghouse nearby. Everything would be fine. London was the perfect place. Murders occurred there all the time. No one would suspect him if some guy died. After all, he was just a man in the wrong century, with no past and no way to be traced.

Unlocking the door to his room, David threw his clothes into a satchel and hurried to the stables to find his new servant, Jack. Jack was a fierce-looking brute, but he had the brain of a gnat. David could sense that Jack was in desperate need of money and someone to look after him. Jack eagerly accepted his offer of employment.

Jack's first day of employment was less than exemplary. He failed to have David's horse saddled at the designated time. David struck him with a riding crop, leaving a bloody gash across his stunned face. From then on, Jack quickly accomplished whatever task was given to him.

David tossed Jack his bag. "Get the lead out of your pants. We're leaving for London. You can ride the gray gelding." Jack stood with his mouth hanging open. "Do you want to stay here and starve or come work for me?"

Jack stammered. "N-never been to London before. Where would I stay?"

"With me, you idiot. I need someone to help me with a project. All you have to do is follow my instructions. Can you do that?"

Twisting his cap with large callused hands, Jack smiled. "Yep. I can do that."

Impatient to be on the road, David gritted his teeth. "Then get going. I haven't got all day."

The two men galloped toward London. David had recently sold most of his belongings, and hoped that the money would allow them to rent a modest home in the West End of London.

David mentally refined his plan of terror. His excitement was building. It was almost as gratifying as a sexual release. One day he and Ann would meet again. He would kill Patrick first and make Ann watch. It wasn't right that she loved Patrick. He had met her first.

The headache had returned. He bent forward, wincing from the excruciating pain. Damn headaches! They seemed to happen when he thought about Ann. Gripping the reins, he held on, fearful that he would tumble to the ground. If he fell, Jack probably wouldn't even notice. Sweat trickled down his face, and his stomach roiled with every movement the animal made.

No longer caring where they were or what time it was, David knew he had to get off this damned animal or become violently ill. By the volume of traffic on the road, he judged they were on the outskirts of London. Spotting an inn ahead, he motioned for Jack to stop. David clung to the saddle as he slid to the ground. He had to get out of the sun.

David stumbled to a table in a darkened corner. He covered his head with his hands. "Get me a room for the night. Take care of the horses and take my bags to the room."

Jack shuffled from foot to foot. "What about me?"

"You can sleep in the stables. Now leave me alone."

Picking up a glass of beer that the owner had set in front of him, David sipped cautiously. Now that he was inside and off the horse, his pain receded. A buxom server stared from across the room as she wiped off the tables. Winking, she bent over to clean a table. Her blouse slipped lower, revealing bountiful breasts.

He created a mental fantasy about what he could do to the woman to make her scream.

Suddenly, a booming voice drew his attention. The innkeeper anxiously greeted the new guest. "Lord Montgomery, it's good to have you visit again. Come and sit down. Your room is ready."

The man sat down and surveyed the other guests with disdain. "Where is the young woman who works here?"

"You mean Martha. She's in the kitchen."

"See that she comes to my room after dinner. She's a nice little thing."

David overheard the new arrival and rolled his eyes. Who was this Montgomery guy? It was obvious that he had wealth and prestige by the way the owner catered to him. David watched the heavyset man through hooded lids.

The owner set a bottle of port on the table. "Anything else, my lord?"

"No. Just see that Martha is available."

Montgomery glanced in David's direction. He tottered over to the corner. "Have we met before?"

David stood and held out his hand. "I don't think so. I'm David Stewart, and you are …?"

Sitting down, William sniffed the contents of David's glass. "Lord Montgomery. William to you. Get rid of that slop you're drinking. Try mine. They keep it here just for me. Now tell me, are you on your way to London?"

Unsure of how important this Montgomery fellow was, David hesitated. He was confused about all the damned titles the English used: baron, lords, earls. What was the difference? "Yes, I am. Is it difficult to find a decent place this time of year?"

William chuckled. "Difficult? It's darn near impossible. How many are in your party?"

"Just me and one servant. Are you traveling with your family?"

"My daughter is married and will be arriving in London shortly. I don't much care for my son-in-law, but you can't always pick your relatives, if you know what I mean. Are you related to the Stewarts in Essex?"

"No, I'm from America. I thought I would visit England and locate some of the old family. I don't suppose you happen to know Lord Marshall?"

Ordering another bottle, William snorted. "I knew his father. Edward is a strange sort. All straightlaced and righteous, not like his father at all. Never liked the lad myself."

Smelling an opportunity, David's mind took off on a new strategy. "He's one reason I'm going to London. His father left me some money in his will. When I confronted Edward, he accused me of being a cheat and liar. He only gave me a fraction of my inheritance. I'm determined to get what is owed to me. I could use any help that you would care to suggest."

"Come with me to London." Before David could respond,

William boasted, "I'm not without power and influence. I have a large house, and most of the rooms sit empty. I insist that you be my guest."

David shook William's hand. "I'm honored. If only there were more men like you, the world would be a better place."

William grinned. "Let's retire to my room for dinner. Then if you don't mind sharing, I have a special little treat for you."

Envisioning the treat that William had in mind, David laughed. "If you're suggesting that the two of us keep Martha entertained, then you are a man after my own heart."

By evening, David wondered how William continued to drink so much and stay on his feet. Even though he was deep in his cups, William managed to chase the plump maid around the room. With great pretense, she cried out in protest as her clothes were ripped from her sagging body. Obviously, this was a game the two of them had played before while appeasing their undisguised lust.

With a final thrust, William rolled off Martha. Staggering to the table for another drink, he nodded to David. "She's all yours now. The rougher you are, the better she likes it."

The unclothed woman winked at David. The odor of sweat, sex, and liquor filled the room.

"Go wash yourself. Make sure you are clean before you come back," David ordered.

Chortling aloud, William winked. "A little picky, are we? Well, it doesn't offend me. I'll sit here and watch you two young people. It reminds me of earlier times with my son. Pay no mind to me."

Wary of participating in a spectator sport, David shrugged. If the old man wanted to watch, so be it. It was doubtful that he would stay conscious anyway. At the moment, David was too excited to deny the old man his pleasures.

Impatient for Martha to join him, he rubbed himself. He must be getting desperate to bed this whore. She was nothing like the women he was used to. Not wanting to dwell on his past life, David concentrated on starting a new life in London and making his enemies pay for his humiliation.

Chapter 37

ANN WAS GOING TO have more gowns than she could ever wear. The dressmaker had tried to convince Ann that blue was all the rage. She quickly learned that the lighting, whether it was candle or gas, tended to distort the color of most gowns that weren't a shade of blue. Ann had the necklines raised on several dresses, but it still felt as if her breasts were going to topple out of the gowns. She felt decadent spending his money, which in her time was considered a fortune.

Dressed only in her chemise, Ann shivered as a draft of cool air wafted about her. She turned and saw Patrick standing in the doorway. His heated gaze warmed her heart.

Unable to tear her gaze from the commanding figure in the doorway, Ann asked the dressmaker, "Can we finish this later?"

The woman nodded, starting to gather up supplies. "That won't be necessary. I have enough measurements to complete the gowns. I'll return in a day or two."

Patrick helped the woman collect all her items. "I'm very sorry for the interruption. Something has come up."

After the woman left, Ann flopped on the bed. "Such finesse. Did you notice that you made her blush? I suppose I should get used to women throwing themselves at your feet."

Locking the door, he quickly shed his clothes. He lunged at Ann, rubbing his whiskers across her stomach.

Rolling to her side, she found a pin. Holding it in her hand, she pretended to poke Patrick.

"Watch it! If it's a poking you want, it's a poking you'll get."

He snatched the pin from her and tossed it across the room. Grabbing her wrists, he held them above her head. Her laughter faded when his lips met hers.

Shifting to his side, Patrick trembled as he caressed her face. "I want to make love to you every day for the rest of our lives." With a groan, his hand pressed between her thighs. His eyes glinted with desire. "You're wet for me." Slowly he rubbed between her legs, smiling at the tremors coursing through her. "What an eager wench you are." He pressed two fingers in her heat, increasing her tension.

Her legs tightened around his hand, squeezing with each convulsion. Barely able to speak, she whispered, "I thought you liked eager wenches, darling."

His hand drifted up her narrow waist, lingering at sensitive nipples before settling on her lips. He slowly rubbed his fingers across her lips, inserting one in her mouth. He glided in and out as she sucked on his finger. Her hips bucked with the motion of his finger. Without warning, he flipped her on her stomach. He pulled her hips up to him and thrust her legs apart. A deep groan of pleasure split the air as he thrust in her heat.

Ann gripped the sheet as she jerked with each movement. Her body was not hers to command. Every touch, every look was filled with need and desire. She knew Patrick was her destiny. Though separated by time, they had somehow found one another. Ann succumbed to the roaring passion that demanded satisfaction. Crying out her release, Ann drew Patrick closer. Their hearts beat as one. Their souls fused together for eternity.

The entire household was in an uproar as the carriages were loaded for the trip to London. Patrick rolled his eyes as another trunk was brought outside. "Do you have to take everything you own? We'll only be gone for a couple of months."

"You're the one who encouraged me to get those extra dresses. I can't wad them up and stuff them in one trunk. That's why we need so many trunks."

He threw up his hands in mock despair. "I should have learned years ago never to expect to win an argument with a woman."

She stuck out her tongue at him. The servants loading the carriage burst out laughing at the surprised look on Patrick's face. Ann ran to the house as Patrick stalked after her, muttering about disobedient wives.

She was going to London! The stories she could tell her future grandchildren. Her smile faded as thoughts of Mark and Jessica flashed before her. Suddenly, the trip held no interest. She leaned back against the tufted leather cushions and closed her eyes.

"What's wrong, dearest? You look sad all of a sudden."

"I was thinking of the past ... I mean the future. Whatever it is! I miss Mark and Jessica. I love them so much."

Patrick massaged her tight shoulders. "Of course you love them. That is one of the reasons that I love you. But if you went back to your old life, I would go insane. I can't believe this miracle would have happened if it wasn't going to work out in the end. Perhaps this is some test that the two of us must endure."

Ann wiped the tears trailing down her cheek. "I get so impatient. If we only knew how things were supposed to be. I guess there are no certainties in this life, are there?"

Patrick kissed her gently on her forehead as she drifted off to sleep.

It was dusk before they arrived at the towering limestone house located near St. James's Park. The neighboring homes all exhibited the opulence of the era. Ann stood on the walk, gawking at the picturesque surroundings. Nannies hurried past with their charges as darkness set upon them. Young girls in pinafores called good night to each other. Elegant carriages rolled down the street, transporting their passengers to their homes.

Ann was dazzled by the vision. "I feel like Alice in Wonderland."

Patrick flashed a disarming smile and took her elbow. "Come, let's go inside. The fog is rolling in."

She pulled back and tilted her head, gazing up at the outside of the three-story house. "I can't believe you own this wonderful house."

"The house may be wonderful, but it is not as beautiful as you, my darling."

"Are all men in the nineteenth century so complimentary?"

"What's wrong with letting my wife know how I feel?"

"Thank you. You're right. I can't believe my luck in finding such a wonderful man." Ann touched his whiskered cheek. "Oh dear, I believe you are blushing."

"Humph," Patrick muttered as he led Ann to where servants were lined up for introductions. The housekeeper, Maggie, had arrived ahead of them and galvanized the entire household. Taking their wraps, a maid led them to the sitting room. It was a large airy room with a huge bay window facing the street. Numerous potted ferns adorned the corners. The sofa and chairs were a soft cream color, which offset the dark blue velvet drapes that dressed the windows.

Maggie briskly addressed one of the nearby servants. "Lizzie, please bring in the tea and brandy after you put the coats away."

Patrick walked toward the window, briefly glancing outside before drawing the curtain closed. "How are we doing, Maggie?"

"Everything is in order. I'll send someone to the market tomorrow for fresh provisions. Perhaps Lady O'Neil and I could sit down in the morning and go over things."

Ann rubbed her hip. "If I can walk again. I had no idea that riding in a carriage all day could be so painful."

Noticing the housekeeper's puzzled look, she hastily added, "It has been so long since I have ridden that distance in a carriage. I had forgotten how tiring it is."

Maggie gasped. "Oh my. I will have a warm bath drawn immediately to help you relax."

After the servants left, Ann slipped off her shoes and sipped the hot tea. Peeping over the brim of the teacup, she watched Patrick. "Why were you looking out the window a few minutes ago? Is there anything wrong?"

Patrick stiffened as he turned toward her. "Just gazing about. Edward's home is across the park. I was curious to see whether he had returned to London yet. He and I frequently visit White's together."

"Isn't White's one of those men's clubs?"

"Yes, it's the oldest club in London. It was built in 1693." Patrick frowned. "I know what the impish look on your face means. Forget it. You cannot visit the club."

"Heaven forbid that a woman invade a bastion of male dominance. Just you wait until the next century, Lord O'Neil."

Patrick kissed the tip of her nose. He returned to the window several times before drawing the curtains.

Patrick looked worried about something. Ann said, "You keep looking out the window. Is someone out there?"

"I'm not sure. I thought I spotted someone watching the house earlier. No one is there now."

Ann wondered if it could be David. For his sake, she hoped not. Patrick would kill him. Yawning, she covered her mouth with her hand. The next thing she knew, Patrick was carrying her up the stairs to bed. Traveling in the nineteenth century was exhausting.

At breakfast, Ann discovered that Patrick had left the house to take care of business matters. Ann found tidbits of society gossip in the newspaper. It detailed who was marrying whom, who was entertaining guests from other countries, and who was who in society. Intrigued, she studied the paper, trying to sort out the players in her new social sphere.

After reading the paper, Ann spent time exploring the house. She loved the spaciousness of the sitting room and the large windows that nearly reached the ceiling. The street flowed with activity of everyday life. Carriages rolled up the street, making frequent stops.

What was going on? A carriage stopped in front of their house. Minutes later, the bell rang. Curious, she resisted the temptation to answer the door herself. Minutes later, the butler entered and laid several cards on a salver.

Ann picked up the cards and smiled. She remembered reading about calling cards in etiquette books. Turning over each card, she recognized many of the names from the newspaper. Edward had sent a card announcing that he was in town and wanted to get together soon. Ann gazed out the window again and sighed wistfully. Boredom had set in. She would surprise Edward with a visit. Ringing for her maid, Ann hurried to change clothes. She had learned that there was a dress for every occasion.

Ann was fastening her cloak when she saw Maggie passing down the hall.

"My lady, are you going out?"

"Yes. A card arrived from Lord Marshall. I thought I would stop by and say hello."

Maggie's brows shot up in surprise. "Ma'am, it's not even one o'clock. If you insist, I will have Blanche accompany you. You mustn't visit a single man unaccompanied."

"Why not? We've been introduced, and he's a friend of ours." Ann grew frustrated. "I can't believe all the crazy rules you have for women. In my time, I ..."

Maggie stared questioningly at her. The sound of male voices drifted up the stairs. Ann rushed to the hallway and peered over the banister. Her husband handed his coat to the butler, his dark hair gleaming in the morning light. Ann hurried down to meet him, her feet barely touching the steps. "Patrick, I need to talk to you."

Ann waved a card in front of his face. "See this? Edward sent us a card. Being courteous, I thought I would visit him and invite him to dinner. Maggie has suggested that I should not go out of the house alone. And by no means should I visit a single man without a chaperone. I don't know that I can live like this." By the end of her tirade, her face had become flushed.

"Let's go into the library." Shutting the door behind them, Patrick held up his hands, fending her off. "Hold on. I don't make the rules. If a woman visits a single man by herself, then people probably will think the worst. I learned a long time ago that I had to follow the rules set by a pack of hypocrites if I was going to be accepted in society. I'll admit that men break many of the rules and do not suffer any consequences, especially if one has lots of money."

Ann squared her shoulders. "That's not fair. I'm used to taking care of myself and going where I want. You didn't marry a conventional woman."

He ran a finger lazily down the side of her cheek. He could only guess at the thoughts brewing in that brain of hers. "What does that mean, if I may inquire?"

"I'm just saying that I don't agree with all of the rules. So don't worry if I go out by myself."

The urge to throttle his fiery wife was growing stronger by the minute. "May I remind you that you are my wife? It is my responsibility to protect you from harm or gossip. At this moment, I am finding it difficult to remember that you came from another century. All I ask is that you use your head and do nothing that will create a scandal or bring harm upon yourself."

"I'm not stupid. I won't do anything to harm the O'Neil name. If I knew you were going to be so stodgy about this, I never would have brought it up."

A feeling of guilt washed over him. He could be domineering from time to time, but that was a man's right. A husband needed to protect his wife, even if she thought she didn't need protection.

Wanting to create a diversion, he snatched her hand and headed for the door. "Come with me. I'm going to show you the real London."

Somewhat mollified, she shrugged her shoulders. "Anything is better than sitting here all day."

Before their carriage pulled away from the house, another carriage drew alongside. Hearing a voice call Patrick's name, they turned to see Edward waving at them.

"I see we're all out making the rounds. Good day, Lady O'Neil. I didn't see you. I hope you're doing well."

Ann smiled and leaned past her husband. "I am. Thank you. I was going to call on you today and invite you for dinner."

"Wonderful. I have some surprising news to share with you. My wife and I would love to join you for dinner."

Patrick began to choke. "Excuse me! Wife? Who is she? Wait—let me guess. Viscount Bramberly's daughter? If I remember correctly, she is a fair brunette with a pleasant disposition. She has suitable family connections and decent income from a trust."

Edward shook his head. "I married Lady Paxton."

Patrick remembered to close his mouth. He knew that the two of them had an on-and-off relationship. Why did he marry her? Unfortunately, the middle of the street was not the place to discuss this private matter.

Patrick managed a few words. "Congratulations. We would still like the two of you to join us for dinner tomorrow."

Edward accepted and waved as his carriage pulled away. Before Patrick could say anything, Ann's elbow jabbed him in the ribs.

"Pleasant disposition! A decent income! It sounded as if you were discussing a broodmare. Good heavens, I can only imagine what you men say when there aren't any women around."

"Did you hear what he said? He married Katherine! She'll destroy him. How can he trust her? What does he see in her?"

"You men always go for the women who are stacked."

"Stacked?"

"You know. Women with prominent breasts, big boobs, or whatever else you call them."

Winking, he asked. "What's wrong with *big boobs*? I personally like a nice handful."

Ann's chin jutted upward. "Hush, Patrick. You're going to get it."

He pulled her onto his lap, ignoring her protests. Brushing aside silky curls, his lips nibbled her ear. "Get it? Madam, I am looking forward to *getting it* tonight." His tongue swirled the contours of her ear.

He concentrated on giving her something else to think about. So she thought he needed to be educated about women's rights ... That would be a challenge he'd look forward to.

Chapter 38

THE JOURNEY TOOK THEM down Bond Street and Regent Street, where many of the posh shops were located. It wasn't an outlet mall, but it would suffice. Past Buckingham Palace and over the Thames River they went. Ann stared at the activity along the streets. Children ran about playing games when they should have been in school, except there wasn't compulsory education until 1880. At one point, she covered her nose to block the stench of manure and sewage. The privilege of wealth definitely had its advantage.

She and Patrick had a great time taking in all the sights. She could not imagine a life without him. Ready for a stretch break, Patrick suggested they stop at a coffee shop for refreshments. Alighting from the carriage, they spotted Anthony and a young woman.

Clapping each other on the back, the two men greeted one another. Anthony kissed Ann on the cheek. "I understand that you two have met Miss Eleanor Curtis."

Patrick nodded to the young woman. Ann greeted her warmly. "Yes, I remember meeting her and her family at the wedding. It is so nice to see you again. Anthony, I wasn't aware that you knew Miss Curtis."

Ann had to bite back her giggles, as Anthony looked a little surprised at her comment.

"Miss Curtis and I had the opportunity to speak on several

occasions last season. Her father is one of my business associates. Not to change the subject, but you two look positively beaming. It's good to know that marriage is not too much of a drudgery."

Patrick draped his arm over Ann's shoulder. Joking with Anthony, he remarked, "I have married a most independent woman. When you get married, I'll have several pointers for you, specifically about business matters. Ann wants to know everything about my business. She has threatened to bash me with an umbrella if I don't share information."

Eleanor studied Lady O'Neil. "Surely you jest, Lord O'Neil. Your wife certainly realizes that business matters are better handled by the husband."

Patrick threw his head back, roaring with laughter. Ann punched his arm. "Ignore my husband, Miss Curtis. It would behoove more women to take an interest in their husband's business. If something happens, you will have the ability to step in and manage things. Besides, you want to make sure that you are not being cheated."

Ann liked Eleanor's looks. She was attractive, with sandy brown hair, hazel eyes, and a creamy complexion. She was not like the sophisticated women Anthony frequently escorted about town.

Patrick and Anthony were now laughing, and Ann sent Patrick another warning look.

"Allow me to clarify the situation, Miss Curtis," Ann continued. "Women must bear the burden of marriage. *Our* lives are changed, not theirs. *They* continue with their daily routine while we're left at home. Patrick likes to joke, but if I tried to bash him with anything, he would probably lock me in the bedroom."

Anthony took Eleanor's elbow, leading the way into the coffee shop. "Stop. You two will frighten Miss Curtis. Heaven knows what she already thinks of you."

With a wicked leer, Patrick swept his wife into his arms and branded her with a deep passionate kiss.

Minutes went by before Anthony nudged them. "Come, come. You have the rest of your lives to do that. Miss Curtis and I are thirsty. Are you joining us?"

As the men ordered their drinks, Eleanor leaned closer to Lady O'Neil. "Is your husband always so demonstrative?"

"Believe me, you want a man that tells you he loves you and needs you. Though he takes me by surprise at times, it's fun not knowing what he's going to do next."

Ann saw Eleanor glance at Anthony. The young woman was definitely attracted to the dashing Lord Aylesbury. The longing on Eleanor's face was visible for only a second. Ann laid her hand on Eleanor's. "Forgive my boldness but Anthony seems taken with you. If you care as much as I think you do, then don't hesitate to let him know. Surprise him."

"I'm not sure I understand."

"Sure you do. Let your heart guide you."

Ann enjoyed the visit with Anthony and Eleanor. She'd missed Stacy and their private girl talks. Maybe Eleanor would fill that void.

Early the next morning, the bell rang. It was an invitation from Eleanor. Patrick frowned as Ann planned to go out for a drive. He wore a disapproving husband look.

"Oh, don't be such a fuddy-duddy. What harm can come to two women in broad daylight?"

"You know that I have hired an investigator to find David. But you're probably right. Be careful and do not go wandering off on your own. Take a servant with you."

After lunch, Patrick left to meet Anthony at White's. Ann wasn't quite sure what one did at those bastions of male dominance but it would be interesting to walk in and see for herself. Amusement lit up her face as she imagined walking into White's coffee room and demanding to be served. Playing a docile wife in public was stretching her acting abilities.

When Eleanor's carriage pulled up, Ann darted out the door before the driver could ring the bell. Ann tucked her skirts about her, smiling at her companion. "This is a wonderful idea! I couldn't stay in that house any longer."

Eleanor sighed. "My mother suggested that a ride would put color in my cheeks. She wants me to be seen in the best possible light for fear that no man will declare for me otherwise. She is afraid that I will have my heart broken by Lord Aylesbury."

Ann patted the girl's hand comfortingly. "I thought you had a crush on Anthony."

"I assume by a crush, you mean an attachment. I do care," she pouted, "but he thinks that I'm a child, not a woman. Could you help me win his heart?"

Ann smiled. The wheels in her brain churned away. "I'd love to. Now that you and I are friends, what would be more natural than your coming to dinner when Anthony happens to be there? I'm the perfect chaperone. Even your mother will approve."

Their strategy completed, the women returned home to set their plan into action. Giving the young woman a thumbs-up sign, Ann hurried into the house and was greeted by the sight of her husband and Anthony.

Tucking a stray curl in place, she grinned impishly at Patrick. "See, I have returned unharmed."

He seized her by the hand and pulled her to his side. "Don't patronize me, my dear. As your husband, I have the right to worry."

She escaped his grasp away while Anthony grinned at their antics. "Patrick, we have company. Behave yourself. Let's sit down and I'll have refreshments brought in."

The men settled back and humored her with the gossip from the club. A mutual friend was being led to the altar.

Anthony shook his head. "I can't believe James was so careless. He should limit his amorous attentions to women who are experienced. Now that I'm the only one from our set who is unmarried, Mother believes she is destined to never have grandchildren."

"Marriage isn't half bad. I endorse it very much." Patrick's warm gaze caressed her from across the room. Ann felt herself blushing from the heat in his gaze. It seemed she wasn't the only one remembering their night in bed. She almost laughed as she watched him shifting uncomfortably in the chair.

Ignoring her husband's predatory stare, Ann turned to Anthony.

"I think you should consider marriage. What about the nice young woman you were with yesterday? She was quite lovely. Don't you agree, Patrick?"

Patrick shot his friend a warning look. "I fear a plot is afoot, my friend. If you're not careful, you'll be married before you know it."

Grabbing the corner of an embroidered pillow, Ann tossed it at her husband while Anthony laughed loudly. "You're giving Anthony the wrong idea. Now Anthony thinks marriage is comparable to being shackled."

Apologetic, Anthony said, "I hate to see a beautiful woman distraught. How can I make it up to you?"

Ann beamed with satisfaction. "Edward and Katherine are coming to dinner tonight. I would be more comfortable if someone else were here to temper the situation. After all, what does one say to her husband's ex-mistress?"

Anthony glanced at Patrick. Smiling, he accepted the invitation. Anthony stood to take his leave "Patrick, I am trusting you to protect me from any of your wife's machinations."

Walking his friend to the door, Patrick reassured Anthony. "You can count on it."

With a wave good-bye, Anthony left.

Alone again, Patrick stretched out his legs and stared thoughtfully at Ann.

"Well," she said, "I should go let Maggie know that there will be extra people for dinner."

"People, as in more than three?"

"I may have invited Miss Curtis to dinner tonight; I really don't remember. Now I have things to do so please excuse me."

Snatching her by the hand as she attempted to leave the room, Patrick's warm lips traced the curve of her palm. Lifting up his head, a lock fell across his brow. "If this evening becomes a fiasco, just remember I told you so. In spite of his mother, Anthony is determined not to marry. Although I think he may have some feelings for Eleanor, I wouldn't want to raise her hopes. Anthony is my friend and I don't want him to feel uncomfortable in our home."

She ran her hand down the side of his jaw, tracing the masculine contours. "Don't worry. I have everything under control." Except her emotions.

Patrick's hand lifted her skirts and inched up her thigh. Concerned they might be discovered, she intercepted his hand.

"I thought women of your time were liberated."

Foolishly, she attempted to wiggle out of his reach. Loose curls fell across her cheek. "I thought men in this time were prudish."

Before she could utter another word, he tossed her over his shoulder. With her head dangling down toward the floor, she bobbed up and down with laughter.

Swatting her bottom playfully, Patrick huskily ordered, "Be still, wife. I'm about to show you how prudish I really am."

More than one servant gaped in amazement as the Lord carried his giggling wife up the stairs. Using his foot, he kicked their bedroom door open. A quick movement shut the door. Tossing Ann on the bed, he jerked up her skirts before her body quit bouncing. He tore the undergarments with one rip. He smiled as he exposed her bottom. Pressing her thighs apart, his mouth pressed to her flesh. Her soft moans filled the air. He could fulfill every fantasy she ever had. He stood long enough to remove his clothes. His heated gaze held her to the bed. Her glazed eyes caressed every muscle on his frame, lingering on his manhood. He slowly lowered himself, pressing into her heat, his gaze never leaving hers.

Every moment spent in each other's arms brought them closer together, forging a unified bond that time could not destroy. Every touch and caress fueled a growing need that neither one could deny.

Damp from their passionate exertion, Patrick pressed a kiss to her forehead. "I'm like a schoolboy with no control over my desires. I can't imagine what the servants are thinking."

Listening to the pounding of his heart, Ann smiled. She never thought that she could be happy in nineteenth-century England, yet she was.

Chapter 39

PATRICK STRODE INTO ANN'S dressing room unannounced. "I see you decided to wear the plum silk. An excellent choice, dearest. You look ravishing as always." With a quick glance at his watch, he smiled. "Are you ready? Everyone should be here any minute."

They descended the stairs as the bell rang. Anthony entered, attired in a dark maroon jacket and black trousers with a tonal stripe up the outside of each leg. His silk top hat had a cashmere-lined brim, just as Patrick's hat did.

Anthony rubbed his hands together. "Good! No one else is here yet. I came early so I wouldn't miss any of the fireworks."

Sparks shot from Patrick's eyes, silently warning his friend. "I think you're blowing this situation out of proportion. Remember, you're here to help, not to add fuel to the fire."

"Tsk-tsk," Anthony admonished. "A little touchy, aren't you?" He stood by the fire, brushing a fine sheen of mist from his brow. "The fog is dreadful. I could barely see your house."

The bell rang again. Patrick tensed. Would Katherine humiliate Edward by flirting with him? Heaven knew what Ann would do if Katherine made any intimate gestures toward him. He rubbed his sweaty palms together.

Minutes later, Edward and Katherine joined their hosts in the sitting room. Patrick greeted them, but his gaze lingered on Katherine.

Ann's elbow hit his side, jolting him into being a gracious host. He broke the uncomfortable silence by offering drinks. Surprisingly, conversation continued without any uncomfortable lapses. When dinner was announced, Patrick looked questioningly at Ann. Where was Eleanor? Ann nodded toward the front door and left the room.

Patrick led the guests into the dining room. Anthony looked at the table with six place settings. "Are you expecting someone else?"

The chatter ceased as Ann and Eleanor entered the room. "I believe everyone here knows Miss Curtis. I thought I invited her to dinner tomorrow night. Silly me, I mistakenly told her tonight. Thank goodness one of Patrick's friends canceled at the last minute and we have an additional setting all arranged. Now, everyone, please be seated."

Patrick warmly greeted Eleanor. Anthony glared at Patrick, who grinned back. Ann flashed Patrick an odd look, noticing that Katherine sat next to him. Throughout dinner, Anthony speared the food on his plate, contributing little to the conversation. Eleanor sat across from Anthony but rarely looked up from her plate. Patrick shot Ann I-told-you-so glances every few minutes.

Patrick broke the uneasy silence. "Edward and Katherine, we were surprised to hear of your marriage. I think I speak for all of us when I say that we wish the two of you a long and happy marriage." Patrick raised his glass with the others in a toast.

Edward gazed at Katherine. "It was sudden, but we've known each other for years and decided not to wait any longer. We are hosting a small dinner party on Saturday. You are all invited, of course." Edward chuckled. "Now that I'm married, Anthony, I imagine your mother is pressing you."

Anthony grudgingly smiled. "Yes. She's convinced that she'll go to her grave with no grandchildren. I avoid visiting her unless absolutely necessary."

Ann quickly added, "Katherine, if there is anything I can do to help you and Edward, don't hesitate to call on me. I know how stressful everything is when you are first married. I'm thankful Patrick and I had some time alone to become better acquainted."

Katherine gave Ann a nod. "How kind. Even though Edward and I are well acquainted, there are adjustments."

As the conversation flowed on about the state of matrimony, Anthony's stomach roiled. He did not know who planned this debacle tonight, but Patrick was going to hear about it. Being a gentleman, he couldn't eat and take his leave. Eleanor would be without a partner for the evening, so he was obligated to stay. Or so he convinced himself.

After dinner, Ann suggested they play a game of charades. She volunteered to go first. Within minutes, the entire group dissolved with laughter. Furtive glances between Anthony and Eleanor were numerous, but by the end of the evening, they had barely spoken to one another.

Finally, Anthony was able to make his excuses and bid everyone good night. He settled back in the carriage, sighing a breath of relief. He was strung so tightly that he didn't know what would happen if he and Eleanor were alone with one another. He felt like a bore for ignoring her, but damn it all, he hated being manipulated.

Her creamy complexion and full lips had invited his gaze more than once. She had the right connections, an acceptable upbringing, and was extremely pleasant to look at. In other words, she was the perfect woman. He wasn't averse to being married; he just wanted to make sure it was the right woman. He had too many friends who married only for money or connections. He was determined not to live under such false pretenses. Now that he was invited to the party at the Marshalls', he would have to put in an appearance, as would Eleanor. With a calculating smile, he realized that he looked forward to seeing her again.

Waving farewell to the last of their guests, a shadow under a nearby light post caught Patrick's attention. In the penetrating fog, the man's features were obscured. For days, Patrick had had the feeling of being watched, but he'd never seen anything out of the ordinary until tonight.

The lights inside the O'Neil home dimmed. The man, lurking in the shadows for hours, waiting and watching, came forward. Pulling the collar of the coat around his face, a sinister smile distorted his features. Dampened locks framed his face. He whistled for the hired coach waiting beyond the corner. This was too easy, he mused.

Chapter 40

THE DAY OF THE Marshall party had arrived. Ann chose an amber silk gown that accented the color of her skin and hair.

Patrick called from downstairs. "Are you ready? We're going to be exceptionally late." His eyes raked her body as she descended the stairs. "I've changed my mind about going out tonight."

"Oh, no. I need to be there for Eleanor."

Draping a cape about her shoulders, he sighed and reluctantly opened the door. "I tried. Our carriage awaits, madam."

They shortly arrived at the Marshalls' townhome. Edward greeted them at the doorway, looking harried. He gave Ann a quick kiss on the cheek. "Katherine is upstairs. She believes the party will be a disaster and that I regret marrying her. Could you try to talk some sense into her?" he pleaded.

She had intended to be friendly to Katherine for the sakes of their husbands, but being confidants was a thought that had not entered her mind. The distressed look on Edward's face convinced her to at least try. "I'm not sure she will appreciate any advice that I offer, but I'll do my best."

Ann knocked softly on Katherine's dressing room door. After a few moments, Ann entered. Katherine sat at the dressing table, tears silently falling.

"Excuse me for intruding. Edward asked that I check on you."

Katherine hastily wiped her eyes and glared at Ann. "Thank you, but it isn't necessary. Tell Edward that I'll be down shortly." She sighed when she realized that Ann was not leaving. "What do you want?"

"I am as uncomfortable about this as you are, but our husbands are friends, so you and I will have to put the past behind us. However, if you ever make a pass at Patrick, you'll have to deal with me. As long as I know that you have no further designs on *my* husband, I believe we can get along quite well together." As a peace offering, Ann held out her hand to Katherine and waited.

Katherine took the offered hand. Suddenly, they both burst out laughing. "You know why I never liked you?" Katherine asked. "I thought you were some timid little mouse with no backbone. Now I think we'll be good friends."

"Let's go join the other guests. I'm sure our husbands are wondering if we've strangled each other."

Both men waited at the bottom of the stairway. Relief shone on their faces as the two women walked arm in arm toward them.

Ann saw the guests streaming through the doorway. That should put Katherine's fears to rest. She knew that many of the women distrusted Katherine, but it seemed they were willing to give her the benefit of the doubt.

Ann couldn't get over the extravagance and wealth of the mingling crowd. Even the wealthiest socialite in the twenty-first century would be in awe. The music room was made to serve as the ballroom. Couples twirled to the latest waltz and followed the intricate steps of the cotillion.

Heat from the numerous candles and the press of people became too much. Ann needed some fresh air. Unable to find Patrick, she walked outside. The cool night air washed over her bare shoulders. Several couples strolled by, oblivious to her presence. She watched the gentle night breeze playfully tease the flowers throughout the elaborate garden. From the shadows, she heard the sound of someone calling her name. Turning she saw only darkness.

"Who's there?" she demanded.

Uneasy, she backed toward the doors. Her heart pounded in her throat. Before she reached the doorway, a hand seized her arm. She whipped around to see William drunkenly swaying.

"What are you doing here?" she snapped.

He tightened his grip. "I'm enjoying the party. It has been a while since you've helped out your father."

Ann struggled to remain calm, when all she wanted to do was scream. "What do you want?" The air reeked of his foul breath. Ann covered her nose.

William was staring at her topaz necklace and matching bracelet. Unconsciously, she raised her hand to cover the large stone gracing her neck.

He boldly stated, "I require additional funds. Epsom Downs has proved unlucky this year. I approached your brother, but he refused me. He had the gall to say that his money had to go for seed next year. The ungrateful whelp. He'll get nothing from me later on, you wait and see."

Ann stared at the disheveled man. His clothes were stained and unkempt. "I gave you everything I could last time. If Patrick ever finds out, he'll be furious. I can't contribute to someone who throws money away on booze and gambling."

He yanked her shoulders and shook her. Ann's head snapped back and forth like a rag doll. Snatching the bracelet off her wrist, William stuffed it in his pocket.

"Bitch, don't argue with me! You'll do as you're told." Straightening his jacket, he swaggered off across the lawn.

Ann felt ill. He was crazy. She had to find Malcolm. He would help her get the bracelet back. Spotting her reflection in the windows, Ann hastily pinned up her hair.

Weaving between couples in the ballroom, she spotted Patrick. From the look on his face, he had been looking for her.

He took in her tousled appearance and growled, "What happened?"

She sagged against his shoulder. "I feel a little faint. I need to sit down."

Patrick helped her to a chair and then hurried off to get some water. He returned with Anthony in tow. Both hovered over her until she convinced them that she was fine. It took an hour before the men left her side and gravitated to other guests.

Ann saw Eleanor standing alone and went over to visit with her. "Thank goodness you're here," Eleanor said. "I was feeling quite alone until I saw you. I believe the entire *ton* is here tonight. Have you seen Lord Aylesbury?"

"Yes, I have. He's coming this way. If you will excuse me, I'll allow you two a moment of privacy."

Abruptly turning, Eleanor slammed against his chest. A crimson flush enveloped her cheeks as she met Anthony's amused gaze. "Oh, excuse me! I was unaware that you were there."

Anthony's pulse raced. "My apologies. I've startled you."

Over Eleanor's shoulder, he spotted Lady Weston and her gangly daughter. Muttering under his breath, Anthony took Eleanor's hand, heading toward the dance floor. Anthony sighed with relief as the music started.

"You can relax now. You've escaped the clutches of Lady Weston."

The woman in his arms surprised him with mischief dancing in her eyes. "I suppose you find it amusing? She is unrelenting. Every time I turn around, there she is, fluttering about and batting her lashes. It's most disconcerting."

Eleanor giggled at his comments. He supposed it was highly amusing that a man of his age and stature could be so intimidated by two women.

The time with Eleanor in his arms ended too soon. The music had barely died away when several young men approached Eleanor for a dance. Annoyed with the bevy of would-be suitors, Anthony reluctantly watched a young man take her in his arms. His gaze followed her slender figure as she whirled about the room. The vein in his neck throbbed when her partner's hand slid below her waist. Damn it all! What was the matter with him? He was too old to be standing here mooning over a girl barely out of the schoolroom. Why should he care? But no matter how hard he tried to pretend indifference, all he saw was her pale skin, which glistened like iridescent pearls. Her breathless laugh made men fantasize about discovering her other hidden attributes. By the size of the group of admirers that seemed to follow her, he doubted he would be able to claim a second dance. Frustrated, he found his way back to his friends.

∞

Ann was acting odd, as if she were hiding something. Her ashen complexion and shadowed eyes worried Patrick. He called for their carriage and wraps, anxious to get her home.

Standing next to him, Anthony asked, "May I ride with you? I don't know why I attend these social functions." Anthony glanced back at the crowded ballroom one last time. "There's little here to convince me to stay. Besides, if I have to listen to Lady Weston praise the attributes of her daughter one more time, I shall commit myself to Bedlam."

The three of them said their good-byes and hurried to the carriage.

Patrick choked back a laugh as he climbed into the carriage. "Social events and balls are one of the hardships you bachelors must endure. I consider myself lucky to have escaped those horrid encounters."

"If you men gave women the same rights that you have, perhaps they wouldn't be so determined to marry. A financially secure woman needs no one but herself." Folding her arms across her chest, Ann glared furiously at both men.

Anthony snorted. "If that's what it takes to get the Westons off my scent, by gads, I shall send a fortune to Miss Weston and sign it from an anonymous admirer."

Patrick and Anthony roared with laughter. As the men bantered, Ann's look of annoyance grew.

Once Anthony was let off, Patrick pulled Ann onto his lap. His lips tenderly brushed her forehead while his fingers stroked the side of her neck. All too soon, the carriage arrived home.

As they readied for bed, Ann sat at the dressing table brushing her hair. The golden highlights in her hair shimmered in the subdued glow of the room. Patrick stared, hypnotized by the movements of the silken strands.

He jerked to his feet when he spotted a red welt on her wrist. "What happened? The scratch wasn't there earlier."

The color drained from Ann's face. "It's nothing. I scraped it." She hurried to the bed and pulled up the covers. She wouldn't meet his gaze.

"Perhaps I should check the bracelet to see why it scratched your skin."

"That really isn't necessary." Pulling back the covers, she seductively arched her back. "Come to bed. I need you tonight."

His body was ready to leap into bed, but his mind was suspicious. Opening the armoire, Patrick removed the locked chest. He wordlessly gazed at her, giving her one last opportunity for the truth. He ripped off the small lock, shattering the hinges. Restraining the impulse to shake his pale wife, he dumped the box in her lap.

"Where is the bracelet?"

Ann shrugged her shoulders and reached for his hand. "Oh, I'm sure it's here somewhere. I'll find it tomorrow. Maybe it fell off in the carriage or at the Marshalls'. Please ... I don't want to talk about it."

What was she trying to hide? She knew the importance of the bracelet. Only a few family jewels had been salvaged when his family left Ireland. The pieces had been in the family for several generations. By God, he must know what was causing her odd behavior.

"Ann, I must know what happened. I'm not a fool. I know when there's something wrong. I mistakenly assumed you were ill earlier this evening, but I was wrong, wasn't I?"

Ann buried her face in her hands. "William has accrued large gaming debts again. Malcolm refused him, so he approached me. He thinks that I can ask you for money whenever I want. Of course, I refused. I tried to walk away, but he grabbed me and ripped off the bracelet. I feel horrible. I should have fought harder."

Patrick clutched Ann to him. "Did he hurt you?"

Ann started to cry. "I planned to contact Malcolm, so he could try to get it back before William sold it."

He tilted back her head, wiping the tears away with his thumb. Examining her wrist again, he muttered an oath. "Never mind the jewelry. Thank God you're safe. William is never to enter our house again."

"If he finds out that I'm not Victoria, it's hard telling what he will do."

"Let me worry about that. Let's get you tucked into bed."

"What are you going to do?"

Patrick bent and kissed her forehead. "I need to work on a few things. I will join you shortly." He pulled the covers around her shoulders, pressing his lips to hers. His gaze locked with hers, and his willpower nearly dissolved. Undeterred, he walked to the door, closing it softly behind him.

He stormed into the library and rang for the butler. The elderly servant took one look at his employer and clearly knew that something was wrong. The dedicated servant hurried from the room with a list of orders. Within minutes, two burly men in his employment stood before Patrick.

"Here is the address of Baron Montgomery. I want you two to watch his house twenty-four hours a day. Report to me twice a day. If anyone enters or leaves that house, I want to know about it. Is that clear?"

Both men nodded vigorously. Dismissed, they almost ran into each other trying to get out of the room.

Patrick didn't know how long he sat in the darkness, simmering with anger. When the partially closed drapes reflected the pinkish glow of the rising sun, he stood. He climbed the stairs to where his wife slept. She was wound in a cocoon of white. Tangled auburn curls covered the pillows. Regret tugged at his heart, for he knew that the situation with the Montgomery family was about to get worse. He knew that Malcolm was like a real brother to Ann, but

Patrick wasn't sure if the two men had contrived this scheme or not. Until the truth was known, he preferred Malcolm's absence.

Climbing into bed, he pulled her closer, kissing the top of her curls. He had to protect Ann by whatever means. Their vow of "until death do us part" was taking on a new meaning, one he refused to accept.

Chapter 41

IF NOT FOR THE indentation on the pillow, Ann wouldn't have known that Patrick had come to bed. She quickly dressed, hoping to visit with him before he left the house. Patrick and Anthony ceased speaking when she entered the dining room. Seeing the grim looks on their faces, Ann felt like an interloper.

She flashed Anthony a smile and helped herself to a warm blueberry scone and coffee.

"Don't let me interrupt. Go ahead and continue whatever you were talking about before I came in."

Ann couldn't interpret the strange glance the men gave one another. Anthony pushed back his chair and announced, "My regrets, but I have a business matter that requires my attention."

After Anthony left, Patrick fidgeted in his chair and continually glanced at the clock.

Ann smiled knowingly. "If you must leave, go ahead. I have things to do also."

His stern countenance softened as he lightly kissed her cheek. "I don't want you leaving the house alone." Nearing the doorway, he turned and flashed a heated look. "Don't make any plans for the evening. We have a rendezvous."

On her own, Ann hurried to the library and dispatched a note to Malcolm. Minutes later, a maid announced the arrival of Eleanor.

Looking positively giddy, Eleanor blurted out, "I apologize for disturbing you this early in the day, but I have the most wonderful news. Anthony has invited me to a recital. He is the handsomest man in London. A true gentleman." A dreamy look transformed the young woman's face.

Ann smiled. "He couldn't take his eyes off you last night. Every time someone asked you to dance, he scowled."

"He did? I wanted him to ask for a second dance, but he left. Did I do something wrong?"

Ann clasped their hands together. Her maternal instincts warmed to the shy young woman before her. "I believe quite the opposite is true. I almost feel sorry for him. He's trying so hard to remain aloof. Instead he is attracted to you like a bee is to honey."

Eleanor blushed. "Mother says I shouldn't get my hopes up, for he is quite a catch. She said that he preferred more mature women."

"Men want a kind, beautiful woman—a woman they can come home to, someone to raise their children, and most of all, a woman who is a friend. In other words, someone just like you. So don't get discouraged! You hang in there."

It was late afternoon when Malcolm's carriage pulled up to the house. He ran up the steps to meet her.

Malcolm wrapped his arm about Ann as they entered the house. "I received your note this morning. I am so sorry that you have to go through this. Have you heard anything from my father yet?"

"No, I haven't heard a word. Now that Patrick knows, we must try to get the bracelet back before someone gets hurt or killed."

Hitting his fists together, Malcolm cursed, "Damn him. His greed will be the destruction of us all." He knelt at Ann's side. Grim lines shadowed his tanned face. "I'm so ashamed. What must you think of me and this world you were suddenly thrust into?"

"I love being here. You've become like family to me. You must concentrate on the good work that you have done."

"What can I do? I thought if he stayed in London, he would realize he had to change or be ostracized. Who would have guessed his greed outweighed his pride?"

"You must find him and see if he still has the bracelet. Offer to buy it back. Give him whatever he wants. I must get it back for Patrick."

"I'll try, but once you offer to buy it, you're setting a precedent. You'll be paying forever."

"Don't worry about that. Patrick won't allow him to get near me again."

"I wish I shared your confidence. I will visit our residence here in London. If he's not there, I shall stay until he returns. You rest and try to relax. I'll call as soon as I have news."

Ann watched Malcolm slam the carriage door closed before it started down the street. His facial features were frozen with determination. He had a terrible burden to shoulder. Ann wished there was more she could do.

Malcolm didn't wait to be announced. He tore through the double doors of the brick town house. He burst into the library and came to an abrupt halt. A young man sat at his father's desk. The man's slender yet athletic build and fair complexion were similar to his own.

"I am the Honorable Malcolm Montgomery, and this is my family home. I'm looking for my father. Who the hell are you?"

"Well, good day to you. I am David Stewart. Your father stepped out for a while. He was kind enough to offer me a place to stay while I'm in London."

Malcolm disliked the stranger immediately. "Wonderful. I'll wait for my father."

David shrugged his shoulders. "It's your choice. Should I ring for something to drink? You look like you could use a stiff one."

Malcolm stared at David. "If you don't mind, I will ring, as this is my home." To break the uncomfortable silence that followed,

Malcolm asked, "Say, were you at Lord O'Neil's wedding? You look somewhat familiar."

Before David could respond, a servant entered with the drinks. When he set the tray on the desk, the bottle precariously tottered back and forth.

David caught the bottle before it fell. "You imbecile. Get back to the kitchen and stay there."

Malcolm watched the hunched-shouldered servant scurry out of the room. "I hate to ask, but do you have any idea who the new man is? He is definitely someone Father would not hire."

David scowled back at him. "He's my servant. Your father's servants got fed up and left. I guess they wanted to be paid. Jack is now butler, waiter, and groomsman—or whatever else we need. Unfortunately, he has the mind of a maggot. All brawn and no brains. Thank God we're not all like that."

Malcolm quietly sipped his drink. Why did David's name sound so familiar? There was something he should remember. What was it?

David quickly downed his drink. "I believe I saw you several months ago at a wedding. I attended the wedding with Lady Paxton. It was quite a shindig. That O'Neil guy must have tons of money." David paused as if remembering something. "I hear that the groom caught his new bride rolling in the hay with another man."

Malcolm nearly dropped the glass, for he had just realized that David was the man who tried to kill Ann. Malcolm gripped the edge of the desk and leaned toward David. "I know who you are and where you're from. You may be able to fool my father, but you are the devil personified. I will be damned if I will let you ruin Ann's life. I demand that you leave this house immediately!"

David's face crinkled with amusement. He walked from behind the desk and flicked an imaginary speck off his sleeve.

"No can do. I don't plan to leave, and I won't allow you to interfere with my plans. Now if you want to try to stop me, be my guest."

David's aggressive stance gave him pause. Torn with indecision, Malcolm felt he could hold his own in any fight, but instinctively he knew not to challenge David. The man was a scoundrel and a murderer. Malcolm had to protect Ann. He couldn't lose her also.

Cautiously, Malcolm backed away. There would be another day, another time to deal with this lunatic. "Just remember, I'll be watching you. If anything happens to Ann, I shall kill you myself. If you come near her, I will make sure you're not welcome anywhere in London."

Alone in his carriage, regret consumed Malcolm. He had let Ann down. He had not recovered the jewelry and he'd let David go free. His eyes filled with tears, despair threatening to overwhelm him.

David was furious. William had assured him that he would have access to the best homes while in London. Damn, the man had better keep his word. David held his throbbing head in his hands, trying to make the pain stop.

In a fit of rage, he threw the brandy bottle to the floor. "They'll regret their actions. All of them! All! All!"

David paced wildly about the room. His glazed eyes fixated. Tonight! He would start tonight and show them all that they had just pissed off the wrong guy.

Chapter 42

KATHERINE'S PARTY WAS THE talk of the town the next day. Even the prime minister had stopped by for a brief visit. She had never been happier. Edward was the perfect husband—patient and understanding by day and demanding at night. She was determined to make her marriage a success.

She glanced at the clock, wishing Edward would return. He had sent a note indicating that he and Patrick were working late. He expected to be home by eight. The grandfather clock in the hallway chimed nine times.

She dismissed the servants for the night so it would be just the two of them when he came home. The thought of what would follow was too delicious to contemplate as she prepared her bath.

Slipping into mountains of lavender-scented bubbles, she leaned back and enjoyed the warm sensations. The tips of her curls draped across her breasts. A feeling of contentment welled up inside. Pressing her thighs together, Katherine smiled seductively as the water trickled down the valley between her breasts. Her eyes drifted shut, imagining Edward's lips following the liquid trail.

A strange sound broke her reverie. She wetted her lips, expecting to see Edward walk through the door. Moments later, she decided it must have been her imagination, for the house was completely quiet. She resumed bathing, amused at her own impatience.

Katherine stepped out of the tub, mounds of bubbles sliding

downward, exposing her rounded bottom. Wrapped in a towel, she sat down in front of the mirror to brush her dampened curls. A draft of cool air grazed her back. She turned to glance at the closed bathroom door. She must be losing her mind. She swore the door had been open a few minutes ago.

She faced the mirror again, choking back a sob of terror. A masked man stood only inches behind her. The sound of his labored breathing filled the room. Though the black mask covered his face, glittering eyes watched her every movement. Instinctively, she swung the hand holding the brush at his head. A rough hand viciously grabbed the brush and threw it across the room. His hand pressed against her mouth before she could scream. A rag quickly took the place of his hand. A feeling of helplessness paralyzed her.

The man bound her hands together with a rope. He pulled her to the bed, where he unceremoniously tied her legs to the bedposts. He stood at the foot of the bed, watching her frightened struggles. A knife glistened in his hand.

The way he caressed the deadly blade filled Katherine with fear. Seized with determination to escape, she frantically pulled on the ropes.

He straddled her writhing figure, slapping her face, making her head snap to the side. "Lie still!" He poised the tip of the blade on her tear-stained cheek.

She panicked, earning her additional blows to her upper body. Defeated, her bloodied body lay still upon the once snow-white sheets.

He slowly lowered the blade, carving something into her cheek. Blood ebbed from the wound, flowing down her neck and shoulder.

"I've branded you with an S. Do you know what the S is for?" Through his muffled laughter, he goaded, "It stands for slut!"

That voice! Although disguised, she could never forget it. It was David! He was a madman. She squeezed her eyes shut, silently praying.

What if Edward arrived and found David in the house? David

would kill him! At that moment, she realized how deeply she loved Edward. Tears seeped from the corners of her eyes. She couldn't lose him, not now.

The wool cap made his face itch. He didn't want Katherine to know who her tormentor was, not yet anyway. He stood near the window, waiting for Edward's return. Apathetic, he stared at the sobbing woman on the bed, observing the blood drying on her face and neck. He wanted revenge for her betrayal and his humiliation at Edward's hands. Perhaps he should slice up the other cheek. Amused at the thought, he turned his sights back to the street below.

A carriage stopped at the front door, and Edward and Patrick hopped out. Damn! Another unexpected snag in his carefully laid plans. He couldn't overpower both of them. He needed to get out of here now. Trying the window, he found it wouldn't open. It was stuck. He grabbed a pillow and shielded his hand as he punched through the glass. He quickly climbed out on the ledge, knowing the noise would draw attention. From downstairs, a door opened, and a voice called Katherine's name. Gauging the distance to the neighboring roof, he paused only for a second before leaping, landing on both knees. Tonight had been the first strike. He slipped away into the ethereal shadows of the night.

Edward knew he was late. In fact, he could almost hear Katherine scolding him. He invited Patrick in for a drink, celebrating the conclusion of their business. Edward knew that in the presence of someone else, Katherine wouldn't fuss at him for being late. Ringing for a servant, he waited several minutes.

"Katherine must have given everyone the night off. She probably went to the opera without me."

Patrick shrugged. "How about a quick drink? Then I should get myself home or I'll have to deal with my own termagant."

Relaxing in front of the fire, the two men drank to their

successful business ventures. Suddenly, the sound of breaking glass echoed throughout the house. Startled, Edward dropped his glass on the carpet, his face ashen. What the hell! Vaulting out of his chair, he quickly removed two pistols from the desk drawer. The men took the stairs two at a time. Upon reaching the upstairs hallway, each went a separate direction to locate the source of the noise.

Horrible thoughts filled his mind as he searched for Katherine. Out of breath, Edward paused as he threw open their bedroom door. All he could see was blood and her unmoving body.

"No! No! Oh, God. Katherine!"

He knelt beside the bed, quickly cutting the ropes, holding his wife's limp body in his arms. Relief flooded him. She was still breathing. He saw Patrick running into the room.

Patrick gently touched his shoulder. "I'll send my driver to fetch a physician.

Edward's voice broke as he tried to answer. "Fine. Ple-please hurry. I cannot leave her."

He heard Patrick storming down the stairs. Minutes later, Patrick returned with a pitcher of water and a rag.

Edward crooned soft words of reassurance in an attempt to calm Katherine. He wet the rag and carefully dabbed the blood from her face. Edward blinked repeatedly, trying to clear the tears from his eyes. He cringed each time he touched her cheek.

As the extent of her injury became apparent, he hissed, "My God! Who would do such a despicable act?" Instantly regretting his outburst, he massaged her hand. "The cut doesn't appear to be very deep, darling. Are you hurt anywhere else?"

She took a deep breath, visibly trembling. "No, but I was so afraid."

As painful as it was, Edward had to ask. "Did he touch or violate you in any manner?"

She buried her face against his chest. "No. He heard you return and left through the window. I'm so thankful that you arrived when you did. I don't know what would have hap ..." She broke into tears once again.

Edward tightened his embrace, grateful that she was alive.

The bell rang, heralding the arrival of the physician. Within minutes, the unruffled man entered the bedroom. He thoroughly cleansed the wound and bandaged it. Taking a bottle of laudanum from his bag, the physician poured a few drops and mixed it with water. "Here, drink this. It will calm your nerves and help you sleep. I will stop by tomorrow to see how you are doing." Shutting his bag, he motioned for the men to join him downstairs.

Edward first helped his wife to a chair. He quickly stripped the bed of the sullied sheets and attempted to put clean ones on the bed. Under the effects of the quick-acting drug, Katherine fell asleep immediately. Carrying her back to the bed, he was able to get her into a clean nightgown.

He tucked the comforter about her and kissed her forehead. As he was about to turn away, she murmured, "It was David. David did this."

Gripping the bedposts, Edward was filled with rage. He had greatly underestimated David, and Katherine had paid for his error in judgment. Guilt consumed him. Never had he wanted to kill a man so badly. Right there, he vowed to avenge the attack on his wife.

Joining the men in the library, Edward's face reflected the grim situation. "Katherine just told me that David attacked her." Edward turned to his friend. "Patrick, I think you should go home. We'll be fine. I doubt that he will return tonight. I will find the bastard even if I have to tear this city apart."

Patrick shut his eyes, anxious to get home to Ann. Once home, he flew through the doorway, calling her name.

Ann peered over the banister. "What is it? You're scaring the living daylights out of me."

Just seeing her stand there, safe and unharmed, was all the assurance he needed. He handed his coat and gloves to the bewildered butler and slowly walked up the stairs. He brushed back his hair from his brow before leading her into the bedroom.

As she sat on the edge of the bed, he kneeled down before her. Patrick searched for the right words.

"Something terrible has happened. I don't want to alarm you, but I think we may be in danger."

Ann gripped his hands. Fear filled her eyes. "Please tell me."

"David broke into the Marshalls' home and attacked Katherine."

"How bad was it?"

Patrick tenderly caressed her cheek. His throat tightened with emotion. "He took a knife and cut her face. She is in shock, but the cut does not appear to be deep. If we hadn't arrived when we did, who knows what would have happened. I am so thankful it wasn't you. I couldn't bear it if you were hurt."

Clenching her fists together, she swore, "I wish for one day that I was a man. I would love to beat him until he cried for mercy. If it weren't for me, none of this would have happened."

Patrick shook his head. "Don't say that. You're not to blame for any of this."

He rose and sat next to Ann, lifting her to his lap. With her head against his chest, he held her tightly. "This isn't your fault. Besides, if you had not been so persistent in researching your family history and buying that book, we never would have found each other. David is like a bad recurring dream, and someday justice will prevail. Edward and I will find him. I do not want you to leave the house unprotected. Is that understood?"

She nodded. Her fingers nimbly unfastened the top buttons of his shirt. His breathing deepened as her fingers inched toward his waist. He inhaled her scent, holding her a little bit closer to his heart. This is what heaven felt like. He was sure of it.

Chapter 43

THE NEXT MORNING, THEY lingered in bed, both exhausted from yesterday's events. Patrick gazed down at her. "I received a report about Victoria yesterday. I thought you would want to know."

Ann searched Patrick's solemn face. "Of course I do. I know how worried you've been. When you grow up with someone and care about them, it's only natural to want to make sure they're safe."

He took a deep breath. "I need for you to understand that what I have done has been for the benefit of Victoria. Malcolm said that Victoria left on her own and was safe. I may have been wrong about him. He obviously cares for you, and he has been a good friend to both of us. Still, call it my suspicious nature, but I've had him followed for several weeks."

Ann rolled out of bed, grabbing her robe. "You what! I can't believe you would do that. What do you think he did?"

"It's not that I think him capable of any misdeed. It's my concern for Victoria that impelled me to pursue this course of action. You never knew her. She was so timid that she could barely look at my face. She was rarely let out of her father's sight. The fact that William still believes you are his daughter means that whatever happened to Victoria, only Malcolm knows the truth. As I said, my men have followed Malcolm for weeks. He never leaves the estate except to visit you. Do you find it odd that such a considerate, thoughtful brother would never visit his sister?"

Doubts assailed her. She loved Malcolm like the brother she never had. She wouldn't have adapted to life in this century without his support and guidance. What Patrick suggested was unnerving. "Are you saying what I think you're saying? Malcolm couldn't hurt anyone."

He tugged at his hair. "I don't know what I am saying. She was last seen the night you arrived. It has not gone unnoticed that *Victoria* has changed recently. We both know that people think you are Victoria."

Filled with anguish, Ann whispered, "Do you think that my coming here caused something to happen to Victoria? If that's true, I'll never be able to forgive myself. I feel terrible. Look at the lives that changed because I was sent here."

His eyes misted over. "Without you, my life would have been a horrible pretense and nothing else. We don't know what happened, so let's not assume the worst. It's most likely a misunderstanding. Malcolm probably has some reason for being so secretive."

Ann was more confused than ever. Patrick had raised valid issues. If she believed what Patrick suggested, then she had to believe that Malcolm had done something very wrong. Could she accept that? She had to find out the truth.

Later that week, Ann sat down for breakfast feeling as if she had been run over by a truck. She had tossed and turned every night since Katherine's attack. Each time sleep claimed her, the tortuous nightmares about David would wake her.

Her stomach churned. She could only manage a cup of tea for breakfast. Maybe if she started a journal, it would become easier to decide what to do. Or she could do a timeline on the laptop. But what if while using the future technology, she was somehow sent back to the twenty-first century? Deciding it was a risk she had to take, she hurried upstairs.

She stared at the black case for several minutes before tearing open the Velcro tabs. Smiling, she wondered what would happen if she could send Stacy an e-mail. Too bad there were no wireless networks in this century. Ann laughed aloud. Back to the task at hand, she tried to develop a timeline of events that brought her to this century. Once again, she had to wonder why she came to this specific time and place. Was it because something had happened to Victoria? Or was it because of Patrick? Was she meant to live in this century?

Her maid's voice interrupted her thoughts. Ann slammed the lid down and shoved the computer under the desk. "Yes, come in."

"My lady. Your father is waiting downstairs. He said it was quite important. I tried to get him to leave, but he started such a ruckus that I thought I should tell you."

Ann thanked the woman. Where was Patrick when she needed him? She entered the room in time to see William helping himself to the liquor cabinet.

Holding up the glass in her direction, he waved her in. "So ... my daughter has decided to grant me the honor of her presence." With a weasel-like grin, he poured a brandy.

Ann refused to be intimidated. "Why are you here? I'm not giving you any more money."

William sneered at her. "Missy, your husband may appreciate your sass. I do not. The grocer won't make any more deliveries until his bill is paid. I don't know what this world is coming to when a man thinks he is above his superiors."

"It doesn't get any better in 2013 either," she muttered under her breath.

Leaning forward, he repeated, "In 2013?"

"Never mind. I guess I cannot have you starving to death. I will take care of the bill, but that's all I'm paying for."

Ringing for Maggie, Ann quickly whispered instructions to the housekeeper. Patrick would not be pleased at this turn of events.

Setting aside his glass, William smiled. "Since everything is settled, I will take my leave." He strolled to the door and stopped. "Oh, I almost forgot. I plan on going to the track and will require a small amount of funds to cover my customary bets. Let's say one hundred pounds?"

Ann brushed aside the curtain and looked down to the street below. In a high-pitched voice, she announced, "Here comes Patrick now. Why don't you ask him for the money?"

William sauntered toward her, guffawing. "Poor Victoria, do you really think you can fool me? You know better than that. To make sure I have my demands met, I planned today's visit down to the last detail."

Suspicion reared its head. "What have you done?"

His fleshy arm snaked about her shoulders. His putrid breath made her wince. "Nothing serious. Lord O'Neil had a carriage accident, that's all. Now, let's finish this distasteful exchange and I will be on my way."

"An accident!" Her shrill voice rang through the house. "If he's hurt, I'll shoot you myself. Get out of my house! I wouldn't give you a penny now if my life depended on it."

His eyes had an eerie gleam. "Ah, but your life does depend on it—and so does your husband's. Don't be so difficult." Squeezing her forearm, he shoved her toward the stairway. "Get the money or I'll wait here until Patrick returns. When he opens the door, I shall be forced to fire my gun. Of course, I will explain to the magistrate that while visiting my daughter, we suspected the same man who attacked Lady Marshall of trying to harm you. No one will blame me. You will be distraught and I will be named executor of the estate. It is your choice as to how the game is played. What shall it be?"

Barely able to comprehend the horror of his words, she stared at him. This was no idle threat. In this era, most men would take William's word over hers. What chance would she have in court? Unwillingly, she made her way upstairs. Opening the jewelry case, she was unable to decide on what piece to hand over to William. She couldn't stop thinking of Patrick.

Ann choked back a scream when William suddenly pushed her aside. He fingered all her rings and bracelets. He shoved several expensive pieces in his pocket.

She lunged for them. "You can't take those. They're worth a fortune!"

"Precisely my thought." He headed downstairs toward the door, calling back over his shoulder, "Cheer up. Perhaps I shall win and won't have to bother you for several weeks."

Sick to her stomach, Ann scrawled a note to Anthony. Less than an hour later, he arrived. Ann ran to his side. Sobbing, she embraced him tightly. "Thank God you're here. I think something has happened to Patrick."

"Your message indicated that William has harmed Patrick. What happened?"

"I don't know. William made sure Patrick wasn't at home this morning when he came by to ask for more money. He has been blackmailing me. Either I give him money or he will kill Patrick."

"Come now. Do you really believe he could hurt Patrick? Patrick is cold-blooded when it comes to dealing with those who threaten him. I don't know anyone crazy enough to challenge your husband."

Ann snapped, "Anthony, don't patronize me. I'm not a child. If you had heard William, you would be just as alarmed as I am. Now, do you know where Patrick went today?"

Anthony looked stunned at her outburst. "Excuse me. It was not my intention to offend you. I will check the club. Usually he stops for a drink with friends after leaving the office. I'll go see if I can find him."

Loud voices and pounding in the foyer brought the two running toward the noise. Assisted by men on each side, Patrick stumbled through the doorway. The sleeve of his shirt was ripped and bloodied, his face blackened with dirt.

Smothering a cry, she rushed forward to help him. Bruised and battered, Patrick collapsed in the nearest chair. Ann quickly removed his bloodied shirt, checking for injuries. Assured the wounds were minor, she allowed herself a sigh of relief.

Anthony handed him a glass of brandy. "For God's sake, man, tell us what happened."

Patrick squeezed Ann's hand. "I don't understand it. The axle on the rear wheels snapped. Luckily, I was thrown free. Before I could get up from the road, a pair of black horses came barreling toward me. The carriage was unmarked and the curtains drawn, so I could not see who was inside. It was as if they were deliberately trying to run me over."

Ann clasped a hand over her mouth. William's threats weren't in vain after all.

Patrick drew her closer. "Anthony, I thought you had an appointment to go riding with Miss Curtis today."

Anthony patted Patrick's shoulder on his way to the door. "I believe I shall leave the explanation to your wife. Call if you need anything and be careful."

Patrick stared at Ann. "Why do I have a feeling that I do not want to hear this?"

Ann bravely recounted the morning's events.

Throughout the recital, Patrick's emotions went from anger to that of pure rage. It was all he could do not to race from the house and end William's miserable life. Instead, he enveloped Ann in his arms.

"Forgive me. I should have left someone here to watch over you. He shall not catch us unaware again."

"Shouldn't we call the police, the bobbies, to report what has happened?"

Surprised with her familiarity of terms for law enforcement, he asked, "How do you know they're called that?"

"They're still referred to as bobbies in my time. Is it true that they use that name because Sir Robert Peel organized the police a few years ago?"

He glanced at the wet rag on his arm. The bleeding had quit. He set aside the dirty rag. With a small groan, he shifted to a more comfortable position. "Yes, but it was a little more than a few years ago. It was 1829 to be precise. And yes, they were named after him. Since they witnessed the accident today, I'll work with them, but that will not stop me from pursuing my own justice. Montgomery will regret his actions."

"He took several pieces of jewelry. I tried to stop him, but he threatened to kill you. I was so afraid that you wouldn't come back to me."

Patrick couldn't speak. His emotions felt too close to the surface. He buried his nose in her tousled curls, taking a deep breath. He was home with Ann.

His servants were due any moment with their report on the Montgomery house. He would not take any further chances with Ann's life. She would probably chafe at his orders, but as her husband, he had a responsibility to make sure she was protected.

A subdued knock on the door interrupted them. Maggie entered. "Sir, men are waiting in the library. Will you be requiring anything else?"

"No, that's all for now. Tell them I'll join them shortly." He placed his thumb under Ann's chin and slowly raised her face. Tenderly his lips joined hers. "I need to see if they have any new information. Why don't you have a warm bath readied and you can wash my back?"

She stood and placed her fists on her hips. "Although I am tempted, no. I want to go with you. We both have a lot to lose. Besides, maybe I can help. I know David better than anyone else."

Reluctantly, he nodded and led the way to the library. Most women he knew would be terrified under the circumstances and would be more than willing to let their husbands handle matters. He wondered if he would ever get used to independent women.

The men jumped to their feet as the door opened. Patrick's spirits soared at the sight of their smiling faces. "Well, gentlemen. Tell me you have good news ..."

Grinning like a cat that caught the canary, the older man's head bobbed up and down. "You was right, sir. We kept our wits about us, like you said. I wrote down notes as you ordered. Do you want me to read them?"

"Go ahead, but keep in mind that my wife is here."

Politely nodding in her direction, the man continued. "We saw Montgomery. He packed up a carriage earlier today and left. There was a servant looking about outside. We thought he spotted us once and had to duck back in the shadows for a spell. A big mean brute he was. As tall as you, my lord. Never catched his name."

Ann timidly suggested, "Malcolm may know who it is."

Patrick curtly replied, "We'll leave your family out of this matter."

As she opened her mouth to protest, Patrick cut her off. "Anything else?"

The younger man, just as brawny as his brother, replied, "Just as we was leaving, a young gent gets out of a carriage and walks up to the front door as bold as he pleases—and he's let in. If you ask me, he looked like some fancy lord or something. Fair hair and those kind of looks that ladies fall for, if you get my meaning."

Jabbing his younger brother in the ribs with his elbow, the elder one apologized. "Sorry, my lady. He sometimes forgets his manners."

Ann met his gaze. He'd easily read her mind. It had to be David. Thanking the men, Patrick paid them handsomely for their work and escorted them to the door.

Patrick returned to Ann's side and gripped her shoulders. "You don't have to be afraid. Now that I know where he is, he will be picked up and put in prison. That will be the end of David Stewart."

Ann leaned against him. "I wish I could be as confident as you. Something terrible is going to happen. I feel it."

Dismissing her fear, Patrick whispered soothing words in her ear. He cradled her to his chest and carried her upstairs.

Patrick watched Ann as she undressed. She had *that* look on her face. Their problems temporarily forgotten, Ann nuzzled his neck, causing his pulse to pound. Surely fate didn't bring them together to find love only to snatch it away? Not even fate could be that cruel.

Chapter 44

IN THE MORNING, PATRICK and Ann childishly rolled about, tickling and delightfully tormenting one another. After satisfying their desire last night, they had stayed up and talked for several hours. They decided that they were not going to be bound by William's or David's actions. If they acted prudently and took precautions, they would live their lives as normal.

Enjoying a lull in their antics, Patrick's sated body sprawled across the bed. He could feel Ann studying his profile. Worn out from yesterday, his eyes drifted shut.

When a wet object hit Patrick's forehead, his sleepy eyes jerked open. Crouched above him was his wife, armed with purple bullets. Her face was aglow with mischief and wantonness. Thick auburn tresses framed her face. The sheerness of her gown left nothing to his imagination. His shaft jumped to life. He eased the gown off her shoulders. With hooded eyes, he stared at the luscious fruit her body offered.

He would play her game for a few minutes. Unfortunately, the next five grapes missed his mouth. His patience at an end, he grabbed the fruit and tossed it out of her reach. He pulled her down next to him, raining kisses along her arched neck.

Trying to escape his arms, she moaned. "Stop! You're getting grape juice all over everything."

He flashed a grin. "Perhaps you should have thought about that sooner. You must pay a price for waking your hungry husband."

Picking up a ripe grape from the pillow, he positioned it above her face and squeezed until purple juice trickled down to her pouty lips. Ignoring her giggles, he licked the juice from her lush mouth, pressing closer and deeper to feel the sweetness between her legs. His body trembled. He refused to surrender to the need of completion. He wanted to last forever. In and out. Fast and then slow. He showed no mercy. Lunging hard a final time brought his pleasure and hers.

Surrounded by purple-stained sheets, Ann purred, "That was nice."

"I don't think I can walk again. I'll have to stay here and keep you beneath me," mumbled Patrick, his whiskers tickling her shoulder.

Her hips shifted upward, keeping him imbedded deep inside of her. "That would be fine with me. But I have a feeling you would eventually become bored and leave me."

He growled deep within his throat and rolled over on his side. "Never. When I'm an old man, I will still desire you."

The sound of heavy footsteps echoed from the hallway. A knock broke their tranquility. Quickly jumping out of bed, he pulled on his trousers. "Who is it?"

Anthony's voice rang out. "It's two in the afternoon. What are you two doing?"

Patrick tossed a heavy book at the door, laughing when he heard Anthony step away from the door. "If you wish to see what we're doing, just stay there while I open the door. Otherwise, I suggest you wait in the library."

Ann fastened her silk robe. "I think reality has intruded. Go see what he wants. It must be important if he came barging upstairs."

Grabbing a starched shirt from the armoire, he blew her a kiss and hurried from the room as the maid entered. Patrick glanced back at the bed. Good Lord! There were purple stains everywhere.

He chuckled, thinking about the comments that would be repeated in the servants' quarters.

Patrick and Anthony were finishing up a light repast when Ann joined them. "Well? Do you have news about David?"

Anthony glanced at Patrick before replying. "Yes. The authorities have been watching your father's house, and David is living there. An hour from now, an arrest is planned. They had to wait to bring on extra men before they could completely surround the house. I thought Patrick might want to be there."

Ann exclaimed, "Of course we'll be there. When do we leave?"

Patrick shook his head, speaking in a tone that brooked no argument. "You will remain here. Shots may be fired, and I won't risk your life. Anthony and I will make sure he does not evade capture."

"You're teasing, right? I can't wait here. I'll go crazy." She glared at him.

Anthony stepped between them, flashing a beseeching smile at Ann. "Perhaps you could send for Miss Curtis. The two of you could keep each other company. After we return, we could enjoy dinner together."

Ann clasped Anthony's hand. "I didn't know you were seeing Eleanor."

With a red face, Anthony mumbled, "Since you are fond of her, I made the suggestion to ease your anxiety. Are you coming, Patrick?"

Ann threw up her hands in capitulation. "Fine. You two go and leave me here. And, Anthony, I'm holding you to your promise of dinner tonight with Eleanor."

In the carriage, Patrick glanced at his friend, who seemed determined to ignore him. "Miss Curtis?"

Anthony snorted and jerked aside the curtain on the window. "It's not what you think. It was the only thing that crossed my mind at the time. Your wife seemed set on going, and you were just as determined that she stay at home, so I proposed a diversion."

His hand covering the lower half of his face, Patrick struggled to contain his amusement. "So kind of you to think of saving my marriage. I imagine you will have to take her home later this evening. Clever idea, Aylesbury."

Anthony gave a faint smile. "Yes, it was quite clever, wasn't it?"

By the time they reached the Montgomery townhome, twenty men had surrounded the house. Striding up to the officer in charge, Patrick demanded, "Are you sure he's inside?"

The portly officer respectfully nodded. "Yes, my lord. We've had the house under surveillance since you filed the complaint. No one has entered or left since my men arrived. We are about to enter the house. I suggest you stay here, out of danger."

Patrick bristled at the request. His flinty gaze never wavered from the house. "No mistakes. I want Stewart in custody today."

Two groups of men swarmed the house. On cue, they burst through the front and rear doors. From inside, the sounds of voices and shattering glass were heard.

Patrick surged forward, only to have Anthony grasp his elbow. "Let's wait."

Patrick swore under his breath, shaking off Anthony's hand. Minutes later, a few officials exited the door.

Patrick rushed forward. "Well, where is he?"

The official cleared his throat; his look apologetic. "Only one servant was found in the house. Mr. Stewart wasn't there. In fact, all his clothes and belongings are gone. Appears he left quite abruptly."

Patrick threw back his head and squeezed his eyes shut. He wanted to scream to the heavens. To be so damn close to catching the bastard yet he still escaped.

Patrick shoved his way into the house to find the authorities questioning a servant. He stepped forward, towering over the bewildered man. "Where is Mr. Stewart?"

The trembling servant lifted his face to look at Patrick. Patrick felt pity for the poorly dressed man. "What's your name?"

The man cowered. "Jack. Who are you?"

"I am Lord O'Neil. Do you think you can help us find Mr. Stewart?"

Jack nodded, seeming eager to help. "He was here this morning. He had blood all over his clothes. Smelled bad too, like the perfume those women near the dock use. You know the ones I mean?"

Ignoring the smirks of the officers, Patrick nodded. "So he came back here to sleep. Are you sure you didn't see or hear anything else?"

Jack shook his head, pointing to the stables out back. "No, I was cleaning out the stalls. Mr. Stewart gets mad if they ain't clean. I don't like it when he gets angry. He scares me."

Patrick swore, pounding his fist on the stained walnut table. "Someone must have tipped him off."

"Perhaps he left the city," one officer suggested.

"If only I could believe that, but you don't know him like I do. He has already tried to murder two women, one of which is my wife. The man's extremely dangerous."

Patrick joined Anthony, who waited outside, dodging questions from the curious crowd who recognized O'Neil's carriage.

"Well, any news?" Anthony asked.

"No, he's gone. He has more luck than a cat with nine lives. I don't know how I will face my wife or the Marshalls."

"It's not your fault. Everyone is doing his best to capture David. He'll make a mistake, and we'll be there waiting."

Chapter 45

As PATRICK AND ANTHONY rode home from the failed attempt to capture David, a misting rain enveloped the entire city. Low gray clouds skimmed over rooftops, making it appear as if the world were closing in. The dismal weather echoed Patrick's mood.

Ann ran to Patrick when the door opened. She took one look at his face and pressed the back of her hand to her mouth. Her eyes welled up with tears.

Patrick embraced Ann. "I'm sorry, darling. Somehow he escaped." Patrick drew up when he saw Edward standing nearby.

Edward cleared his throat, drawing the attention of the others. "I hope you don't mind my being here. I wanted to come and support Victoria."

Patrick hugged his friend. "Thank you."

Ann flashed Patrick a fiery look. "Well, what's next? David ruined my last life. He is not going to ruin this one."

In unison, Patrick and the other two men whipped toward her and stared, their eyes bulging with disbelief. What did she just say?

Patrick reacted first. "What my wife means is that he attempted to ruin our lives in the country and now he's attempting the same thing again."

Ann shook her head at Patrick. He could tell by the look on her face that the time for the truth had come.

Patrick motioned toward the sitting room. "Why don't we sit down? Ann and I have something important to tell you. I hope you will give us the benefit of the doubt and not interrupt until we're done."

∞

For the next hour, Ann shared the story of her life. She laid out fact after fact to support her case. The looks on their faces went from amusement to skepticism and finally curiosity. Exhausted, she sat back and quietly waited.

Edward walked to the tea cart, picked up a cup, and filled it to the rim with brandy. He brought it to his lips and gulped it down. Walking back to his chair, he looked from Patrick to Ann and back again. "God help me, I think I believe your outlandish tale."

Anthony stared at Patrick. In a terse tone, Anthony snapped, "I cannot believe you didn't trust us sooner." Anthony loosened his collar and rested his head on the back of the chair.

Patrick calmly remarked, "I'm sorry. It was important that I protect Ann."

Anthony leaned forward, sitting on the edge of the chair. "I don't know how I missed the differences. I do appreciate your telling us the truth. I just wish you had done it sooner. I can only imagine the things Ann could tell us. I have thousands of questions about the future. What wars have been fought? What scientific breakthroughs were made? I could stay up all night talking about this."

Patrick laughed, taking the tension out of the room. "Well, you're not spending the night with my wife." He quietly added, "I think we all agree that what you've just heard must go no further. To do so would jeopardize Ann's safety."

Their friends heartily agreed.

Ann rose to her feet. "I suspect I'll see you gentlemen tomorrow. Thank you for believing in me. It's been a long day. I bid you good night. Oh, Anthony, I forgot. Miss Curtis already had plans for the evening and couldn't join us."

Anthony nodded. The men drew their chairs closer together

after Ann left the room. Anthony spoke first. "Will Ann be sent back to her time?"

Patrick shrugged his shoulders. "I ask myself the same thing. I hope and pray that it won't happen, but we cannot be sure."

Edward, always an optimist, added, "Of course it won't happen. Ann acts and looks like a woman born in this century. I never suspected otherwise."

Patrick smiled at Edward. "Thanks for the encouragement. I need Anthony's assistance. You have enough to worry about without my adding to it." Patrick went into detail about how William had been threatening Ann and blackmailing her.

"Blast the man!" Edward exclaimed. "I assume you've contacted the authorities."

"She's worried about Malcolm. She believes that he isn't involved."

Edward jumped up and paced before them. "We need to get William away from Ann. I have a villa in northern Italy that is quite secluded. I guarantee that he would be closely guarded and wouldn't bother Ann anymore."

Patrick wondered if it would work. Could he assure Ann's safety? Anthony nodded his approval. Patrick freshened their drinks, encouraged that they had an idea for a plan, but it would take time to pull it together. He hoped there was enough time.

Anthony swirled the amber liquid in the glass. "Where is Victoria? How will you explain this to her when she returns?"

Patrick rubbed his tired eyes. "I've been searching for her. No one but Malcolm has seen her since the ball. He assures me that she desires privacy and is well cared for. I don't know when or if she will return."

"From your tone, you suspect Malcolm of some nefarious act?" Edward inquired.

"I don't know what to believe anymore. If you would have told me a year ago that I would be married to a woman from the future, that William would be trying to kill me, and that we were being stalked by a crazed man from another time, I would have declared you quite insane."

Anthony stated, "I cannot believe Malcolm would harm his own sister. He is a changed man."

Anthony rose and rang for his carriage. "It's late. I need some sleep before meeting Eleanor tomorrow. Would you two care to go riding with us tomorrow?"

Patrick silently weighed the situation. "We might as well. If we're out in public, perhaps William and David will show themselves."

Edward echoed, "Fabulous idea. Katherine needs some fresh air. I have not been able to get her to leave the house since the attack. With the other two women, she'll be much more relaxed."

They quickly agreed on a time, and Patrick bid his guests farewell. As he crept into the darkened bedroom, he found Ann fast asleep. He undressed and slid next to her. The warmth from her body permeated his. She was like a cuddly kitten seeking the warmth and comfort of his body.

She drowsily murmured, "I can't believe they took the news so well. I'm glad they know the truth. Now I won't worry about doing or saying something inappropriate."

Kissing her forehead, he muttered wearily as exhaustion enveloped him. "Now they know. I disliked keeping the truth from them."

"I wish we knew where Victoria was." Looking perplexed, she wondered aloud, "Am I really so different from Victoria?"

He mulled over his response. "On the outside, you two are much alike. I'm not sure why you are asking, but I have no desire to be married to anyone but you. You will always be my heart's desire. Now, are you satisfied?"

"Yes, kiss me good night."

His halfhearted attempt to prolong the kiss into something more intimate fizzled as her eyes drifted shut. His brows lifted in puzzlement. Nudging her gently to see if she would waken also proved ineffective. He tossed for a few minutes before falling asleep.

His dream returned. Ann was running from someone. No matter how hard he tried, he couldn't reach her.

Chapter 46

PATRICK WOKE WITH A start. He looked about the room, trying to shake the dream from his mind. The clock on the landing struck eleven times. The bed was empty. He bounded from bed and rang for a bath. As soon as he was done, he hurried downstairs for breakfast.

"Just coffee and toast," he requested of the waiting servant. Patrick grabbed the paper and sat next to Ann.

She rubbed his whiskered cheek. "I wondered when you would wake up. You kicked and moaned all night. Did you have a bad dream?"

"Not that I can remember. I forgot to tell you that our friends will arrive any minute for a drive about town."

Ann playfully punched his arm. "Thanks for the notice, O'Neil." Tossing aside the napkin, she hurried up the stairs to change clothes.

As Ann descended the stairs, Patrick had just greeted Anthony and Eleanor. Ann wore a light violet dress with matching shoes. She carried a deep purple floral silk shawl. She looked like spring.

Ann's melodious laughter trickled down the stairs. "Eleanor, what a nice surprise. Let's go in the parlor while we wait for Edward and Katherine."

Anthony clapped Patrick on the shoulder. "How about a drink?"

Patrick led the way to the library, sensing that something was distressing his friend.

"Anything wrong?"

"How did you know that Ann was the right woman for you?"

Patrick sputtered, almost dropping his drink. "I think it came gradually. I sure couldn't stop thinking of her. I had my doubts when we were first married. Thankfully, we worked through it. Why do you ask?"

Anthony took a sip from his glass. "Just curious. We have so many friends who marry for connections and positions, and I want to make sure I don't fall into that same trap."

Patrick bit back his smile. "You're thinking of marrying the lovely Miss Curtis?"

Not meeting Patrick's gaze, Anthony suddenly became interested in the newspaper on the desk.

"Whatever gave you that idea? I just wanted to assure myself that you were happy."

Patrick chuckled aloud. "Sure you were."

The Marshalls' arrival prevented Patrick from cajoling further information from his friend.

The sun was in full glory. The pale blue sky was a welcome sight after days of drizzle and fog. The group converged on the waiting carriage. After seating the women, Patrick closed the door.

Ann looked curiously at him. "Aren't you joining us?"

"We will let you ladies gossip to your heart's content. Our horses are being brought around. We'll follow right behind the carriage."

Eleanor could barely sit still. "Just think! I will be seen on Rotten Row with Lord Aylesbury. Mother was beside herself this morning when he came to call."

The young woman's excitement was infectious. Ann glanced at Katherine, who sat quietly in the corner with a veil over her face. Through the layer of silk, even Katherine looked amused.

Dubious, Ann asked, "Rotten Row? It sounds like a place we should avoid."

Both Eleanor and Katherine smiled. Eleanor gushed, "Rotten Row is only for the elite of London society. It is a place where one goes to be seen. It's a favorite of the *ton*."

"I wonder why Patrick hasn't taken me there before now." By the puzzled look on Eleanor's face, she knew she had goofed again.

Eleanor excitedly told her, "Rotten Row is mostly popular May through July. The most important people ride at certain times of the day. Now that it's nearly one o'clock, it shall be somewhat crowded. A few do show up in the late afternoon, but the earlier hours are much more preferable."

Ann was in awe as carriages and riders on horseback stopped to exchange pleasantries with one another. When they passed a regal-looking carriage, Katherine and Eleanor nodded as they passed.

Ann was curious. "Who was that?"

In unison, Eleanor and Katherine responded, "Duchess of Winscott."

Katherine added, "Her annual ball is the most sought-after invitation of the season."

Ann turned around and stared at the departing Winscott carriage. Even she had heard of the Winscotts. Ann caught the eye of her husband, who waved and smiled.

The three men rode side by side, nodding to the numerous women who made it a point to draw their attention.

Ann frowned as she turned to face the women again. "In case you ladies haven't noticed, the women around here are practically tripping over themselves to stop and speak to our men."

Katherine glanced back at Edward, who gallantly tipped his hat. "Perhaps we should be friendlier to the men who are hoping to catch our attention."

"Oh, no." Eleanor shook her head. "We can't do that. I don't want to appear brazen. Anthony will think poorly of me."

"Dear, you can't let men control every situation. Trust me when I say that a man likes a little spice in the relationship."

Eleanor blushed at Katherine's remarks. Ann nonchalantly turned to see Anthony smile at Eleanor. He did look quite dashing, though not as good as Patrick did. She wondered if Anthony would think Eleanor was too young for marriage at the age of seventeen.

Patrick approached the open carriage on horseback. "We should turn back. I fear rain is headed our way."

As the carriage made the last turn around the path, Ann glanced at a nearby grove of trees. Half hidden behind the lush greenery, a man mounted on a horse stared at her. Ann lifted her hand in greeting, believing it was Malcolm. When the man shifted in the saddle, Ann gasped. It was David!

She stood and screamed for Patrick. There was no way to predict David's next move. He could have a gun aimed at them this very second.

Patrick hurried to the side of the carriage. Fear was in his eyes. He shouted, "What's wrong?"

She pointed to the trees they had passed. "Back there ... I saw David!"

Katherine moaned. Her hand flew to her chest. "I need Edward!"

The men quickly agreed that Anthony would escort the women home to safety while Patrick and Edward went after David. Ann tried to object, but they had already turned the horses and were flying across the grassy mounds to the grove.

Chapter 47

ANN INSISTED THAT EVERYONE come inside their home to wait together. In tears, Katherine was in no state to be left alone.

Feeling useless, Anthony headed for the library. Damn, but he needed a stiff drink. He should be with Patrick and Edward. He stretched out in a wing-back chair near the fireplace.

As he quietly sipped his drink, his thoughts wandered. Hearing a noise, he watched as Eleanor entered the room. His eyes narrowed as she took a piece of paper and wrote a note.

As she turned to leave, his deep voice made her jump. "Care to join me?"

She slowly turned and saw him sitting in the far corner of the room. "Oh, excuse me. I did not know you were here. I thought I would come in here and look for paper. I wrote Mother a note so she wouldn't worry."

By her rambling statement, his presence obviously disquieted her. She appeared reluctant to leave. He rose, silently walking toward her. Her innocent eyes were frozen on him. She then lowered her gaze, looking unsure of herself. She turned toward the door.

"Wait! Please sit with me."

"Lady Marshall is distraught. I should help Lady O'Neil."

He scrutinized Eleanor, who appeared anxious to leave. She was as skittish as a young filly. Maybe he had misread her interest in him.

Exasperated with his thoughts, he scoffed aloud. Hell, he knew she should leave. At this moment, he wasn't sure he trusted himself. His best friends' lives were in danger at this very minute, and he could do nothing but wait. His whole body burned with frustration. Whether it was from this forced inactivity or the presence of Eleanor, he wasn't sure.

He was unable to tear his eyes from her willowy figure. He relentlessly stalked toward her, fascinated by her tempting cherry lips that parted ever so slightly, fanning his desire to a fever pitch.

She stepped backward until her back pressed against the bookcase. He had never looked at her so closely before. Wicked thoughts made his body come alive. Closer he came, his face inches from hers. He cupped her chin tentatively, brushing his lips against hers. He parted her lips with his tongue, seeking her warmth.

She reached up and pressed her hands against him. As her hands explored his chest, his muscles involuntarily trembled. Surprised, he let her hands slide down his back to a tapered waist.

Her inexperienced hands strayed over his body, yet it was enough to cause his blood to boil. How could one so young and naive be so skilled? Pressing his entire body forward, his lips branded her as his. She wrapped her arms tighter around his body. Her trembling body brought a moan to his lips.

The sound of his raspy breathing filled the air. He was losing control. He dropped his arms and turned away. Damn it all—he was seducing a virgin!

"I think it would be better if you joined the ladies after all. Please forgive me for taking advantage of your inexperience." His voice sounded harsh even to his own ears.

Eleanor couldn't move … wouldn't move. All she could think of was the way his lips had conquered hers only moments before. Now he was telling her to leave? He must be disgusted by her pathetic attempts at kissing. She was such a fool. Her pride in tatters, she started for the doorway.

Before she could open the door, the woman inside broke free. She had to feel his lips on her body. Eleanor boldly locked the door. She wouldn't allow another woman to take the man she had claimed as her own. Heart pounding, she leaned against the wooden barrier.

With his back toward the door, Anthony stared out the windows. Anthony shrugged off his jacket and slumped into the leather chair at Patrick's desk, still staring outside.

Eleanor silently glided across the carpet toward Anthony. She couldn't believe he failed to hear her pounding heart. What would she do if he turned and demanded that she leave? *No!* her mind cried. She wouldn't consider defeat.

With each step, she unfastened another button, until her bodice slipped quietly to the floor. Pulling the pins from her hair, Eleanor shook out her waist-length sandy-colored hair. The curtain of silk shielded her sensitive nipples from view.

Without warning, Anthony spun around in the chair to face her. His fingers turned white as he clenched the arms of the chair. He seemed to be trying to hold himself back.

When she licked her lower lip, he moaned aloud. Oh my, he was definitely interested in her actions.

Her arms raised above her head, lifting her hair. As her arms lowered, the strands fell like a waterfall about her body. He jerked to his feet, walked around the desk, and roughly pulled her to him, ensuring that every inch of his body pressed against hers.

His predatory eyes bore into hers. "Do you know what you're doing?" he growled.

She tossed her hair over her shoulders, revealing her breasts to his perusal. "No, but I know that I love you and that I may only have this one opportunity to show you how much I care. I want you to teach me how to please you."

With a wicked glint in his eyes, he lifted her to the uncluttered desk. His warm lips grazed her shoulders. "Darling, you take my breath away. Let me give you a taste of the pleasure a man can bring to a woman."

He eased up her skirt and petticoat. The warmth of his fingers sent shivers through her body. When he uncovered her knees, she fought the impulse to jump off the desk and run from the room. How could she be so wanton? When she met his simmering gaze, she knew why.

His hair fell across his brow as his tongue traced the outline of her lips. She reached up and slowly pushed back his hair. Her fingers lingered, memorizing the texture of the glossy strands, and then strayed down his neck, where his pulse pounded out of control.

His insistent hands pressed her thighs apart. She instinctively jerked away from his touch. He huskily murmured, "Shhh. I will not hurt you. If you want me to stop, I will."

The desire etched on his face made her shudder with pleasure. She entrusted her body to his sexual machinations. No one had ever touched the place between her legs. Unbidden, her hips sought out his touch. Excitement coursed through her as his finger thrust in and out. Eleanor clenched her thighs around his hand. Soft moans escaped her. What was happening to her? Her body was spinning out of control. She wanted to scream but didn't know why.

Intense spasms seized her. Her hips pushed against his fingers in an uncontrollable frenzy. She buried her face against his shoulder to squelch the cry of joy that threatened to escape.

He held her tightly. She could feel his manhood throbbing.

Anthony pulled out a handkerchief and mopped his dampened brow.

Mortified by her behavior, she silently gathered her clothes. Why didn't he say anything? Had he turned his back to give her privacy or because he regretted his actions? She must have done something wrong. He was probably disgusted by her eager response. How could she forget her mother's advice about marriage? A wife was to lie still and endure her husband's touch.

Once dressed and her hair repinned, Eleanor stood by the door. "I must go. I don't know what came over me. Please forget that today ever happened." With that, she opened the door and ran from the room. Before entering the other room to meet her friends, Eleanor asked a servant to call for her carriage.

"Are you ill, Eleanor? You look flushed," Ann solicitously said a moment later.

"No, I'm just tired. I was going to send a note to Mother, but if you don't mind, I have had the carriage brought around. I'll go home to rest. I hope that I haven't been any trouble."

She turned on her heels and left before Ann could ask any more questions or see the tears that threatened. In the carriage, Eleanor risked a glance up at the library window. From parted curtains, Anthony stared down at her. As the curtains fell in place, her tears fell in earnest. She felt so foolish. It was little wonder that her heart was breaking.

Chapter 48

THE PAST FEW DAYS had been filled with disappointment. Patrick and Edward had returned from chasing David, only with news that he had escaped them. Ann and Katherine broke into tears at the bad news. David had disappeared again. No one could find him. It was like déjà vu. Only this time instead of being 2013, it was 1871. It was hard to believe she had been with Patrick for almost an entire year.

Although Patrick tried to boost her spirits, Ann had moped around the house, refusing to go out for days. This morning, she woke with a lighter heart. She was tired of living in fear. Today she was taking control once again.

The morning started with the delivery of the prized and much sought-after invitation to the Winscott ball. Waving the invitation in her hand, Ann cheerfully announced, "Guess what just arrived."

Patrick set aside the newspaper. "Surprise me."

"The invitation to the Winscott ball! Katherine and Eleanor told me all about it. They said it is the most glamorous social event of the year. We're going, aren't we?"

He smiled. "Even though I hate those stuffy formal engagements, I will gladly escort you to the ball."

Squealing with delight, she gave him a quick hug and kiss. "Great! I'll let them know we're coming." Faltering in midstep, her hand flew to her chest. "What should I wear?"

Patrick laughed heartily. "Have a new gown designed, something spectacular."

Ann hurried to her writing desk to pen their acceptance. Later that morning, the butler announced the arrival of Malcolm.

Ann rose to greet him. "Well, this is a surprise! What's the occasion?"

"I missed your saucy attitude." Malcolm draped his arm about Ann. "Actually, I needed a new overcoat, so I decided to stop in. All the young men seem to follow *Harper's Bazaar* fashion style. Rather than black this time, I am thinking of a tan overcoat. Do you think it's too gaudy?"

"Tan would be very nice, especially with a brown pair of leather gloves. Does this mean you will begin socializing again?"

"Only because of the Winscott ball," he sardonically answered. "I assume that you have received your invitation. Being Lady O'Neil does grant you some privileges."

Malcolm needed to lighten up. He worked from sunrise to sunset and the hard work had taken its toll. "I'm glad you're going. Have you heard from your father lately?"

Malcolm groaned. "Just the usual. Bill collectors came last week trying to get money from me. I tossed them off the property, but I know that others will soon be knocking at the door."

"Do you want me to ask Patrick for help?"

"No, he's my father, and I shall deal with him. I do need to get word to him that the Winscott invitation was only addressed to me. We have both attended in previous years. With all the gossip and such this past year, it comes as no surprise that he wasn't invited. I don't want him creating a scene at the ball."

"Don't look so guilty about it. You're not responsible for your father. I wish you would let me help."

"No, you have enough to worry about. Just leave it be."

She wouldn't interfere, for now. As they visited, Patrick entered the room.

Stretching out a hand to Patrick, Malcolm smiled. "I thought it was time to see how you two were doing. Besides, I have to wait for the tailor to finish my jacket. Ann tells me you're going to the ball."

"Ah, the ball. I fear that will be all I hear about for twenty-four hours a day. Ann and I are visiting the dressmaker this afternoon. You are welcome to join us and stay for dinner. Some male company would be appreciated."

Clasping Malcolm's hand, Ann begged him to come with them. To her delight, he agreed to spend the day with them.

"I will meet you at your dressmaker after my fitting."

Ann watched from the door. Malcolm seemed to have a bounce in his step today. He hopped into his carriage. He was a part of her new family. Her chest tightened as she thought about Mark and Jessica. She was not going to cry today. She had caused Patrick enough worry.

Ann followed Patrick into the library, where he was relaxing in his favorite chair. His eyes were closed, but his serene pose didn't fool her. She suspected that he still harbored suspicions toward Malcolm.

"Are you sure you want Malcolm to spend the day with us? I can send him a note explaining that we decided to stay home."

"No, that's not necessary. I know you enjoy his company so let me be the gracious husband."

The shopping excursion turned out to be a wonderful diversion. The two men poked fun at the outrageous gowns and hats that women were ordering. Ann tried on several styles of gowns, trying to judge which one suited her best. One gown had a neckline that plunged to the tops of her nipples. Both men jerked to their feet when she came out to model it, immediately ordering her back to the fitting room.

Finally, Ann selected a style that she liked and the men approved of. The dress was a soft peach color and had a scooped neckline. It was elegant yet modest. Best of all, there was no bustle. Ann remembered reading that bustles were going out of style and would not make a comeback until the 1880s.

∞

It was late in the day when they returned home. While Ann was upstairs changing, Patrick offered Malcolm a drink. Malcolm fidgeted under Patrick's scrutiny.

Malcolm loosened his collar. "It's rather warm in here."

"Is it? Ann enjoyed your company this afternoon. How any woman can enjoy shopping is beyond me."

"I forgot how women like to stand and look at things." Stretching out his legs, Malcolm eased his head back on the chair.

"I suppose you take Victoria shopping?"

Malcolm gazed up at the ceiling, hesitating before responding. "Yes, we've shopped together several times. She was so quiet that it was difficult to know what she liked or disliked. Quite different from Ann."

Patrick surged to his feet. "I always had the impression that Victoria was afraid of something. Do you know what it could be?"

Malcolm slammed the glass on the silver tray, spinning toward his accuser with flashing eyes. "Why don't you just say what you think I've done? I caution you to watch your words. I know that Victoria cared for you, so I'm making allowances for your impudence. Though I will not stand by and allow you to humiliate me."

Patrick lowered his voice. "You become defensive every time Victoria's name is mentioned. For God's sake, I know you're hiding something. Whatever happened, I can help you."

Malcolm's body trembled with rage. "No one can help me. No one, do you hear!"

"Malcolm, we've been friends since we were young boys. Allow me to help you."

Malcolm shook his head. "Even the powerful Lord O'Neil cannot help me. You have no idea the demons I faced once you went to Oxford. I imagine that you never thought of me until you wanted to marry Victoria. My father ruined my life. By the time I was fifteen, he was dragging me to the worst kinds of brothels. Can you envision being thrust into a world of whores, drunkenness, and opium? If I ever expressed any hesitation about going on these little excursions, I got to taste the leather strap. So you see, I learned very early to bury any emotional pain."

Patrick was clearly appalled by what Malcolm had confessed. Patrick reached out to comfort him, but Malcolm jerked away. Both men froze as a gasp came from the doorway.

Ann stood facing them with tears coursing down her cheeks. "Oh, Malcolm! I had no idea that William was so cruel."

Malcolm angrily grabbed his coat. "I do not want your pity. If only I had been stronger, then ..." Without finishing, he rushed past them. A few seconds later, the door slammed.

Chapter 49

WIPING THE TEARS WITH the back of her hand, Ann hissed, "What did you say to him?"

"All I did was ask about Victoria. I wish Malcolm had confided in me years ago. I could have intervened. Damn it all!"

Her loyalties were torn. She loved Patrick, and he distrusted Malcolm. Yet how could he continue to torment Malcolm?

"You must stop torturing him. You heard how his father treated him. Do you really believe he would hurt Victoria?"

Raking his fingers through his hair, Patrick groaned. "I don't know what to think. I thought that by talking about Victoria, he would reveal where she is."

"Why are you so concerned about Victoria? Sometimes I think that you care more about her than me. Maybe you should have married her." She ran from the room with tears streaming down her face.

The next week, Patrick and Ann saw very little of each other. Their conversations were polite and brief. Ann sat and gazed out the front window for hours at a time. She refused to talk about Victoria. Ann was at a loss on how to breach the void that grew between them.

Even though he denied any deep affection for Victoria, Ann suspected that he cared very much. Why else would he be so obsessed with finding her? If he had married Victoria, would he have been happier? After all, Victoria was a true lady.

Feeling confined, Ann kicked at the material of her skirt. She wanted to scream. Something had to change ... and soon.

Dinner began as usual one evening. No one spoke. The servants glanced uneasily at each other. Sitting at opposite ends of the table, Ann and Patrick stoically picked at the food set before them.

Ann peeked at Patrick. He appeared just as miserable as she was. She dismissed the servants. "I can't stand this tension between us any longer. It's been a week of us avoiding each other. We need to talk."

Patrick pushed back from the table, tossing the napkin on the table. "I've tried several times this past week to speak to you, but you chose to ignore me."

Ann twisted her napkin into a knot, her palms sweaty. "I know, and I'm sorry. There are so many things to think about. I don't even belong in this century. If you're unhappy and want to marry Victoria, I will try to understand."

He stood and solemnly walked toward her. "What am I going to do with you? Haven't you heard anything that I've said these past few months?"

"Then you're not angry with me?"

"No, I'm not angry. You have to believe me when I say I love only you. I have no interest in anyone but you."

She wrapped her arms around his neck and breathed deeply, memorizing his scent. "Let's go back to the country. I want to lock out the world."

He peered down at her. "What about the ball?"

"You're not getting off that easily. We will come back for that. Besides, I promise to make the trip to the country worth your while." With a saucy wink, she soundly kissed him.

The next morning, they hastily packed and left London.

Anthony grinned as he read Patrick's hastily scrawled note. He and Ann were leaving London until the ball. He would celebrate his own wedding before long. He had gathered up the courage to speak to Mr. Curtis about his intentions. Eleanor was reserved at first, but he was an expert in melting a woman's resistance. His own mother beamed brighter than any diamond when she learned he had formed an attachment. The news had reached White's. As an affirmed bachelor, numerous wagers were placed on whether he would make it to the altar.

Anthony had invited Eleanor to accompany him to the Winscott ball. The more Anthony mulled over the idea of marriage, the more appealing it became. With Patrick happily married, Anthony's umbrage to marriage was evaporating.

Marriage had made Katherine more popular than ever. She seemed to glow with happiness, and Edward clearly worshipped her. The *ton* was in the palm of her hand. He had even heard that the duchess of Winscott consulted Katherine regarding the planning of the ball.

Anthony and Edward met with the police while Patrick was in the country with Ann. The report was always the same. David had vanished. The authorities suspected that he had left London, if not England. He had also called upon his fencing instructor to see whether any of his cronies knew a David Stewart. Nothing turned up. Anthony had tried everything he could think of to help Ann and Patrick find David.

It was the day before the ball, and London buzzed with excitement. No sooner had Ann and Patrick walked through their door than Anthony rushed in after them. He swept into the drawing room and grabbed Ann, swinging her around in a circle. Chortling, Anthony fell to the sofa with Ann in his arms.

With his hands on his hips, Patrick watched the pair with his arms folded across his chest. "Unhand my wife, you lummox. You'll fall and crack both of your heads."

Ann swatted Anthony's hands. "I'm so dizzy!"

Sprawled out on the sofa, Anthony flashed a lopsided smile. "Eleanor has accepted my offer of marriage. It took a lot of persistence to convince her father that I was serious. Of course, Mother has started planning the nursery already."

Ann leaned over and kissed him on the cheek. "I'm so glad. I hoped that the two of you would hit it off."

Patrick shook his hand. "Congratulations. I think this calls for champagne."

After the drinks were served, Anthony asked about their trip.

"It was wonderful." Ann glowed as she looked at her husband. "Patrick was so romantic. I wished we could have stayed at Epsom Hall forever."

Patrick gazed affectionately at Ann. "Me too. We will return after the ball. Now, Anthony, tell me whether there is any news of David."

Anthony shook his head. "You have to speak to Edward. He has been in constant contact with the authorities. They seem assured that the man is gone for good."

After their friend left, Ann looked at Patrick. Neither of them believed David had left, but there was no use worrying, for there was nothing that they could do. David would show himself eventually.

After Patrick retired for bed, Ann jotted a note to Malcolm. She wanted to know if he still planned to attend the ball and to reassure him that he was always welcome in their home.

Chapter 50

MALCOLM GAZED WEARILY OUT the library window. The morning sun glowed upon the sprawling green pastures. Rubbing his head, he tried to concentrate on the papers scattered about the desk. It was no use. He ordered a horse saddled and brought around to the front. He needed fresh air.

Several tenants waved as he rode by. Nodding politely, he continued until he reached the destination where his life had changed. His secret was buried here, as well as his spirit. Dismounting, he trudged to the mound of dirt, which was now covered with wild violets. He knelt down and ran his palm over the top of the grave.

His eyes filled with tears. His hoarse whisper broke the silence. "Victoria, my sweet Victoria. I miss you more each day. Only the thought of you keeps me from ending my life. You were right. I should have stood up to Father years ago, when he beat your mother. Perhaps then you would be here with me today. Instead, I am an empty shell of a man, hoping that I hear your voice or see you lingering in the shadows."

Tears stained the earth below him. Using his sleeve, he swiped the moisture from his face. He staggered to his feet and picked up the reins. The peaceful, remote glen was imprinted in his memory. This would be as close to heaven as he would ever get.

When Malcolm returned home, a message from Ann was

waiting. Quickly scanning the note, he smiled. She wanted to make sure he was coming to the ball. He wondered if Patrick knew that she had written. He doubted that Patrick had given him absolution regarding the disappearance of Victoria. Knowing Patrick as he did, it wouldn't be long before the truth was revealed. He no longer cared what happened to himself. Ann was the only one who trusted and believed that there was good in every person, even him. Malcolm thought of the impending scandal. His father would be furious and humiliated, and that brought a reluctant smile to his face.

Malcolm worried about Ann. As long as David remained free, her life was in danger. Wadding up the paper, he threw it in the fireplace. Hell, he would have to go just to keep an eye on Ann. He prayed that Patrick wouldn't badger him with questions. He couldn't keep up the pretense much longer.

Malcolm ordered his bags packed for the brief trip to London. His father's booming voice greeted him as he walked into the dining room.

Out of breath, William swayed as he tried to sit in a chair. Waving a fleshy hand at the butler, William demanded a drink.

Malcolm calmly sat down at the table. "Have you forgotten how to make pleasantries? And judging by your condition, your finances have taken a tumble."

William scowled. "Not that you care. After dinner, I want to look at the financial records."

Malcolm abruptly pushed back his chair and stood. "I control the estate now. Since you have continually gambled away more money than I care to think about, I have started proceedings to declare you incompetent."

With a swipe of his hand, William's glass crashed to the floor. His face turned red with anger. "By God, I will not tolerate this! No son of mine will be stealing what is rightfully mine." His arms flailed wildly as he advanced toward Malcolm. He raised his fists, ready to strike his son.

Malcolm didn't flinch. Instead, he coolly stated, "Hit me and

I will throw you from this house and forget that you are my father."

William's fists fell to his sides. His chest deflated like a balloon leaking hot air. "Come now. What are we doing? Family shouldn't be threatening each other like this. Let's both calm down and discuss this like men."

Malcolm let out a deep breath, unaware that he had been holding it. He was suspicious at the sudden change. "I thought you were staying in London. Why did you return to the country?"

William's eyes shifted from Malcolm's face. "I decided to try my hand at the race track again. I heard that you had the estate flourishing again. I would be negligent not to stop by and see for myself."

Malcolm flashed an irritated look at the older man. "I stopped by our town house and saw that you had a house guest. Did you leave him there alone?"

"Of course. He's one of us. Our tastes are quite similar, if you get my meaning. Now that you and I do not go about together anymore, I enjoy his company. He has experienced a bit of bad luck so I invited him to stay with me. Why do you ask?"

"Haven't you heard the latest rumor about Mr. Stewart?"

"There are always rumors. What have you heard?"

"Lady Marshall reported that he broke into their home and attacked her with a knife. Several days after the incident, your son-in-law and Lord Marshall chased him out of London. It was a terrible scene. People were literally being run off the road. From what I gather, O'Neil and Marshall are being hailed as heroes for giving chase."

William sputtered, "Don't say! I knew the young man had some rather peculiar tastes and all, but I had no idea that he would go that far."

"I suggest that you return to London to make sure Mr. Stewart and his belongings are removed from the house. If you are associated with him in any manner, it will be your complete ruination. By the way, the invitation for the Winscott ball was delivered last week."

William clapped his hands together. "Good! There will be a great deal of wagering in the card room. With the high stakes, I should be able to recover my recent losses. When is it?"

A twinge of remorse filled Malcolm. "The invitation was addressed to me only. Word of your bad debts and erratic behavior has reached the ears of London. I tried to warn you."

William's cheeks puffed out like balloons. "I'm not invited?"

"Father, I don't know how to put it any plainer, but the answer is yes. If you would change and be more respectable, perhaps next year will be different."

The portly man crumpled before Malcolm's eyes. Not saying a word, William shuffled from the room. Humming a nonsensical tune, William trudged up the stairs to his room.

Watching the beaten figure, Malcolm regretted the firm manner in which he'd handled his father, but if he had done any less, William would have destroyed their chances for financial success.

Malcolm checked in on his father before leaving for London. He was appalled at how quick William's condition had deteriorated. William lay curled in a fetal position, rocking himself on the bed. The odd humming noises continued uninterrupted.

"Father, can you hear me?"

Getting no response, he sent for the physician. The elderly physician arrived with his black leather bag in hand. Malcolm rushed the man upstairs. They found William sitting motionless, a vacant stare in his eyes.

The physician frowned as he assessed William's condition. Motioning for Malcolm to step out to the hallway, the physician whispered, "The ailment is not physical. His mind has been afflicted. Whether this is permanent, I cannot say at this time. I suggest we keep him comfortable and calm for now. I will leave laudanum. Four drops every few hours and he will sleep like a baby. I will check back tomorrow."

After the physician left, Malcolm glanced at the closed bedroom door. Should he stay here or go to the ball as he'd promised Ann? There was no choice. He had to watch over Ann. Peter could watch William and send word if his condition worsened.

It was too late to leave for London today, so Malcolm sought out the comfort of his room. He would leave at first light. Peace was as elusive in sleep as it was during the day. He tossed, turned, and fought the tormenting demons that haunted his world. Drenched in sweat, he awoke sensing that a major precipice was at hand.

Malcolm dressed, filled with an urge to quit this house and never return. He checked on his father one last time. Peter, William's valet, jerked awake as Malcolm entered the room. "How is he? Did he sleep well last night?"

The valet nodded. "He woke once. I gave him the medicine like the doctor ordered. I'm sure he will be fine."

Malcolm glanced at the sleeping man. His breathing was labored and shallow, though his color much improved. "You know where I can be reached. Make sure you do not leave him alone. He may harm himself."

With everything secured, Malcolm headed toward London, anxious to be far removed from his home.

When William roused, his valet quickly came to his bedside.

"Sir, how do you feel? Can I get you something to drink?"

William blinked repeatedly. "Where am I?"

"Your room, sir. You're home where you should be."

William sat up. Rubbing his head, he moaned. "I've a splitting headache. What did you give me to drink last night?"

Peter recounted yesterday's events. The argument with Malcolm came flooding back. Now he remembered. He was being written off, ignored by his former friends. His life had deteriorated since Victoria's marriage. There were increasing financial difficulties and Malcolm's new devotion to morals. Everything had changed since Victoria married Patrick.

"Prepare my bath and bring me the best bottle of port that's in the house."

As William soaked in the tub, his thoughts continued to dwell on how much better the past had been compared to his current situation.

The effects of the laudanum lingered, and combined with the port, it distorted William's thoughts. He felt light-headed.

Hours later, William sat in the library with the financial records spread out before him. His son had amassed a small fortune in the past few months. In a queer way, he was proud of him. That thought quickly fled and was replaced with visions of using this money for the gaming tables and horses. He could double or triple the money within weeks. William gleefully cackled, rubbing his hands together.

He scribbled a note to the solicitor, requesting a large advance. In a celebratory mood, he rang for another bottle. By late afternoon, his confidence had dwindled. Finally, there was a knock on the door. "Enter."

Peter held an envelope. "Sir, this was just delivered."

He rose to his feet, trying to steady himself. "Is that all? No one is here to see me?"

"No, sir. Just this."

William ripped open the envelope from their solicitor. He blinked with disbelief. No money would be sent to him without Malcolm's signed authorization. The paper slipped from his hand and fell to the floor.

"Did you get the money?"

"Get out, you impertinent bastard!"

Peter fled from the room. William stumbled about the room. His pulse pounded in his head. He would show them all! He would go to London and attend the ball. They would not dare deny him entry, for to do so would create a scene. It was time to put his plan into motion. Once he got his hands on the O'Neil fortune, nothing would be denied him.

He unlocked the bottom desk drawer and pulled out a pistol. In a crowded ballroom, no one would see who pulled the trigger. Tomorrow he would become the executor of Victoria's estate.

Chapter 51

DAWN BROKE, REVEALING AN endless blue sky and brilliant sunlight. Ann was filled with excitement. The ball was tonight! If only Jessica and Stacy could be here to enjoy the thrill with her. Ann's lower lip began to tremble. She brushed aside the thoughts of the past. Tonight was a fairy tale coming to life. She wouldn't let her emotions ruin the day.

Ann was growing quite accustomed to the daily rituals of an English lady. There was a time when she believed that she couldn't live without a microwave or blow dryer. Amazingly, she had survived without the luxuries of the twenty-first century.

Ann was surprised when Katherine dropped in for a visit that afternoon. Her guest's unsmiling face sparked concern. "I thought you would be getting ready for the big night. Is anything wrong?"

Katherine removed her hat, patting her gold-spun coiffure into place. "No, everything is fine. Let's sit down. I wanted to speak with you privately, to thank you. You will never know how much I have appreciated your kindness. I have had few friends until now. I will always treasure our friendship." Katherine bit her lip. "Edward told me about your past."

Ann coolly replied, "I'm not sure that I understand what you're saying."

Katherine took Ann's trembling hand in hers. "Don't be afraid.

I will not say a word. Edward swore he would divorce me if I did. He thought I should know the truth about David. I knew there was something different about you. I just could not put my finger on it. You must not blame yourself for what has happened. Men like David exist in this world as they do in yours."

Ann didn't know how to respond. Just because Edward trusted Katherine, could she? Could life be any more complicated? Tears blurred her vision.

"Thank you. You can't believe how hard it was to pretend that I was Victoria. Without Patrick's help, I would have been lost. I'll let you in on a little secret. Women in my time are completely independent from men. I think you would enjoy living in the future." Katherine doubled over with laughter when Ann explained that some women actually shaved their heads or dyed their hair shades of blue or green.

Ann spotted Patrick standing in the doorway watching them. One look at his puzzled face caused Ann to burst into another round of laughter.

"Would you mind telling me what is so funny? I could use a good laugh."

Between hiccups, Ann explained that Katherine knew about her past and they had been comparing notes on men.

As Patrick sat down and stretched his legs, he muttered, "I hope you know that we men do not sit around discussing women."

With a side-glance at Katherine, Ann started laughing again.

"Well, I can tell when I am not appreciated." Patrick left the room shaking his head.

Entering his dressing room, Patrick saw that Carrick had laid out his evening clothes. He stripped off his clothes and slid into the waiting bath. The moist steam swirled about the room. Thinking that Ann would join him, he leaned back and relaxed. As the water grew tepid, he gave up waiting and finished bathing. With the towel wrapped snugly about his waist, he stood in front of the mirror and began shaving. He nearly dropped the razor as Ann burst into the room.

Her hungry gaze studied his naked body. Ann sauntered toward him, grabbing a towel to blot the drops of moisture glistening on his chest. Her hands glided over his chest. Unconsciously, he sucked in his breath.

He turned toward the mirror and resumed shaving. "You're too late."

She stared at his back. "Late for what?"

"To scrub my back."

She wrapped her arms around his lean waist. Resting her head against his muscled back, she purred. Carefully, he set the sharp razor aside. With shaving cream still lathered on one cheek, he turned and pressed his face to hers.

She grimaced, wiping away the cream that stuck to her mouth. "You rat! You're lucky I haven't started dressing yet." Glancing at the clock on the table, she shrieked. "Why didn't you tell me it was this late? We're supposed to meet everyone at nine."

Flying out of the room, Ann yelled for her maid. Minutes later, the entire upstairs was a hub of activity.

Two hours later, Patrick stood alone at the foot of the stairs. Pacing back and forth, he glanced upward, expecting to see Ann at any minute. There was no use getting in a dither. He had learned many years ago that it was useless to try to hurry a woman.

At last, he heard her footsteps. He froze as she approached. She looked exquisite. His pulse quickened as he lifted his hand to support her down the last few steps. She wore his mother's pearls. A pang of loss struck him as he remembered his mother wearing the same necklace and earrings at many events.

He raised her hand to his lips, caressing her creamy skin. Goose bumps popped up on her arm. He gave her a smug look. He liked the idea that he could still titillate his wife.

∞

Climbing into the carriage, Ann shivered. A dense fog swirled around the carriage, almost obscuring everything from view. It was creepy. It reminded her of one of the Halloween slasher-type movies.

Patrick's warm, assessing gaze enveloped her. Brushing aside her imagination, Ann nestled next to him. Tonight was a fairy tale, and nothing could spoil its magic.

Carriages were lined up for two blocks in both directions. Multitudes of glittering lights from the Winscott house lit up the entire block. The stately gray stone mansion stood three stories high. Ann was duly impressed as one of the many costumed footmen wearing the old-fashioned livery and wigs magically opened the carriage door. Amazingly, they were all the same height. She had read that many of the households wanted their footmen to be near the same height.

Once inside, they were directed to the receiving line. At least fifty people milled about in the spacious foyer, waiting to be greeted by their hosts.

Patrick smiled at the duke. "Your Grace. You have quite a showing tonight."

Beaming his approval at the young couple, the duke of Winscott shook Patrick's hand. "Glad you made it. If I can get away later, I would like to speak to you privately."

"It would be my pleasure, Your Grace."

The sight that greeted Ann's eyes when they entered the ballroom was one she had only seen in the movies. A small orchestra entertained the ensemble in the upper balcony. Brightly colored dresses blended together like a kaleidoscope as the couples swirled gaily about the floor.

Weaving their way through the crowd, several women flashed assessing glances at Patrick. The women went out of their way to present themselves to him. Brazenly they approached, tittering and brushing against his body.

Resentment coursed through her. Ann tried to pull away, but Patrick gripped her elbow tighter. It made her mad that some of these people assumed that Patrick would be looking for a mistress. Those women obviously didn't know that she had claws and wasn't afraid to use them.

Politely nodding as they jostled through the wall of people, he muttered under his breath, "Calm down. It's not what you think."

"How do you know what I think? Those women practically rubbed up against you, and you just stood there and smiled."

Patrick reached for a glass of champagne from a passing servant. Downing it quickly, he replied, "I was only being polite. How would you suggest that I handle the situation?"

The puzzled look on his face made her smile. "I'm sorry I overreacted."

"I didn't realize you were the jealous type." He gently tipped her chin, kissing the tip of her nose.

Several elderly women sitting nearby sighed in unison as Patrick kissed her. Wow! What a mood booster!

Patrick nodded toward the doorway. "I see Anthony and Eleanor. I'll let them know we're here."

"Hurry back." Standing alone, a sense of uneasiness filled her. She regretted her decision to wait for Patrick. Ann jumped when someone touched her arm. Malcolm stood grinning at her. Flooded with relief, Ann tightly embraced him.

Malcolm blushed. "What's this? If you're not careful, rumors will sprout up like mushrooms."

Playfully tapping his forearm with her fan, Ann boasted, "I knew you would come. You look so handsome. Now admit it—don't you feel better just getting away from that house?"

He replied, "Quite right. Wonderful idea. Instead of standing here feeling conspicuous, shall we dance?"

"I'm still a horrible dancer, but if you're game, so am I."

Ann took pleasure at the serene look on Malcolm's face as they glided across the floor. A boyish smile transformed his normally stoic face. If only he could meet someone and fall in love.

Malcolm stiffened. His gaze focused on a nearby window.

"What's wrong? You look as if you saw a ghost." Ann nervously glanced outside.

Malcolm led Ann away from the other dancers. "It's worse. I think I just saw my father."

"Oh no. What does he want?"

Malcolm planted a quick kiss on her cheek. "I intend to find out. Please excuse me."

Ann made her away to the other side of the room, to where Patrick and their friends were visiting. Ann noticed that Katherine was without a veil for the first time since the attack. The faint scar on her cheek was barely visible.

Ann whispered the disturbing news about William to Patrick.

Groaning, he said, "I'll see if I can find Malcolm. Stay here. I shall return soon."

Ann struggled not to panic, not wanting to ruin the evening for their friends.

In hushed tones, Katherine drew Ann and Eleanor to her side. "See the gentleman in the dark blue jacket? You must not accept a dance with him, especially you, Eleanor. Lord Eden is a reprobate of the worst kind. I know for a fact that he ruined a young lady last season."

"By all means, Miss Curtis will not dance with him." Anthony took Eleanor's hand and placed his hand slightly on her waist, pulling her closer than normal.

Blushing profusely, Eleanor seemed transfixed by Anthony's intent stare. Ann smiled as she thought of the couple's odd behavior at her house. From the looks on their faces, Ann knew they were deeply in love with each other.

Ann's astute gaze followed Anthony and Eleanor as they danced. "I cannot ever imagine blushing like that, can you, Katherine?"

Before Katherine could respond, Patrick captured Ann in an embrace. "Shall we dance?"

As soon as they were away from their friends, Ann prompted, "Well?"

Patrick looked frustrated. "I couldn't find either one of them."

"Maybe Malcolm found William and took him home."

Patrick tightened his hold around her waist. "Perhaps."

She rested her cheek on his chest as they wove around the crowded dance floor. She pushed aside unhappy thoughts, concentrating on her handsome husband. Surprisingly, his deep rumbling laughter drew Ann's attention.

"What's so funny?"

"We're causing a scene with our close embrace. Haven't you noticed the raised eyebrows cast in our direction?"

Sure enough, several women stared with their tight lips scrunched together. Mischievously, Ann pressed her hips closer to Patrick. "Good heavens. It's not as if we are strangers. Besides, I like the feel of you against me."

He pressed his arousal against her. His hot breath grazed her ear. "You vixen! Just you wait until I get you home."

Distracted, she stumbled and stepped squarely on his foot. "Quit talking like that. See what you've done? I'm trying to remember the dance steps you taught me. Everyone will think that I'm the biggest klutz in the world."

Patrick's response was to twirl her faster around the floor. Ann's giggles lit up Patrick's face and drew the attention of the other dancers. As Ann swirled in Patrick's arms, she caught sight of an elderly woman. Tingles ran down Ann's spine. Her head whipped around, trying to catch sight of the woman. Who was she? At that moment, she saw the woman across the room. The woman's sparkling eyes were fixed on her. Ann's mouth dropped open. It was the elderly woman from the bookstore. Holy moly!

Chapter 52

COMING TO A COMPLETE stop in the middle of the dance floor, Ann turned in a complete circle, trying to find the woman again. Ann's stomach felt queasy. Patrick was looking totally bewildered. Other couples nearly collided with them as they stood unmoving in the middle of the ballroom.

She pasted a smile on her face as they walked out of the ballroom. She had to find the woman—to know if it was really the same woman.

"What's wrong? You look as if you've seen a ghost."

Ann pointed toward the veranda doors. "Did you see an older woman with a gaudy headdress?"

Patrick glanced around the room. "I see several women who fit that description. Why?"

Ann felt numb. How could the woman from the bookstore be here? Ann shivered, mentally rejecting the thought. "Never mind. I'm probably hallucinating. Let's go eat."

Sitting with her husband and friends, Ann paid little attention to the conversation around her. Several of Patrick's acquaintances approached, and within minutes, they were deep in discussion on the merits of rail transportation. Ann excused herself and walked outside to the balcony.

She had just determined that her imagination was on overload when a strange thumping sound drew her attention. How odd. It reminded her of the old woman from the bookstore when her cane hit the floor. Ann turned, searching for the source of the sound. The crowd of people near the doorway parted. Ann shivered with anticipation. The woman's cane hit the floor with every step. Her white hair was coiffed into a sophisticated French twist. The woman appeared to be the epitome of a rich society woman, nothing like the woman from the bookstore. Sighing with relief, Ann had just started to turn away when she saw the tips of black boots peeking out from under the woman's gown. Those couldn't be the same boots ... but they were! Every scent, every minute spent in the bookstore came rushing back to Ann.

The woman glanced over her shoulder at Ann and walked out to the balcony. Ann quickly hurried after her, afraid she was having a nervous breakdown. Out of breath, Ann came to a halt as she saw the woman waiting for her.

"Hello, dearie! I've been expecting you."

Ann gulped. She was real. The woman was talking to her. "Hello." Ann couldn't think what else to say.

Leaning on her cane, the woman studied Ann. "You have done well. You look like a grand nineteenth-century lady. You and Patrick have married, I see."

Ann could only nod. Her eyes widened as a gray cat appeared beside the woman's feet. A loud purring sound erupted as the cat rubbed against the woman. Bending over to pet the cat, the woman gave her a sly look.

"You must have a few questions for me."

"Who are you?"

The woman shrugged. "That's not really important, is it? You can consider me your special angel."

"Angel?" Ann croaked.

The woman's harsh laughter surprised Ann. "Your soul didn't want to stay in the twenty-first century, so I helped matters along. You and Patrick needed each other."

"But why me?"

A sad look graced the woman's face. "Why not? Although there was a glitch. David Stewart wasn't supposed to come back in time.

Fate will have to resolve that matter. Now I must go. I have many projects, you know. I want you to know that you are meant to be here. Be happy, my dear. Please enjoy the life you've been given."

A sudden gust of wind blew fallen leaves in Ann's face. When she opened her eyes, the woman and cat were gone. A broken sob escaped Ann. In a way, she now had some answers. Now it made sense to know why she was always drawn to Patrick.

She heard Patrick calling her name. Wiping the tears, she turned to see his silhouette fill the door behind her. Lifting her skirts, she ran into his waiting arms.

"Is something wrong?" His gruff voice tickled her ear.

"Everything is right, as it should be." Her lips met his. Moments later, she took his hand. "Let's go inside. We have a ball to enjoy."

Just as they were about to enter the ballroom, Ann caught a sound in the wind. It was the sound of a cat. *Meow.*

Once inside, they were joined by the Marshalls, Anthony, and Eleanor. Ann watched several high-ranking parliamentary members walking into another room. "Where are those people going?"

Katherine glanced toward the exiting guests. "Julia Cameron is in the other room. It's a great honor for her to attend this type of function."

"Is she royalty?"

Katherine's smile broadened. "Gracious no. She is a renowned photographer. Mostly she photographs important men in government and such. She has a flair for experimenting and trying new things. She has requested certain people to sit for her tonight. The duchess has asked Miss Cameron to take some photographs of the ball for her personal records."

A sense of apprehension enveloped Ann. The faces and voices around her drifted away. She remembered reading about Julia Cameron in a college class. What was happening?

Patrick gripped her hand. "Are you ill? You look quite pale."

Ann tried to smile, shaking off the eerie feeling. "I was just thinking about photos." She wrapped her arm in Patrick's. "Take me outside, please. I need some fresh air."

Patrick took on a roguish mien, winking invitingly. "Is this a proposition, madam? I will gladly oblige after we take care of one little matter."

Ann couldn't imagine what he meant.

"We've been asked to pose for Miss Cameron."

Ann's mouth opened and closed without uttering a sound. Then she sputtered, "You're kidding! Why us?"

"She mentioned something about lighting and the color of your hair and dress. She hinted that you would be an interesting subject."

"Where are we supposed to go?"

"She wants to take the photograph while we are dancing and then do some still shots."

Patrick took Ann in his arms for the last waltz. Lost in the rhythm of the music and the warmth of Patrick's arms, she forgot all about Malcolm, William, and their problems.

Ann could see Miss Cameron setting up in the corner of the ballroom. Minutes later, the blinding flash of the camera brought Ann's life into focus. She and Patrick posed for several shots, facing the camera together. The photographer also took several shots while they were dancing. One photograph was of Patrick holding her in his arms, dancing with her back to the camera.

Her mind whirled with the implications of that shot. The picture in the book! It had to be the picture in that old album that gave her the nightmares. Ann knew that Patrick held a woman in the picture, but she had never closely examined the woman. If she were able to look at the album again, would she recognize herself? My God! She was *the* Lady O'Neil, the creator of the album. Her pulse raced. Her head pounded. If she was the woman in the picture, then the old woman must have been correct. She was meant to be here. She needed to start a diary and album right away, starting with the pictures taken tonight.

Chapter 53

THE SOUND OF MUSIC drifted away. Patrick led Ann outside to enjoy the cool night air. Running his finger under the collar of his shirt, he groaned. "I swear everyone in London is here tonight. I detest coming to these things. Beneath all the glitter and polished manners, people relish in the misfortune of others. You cannot believe how many people have asked me about William."

Standing next to one another, they looked out into the darkened gardens. When a sound came from the nearby bushes, Patrick turned. A man lunged out of the shadows barreling into Patrick like a battering ram. Unprepared for the attack, Patrick's head slammed against the marble railing. He struggled to remain on his feet, gasping for breath. Blood trickled from a cut on his forehead.

"Patrick!" Ann tried to rush to Patrick's side, but a rough jerk brought her to a stop.

She was shocked to see that William held her arm. He tightened his grip around her arm. His eyes were unnaturally bright as he pointed a pistol at Patrick's chest.

Without warning, William's fist struck the side of her face. Dazed, Ann fell to the ground, disoriented and bleeding.

When Patrick attempted to come to her defense, William lunged and clubbed him over the head with the butt of the weapon. Patrick crumpled into a heap.

Specks of light danced before her eyes. She slowly pulled

herself up, leaning against the railing. William's raspy voice filtered through her numbness.

"In a few moments, I will kill your husband. Then you will stumble into the house and claim to have discovered his body. My plan is foolproof. That Stewart fellow will be blamed. You will inherit everything, and I will be named as executor. We will have enough money for a lifetime. Do as I say and we both can go our separate ways and never see one another again."

Sickened by his evil intentions, Ann leaned over the railing and took several deep breaths, hoping to clear her head. With the pistol aimed at Patrick, her choices were limited. She had to pretend to go along with his scheme until she could disarm him or Patrick came to.

William bent over and tied a rope around Patrick's ankles. Straightening, he motioned with the gun for Ann to follow. He dragged Patrick's limp body into the darkness. Glancing helplessly toward the house, she unwillingly followed into the darkness.

William stopped near a row of hedges. Only the sound of his raspy breathing broke the quiet of the night. "This looks as good as anywhere else."

Ann fought to keep her hysteria at bay. The hopelessness of the situation prevented any rational thought. "You're crazy. This is murder! Spare Patrick and I will get you as much money as you want."

William mimicked her voice. "Yes, I'm sure O'Neil will just turn over his money to me. You must think that I'm a fool. I will have his entire fortune."

An unexpected voice came out of the darkness. Ann sent up a silent prayer.

"You won't need any money where you're going." Malcolm came into view.

William waved the gun at Malcolm. "Leave us. This doesn't concern you. You can have the estate, and I will have the power and influence that I deserve."

Palms upturned, Malcolm slowly approached William. "You're

wrong! This does concern me. Put the gun down and walk away before it's too late."

William's laughter filled the air. "You idiot. It is already too late. This is my last warning. Leave now or you can join O'Neil."

For a moment, time was suspended. Ann would remember the next few minutes for the rest of her life.

Malcolm lunged forward, grabbing for the pistol. The two men rolled on the ground, wrestling for control of the weapon. Ann moved closer, hoping to get an opportunity to help Malcolm. The barrel of the gun jerked in her direction. Ann fell to the ground, trying to get out of the line of fire. Unable to force the gun from his father's grip, Malcolm smashed a fist into his father's face.

Stunned, the gun fell from William's hand. Blood gushed from his nose. Spittle dribbled from the corner of his slack mouth.

Malcolm tossed the gun aside. In a blink of an eye, William attacked Malcolm. Hit with a disabling blow to the midsection, Malcolm fell to his knees, clutching his stomach. He stared at his father with a hatred-filled look as he staggered to his feet.

William scooped up the gun, pointing it at Malcolm. "You always were a fool." William squeezed the trigger.

"No!" she screamed.

Malcolm jerked. His eyes widened as a red stain blossomed across his chest. He held out a hand to Ann while slipping to the ground. For Ann, everything seemed to be happening in slow motion.

Ann fell to the ground beside Malcolm. Frantic, she pressed her hand over the gaping wound, trying to stop the flow of blood. Why Malcolm? He had changed and was doing so much good. She should be the one lying in the pool of blood, not him.

William stood above Ann, pointing the gun at her. "Sorry, my dear. I hadn't planned to kill you, but now I have no choice."

The sound of voices drifted toward them. Thankfully, the gunshot had drawn the attention of the partygoers.

As the click of the hammer echoed in her ears, Ann squeezed her eyes shut. *My God, I'm going to die!* Her entire being screamed with the injustice of the situation. Evil people were supposed to die, not the good ones. Not Malcolm! Not Patrick! A minute passed and then another. Ann cautiously opened her eyes.

William's body wavered before her. He tried to reach behind him. He fell forward, screaming in agony. With a loud ragged breath, he lay motionless on the dew-covered grass. A pearl-handled knife stuck out of his back. The blade was buried deep within his flesh.

Patrick had regained consciousness and was propped against a nearby tree. She knew that he had thrown the knife. His loving smile was the best thing she had ever seen. Ann crawled to his side, sobbing with relief. She threw her arms around his neck, wanting to blot out the gruesome sight of William's twitching body.

Patrick held her tightly. Still clutching Ann, Patrick edged to Malcolm's aid.

Malcolm's eyes fluttered opened. Pain filled his eyes. Malcolm wanted to put his conscience to rest. "You were right about me. You do not have to worry about Victoria any longer. She and I can now be together forever."

Patrick leaned over, gently brushing dirt off the dying man's face. "Victoria is dead?"

Malcolm wearily nodded. "Yes, there was an accident, and she fell. I swore that after that night, I would be a better person. I tried hard to live without her, but I just couldn't."

Malcolm reached out for Ann. She had to bend close to hear his whispered words. "I wish we could have spent more time together."

He began to cough, splattering blood on Ann. Unable to breathe, he brokenly muttered, "You must do everything in your power to stay with Patrick. He loves you."

Her throat tightened with emotion. Ann kissed him gently on the cheek. "You were the brother I never had. You shouldn't have tried to save me. I will miss you." Choking back a sob, Ann fell to Malcolm's side.

The flash of lanterns drew nearer. Patrick tried to pull Ann away from the grisly scene. Malcolm's chest no longer rose and fell so painfully. Frozen in death, he had a slight smile on his face. Surely he was in a place where he could find happiness again.

Anthony burst through the hedges. He came to a sudden halt at the sight of the bodies. "What the hell happened?"

"I'll tell you later. Help me get Ann inside," Patrick brusquely replied.

The duchess met them at the doorway and quickly away from the hordes of curious eyes. Gossip would run rampant by morning. Eleanor and Katherine followed, alarmed by the blood on Ann's clothes.

Ann reassured everyone that she was fine, but the tears would not cease. In shock, she kept reliving the scene when William shot Malcolm. Poor Malcolm! He'd tried to rescue them and ended up losing his own life.

Patrick held Ann in his arms as she sobbed for her loss. Hours later, Patrick finally relinquished his hold. "I must go and explain what happened. I'll return shortly."

Ann nodded. She closed her eyes, willing the memory of the night to fade into oblivion. Katherine and Eleanor sat nearby, guarding their friend from curious onlookers peeking inside the room.

By dawn, the bodies were removed and the statements and evidence were gathered. As the dawn broke through the clouds, Ann and Patrick were allowed to return home.

The next day, the entire city knew what had happened. People deeply sympathized with Ann, for they believed she had lost both a father and brother. Patrick had made it clear in his report that without Malcolm's intervention, Patrick and Ann would both be dead.

The days blurred together. Well-wishers and the curious came and went. Katherine and Edward played hosts as Ann stayed in her room. Patrick made the funeral arrangements. Ann refused to discuss the events of that night. She wanted to forget that awful night.

Throughout Malcolm's funeral, Patrick remained at Ann's side. Once the service ended, Ann escaped to the solitude of her room.

Everyone's attempts to talk to Ann were met with failure. Day after day, she sat woodenly gazing out the window. Didn't these people get it! She was in a world not of her own, and it could be taken away at any minute. The thought of leaving Patrick was too much to bear. The old woman could be wrong. No one knew what was going to happen.

David waited across the street in a hired carriage. He shoved the curtain aside so he could view those coming and going. He had been in the country, letting the police and O'Neil cool their heels. Bored with rural pleasures, he had returned to London and learned of William's untimely death. It was so easy to become lost in this bustling city. He was confident in his ability to avoid the police.

David hated living in the nineteenth century. He wanted to enjoy modern conveniences again. He would choose a car over a horse any day. Damn animals were always crapping right where he stepped. David had given much thought to his dilemma and deduced that there was only one way to go back to 2013. The timing had to be just right. If his calculations were correct, he had been here almost a year. The pinnacle of his future was fast approaching, and he would be ready.

Chapter 54

IT TOOK A MONTH before Ann felt like her old self. Just being outdoors boosted her spirits immensely. She felt horrible about how she had treated Patrick since Malcolm's death. She had been self-centered, not considering his emotions. She had to figure out a way to apologize.

She settled back in the carriage, enjoying the short ride to Katherine's. The gray cloud of fog and smoke that typically hung over London from the coal was nonexistent this day, allowing glorious bright rays of sunlight to bring life to Ann's world.

Reconciliation had not come easily, if at all. Her nights were tormented with Malcolm's needless death. Yet the past could not be undone. She could only try to outwit fate and prevent any additional calamities.

She breezed into the Marshalls' drawing room and found Eleanor, who had also stopped to visit. Handing her wrap to a waiting servant, Ann smiled at her friends. "It is so nice to see you two again. I'm excited to hear of your wedding plans."

Eleanor frowned, nibbling on her lower lip. "I am afraid that Anthony is out of sorts with my mother. She can be quite determined. Her plans for our wedding are very grand. She said that if I am to marry an earl, then we must have an appropriate ceremony. I fear there will be a great brouhaha when Lady Aylesbury and my mother meet."

Ann chortled aloud. Lady Aylesbury was a steamroller. It was a wonder that Anthony had remained single so long with a mother so determined to get her way.

Ann wiped the tears from her eyes, struggling to regain her composure. "This is the best I've felt in weeks."

After lunch, when Ann prepared to leave, Katherine pulled her aside. "We were so worried about you. Patrick believes he is to blame for Malcolm's death."

How could Patrick even think such a thing? It was her fault, not his. If she had screamed or run for help, Malcolm would be alive today. She had made a terrible mess of things. A chasm had grown between her and Patrick, jeopardizing their relationship. She had to make things right.

Hurrying home, Ann rushed past the surprised butler. Picking up her skirts, she raced upstairs. Patrick would be home soon, and she planned to seduce the pants off him. He was going to know, without a doubt, how sorry she was … and that she needed him.

Patrick stood on the steps leading to his house. He ran his hand through windblown hair and glanced up at their bedroom window. He wanted his vivacious wife back—the one he could not predict, the one who could make him laugh aloud, the one with the sultry looks—the one who could bring him to his knees within minutes.

Standing in the foyer, silence met his ears. He strode to the library, his frown growing by the minute. Damn, he couldn't stand living like this. One minute he wanted to shake some sense into her, and the next, he wanted her lying in bed with him.

Determined, he went to find Maggie. His presence in the kitchen caused some of the servants to look up from their duties. Maggie looked toward the doorway, gasping, "Lord O'Neil."

Authoritatively, she took his arm and led him away from prying eyes. Maggie scolded, "What's wrong? I haven't seen that pouty look of yours in years."

Feeling penitent, he asked, "Is Lady O'Neil in?"

"I heard her come in some time ago. Shall I send someone for her?"

"No. How is she feeling today?"

Maggie patted his arm and flashed him a smile. "Well, she's been prancing around and singing since she returned. It's as if she's anxious to see someone."

Patrick threw his arms around his faithful housekeeper and kissed her soundly on the lips.

"Merciful heavens!" she shrieked.

Maggie's laughter followed him down the hallway. Patrick ran up the stairs, taking them two at a time. The glow from a banked fire warmed the bedroom as he opened the door. Next to the bed sat a bottle of wine and two glasses. The covers on the bed were turned down.

The dressing room door slowly opened. Ann wore a paper-thin cloud of violet silk. Her arms fell to her side, revealing a plunging neckline. She glided across the room and stood in front of the fire to warm her hands. Her slender thighs were silhouetted through the sheer gown. Patrick's breath caught in his throat as she turned toward him. The light from the fire enabled him to clearly view the curves of her hips and the swell of her breasts.

Unbuttoning his shirt, he tossed it on the floor. His chest muscles tightened involuntarily. Her eyes darkened with anticipation. He wanted to devour her. His fingers slowly loosened the buttons on his trousers. He watched Ann's eyes widen as his pants slid to the floor. He didn't know if he could wait much longer. His member pulsated wildly. A hoarse sound escaped his throat.

He proudly stood before her, his need obvious. He waited for her to come to him, every muscle wound tighter than a spring.

She slipped her hand in his. With a coy glance, she led him to the bed. She slid onto the satin sheets "Are you going to join me?"

Her sultry voice heightened his anticipation. Heat radiated from his body as he inched toward her. "Are you sure this is what you want?"

Ann drew him closer, pressing against him. She rained feather-light kisses on his face, starting with his brow and working down to his waiting lips.

At the first touch of her mouth, his passion burst forth like an untamed beast. Ravaging, plundering, his body urgently sought hers. Her fingers were like torches. Everywhere they touched, his body burned with need. He parted her thighs, easing a finger gently inside. The slow, sensual rhythm of his hand rocked her body.

Panting, Ann slipped from his arms and pushed him on his back. She yanked off her gown and straddled his waist. Her hands glided across his chest. His muscles tightened with every touch. Her breasts teased his lips.

He eyed her budding nipples speculatively, hoarsely whispering, "Are you trying to finish me off for good?"

"Can't a woman enjoy herself? I love touching you. Men are so different from women. I can't resist touching you."

Patrick took a deep breath. At this rate, he would explode before entering her. "Since you love touching me, may I make a suggestion? I have a certain body part that craves your touch." To emphasize the point, his penis jerked against her thigh.

Reaching between them, she wrapped her hand around him. Ever so slowly, she slid her hand up and down, watching his face with every movement. Never a patient man, it was only minutes later before he rolled her beneath him. In an instant, they were joined. Ann trembled as he throbbed inside of her.

His thumb brushed against her lower lip. "Never shut me out again. I don't think I could bear it."

She pressed her hand against his whiskered cheek. "I love you. Will you forgive me?"

"Of course. Now, no more talking."

Feverishly, he branded her with his touch and body. Lost in the haze of passion, the two of them reached the pinnacle of desire together. Wrapped in a cocoon of love, they passed away the hours of the night fulfilling the needs of their souls and bodies.

When the sun peeked through the curtains, Patrick stirred. Careful not to wake Ann, he eased out of bed. They would leave London, get away from the reminders of Malcolm's death.

Several hours later, Ann strolled into the library to find Patrick. Recognizing her footsteps, he looked up from his paperwork. She looked radiant. Gleaming strands of auburn curls framed her swanlike neck. Her lips were red and swollen from his kisses.

"I have a surprise," he said. "Would you care to guess?"

Ann studied his schooled expression. "I don't have a clue, so tell me."

He swooped her off her feet and onto his lap. "I would like to return to the country. Do you have any objections?"

Ann gave him a tentative look. "No. Right now London is full of bad memories and the loss of Malcolm. I think a change in scenery would be a good thing. When do we leave?"

Patrick rose, nearly dumping her to the floor. "How about one hour? I've already given Maggie orders to start packing."

"You rat! What made you think I would agree?"

"After last night, I figured you would follow me anywhere." After leaving the room and quickly closing the door behind him, he heard a loud thump on the other side. His wife loved to throw shoes! A second later, he stuck his head around the door. "Could you write a note to the Marshalls and Anthony and let them know that we're returning to Epsom Hall?"

Ann was already sitting at his desk, writing notes. He blew her a kiss and went about closing up the town house.

Patrick was outside, checking on the loading of the trunks, and he waved as Anthony approached. "I see you received Ann's note."

Anthony pretended to look horrified at the number of trunks being loaded. "I had no idea that women required so much clothing. How do you manage?"

Amused, Patrick reassured his friend. "Don't worry. I'm sure that Eleanor is sensible about these things."

Anthony fell into step beside him. "There is still no word on Stewart. The authorities still believe that he has returned to America. Personally, I have my doubts."

Patrick glanced briefly toward the house. "I agree. I want to be gone before there is too much activity on the streets. I hope it may be days before anyone knows we are gone. At least there, I can control who comes and goes. I plan on having men on guard around the clock."

"What will Ann say about the guards?"

"As far as she is concerned, they're just men who work for me, doing odd jobs about the place. I don't want to burden her."

"Bloody hell!" Anthony swore. "I cannot believe that David has simply disappeared. If you need anything, you must promise to send word immediately."

Solemnly, Patrick agreed. He warily glanced around at the surrounding shrubs and hedges. Patrick often wondered if David lurked nearby, laughing at them all.

Upon returning to the house, the men found Edward and Katherine enjoying tea with Ann.

Patrick threw his hands up in the air. "Ann, you do know that we're leaving shortly?"

Before Ann could answer, Katherine interrupted. "Now, Patrick, we just stopped by to say our good-byes."

Patrick bowed to Katherine, capitulating. "I withdraw my comments. You are right, of course."

Edward stifled a chuckle. "Don't be too apologetic. Women will start expecting that kind of stuff, you know."

That brought instant denials from the women and laughter from the men. Ann promised a weekend party at their residence next month so that they could all get together.

When their friends departed, Patrick flashed a quick glance up and down the street. Hundreds of hiding places lined the street.

"I know you're out there somewhere, you bastard!" Patrick exclaimed. "If you make the mistake of harming Ann again, it will be your last mistake."

From the foyer, Ann called. "Did you say something, darling?"

"No, just talking to myself. I'll be up in a few minutes." He felt edgy. His instinct warned him of impending danger.

Chapter 55

THE SUNNY DAY HAD turned into a gentle mist and gray overcast skies by the time they loaded the carriages. The gloomy skies couldn't dampen Patrick's spirits. They were leaving London. There were too many dangers in London. He could keep her safer at their country home, Epsom Hall.

His aunt Lady O'Neil awaited their arrival. She had returned from her tour of Europe. Mary greeted them at the door, hugging them both.

Ann sighed with pleasure. "It's so good to be home. I feel better already."

"You poor dears. You had such a bad time of it in London. Well, now that you are here, I will look after the both of you."

Patrick hugged his aunt and pressed a kiss to her cheek. "I love you, Auntie. Now tell me there are hot scones ready to eat."

Ann headed for the stairway. "I need to freshen up."

Patrick agreed. "I couldn't agree more. Why don't you take advantage of the hot bath I know Maggie has waiting for you. I'll join you shortly."

With responsibility weighing heavily on his shoulders, Patrick turned toward the library and locked the door behind him after entering. Waiting in chairs by his desk were two of the guards that he'd hired. He motioned for them to remain seated as he poured a drink. Ignoring the customary pleasantries, he impatiently asked, "Well, did either one of you see anything on our way here?"

Both men shook their heads. Patrick fixed his gaze on them. Thomas, the more experienced guard, finally spoke. "We made a thorough search of the grounds after arriving, just like you ordered. No one has seen any strangers in the area."

Patrick's emotions were stretched to a thread. He knew that David was too smart to be seen. "Are the guards posted around the grounds as I requested?"

"Yes, sir."

Patrick dismissed the men. "Keep me informed of anything out of the ordinary."

Patrick sat alone for hours, his head resting on the back of the chair and his eyes squeezed shut. When he opened them, it was dark outside. Every instinct told him that David was closing in. Should he warn Ann? There was no reason to make her miserable or afraid of every shadow that moved. For now, it was best if he kept his suspicions to himself.

Entering the bedroom, he quietly shed his clothes and slid into bed. He cradled Ann's body to his, listening to the nocturnal sounds that echoed through the huge house. Those odd noises had never unnerved him until tonight. No matter how hard he tried to remain awake, the need for sleep overcame his desire for vigilance.

The next couple of weeks passed without incident. The staff and guards fell into a relaxed routine. Even Patrick had to admit that perhaps he had been overreacting. Anthony had sent a note indicating that he and Eleanor planned to visit the following weekend. Luckily, her mother was allowing Ann to act as chaperone.

It was as if David had completely vanished from the face of the earth. Could he have been sent back to 2013? Could they be that lucky?

The time with Ann was more than he could have hoped for. Every morning Ann woke him by playing seductive little games that heightened his desire. She constantly amazed him. Only yesterday, he awoke to find his arms loosely tied to the bedposts.

Testy from the lack of sleep, he growled, "Ann, untie the ropes. I'm not in the mood." Impishly, she shook her tousled hair. Her yellow silk gown hid nothing from his sultry gaze.

Positioning herself across his thighs, her hands and mouth teased and tormented every part of his straining body. At the last minute, she relented and freed his hands. His arms snaked out, and he snatched her waist. Once in control, Patrick punished her the best way he could think of, with his body. Merciful heavens, the woman was going to wear him out before he turned thirty. What a way to go!

That afternoon as Patrick worked in the library, Ann took out the laptop. It had been months since she had turned it on. She waited. Nothing happened. Not a light, not a noise, nothing. Turning the switch on and off several times, Ann's frustration increased. This was her only link to her previous life. It proved she had really come from the future. Now it was just a piece of plastic.

She hurried to the dressing room to find her bag. She needed assurance that her former life had existed, that she had two wonderful children who missed her terribly. Clutching her billfold, she yanked out her driver's license. All that remained was a blank plastic card. No numbers, no words, and worst of all, no dates. Nothing to prove when her real birthday was. Her frantic brain couldn't comprehend what her eyes were seeing.

Ann ran downstairs. Startled from his musings, Patrick glanced up as Ann flung herself into his waiting arms. He whispered soothing words while stroking her shaking body. "What's wrong?"

Ann couldn't speak. She held out her driver's license, letting him examine it.

"What is it?"

Tears blurred her vision. Ann wailed, "It's my driver's license. Remember, I showed it to you to prove when I was born. Now it's blank! Everything has disappeared. The laptop isn't working either.

Now I can't open any of the files containing our family history. I don't exist anymore."

"Ann, you do exist! You exist here, now, for me. Do you want to return to the future?"

His hands massaged the back of her neck and shoulders.

What was wrong with her? She hadn't thought about the impact of her words. She wished there were rules on how a person who was zapped to another century should act.

Ann held his face in her hands. "No, I never want to leave you, but now it's as if I never existed. I don't even know if my children exist." Burying herself against his chest, the tears returned.

Patrick's deep voice soothed her raging emotions. Gently tipping her chin so she would look at him, his lips drifted down to hers. "Your presence here was never an accident or a freak happenstance. You and I both know there is a higher being than us. Do you think God could have made a mistake?" Seeing her halfhearted smile, he continued. "I know in my heart that nothing has happened to your children. When we have children, I know that you will love them as much as you love Jessica and Mark. You will always have your memories."

She snuggled closer. "Of course I will. I will cherish any child that is ours. Do you think I'm being melodramatic?"

He threw back his head and burst out laughing. "If you think I will answer that, you're crazy." Helping her to her feet, he held out his hand. "Come—let's take a walk in the gardens. Fresh air would do us both good."

The week drifted by. The two of them fell into a comfortable pattern and savored every moment together.

On Saturday morning, the sounds of carriages and barking dogs interrupted their meal. Anthony, Eleanor, and the Marshalls filled the foyer, and the servants brought in the luggage.

Anthony's face lit with amusement at the baffled looks on Ann's and Patrick's faces. "Come now. You can't be that surprised. You two have been alone far too long. So we have taken the liberty to come and entertain you."

Patrick strode forward, playfully punching Anthony's shoulder. The next second, they hugged each other tightly.

Edward dryly remarked, "So, Lord Aylesbury, you sent word ahead, did you? You're lucky I don't box your ears myself."

Ann drew both women to her side. "Let's leave these boys to themselves. After we get you settled, you can tell me about the progress on the wedding and the latest tidbits from London."

Dinner was a joyful coming together of friends. Ann was amused by how much Anthony watched Eleanor. Eleanor was becoming bolder and more self-assured every day.

After dinner, they all withdrew to the parlor for a game of commerce, or what Ann referred to as poker. Once they were seated, Edward cleared his throat. "Before we begin the evening activities, I would like to make a toast. Katherine and I have decided that there is no better place to make this announcement than with our closest friends." Holding his glass in the air, he announced, "We are expecting a child."

Ann shrieked with joy and rushed over to embrace Katherine. Edward beamed like a proud father.

Patrick looked surprised and then shook Edward's hand. "When is the big event?"

Glancing toward his wife, Edward looked chagrined.

Katherine sighed. "My word, Edward, did you forget already?"

Ann felt a sudden sense of remorse. She thought about her children. When would she and Patrick have children? Would their child have her reddish hair or his raven locks? She prayed for the opportunity to find out.

Chapter 56

ANN ROLLED OVER AND saw that Patrick was still sleeping. She rose and stretched. She was just starting to get this new body toned. Patrick didn't object to her running as long as Robert, her guard, went with her. Quietly dressing in a tank top, shorts, and Nikes, she headed for the kitchen to get something to eat.

Maggie shook her head. "I'll never get used to seeing those bare legs and arms of yours, m'lady."

"I know, but if you ever want to go jogging with me, let me know," Ann teased as she headed for the door.

Maggie's face turned red. "I don't think I would look quite as attractive in that costume of yours. Since Lord O'Neil doesn't mind your running around in such a state, I guess I shouldn't worry."

Her reluctant running companion, Robert, was nowhere to be found. The grounds appeared to be deserted. Ann called out his name. Where was he? Robert was always ready when she left the house, though she knew he hated jogging. She opened the stable door and called out again. No answer. Where were all the servants?

Maybe she should ask Patrick to run with her. But she hated to wake him. He had enjoyed one too many toasts last night. Ann shrugged away her doubts and followed the trail leading toward the woods. It was a beautiful day, much too nice to stay indoors.

She would cut the run down to thirty minutes, and Patrick would never know she'd jogged alone.

Caught up watching the chattering squirrels as they jumped from branch to branch, she suddenly tripped. Arms flailing, Ann screamed as she lost her balance and fell flat on her stomach. Winded, she could barely move. Ann could see a rope drawn taut across the trail. A shadow fell across the trail.

Ann moaned, "Robert, help me up. I think I've hurt myself."

He clasped her hand and jerked her to her feet. Bent over, Ann fought a wave of dizziness. Staring at the black polished boots before her, Ann realized that her rescuer was not Robert. He did not own a pair of dress boots of this quality. Fear coursed through her. Why hadn't she waited? Patrick was going to throttle her. She slowly straightened and found herself staring at the one person she never wanted to see. David!

Ann jerked her hand out of David's grip. She swung around and started running. She only made it a few steps before David tackled her from behind. Slamming into the ground, her face took the hit. The taste of blood coated her tongue.

David pulled out a rope and quickly wrapped it around her wrists. He jerked a black hood over her head, completely blinding her. With no holes to breathe through, panic consumed her. She violently shook her head, trying to remove the smelly fabric. When she raised her arms to try to grasp the hood, David yanked on her wrists.

His laughter echoed through the trees. "Oh, no, you don't. I'm using you for bait. Thanks to you, I'm in the wrong century. The way I figure, I need you to return."

Hysteria rose up in her throat. Ann screamed as loudly as she could. She kicked her leg, hoping to connect with David, throwing him off balance.

"We've been gone almost a year, and I want my life back. Once I'm back in 2013, I can resume my life and no one will be the wiser, providing that you're dead."

"No, I have to stay here! I'm not going back."

"Yes, you are."

Ann dug in her heels, making the ropes squeeze tighter around her wrists. "Stop! Just let me go. You don't need me."

She couldn't go back. It was better to die here than to disappear and leave Patrick wondering what happened to her.

Patrick's arm flung across the pillow. By the position of the sun, it was late morning. He rubbed his pounding head. His brows scrunched together when someone knocked on the door. "I hope it's important," he grumbled.

Carrick entered the room, announcing, "Sir, Lady O'Neil went running over an hour ago and hasn't returned."

Ignoring the sickening sensation in his stomach, he yanked on his trousers and threw open the door. "Where's Robert?"

"I haven't seen him. Maggie says Lady O'Neil has never been gone this long. The staff's worried."

Patrick grabbed a shirt before pounding on Anthony's door. Patrick barged in without waiting for a response.

Anthony jumped out of bed, hastily covering his nakedness. "What the hell is going on, O'Neil? Can't a guest of yours get any peace and quiet?"

He tossed Anthony his clothes. "Meet me downstairs as soon as you're able."

He went down the hall and pounded on Edward's door next.

Patrick was standing in the middle of the room reading a letter from Ann when Edward and Anthony joined him. A servant had found the paper at the front door and delivered it immediately to Patrick.

Crumpling the paper in his fist, Patrick snatched up an Oriental vase sitting on the table and hurled it against the wall. Shards of glass littered the carpet. The pain in his chest was unbearable. His throat tightened as he withheld the sobs that threatened to destroy his remaining composure. He collapsed into a chair.

Anthony and Edward looked stunned. Anthony rested his hand on Patrick's shoulder. Patrick raised his head, his eyes filled with unshed tears.

Edward gruffly asked, "For God's sake, what happened? What can we do to help? You name it and we'll do it."

Feeling sick to his stomach, Patrick rose. "No one can help me. I'll have the servants help you pack so you can leave right away. I don't want you here."

Anthony folded his arms across his chest. "Damn it! We're not leaving you in this condition. We are your friends, and we're staying to help. Where is Ann?"

Patrick knew it would be futile to argue. He nodded to the piece of paper lying on the floor. Anthony walked over, picked it up, and gave it to Patrick. Unfolding the paper, he read the note aloud while Anthony and Edward stared over his shoulder:

Patrick, I can't stay here. I've tried to love you, but I can't. You will be happier without me. I am leaving to return to my own time.
Ann

Anthony glanced at Patrick. "You believe these lies? Have you completely lost your mind? I cannot believe you bought this rubbish."

Patrick jerked from the scathing comment. His glare riveted on Anthony. Leaping to his feet, Patrick grabbed Anthony's shirt and shoved his friend into the wall, sending a picture crashing to the floor. "Do not challenge me. You cannot begin to know the difficulties, the hell, we've faced."

Always the mediator, Edward stepped between them. "Before you kill each other, listen carefully to the words. He read the note again. "Patrick, this is a forgery," Edward softly admonished.

Patrick's exploded with a sarcastic lashing. "Forgery? Who do you think wrote the note? A servant? Or perhaps Katherine wrote it. Or even better yet, Eleanor may have written it. For God's sake, both of you get the hell out of here."

Katherine and Eleanor burst into the room through the open door, startling the men. With hands on her hips, Katherine glared at Patrick. "What do you mean by saying I wrote it? I demand to see what you're accusing me of."

Edward handed her the letter. Patrick rolled his eyes. "Bloody hell. Must everyone witness my humiliation? Let's call in the servants too."

"Be quiet, Patrick. I want to read this." Katherine studied the letter. She handed it to Eleanor, who was clearly just as curious.

Katherine shook her finger at Patrick. "I suppose you think Ann wrote this? Ah, I see that you do. Have you compared the writing to Ann's? I have never seen a woman write with such bold, blunt letters. What do you think, Eleanor?"

Eleanor nodded, looking too afraid to say anything.

Anthony searched the desk for one of Ann's letters. A menu lay in a pile of papers. Anthony waved it in front Patrick. "Is this her writing?"

Patrick studied the paper. Perhaps it was his imagination, but the writing did seem different. Setting the two papers side by side, Patrick studied them with new hope. Edward and Anthony peered over his shoulders. The writing was different! Dragging his fingers through his uncombed hair, the realization hit him. If she didn't write this letter, then who did?

Unlocking the gun cabinet, Patrick quickly loaded a pistol. "David! The bastard has Ann!"

Chapter 57

As soon as Patrick announced that David had Ann, chaos broke out. Katherine collapsed on the settee, crying out in terror. Edward went to her side, trying to calm her. With her pregnancy, she needed extra care. Poor Eleanor looked lost. Anthony grimly escorted Eleanor to her room.

Patrick sent a servant to wake his aunt to take care of the women. Patrick was filled with an urgency to find Ann. After safely ensconcing Katherine and Eleanor upstairs, his friends returned to get several weapons and enough ammunition for an army.

Patrick stormed through the house to the rear doorway. His group of friends spilled out the rear door. Patrick abruptly stopped. "Does anyone see anything unusual?"

Anthony paled, looking around the grounds. "Where are the servants? Don't the groomsmen work the animals this time of day?"

After silently motioning to the others, Anthony crept toward the rear stable door. Edward and Patrick approached the front entrance. Silence greeted them. They inched forward, checking every stall and hiding place, but they found nothing. They reached the storeroom at the same time. Patrick took a deep breath and swung open the wooden door. Three pistols trained into the darkened room. The muffled sound of voices greeted them. A man with his feet and hands tied together rolled through the doorway, startling the three men. Robert lay at their feet.

All the groomsmen were tied and gagged. Swiftly untying the men, Patrick demanded answers.

Robert held his chest as a violent cough shook his body. "I don't know what happened. Someone got behind me and held an awful-smelling rag to my face. The next thing I know, I'm tied up and locked in here."

Patrick spotted the damp rag and picked it up. After one sniff, he said, "Ether. No wonder David was able to overpower everyone."

Patrick and his friends helped the injured men to the kitchen. Gripping the back of a wooden chair, he tried to think. Where was Ann? He had to create a plan. Hearing a noise, he turned to find his aunt and most of the servants filing into the room.

"I want Robert and his men to search the grounds. Maggie, you take the servants and search the house. Leave nothing untouched. Once the house is secured, all doors and windows will be locked on the ground level. My wife has been kidnapped. We must find her. I've sent for the local magistrate. Auntie, notify me as soon he arrives."

"Patrick, you'll find her. I know it." His aunt's cheeks trembled as she fought back tears.

Flinging the door aside, Patrick rushed outside, gulping deep breaths of air. He felt like a puppet being manipulated by David. Patrick forced the rage aside. Time was of the essence.

Anthony and Edward followed Patrick down the path that Ann used for jogging. They looked for any clue that would lead them to Ann. After a quick snack, they searched by horseback until twilight. In the end, they returned to the house empty-handed as darkness prevailed.

Patrick knew that the scowl on his face discouraged any conversation. Patrick's facade of control was slipping away. He had to find Ann.

Ann struggled to clear the heaviness from her eyes. The blindfold had been removed. Her mouth was dry, as if it had been packed with cotton. Pain tore through her wrists with each movement. Where was she? Footsteps approached from the other room. Immediately she called out, "Help! Please help me."

David stood in the doorway watching Ann. "Quit your whining! No one can hear you, so you might as well be quiet. By tomorrow night, I'll be back in the real world."

"I'm not going back! My life is here with Patrick. If you have any compassion, please let me go. If I stay here, I'm not a threat to you."

David slowly shook his head. "What will you do if I agree to leave you here? I can't take a chance that you won't tell anyone. You're too late to be discussing options. I've decided that once I get back, I'll look up your daughter. Do you want me to give her a message?"

The ropes cut into her skin as she jerked toward him. "Damn you! Leave her alone. She's never done anything to you. If you touch her, I'll kill you myself."

"Tsk-tsk. You won't be around to see her suffer, so why worry?" He slithered closer, sliding his hand up her thigh. Ann twisted and turned, attempting to draw away from his touch. He reached down, picked up a piece of rope, and looped it about her neck. He pulled the rope until she gasped for air. Loosening his hold, he ran his tongue down her neck.

"Isn't this better? If you don't listen to me, then I have no choice but to remind you who is in charge."

The mindless fog from the ether closed in again.

Robert and the men returned that evening. They had searched the grounds and found nothing. Patrick was at a loss. Where could she be? He had never felt so helpless.

Dinner was a somber affair. Patrick gloomily stared out the

window, not touching any of his food. He paid little attention to his guests. Half listening to the conversation at the dinner table, he saw Anthony lean over to speak to Eleanor. He said softly, "I think you should return to London tomorrow."

Patrick startled them by speaking. "Ann might need Eleanor and Katherine when she returns. Let them stay if they wish."

Patrick stared unseeingly into the night. Had David hurt Ann? Tormented by his deepest fears, Patrick's fingers tore through his hair. His spirit withered while tendrils of fear ate away at his soul. How long he sat alone, he didn't know. Until Anthony's hand touched his shoulder, it was as if reality had disappeared.

Anthony stirred the dying embers in the fireplace before sitting down. Several moments passed before either spoke. "You mustn't give up. Ann will make it through this. She has more stamina than most men."

"Where could they be?" Patrick said. "It's like they vanished off the face of the earth."

Edward ground out his cigar. "We will find her. She wouldn't leave you … if she had a choice."

Those words hung in the air as they all stared at one another. It was highly probable that they had vanished, right into another century. The grandfather clock in the upstairs hallway struck midnight. The chimes rang throughout the house, reminding the inhabitants of the lateness of the hour. There was nothing further to be done this night. Reluctantly, Patrick, Edward, and Anthony dragged themselves to bed.

Patrick stared up at the ceiling as he lay in bed. He couldn't afford to be weak. Ann needed him. Even with his eyes closed, sleep eluded him. Impatient when the first rays of light broke through the darkness, he dressed, not thinking of anything but finding Ann. At the bottom of the stairs, his two friends stood, dressed and waiting.

"What are you two doing?" Patrick growled.

Edward handed him a cup of dark coffee. "We knew you would be up at the crack of dawn. You need us so lead the way."

Robert was waiting outside with three saddled horses. Patrick organized the men into groups. Patrick turned to his faithful servant. "Remember, I want David alive."

Patrick and his friends headed off alone. Patrick's jaw was clenched so tightly that his teeth hurt. When an old hunting lodge came into view, they quietly dismounted. The dilapidated building was quickly surrounded. Patrick kicked in the weathered door, his pistol drawn and primed.

"Damn it." Even with a chill in the air, Patrick wiped sweat from his brow.

"I thought for sure we would find them here," Edward muttered. He and Patrick turned to go outside.

Anthony saw a piece of paper lying in the corner. His eyes widened as he read the creased paper. "Patrick, you'd better take a look at this."

Patrick snatched the paper from Anthony. He read aloud:

I know you'll find this. I'm watching you. You're not as clever as you think. Forget about finding Ann. There's not enough time left for you to save her.

Patrick crumpled the paper and threw his head back, roaring with frustration. He stared at the surrounding forest. He didn't see anything out of the ordinary, but he knew that David was out there, watching them and waiting.

By midday, Patrick's group met up with the other men. Weariness and the lack of sleep had begun to take its toll on everyone. Several men slumped forward in their saddles. Without their help, he didn't know if he would find Ann. He didn't even know how much time he had to find her. Damn it all! He pulled Robert aside. "Why don't you have the men rest up for a while?"

Robert folded his arms across his chest; his spine was clearly stiff. "Lord O'Neil, I thought you knew us better than that. These men would lay down their lives for Lady O'Neil. There isn't one of them who wouldn't be insulted at your offer. So I suggest you not repeat it."

Patrick smiled, his voice cracking as he said, "Thank you. Tell them how much I appreciate their efforts."

The afternoon was as unsuccessful as the morning had been. Patrick felt hopeless. In another hour, it would be too dark to continue the search. Edward and Anthony looked as bad as he felt.

Edward broke the silence. "Patrick, we can't go much farther. The horses may stumble, injuring them or us. We can begin again early tomorrow."

Patrick reined his horse to a halt. He knew that Edward spoke the truth, but he couldn't quit. Tonight was the one-year anniversary of Ann's arrival. He hadn't thought about this until now. His intuition warned him that there was something important about that fact. He would keep searching until he found her or couldn't continue any longer.

Chapter 58

A CHILL PERMEATED THE dense forest as the sun dipped lower. A lone owl was heard calling to its mate high in the trees above them. A small clearing lay ahead. The smell of smoke drifted lazily through the trees, wafting around them like a scented scarf. Patrick motioned for them to stop.

Anthony whispered, "Smells like firewood. I didn't know anyone lived in this area."

"No one does." Tying the reins to the nearest tree, Patrick crept forward. Anthony and Edward followed, drawing their pistols. Pushing through the dense underbrush, they reached the clearing.

Light seeped from a boarded-up window. The blackness of the night made the situation even more dangerous. A strange sense of foreboding filled Patrick. It seemed as if unnatural forces were working against them. Patrick held his hand inches from his face, shocked that he was unable to see it. Never in his lifetime had he witnessed such eerie circumstances.

Sounds were heard from within the lodge. Patrick edged closer. He crawled on his stomach, inching forward, ignoring the pounding of his heart. When he reached the wall undetected, he slowly rose to his feet and peered through the window. A crumbling fireplace greeted his eyes. Uneaten food lay on the table. Cobwebs filled the corners of the room, indicating a lack of inhabitants for quite some time. A bed sat in the far corner. At first, it appeared to be covered with piles of old blankets. A slight movement on the bed caught his eye. He froze. Was that a body on the bed? A limp hand tugged at the bindings attached to the bedpost. Was it Ann or someone else?

Ann turned toward the window, meeting Patrick's gaze. Thank God. She was alive.

Where was David? Turning slightly to get a better view of the room, he saw David poke the fire with a stick, stirring up fiery embers. David threw on another log and glanced at Ann.

The sound of distant thunder made David jump. A strong wind whistled around the lodge.

Patrick shivered as he remembered the night that Ann had arrived. This storm was eerily similar to the one that had occurred on the night that Ann had been sent back in time.

Patrick motioned his friends closer. The sudden appearance of the thunderstorm made him apprehensive. Minutes ago, it had been completely clear. The rumbling of thunder echoed through the forest. The howling wind gained momentum. Anthony and Edward got into position, covering all possible exits. Surprise had to be on their side. Otherwise, all could be lost.

A sudden chill filled the air. Patrick blinked several times at the sight before him. A flash of lightning lit up the forest, revealing a strange cloud winding its way through the dense trees. A strange mist advanced toward the lodge.

Patrick stared at the eerie vapor as it came toward him. The cloud wrapped itself around his legs, advancing up his body. He glanced at his friends, who were also surrounded by the mist. Numbness spread through Patrick's body. He knew that if he didn't break free from the tentacles of the mist, he would be unable to move. From the look on his friends' faces, they were immobilized already.

Patrick screamed as he ran to the door, splintering it into ragged chunks of wood.

As he rolled to the floor, David grabbed a knife. The two men viciously landed blow after blow to the other. Blood squirted from

Patrick's nose. Patrick's fist drove into David's stomach, causing him to double over and fall to the floor.

Worried about Ann, Patrick rushed to her side and cut the binding ropes.

"Patrick, watch out!" Ann screamed.

Instinctively, Patrick raised his forearm. Ignoring the agonizing pain in his arm, Patrick tackled his bloodied foe.

The familiar mist made its way inside the lodge. It enveloped everything in its path, making its way toward Ann.

David crowed, "I was right!" David viciously smashed a fist into Patrick's jaw.

Excruciating pain ripped through Patrick. Blood flowed from his mouth as he hit the floor with a thud. His eyes rolled back in his head before closing.

David stalked toward Ann. She screamed, lashing out with her hands. Patrick didn't move.

"Patrick, get up! Help me!"

David closed in. He yanked her toward him, wrapping an arm around her neck. Sporting an unholy grin, he dragged her toward the mist. "You see, Ann, I was right. Now I can go back to where I belong and finish what I started: killing you."

His taunting laughter echoed in her ears. No longer caring if she lived or died, Ann raked her nails down David's face. David wasn't going to get the satisfaction of deciding when and where she died. She chose to die now—here with Patrick.

As Ann struggled with David, the storm grew in intensity. The sound of the droning wind drowned out all other noises. The foundation of the lodge was tearing loose, unable to withstand the battering forces of nature.

Tears coursed down her face. Trembling with weariness, she had no energy to fight any longer. Her body was seriously bruised. She wanted this nightmare with David to end, yet she wanted to stay with Patrick. He held her heart.

Suddenly, the pressure of David's hands about her neck was

gone. As David crumbled to the floor, she saw Patrick standing with a heavy iron pot in his hand. Crying with joy, she threw herself into his waiting arms.

Cradling her face with his bloodied hands, Patrick kissed her quivering lips. His hand brushed across her tear-stained face.

Ann met his gaze. "I'm fine. You should worry about yourself. Let's get you to the bed before you collapse."

Grimacing, he tightened his embrace. He tore his gaze from Ann and turned to stare at David's still body.

Ann shuddered. "Is he dead?"

"I don't think so. Help me find some rope. I don't want him escaping. I want him punished for what he's done to you and Katherine."

As Ann reached for the rope, she realized that the mist had disappeared. The wind was no longer threatening.

Anthony and Edward rushed into the room with weapons drawn. They skidded to a halt upon seeing David's unconscious body on the floor.

Anthony brushed the water off his face. "My God! I cannot believe we're alive after that storm. I have never witnessed such a strange event. I'll be damned. When that fog surrounded us, I couldn't move."

"Me either," chimed in Edward. "How did you manage, Patrick?"

Patrick smiled, embracing his wife. "It would have taken more than that to stop me from getting to Ann."

Ann nodded. "I hope to never see any fog, mist, or whatever that was for the rest of my life. Three times was more than enough."

David moaned, drawing their attention. Patrick tore off a piece of his shirt and wrapped it around David's mouth. Patrick never wanted to hear a word out of that man's mouth again.

The men threw David's bloodied body over a horse. The weary party made their way home. Robert and his men gave a loud cheer when they saw Ann sitting in front of Patrick.

It was late that night before Ann could relax. The entire household had been in an uproar all day. Upon their return, the local magistrate arrived to take David into custody. Forgoing the usual formalities after dinner, everyone agreed that they were exhausted and turned in early.

Ann felt some trepidation as she waited for Patrick to join her in bed. He hadn't asked her any questions. Did he assume the worst?

The door opened. Patrick came toward her. His loosely belted robe revealed the sculptured, tanned body she loved. His hair was still damp from the bath, molded to the back of his neck. She met his gaze. His emerald eyes sparkled with unusual brightness. In one fluid motion, his robe slid to the floor. His desire was obvious.

Patrick took her hand. "Ann, I love you. Nothing will ever change my feelings for you. I'm completely content to sit by the fire and hold you. I just want to touch you."

Nestled on his lap, Ann rested her head on his shoulder. The crackling sounds of the fire filled the room. Patrick wrapped one of her curls around his finger, relishing in the fiery highlights and silky texture.

"I want you to know that nothing happened with David."

Patrick continued to draw the satiny strands into his hands. Minutes later, he bent down, tenderly kissing her brow. "I wouldn't care what happened as long as you are with me. I almost lost you. I was so damn afraid that the mist would take you away from me. I will never forget that moment."

She buried her face against his chest, smiling through the teardrops. This was what she had always desired—to be loved. The kind of love that made you feel as if you could walk on water. The kind of love that made you feel cherished and protected. Patrick would always love her, even if she went a little crazy from time to time, which she was sure to do.

Ann slid off the chair and pulled Patrick to the floor. Stretched out on the plush rug in front of the fireplace, Ann proceeded to show him how much she cared.

This was her place in time, and he was her future.

Chapter 59

THE COURTROOM OVERFLOWED WITH spectators. The curious came from miles around to witness the trial of David Stewart. Speculation ran rampant. He was the brutal slasher who had attacked Lady Marshall in London. He'd kidnapped Lady O'Neil. It was rumored that he was responsible for the deaths of several prostitutes found with their throats slashed. The police called Stewart the Covent Garden Slasher.

Witness after witness came forward with unquestionable proof of these serious charges. By the final day of the hearing, David's appearance had deteriorated. Lank unwashed hair knotted in clumps about his head. His once-swarthy appearance had faded. His face was gaunt and bruised.

David listened to the charges and trembled with rage. How dare these uneducated simpleminded idiots judge him! He wasn't even born yet. The trial was a travesty of justice.

He jumped to his feet, causing the chains binding his hands to clank noisily. "I demand to be released! You have no authority over me," he ranted. "I'm not even from this century! I don't belong here."

The spectators sat spellbound. Sensing a gaining momentum, David pointed to Ann. "Ann, tell them. Tell them the truth. Explain how we traveled through time."

With Patrick at her side, Ann stood and faced her accuser. "Sir, I must deny your accusation. I am Lady Victoria O'Neil and have no skills in card reading or peering into crystal balls. The idea of time travel is too farfetched for me to even imagine."

Chuckles were heard across the courtroom. The idea that people could travel from one time to another was preposterous.

David looked humiliated. Beads of sweat dotted his forehead. He massaged his throbbing temple as if he had a headache.

With no further evidence or witnesses, a recess was called. Since it was early afternoon, Ann and Patrick decided to wait at a nearby inn, seeking comfort from each other. Sitting near the front window, Ann saw Anthony running toward the inn.

Minutes later, Anthony burst in. "The verdict is in."

Patrick tucked her arm in his as they entered the courtroom. A buzz of excitement filled the air. Heads craned toward them as they walked down the aisle to their seats. Ann shivered with nervousness.

The judge glanced at the crowd. Peering over wire-rimmed glasses, he stared at David. "The charges of attempted murder and assault have been made against you. After hearing all the witnesses and viewing the evidence, the court has ruled. Never in my years as a member of the legal system have I been so appalled by such a blatant disregard for human life. The court finds you guilty. Do you have any final words before I sentence you?"

David seemed confused, as if he couldn't believe what he had just heard.

Since David did not respond, the judge continued. "Due to the bizarre accusations you've made and your obvious mental state, I have sentenced you to the Hospital of St. Mary of Bethlehem in London for treatment."

David's face lit up with a big smile.

Ann grabbed Patrick's hand. "A hospital? He'll be out by nightfall."

David winked at her. Ann's fear grew. She could not go through this again.

Patrick leaned closer, saying, "It will be fine. He's being sent to Bedlam."

Ann felt a sense of relief. "Bedlam? Wow. I almost feel sorry for the other patients."

The whispering in the courtroom grew louder. Someone shouted, "Poor devil! He'll not see the sun again once he's inside Bedlam."

David screamed, pounding his fists on the wood railing around his seat. Jumping to his feet, David slammed a fist into the face of the guard and then lunged at the judge. "No! You can't send me there. I am an American. I know my rights."

Several guards struggled to pull David's hands from the judge's throat. Turmoil disrupted the courtroom. Within minutes, David was restrained. Bloodied, he was unable to stand. His cries and threats grew fainter as he was dragged down the hallway to a waiting wagon.

Ann sagged against Patrick. David would never be a threat again. As she thought about his sentence, a chuckle escaped her. How ironic that all David wanted was to return to the twenty-first century, but because of the evil in him, he would remain locked up in the nineteenth century. He would be in a place that every sane person shied away from. The old saying was true after all—you truly do reap what you sow.

Suddenly, she found herself in Patrick's arms. Their laughter echoed through the now-empty room.

"Are you ready to go home?"

Ann pressed a kiss to his upturned lips. "Yes. Let's go home and start our family. I want five sons who look like their father."

A roguish smile lit his face. "Five sons? Well, we'd best get busy." He bent and swung her up in his arms.

As they made their way to the carriage, laughter and catcalls followed. Anthony opened the carriage door for them.

Leaning toward his friend, Patrick announced, "My wife wants

Jan Walters

a baby, and I intend to satisfy her request." His booming voice carried through the crowd.

Embarrassed, she tugged on his arm. "Get in here, Patrick! You don't have to tell the world about our private plans."

Grinning, Patrick jumped in the carriage and proceeded to remove his jacket. He calmly began to unbutton his shirt. Ann's eyes widened.

Anthony quickly shut the door, anticipating Patrick's next action. Ann's shrieks of laughter were heard as the vehicle rumbled away. Anthony chuckled as Ann's shoe sailed from the carriage window. Perhaps he should go to White's and lay a wager on when O'Neil's first child would arrive. Without a doubt, it would be exactly nine months from today.

Epilogue

A YEAR HAD PASSED since the strange disappearance of their mother. Mark and Jessica had come to rely on one another during this time.

They had showed up at Ann's house the morning after the storm, only to find it empty. Remnants of a violent struggle were seen everywhere. Even though David Stewart had disappeared weeks before, Jessica knew that David was at the root of her mother's disappearance, but without evidence or a body, nothing could be done.

They boarded up their mother's house, hoping she would return. Her presence in the house was so real that they believed a miracle could still occur.

On the anniversary of their mother's disappearance, Jessica called Mark. "Let's meet at Mom's house this weekend. I know we decided to keep the house in the family, but since you and Deb have moved out of state, it's too much for me to take care of, especially now that we're trying to start a family."

Mark muttered, "I've got things to do. Some other time."

After a lengthy discussion, Jessica eventually convinced him that it was time to accept reality.

As Jessica pulled up to her mother's house, Mark pulled in behind her. Weeds had overtaken the flower garden. Litter lay strewn about the yard. She cringed at the state of neglect that had overtaken their childhood home.

Jessica brushed back a tear as they entered the house. Books littered the coffee table, exactly where their mom had left them a year ago.

Jessica took a deep breath and began her prepared speech. "Mark, this is as hard for me as it is you, but I think it's time we sell the house and move on with our lives."

Mark glared at her and shook his head. "How can you say that? This is where Mom lived, where we grew up."

Trying to be patient, Jessica asked, "Do you want to move back here to live?"

After several minutes, he finally admitted, "No. I couldn't live here anymore, but it's Mom's house."

Jessica sighed. "I received a call last week from Stacy. You remember Mom's friend? Anyway, she wants to meet us here today. This past year has been hell for all of us. I can't believe she's really gone."

Before she could say more, the doorbell rang. Mark flung open the door and saw Stacy's smiling face.

"My goodness! Look how you kids have changed. You're all grown up," Stacy exclaimed.

Jessica laughed with joy. Stacy was exactly the way she remembered. Stacy set her purse on the kitchen table and opened the windows. "Let's air this place out a bit. I have good news. A friend of mine drove by this house and would like to see the inside. She's interested in moving back here to be closer to her parents. She'd like to buy the house, assuming that she likes the inside. What do you think?"

Mark stared out the window overlooking the back yard. "Everything looks the same, but it isn't. Jess, you may be right." Reluctantly, he nodded. "Sure. Why not? It's probably for the best."

Jessica wrapped her arms around her brother and kissed him on the cheek, trying to ignore the lump in her throat.

Stacy sniffled and reached for a Kleenex. Jess knew that Stacy missed her mom. They had been best friends.

Impulsively, Jessica grabbed Stacy's hand and pulled her upstairs. "We want you to take something to remind you of Mom. Besides, you're like a second mother to us."

The spare room looked the same as it had a year ago—the night of Ann's disappearance. Papers were scattered about, books all over the floor. The three of them paused in the doorway, hesitant to enter.

They sifted through a pile of books and photos, each remembering special times with Ann. Jessica spotted an antique-looking album lying in the corner. Curious, she flipped through the pages. She choked back a cry.

"Sis, you look like you saw a ghost." Mark leaned over her shoulder, trying to get a better look.

Tears sparkled in Jessica's eyes as she held up the book. "Remember Mom talking about her genealogy research on one of our distant relatives? Well, here it is. A woman by the name of Alice O'Neil wrote about how the family had lost the family home in Ireland and moved to England. Oh, look! She writes later that she had a son, Patrick O'Neil."

Stacy gasped, hearing Patrick's name after all this time. Jessica's head whipped toward Stacy. "You act as if you've heard that name before. Did Mom mention something about Patrick O'Neil?" Jessica probed.

"I guess there's no harm telling you now. Your mom was having weird dreams after she brought home an album called *Lady O'Neil's Memoirs*. She believed the album somehow caused the dreams. I know this sounds like something out of a science-fiction movie. Before she disappeared, your mom believed she had gone back in time and met Patrick O'Neil. His picture is in the book. She was so sincere and convincing that I began to believe it really happened."

Jessica stared numbly at Stacy. Mark, always the skeptic, laughed out loud. "No way! If Mom had really believed that, why didn't she say anything to us, her own children?"

Stacy touched Mark's arm. "I don't know. Maybe she wanted more proof. Or maybe she wasn't fully convinced herself, but don't you find it a little strange that her body was never found? If she were alive in this century, you know that she would do anything humanly possible to contact you kids. The police have said a hundred times that they can't be 100 percent sure what happened. What if she's in another century, where there are no phones, no airplanes, and no way to contact her family because neither one of you exist?"

Mark angrily kicked a book lying on the floor. Infused with energy, Jessica began opening desk drawers, looking for the tiniest piece of evidence or clue.

Mark jammed his fists in a pocket of his pants. "What are you doing? There's nothing here to tell us what the hell happened. You're wasting your time and mine if you believe in this ... this fairy tale."

Quickly flipping through the numerous books, Jessica found one stuffed away on a shelf. In the middle of the book, a corner of the page was folded over as if to draw attention to it. She turned to the page.

Holding the old album out to Mark, Jessica cried, "Look at this."

Trembling, he took the album, looking at the large picture. His eyes widened with amazement. A photograph showed couples dancing at some type of formal event. The two people in the center of the picture captured his attention. There was a woman who looked exactly like a younger version of his mother. Her elaborate hairstyle gave her a regal look from an era long gone. The young woman seemed to be looking directly into the camera, trying to convey a silent message. A man stood close by, his hand resting protectively on her shoulder. His eyes gazed lovingly at her.

Mark choked back sobs. He flipped to the back of the book and found a note. Jessica gasped, recognizing her mother's handwriting. Mark wiped away tears. Unable to speak, he gave the book back to Jessica, who read the words aloud.

Dear Jessica and Mark,
I trust you will find this message that I have left for you.
I miss you both dearly and love you more than you'll ever
know. I want you to know that I have fallen in love with
the most wonderful man in the world, Patrick O'Neil.
Don't ask me to explain how all this happened, because I
don't think I will ever know. Don't be angry or upset with
me, for I couldn't wish for greater happiness. Now that
both of you are grown and on your own, I have complete
faith that you will continue to live your lives and cherish
the time with your own children. I will always love you.
You will never be far from my thoughts. Tell Stacy that I
love her and hope she has found the love of her life.

"It's signed Ann Roberts O'Neil," Jessica added.

Stacy blew her nose, dashing away a flood of tears. Mark reached out and touched the faded picture of his mother. Jessica leaned on her brother's shoulder and sighed. "I feel so blessed. We know Mom is alive and happy."

Stacy stared at the picture of her best friend and the man next to her. Smiling, she began laughing uncontrollably. Ignoring the puzzled glances from Jess and Mark, Stacy crowed, "I always knew you'd meet someone absolutely gorgeous. Patrick is as handsome as you said he was. Good-bye, kiddo. You enjoy every minute of the rest of your life." Stacy pressed a kiss to her finger and laid it on the cheek of her smiling friend in the photograph.

Impishly, she suddenly knew what her vacation plans for the summer would be. She had always wanted to visit England. Now there was a reason for doing so.

CPSIA information can be obtained at www.ICGtesting.com
Printed in the USA
LVOW06s1654090913

351652LV00005B/820/P